The Society for Single Ladies is a crime-solving club founded by the wealthiest woman in London. Yet even Miss Angela Childers' charming detectives are not immune to the forces of love . . .

Dorothea Rowland attends a country house party to investigate a long-lost heir—not to find a husband. But when the dashing American claimant discovers her prowling for clues, she is startled—and then seduced—by his provocative kiss. It's all Dorothea can do to remember her mission. Especially when a series of accidents adds up to something far more dangerous . . .

Benedict only meant to silence lovely Dorothea—not find himself enamored. What's a gentleman to do but join forces—and propose to the clever beauty? Yet as Ben and Dorothea pursue the truth about his inheritance, their faux betrothal threatens to become the real thing. Soon Ben's plan to return to his life in America is upended—not only by his deepening bond with his bride, but by someone who wants his fortune badly enough to jeopardize his future—even end it. And Dorothea can't let that happen. Not for the title, but for Ben . . .

Visit us at www.kensingtonbooks.com

Books by Lynne Connolly

The Society of Single Ladies
The Girl With the Pearl Pin
The Making of A Marquess

The Shaw Series
Fearless
Sinless
Dauntless
Boundless

The Emperors of London Series
Rogue in Red Velvet
Temptation Has Green Eyes
Danger Wears White
Reckless in Pink
Dilemma in Yellow
Silk Veiled in Blue
Wild Lavender

Published by Kensington Publishing Corporation

The Making of A Marquess

The Society of Single Ladies

Lynne Connolly

LYRICAL PRESS
Kensington Publishing Corp.
www.kensingtonbooks.com

LYRICAL PRESS BOOKS are published by
Kensington Publishing Corp.
119 West 40th Street
New York, NY 10018

All Kensington titles, imprints, and distributed lines are available at special quantity discounts for bulk purchases for sales promotion, premiums, fundraising, educational, or institutional use.

Special book excerpts or customized printings can also be created to fit specific needs. For details, write or phone the office of the Kensington Sales Manager: Kensington Publishing Corp., 119 West 40th Street, New York, NY 10018. Attn. Sales Department. Phone: 1-800-221-2647.

Lyrical Press and Lyrical Press logo Reg. U.S. Pat. & TM Off.

First Electronic Edition: March 2020
eISBN-13: 978-1-5161-0953-1
eISBN-10: 1-5161-0953-8

First Print Edition: March 2020
ISBN-13: 978-1-5161-0956-2
ISBN-10: 1-5161-0956-2

Printed in the United States of America

To you, the reader. Without you, I wouldn't be here, doing this.

Author's Foreword

Now I'm into my stride, and the story of the mysterious claimant to a title and the single lady investigating his claim led me on an adventure I didn't want to end!

Chapter 1

Spring, 1743

Benedict Thorpe, Lord Brocklebank, heir to the mighty marquessate of Belstead, braced himself against shivering, despite the chill of the early morning. This April had been wet and cold. Today would be no exception. The people standing around would think he was afraid. He was not. Not one bit. Already in his shirtsleeves, facing his cousin Louis, Ben squared his jaw. If he died this morning, he'd do it staring down the man who'd dared to insult the woman who meant more to Ben than anyone else. His betrothed, the woman he would marry next week.

If he lived.

The great oak tree above them had witnessed many of these encounters. A dozen men stood around, their soft voices breaking the natural peace of dawn. They were placing bets and calling out encouragement to their favorite. Quietly, because dueling was illegal. If the authorities caught them everyone would be in trouble. Ben and Louis most of all.

How had they come to this? Louis had spent so much time in Ben's childhood home, he was all but a brother. Watching Louis divest himself of his blue riding coat and hand it to his younger brother, William, Ben recalled childhood moments with his two cousins. Carefree times playing Robin Hood on the grounds of Cressbrook House. William and Louis had made his childhood bearable. If not for them, the expectations heaped on his shoulders would have overwhelmed him. Then Louis and he had roared their way around Europe, while William had started his longed-for army career.

So short a time ago. A year after they'd returned home, everything had gone wrong. To be more precise, ever since they both set eyes on Lady Honoria Colt.

Now look at them. Fighting over a woman. Although Honoria's name had not crossed their lips, everybody here knew the real reason for this duel. And who had persuaded Louis to demand pistols? He had assumed Louis would choose swords, and they'd fight to first blood.

Honoria had accepted Ben's offer of marriage before Louis had said the ugly things that had driven them to stand here. Instead of snuggling in their warm beds, they were facing off across twenty yards of damp grass.

If they'd used swords, one of them could still have died, but pistols made that eventuality even more certain. And yet, after what Louis had said, Ben could not forgive him. He never would.

If he lived. Those three words counterpointed his heartbeat, like some fancy harpsichord piece. They marked the short time from challenge to meeting.

Ben had stripped off his scarlet coat and handed it to his best friend Hal. Disdainful of the practice of reducing the visibility of the target for his opponent by wearing subdued clothing, he'd kept up the color theme. His red waistcoat and full-sleeved white shirt made him a flamboyant presence. He would give Louis every chance. Then he would wing him, and this foolishness would end. Louis was an excellent shot, but Ben was better. Ben didn't think Louis would aim for the heart. Not Louis.

The seconds met in the middle of the field of play, ten yards from the oak tree. This spot had been mute witness to many duels; some were serious, some half-hearted. But if they came here, the people involved were usually in earnest. Impulsive duels were sorted out on the spot, whether that was a gaming den or a gentleman's club. To wait until dawn meant the participants had every chance to make up and shake hands. Many did. Ben and Louis had not.

At two in the morning, in the middle of St. James's Club, Ben had tallied his winnings and told William how much he owed. His cousin should have known that Ben would never demand the reckoning. How could he take such an enormous sum from him?

But before he said anything else, Louis ripped up. "At least I have something you want. Honoria is mine. Yes, that's right, I took her, and I've enjoyed her since the beginning of the year. She's mine. You might have everything else, but you won't get her."

The insult had proved too much to bear and Ben had struck him. Marston had said to Ben, "Do you mean to issue a challenge, my lord?" and that had been that.

His temper roused, his heart sore, Ben had confirmed the challenge, and stipulated that the loser would step aside in the pursuit of Lady Honoria. To do so, the loser would have to be alive, but Louis hadn't taken that into consideration. Pistols at dawn, he'd wanted.

Well, he would get it.

His second, Lord Henry Evington, came across the turf to Ben. His feet left wet footprints in the dew-soaked grass. "No apology. He says he meant every word."

"Bastard," Ben said without heat. He'd expected nothing less. His cousin never backed down from a challenge. "Hal, if I don't get past this, can you ensure Louis looks after her?"

Hal touched his arm. "You'll get through it, old man. Neither of you wants to kill the other."

"Then why the pistols?"

Hal shook his head. "He's a better shot than he is a swordsman. Other than that, I don't know. Let's get through this. I've bespoken breakfast at St. James's Club." When he smiled, the carefree part of Hal shone through. Ben smiled back, a flash of amusement lightening his mood for a moment.

"Yes, let's get this done."

They started on the ritual, as well laid out as any courtly dance. The opponents came together in the middle of the arena.

"Well met, cousin," Ben murmured, low enough for only Louis to hear. Louis said nothing, but set his jaw.

The crowd, now swelled to twenty, called muted encouragement, but not for them to make up. They wanted Ben and Louis to get on with it.

"Fifty on Lord Brocklebank!" someone said. "He's a likely lad!"

"T'other's the better shot!"

His life was worth fifty guineas. Good to know.

Neither man took his attention away from the other. Ben sighed. Their "private disagreement" would be all over town in a few hours.

The seconds collected the case of pistols and returned. As the accused, Louis had the first choice. He selected a weapon after one glance. Ben took the other.

They turned their backs. They stood so close that the heat of Louis's body seeped through Ben's silk waistcoat and linen shirt.

The seconds tonelessly counted to ten. On each number the men paced a step, until they had reached the agreed distance, ten paces. Ben kept his breath steady. He willed his heart to settle to a regular beat, instead of trying to hammer its way through his rib cage.

They turned. Hal and William held a white handkerchief, a corner each. Ben fixed his attention on Louis, letting the flash of white linen occupy part of his field of vision. He held the weapon by his side in the approved fashion, trusting that Hal and William had loaded them properly.

Sometimes the seconds "accidentally" forgot to load the balls. While he wished that to be the case, Ben could not rely on it. Maddening though his cousin was, he had no desire to hurt him. He made some rapid calculations. If he aimed at the right side of Louis's waistcoat, he wouldn't cause any lasting damage. Honor would be served. They would sort out the problem of Honoria another way. In private. They wouldn't need the surgeon, even though they had brought one, as the rules dictated.

She was Ben's. He had claimed her. He would have to bring Louis around to understand that. Louis was lying; he had to be. How could Honoria swear undying love to him and sleep with Louis at the same time?

Anticipation sent a shot of energy through his blood. When Hal said, "Gentlemen, are you ready?" Ben nodded and raised his weapon, holding it steady, aiming it at Louis's chest. He would move six inches to the left. He had no idea what Louis planned, but he refused to believe his cousin meant to kill him.

Except Louis held his gun aimed at Ben. Right at his heart. A touch of concern made Ben waver, but he had no time to change his plan. Not that he wanted to.

"You may fire when you are ready," William said.

The spectators fell silent. It would not be gentlemanly to interrupt the concentration of the opponents. In any case, if someone shouted, they would have to build the distraction into the odds after the event. It might even invalidate some wagers.

They drew back the hammers on their weapons. The click echoed around the sward of Hampstead Heath. Someone standing in the garden of Kenwood House, on the other side of the Heath, would hear it.

The fraught silence lasted for the rest of Ben's life, or that was what it felt like. In this eternal stretch of time, it might be true.

With a clap of wings and a harsh cry, a crow flew out of the oak tree at Ben's right.

A shot followed and a sharp pain blossomed in Ben's side. The shock of the hit made Ben tighten his grip. His own weapon burst into life, the flare of the flint as the hammer hit the pan dazzling his sight.

Dropping the pistol, he fell to his knees and clutched his rib cage. He gasped, forcing himself to conquer the pain, to keep breathing. When his sight cleared, he beheld a scene he would never forget.

Louis lay on the ground, his feet toward Ben, the brown leather of his boots darkened with dew. Two men knelt at his head, the surgeon and William.

Hal rushed to Ben. "What has he done? How badly are you wounded?"

A few deep breaths gave Ben some measure of control. "It hurts like the devil, but I don't think he's done more than graze me."

"He aimed for your heart," Hal said grimly.

"But he missed," Ben reminded him. "Now get a pad of linen for me, there's a good fellow, and find out what has happened to Louis."

Hal tore off his shirt sleeve and roughly fashioned it into a wad of fabric, pressing it to Ben's side. Ben winced, but bore the pain. It was receding now, from blinding to agonizing. Enough for him to take note of what else was happening.

Already the crowd was dispersing. The sound of shots, loud in the quiet morning air, would be enough to rouse the authorities. The spectators would settle their wagers in the comfort of their clubs.

Ben sank back on his heels and breathed deeply. When pain speared him, he bit the side of his cheek to prevent himself crying out. A rib or two was probably cracked or broken. When he moved the pad, the bleeding was settling to a sluggish trickle.

Hal raced back. "We have to go," he said, anxiety creasing his forehead and deepening the brackets around his mouth.

"What?" Ben wouldn't leave his cousin. Their dispute was settled, honor restored. He could make sure Louis was cared for.

"Ben, he's bleeding badly. You shot him over his heart. He's like to die."

Death in a duel, honor or not, was murder in the eyes of the law, premeditated and carried out. If Louis died, Ben would hang, unless he did as Hal urged. "He'll die?"

"The surgeon can't see him surviving. Yes, fool, he will die."

"I didn't mean to kill him..." Ben rose and took a step toward his cousin, but Hal put his hand on his arm.

"Don't go. Don't watch him die. You'll never forget it."

Guilt burdened him, and numbness filled his body until his feet weighed heavy as lead. "It was that bird—"

"Yes. But the damage is done. Come."

This time Ben allowed Hal to lead him to the carriage waiting on the pathway. He climbed in and spared one glance behind him. The people remaining at the scene were crowding around the supine body of Louis. Ben's thoughts whirled, confused.

"This wasn't supposed to happen," he muttered as the carriage drew away. "I was the one who should have died."

Chapter 2

Spring, 1750

Ben threaded his hand through his hair, spreading his fingers out before he reached the bow at the back of his head. If he had a valet, he'd have appalled the man, but these days he rarely bothered with a body servant. No time, no inclination, no reason to have one.

Getting up from his desk, he took a turn around his office, the letter in his hand. Standing before the window, with its spectacular view of the bay, he stared out. From here he marked his ships in the forest of masts, the achievements he'd won with no help from anyone else.

He read it again.

The lines dragged him back to the world he'd left, the one he'd never expected to see again. Or wanted to, for that matter.

Dear Ben,

I need advice.

Events here are coming to a head.

Since the death of your father, Louis has run through as much of your fortune as he can get hold of. Now he wants the entailed property.

The only way he can do this is to inherit. That can only happen if you are dead. Since the last time anyone saw you was the day of the duel, Louis wants you declared dead on the last day of August. That's seven years and a month since you were last heard of.

I did as I promised. I told no one that I know where you are, if you are alive or not. If you wish to remain dead, then you need do nothing.

But Ben, Louis is ruining more than the estate. He is ruining the people who depend on it for their living. The dwellings your steward is supposed to oversee are tumbling down, and so are the walls. Everything except the house is falling into disrepair. He has sold your father's fleet of trading ships. The only reason he has not sold the coal mine is that it is on entailed land.

You may have given him free rein over the estate as compensation, out of guilt or for Honoria's happiness. But he has more than made up for that one moment of madness on Hampstead Heath. It is time you came home. If you do not come now, then there is no point returning at all.

His brother is serving in the army, and can do nothing to help as long as his brother is alive.

If you wish this to happen, then I swear to you I will do nothing. I will watch the destruction continue, or rather, keep as far away from it as I can. But if you are not home by August, you will lose everything, including your name. Even if you return later, you will face a legal battle to regain what is yours. And the way the law is, you will most likely fail. If he claims the marquessate, the law will hold it as his.

I will remain your friend, and I will not say a word, unless you instruct me to. If you choose not to reply, I will count that as a signal of your death. And I will mourn, but I may continue to correspond with my friend in the colonies, Benjamin Thorpe. He is a good man.

Yours,
Henry Evington

Ben carefully folded the letter and put it aside.

Hal had proved the best kind of friend. Although Ben had not seen him since the day he had hastily embarked on the first ship to leave the Pool of London, they had written often. At least once a month, although the letters were long delayed.

After his father had cast him off, Ben determined never to contact the man again. He'd made such a mess, this being only the latest in a series of scandals, that he longed for a clean sheet, a new start.

The night before his rash challenge, his father had carpeted him, threatening to beat him, but it was the grief on his father's face rather than his empty promises that had distressed Ben. He'd spurned the match his parents had chosen for him, deciding that Lady Dorothea Rowland was too staid for his taste, and turned to chasing Honoria instead.

His mother had sobbed out her distress. They were better off without him. And her last words, "You would be better dead, Ben. I fear I have done you a bad turn somehow, that I failed you."

Those words had hurt him more than the opprobrium his father had heaped on his head. That his mother blamed herself.

Consequently, when he'd met Louis, he'd issued the challenge. He had lost his parents' love, so losing Honoria had been the last straw.

After the duel, he'd rushed to the docks and taken the next ship to leave, never minding where it went. It had sailed to Boston on the tide, and here he still was.

Louis had survived, for which Ben was profoundly grateful, but he had no wish to return home, or to contact his cousin. He'd made such a mess of everything; he was better off dead.

Maybe I should go home. Instant discomfort made him shift his stance.

His marriage had ended when his wife died trying to birth their child, and he'd inherited a business from his father-in-law, Jeremiah Foulson, when he'd died shortly after his daughter.

Ben was successful, a merchant in his own right, a life he savored more than he had ever enjoyed his life as the heir of a marquess.

Ben gazed out the window at the ships below. He owned some of them. Men scurried about on the dock, loading and unloading. This country would be far greater than most people in the civilized world imagined. He'd visited the interior, and there was far more of it than appeared on the maps. And he still hadn't reached the other coast. There was so much to do and discover here, unlike his cynical, well-mapped homeland.

But that elm tree in the Home Park—did the initials he'd carved there still exist? And that dip past the rose garden where a boy could hide for hours—was it still there?

If he went home, he'd have to stay for at least a year, maybe more. His duties in Britain would demand his attention. Eventually he could appoint a manager for the estates at home. If Louis had reduced them so much, that was definitely possible.

Maybe find a new wife. Someone intelligent, who could look after affairs at home. If he stayed for the year, he could marry and start his nursery, provide an heir to cut Louis off from creating further depredations. Another duty wife, but this time they would live on opposite sides of the world. More a business partner.

A sense of regret lingered. His dreams of having someone he could share a life with, loving her and having love in return, had vanished. He doubted that would happen now.

Nonsense. Sentimental nonsense at that. Better he put youthful dreams of romance where they belonged; at the bottom of the sea.

Ben would have sworn to hell and back that he cared little for the estate and the title he'd abandoned. But he was wrong. His inheritance burned deep, a part of him. He'd been bred to care for it, to support it, to ensure its health and well-being and that of everyone who belonged to it. If Louis had proved a worthy master, Ben could have kept away with good conscience, but now? He could not do it.

Even if Louis had been near death's door after the duel, Ben had carried that guilt for too long.

Ben stared through the bristling masts to the horizon, where gray sea met gray sky. Already his mind teemed with plans, possibilities. He did not fool himself that regaining what he had lost would be easy. But for his father's sake, or for the name he still bore, he should do it.

He stared back out to sea.

He would go.

Chapter 3

Dorothea Rowland closed the door of the bedroom assigned to her and breathed a heavy sigh of relief. Arriving at Cressbrook House in the early afternoon with a plethora of other guests had exhausted her social tolerance. Now she had some time to herself, and she would make the most of it.

She looked around. Her traveling trunk had not arrived yet, but the maid had promised a footman would bring it up directly, which probably meant at least two hours.

This room was not the best in the house; with prestigious guests included in the party, she could hardly expect that. But it was pleasant enough, if a little spartan, tucked at the end of a long corridor that also contained the rooms assigned to her brother and sister-in-law.

Being, at the age of thirty, an older spinster, destined to become that dreadful thing, an unmarried woman, she had often been placed in less-than-pleasant surroundings. This room would serve her well enough. The old-fashioned four-poster bed at least sported a modern mattress, which boded well for her night's sleep. An upholstered chair was set by the window, and a chest of drawers capacious enough to hold her modest belongings stood against the wall opposite. She had no bureau, but the table near the window would suffice for writing her letters once she'd cleared it of its motley collection of ornaments and empty vases.

Best of all, since she had a corner room she had windows on two sides. Even better, they opened easily and stayed that way, since they were of the old-fashioned latched type instead of modern sashes. Cool air rushed in, bringing a gentle breeze that made Dorothea groan in pleasure. The tiny, airless rooms in the inns they'd used had given her sleepless nights on the way here. She was tempted to lie down on that mattress and send her excuses for dinner.

The windows gave a view of the front of the house, the Home Park stretching to the horizon. The mature elms marching down either side of the drive added a touch of majesty.

The clock on the mantelpiece struck two. Two hours to dinner. Finding her bag, Dorothea plucked out the leather portfolio and opened it to reacquaint herself with the contents. Not that she needed to, but every time she touched the thing a sense of exhilaration flooded her. No more the discarded spinster, Dorothea now had a purpose in life. She was a member of the Society for Single Ladies, and she was here on a mission. She was supposed to meet the officer from the Crown Office, Sir James Hunstone, within the hour. So she could do no more than freshen up before she went downstairs. She glanced at the bed regretfully. No time to rest.

Someone knocked at the door, and Dorothea hastily closed the portfolio and shoved it back in her bag. Her sister-in-law's maid, Brooks, entered, two footmen hauling Dorothea's trunk in her wake. "My mistress says you must use me as much as you wish, ma'am. Would you like to change now?"

Dorothea shook the skirts of her traveling gown ruefully. "I'm afraid it was rather muddy today. What do we have?"

Twenty minutes later, arrayed in her new gown of blue striped lustring, her silver SSL pin tucked behind the robings on the left-hand side, Dorothea set forth to meet the officer of the Crown.

Cressbrook House was larger than she'd been led to believe, but the domestic staff were friendly, if reserved. She got directions to the small green parlor easily enough. Exhilaration filled Dorothea anew. At last, she was doing something useful, something that mattered. Dwindling into an old maid, even with a family as kind as hers, was not a fate she looked forward to.

Her first assignment for the SSL was a personal connection. She'd entered society two years before the beauteous Lady Honoria Colt, and while she had not driven young men to their knees, she'd been noticed. Lord Brocklebank, Ben to his friends, had entered into a gentle courtship with her, and she'd been lost. But her father had bidden him wait for her to grow a little older, and he'd agreed. Although Dorothea knew Ben wasn't in love with her, she'd fallen for him the instant she'd seen him.

She'd never forget her first sight of him. Brocklebank had stood out as the most handsome, the most desirable of them all, tall and elegantly built. A pang had hit her as sharp as a knife between her ribs, and she'd wanted him with every sinew in her young body. He'd been taller than her, a definite advantage, since no man wanted a wife who looked down on him. In her late mother's words, Dorothea was "unconscionably tall." Her quiet happiness at the unspoken arrangement between them had colored her life. She'd had every expectation that their time together would be happy. She had love enough for two. Not that she had ever told him. Her shyness at the time had precluded that.

Then, the next season, Lady Honoria Colt had descended on society and drawn men like iron filings to a magnet. Dorothea had pale hair; Honoria's was of spun gold. Dorothea's features were not remarkable, while men wrote sonnets to Honoria's fine eyes and clear complexion. Ben had abandoned Dorothea—or rather, smiled at her and told her they would always be friends, would they not? He'd left it to her brother to break the bad news to her, that the negotiations for the marriage contract would not now take place.

Dorothea had berated him bitterly, but not to his face, and the negotiations for the marriage settlement melted away as if they'd never been. Lady Honoria became the prize to be won.

Then, after the duel, Benedict had disappeared, never to return. Dorothea had pined for him, but tried to move on. At the time, she'd expected to make some kind of a match, but the seasons had passed without one. There had always been someone more lovely and accomplished than her. And shorter.

Now she would remember her advantages, not her losses. She had much to be thankful for. This investigation would put an end to an unfortunate chapter in her life, as Angela had known when she'd handed her the portfolio.

Dorothea had paid only one visit to Cressbrook House before, but she remembered it well. That summer when she'd been happy. She was a different person now, with a different future to plan for. *Remember that, and finally close the door on youthful dreams.*

Left, then right at the painting of the miserable child—yes, because the second door on her left led to the room she'd been looking for. Unmistakably the small green parlor. The upholstery on the sofa set before the unlit fire was green, the walls were green, and so were most of the ornaments. An edge of shabbiness marked the room, and a dullness signifying that it did not receive much love from the housemaids.

A dapper gentleman sat on the green leather armchair by the fireplace. He rose at her entrance. "Miss Rowland?"

She dropped a short curtsy to match his bow. "Indeed. And you are Sir James Hunstone."

He nodded. "You do not object to spending time alone with a gentleman? I had thought you would bring your maid."

Dorothea gave a most unladylike snort. "And have our business discussed in the kitchen before the day is out? I think not, sir. I doubt you will pounce on me with unalloyed passion."

The gentleman raised a slim brow. "You don't do yourself justice, ma'am." He was about fifty years old or thereabouts, a neat appearance indicating a man who did not allow fashion to rule his life. While respectable, his maroon coat and green waistcoat did not display extravagant embroidery, spangles or gilded buttons, but they were perfectly acceptable. Instinctively, Dorothea liked him.

He sat down and crossed his legs, while she disposed her skirts comfortably. "Shall I begin?" he asked. When she nodded assent, he went on. "Mr. Louis Thorpe contacted the coroner about declaring his cousin dead. That means as soon as the courts confirm the death, Louis can claim the marquessate as the next heir in line. When it is ratified by the Lord Chancellor and approved by the King, he will inherit the estate. However, we are by no means certain that Lord Brocklebank is dead, and if he is, what became of him? Why has nobody heard from him?"

Dorothea ignored the inevitable pang when the prospect of Ben's death was spoken of so calmly. What else did she expect? "I agree. And the usual period to wait until death is declared is seven years after the person has disappeared, is it not?"

Sir James's thin lips flattened. "Lord Hardwicke and I are deeply concerned that Lord Brocklebank met his end, either as a result of injury sustained in the duel, or shortly after. Nefariously. You understand?"

Dorothea nodded. "Yes. Duels are illegal, and if his death occurred as a result, that makes Louis a murderer." The pang turned into an ache. "I never considered that." Surely not. Louis Thorpe was many things, but not a murderer. "Are you considering removing the title altogether?"

Sir James raised his brows. "Not while there is a legitimate heir in Louis Thorpe's younger brother, and after that, his uncle. If we did that, the House of Lords would turn on us like an angry tiger. Or a collection of them." His forehead pleated in a frown. "A herd of tigers? A bunch?"

"A prowl?" she suggested, and received a nod and a reluctant smile.

"We must be sure of our facts, ma'am. If Mr. Thorpe was responsible for Lord Brocklebank's death, we cannot allow him to profit from that. However, the case would be difficult, and we have no wish to drag Mr. Thorpe through the mud if we are not sure of our facts."

"I see." So Ben's death could go unavenged. After all this time, what proof could they uncover? Dorothea tried to think of him as Lord

Brocklebank, nothing to do with her or the man she'd set her girlish heart on eight years ago.

Sir James lifted his hand, turning it in an elegant flip and curving his fingers to her. "And then we have the problem of the estate. Mr. Thorpe's extravagance is growing worse. I would appreciate anything you have to tell me from that aspect of the affair. We are concerned he will create a weak link, that he will plunge a great estate into debt that would enable others to take advantage."

He was listening to her, treating her as someone who mattered. Dorothea knew exactly what she could share with the officer of the Crown. "Thank you for being frank, sir. I will try to be equally honest with you. I am empowered to tell you that Mr. Thorpe has borrowed a considerable sum from Childers's Bank. On demanding payment, Childers's received no answer except for a request for more loans secured on the estate. Naturally, it is reluctant to do that until Mr. Thorpe is confirmed as the Marquess of Belstead. Miss Childers wishes to ensure the security of the existing loans and assure herself that Mr. Thorpe has the security to ask for more."

"Miss Childers is far more formidable than her appearance indicates," Sir James murmured.

Angela was fair-haired, blue-eyed, and very beautiful. Her refusal to marry was because of her vast wealth, not for want of proposals. Her fragile loveliness had caused many people to assume she did not have a soul of iron. She had proved them wrong.

"She is," was all Dorothea said now. "The bank is deeply concerned that Mr. Thorpe will renege on his current debts. If he accedes to the title, the bank will lose the ability to cast him into debtor's prison. Childers's Bank will not enter into unsecured loans."

Sir James touched his lip. "It is almost inconceivable to consider how much money that young man has gone through in the past two years, and his debts have increased recently. His lordship made a grave mistake trusting Mr. Louis Thorpe with his affairs."

The last anyone had heard of Lord Brocklebank was a letter granting his cousin power of attorney in his absence, which had been sent four months after his lordship's disappearance. He had enclosed it in a letter to his mother, begging her forgiveness for his transgressions. Nobody could discern where it had been sent from, since the outer wrapping had been destroyed, and it had magically appeared at the London offices of the estate's man of business. However, the handwriting had undoubtedly been his lordship's, properly drawn up and witnessed, and the enclosed letter mentioned a few matters known only to the family, small incidents from Brocklebank's childhood confirmed by his parents.

"As I recall, Mr. Thorpe had not shown any sign of extravagance before he married Honoria."

"Only the usual rashness of a young man," Sir James admitted. "But he demonstrated a positive gift for it after he had control of the estate. He was trained alongside Lord Brocklebank, with a view to him becoming the land steward to the estate once his lordship inherited, so in a way the decision was a natural one, even considering the circumstances of the duel."

The House of Lords had decreed that the date of the presumed death must be taken from the reception of the letter. So at the end of this month, Ben would be officially dead. He would take all Dorothea's girlish dreams with him.

"Just so."

They were in accord. But the business was uncomfortable for all involved, and a great pity. "This house is beautiful, if a little run-down in parts." Dorothea got to her feet and ran her finger along the windowsill, coming up with a fine film of dust.

Since she had stood, Sir James followed suit. "However, Mr. Thorpe has made many extravagant purchases for the estate, as if he had no doubt he would inherit. He has, as Lord Brocklebank's accredited steward, sold some outlying unentailed assets." He sighed heavily. "I will do my best to get an overview of the accounts."

"If you do, I would appreciate seeing them."

He nodded. "I will ensure you are informed." He went to the door, but paused in the action of opening it. "I would caution you not to go into situations where you might be in danger. If Mr. Thorpe was willing to do away with his cousin, he will not hesitate to do the same to any person who threatens his inheritance. We will try to make sure we have all the facts. When we are sure, the inheritance will most likely go through, but by then Mr. Thorpe would be in prison awaiting trial. So promise me you will not appear to others to be too interested in this case. Does your brother know what you are up to?"

She nodded. "He told me much the same. If there is the least suspicion of danger, I am to back away."

She did not say she would, merely that she had been told to do so. She was not foolhardy, and she had a couple of pistols in her luggage, which she well knew how to use. Since this gathering was designated a hunting party, nobody would see it as very unusual. And travel could be dangerous. But that was not what the weapons were for.

But for the sake of her lost love, the man she'd given her heart to so long ago, she'd do her best to discover everything she could and ensure he was avenged. Of course she was over her youthful passion now. Naturally she was.

"If we need to meet," he continued, "we may as well use this room. It is rarely used and is out-of-the-way enough to avoid attracting attention. If I ask you to meet me, we may merely name a time."

"I agree. We should achieve much more together than we do apart." She liked Sir James, despite his overcautious approach. "Mr. Thorpe has invited his particular cronies, the ones he expects to approve of his actions. Some were on Hampstead Heath that fateful day."

"Indeed. Conversations can be had before we put the enquiry on an official footing. If necessary, I will formally accuse him and call in the local magistrate, although a case such as this could end in the House of Lords."

The Thorpe family must bear a curse. Only Louis's younger brother, William, could save them if Louis was brought to trial for the death of his cousin.

Sir James opened the door for her to precede him. "I appreciate your help, ma'am, and while we may not be able to affect anything, at least we have tried."

* * * *

Dorothea dressed herself for dinner without the help of a maid, but she didn't find the task too arduous. Her dark green satin gown was perhaps not at the height of fashion, but nobody would be expecting her to be the center of attention. Pairing the gown with the white petticoat with the embroidery around the hem that had taken her most of last December to complete gave her at least a respectable presence. She wouldn't powder. Not everybody did in the country. Locating her evening gloves and picking up her fan, she set out. She had no difficulty navigating her way to the drawing room, where the party was gathering before dinner.

The atmosphere in the great drawing room was fraught. Tension snapped in the air as the groups of people, around twenty persons total, chatted quietly. Dorothea had no doubt they were all talking about the same thing. This room was spacious enough to ensure a measure of privacy, but not to prevent threads of words drifting around. She was right. "Marquess" and "new" were two of the words she caught. As always in company, she kept her head down and spoke quietly, listening more than talking. Not that people asked for her opinion very often. But she was used to that. In society, people tended to prefer the sound of their own voices to anyone else's.

Major William Thorpe, brother to Louis, for once not in his regimentals, smiled at her, crossed the room to where she stood, and bowed over her hand. "It is good to see you again, Miss Rowland, after our delightful time together at the Wilkinson rout last year. How are you?"

"Very well." He held her hand for a few seconds longer than necessary. William Thorpe was altogether a different person from his brother. His army career was prospering, and his kindly features belied the warrior he was reputed to be. William would have made a solid, dependable marquess, but he was the younger brother. "Have you been abroad recently?"

"Constantly," he said. "I try to keep myself busy. However, the general has threatened to have me transferred to Horse Guards for a spell." He touched his upper arm. "A wound I sustained refused to heal. It's well now, but a period of enforced rest is called for. Do you spend much time in London?"

"I do, yes. I accompany my brother and sister-in-law when they go to town for the season. Although I'm not on the marriage mart any longer, I find plenty to do."

He raised a brow. "I wouldn't say that. The part about not being on the marriage mart, I mean." He stood to one side of the sofa, as if protecting her, though from what, Dorothea had no idea. Perhaps, at this late stage in her career, she'd finally found another suitor. That would be exceedingly odd, but Dorothea wasn't the idealistic young woman she'd been on her entrance into society. She was no longer seeking passion and love, but a comfortable partnership.

When Louis Thorpe entered the drawing room, his wife by his side, the sound dipped, then rose once more. Mr. Thorpe was his usual handsome self, his smiles proclaiming pleasure in his imminent triumph. Honoria Thorpe had hardly changed from the golden beauty who had taken society by storm seven years ago. Despite giving birth twice, her figure was as elegant as ever.

Smiles and laughter increased, and soon a lively group surrounded the pair. "Of course, I am devastated to have to do this," Thorpe said, loud enough for everyone to hear. "However, my cousin's disappearance is a tragedy that needs bringing to its inevitable conclusion." Regret tinged his voice.

"I wish you would tell us what really happened that day," Lady Steeping said, her cherry-red lips drawn in a pout.

"Most people are aware of the events, which I deeply regret." He glanced around the room, drawing in his audience. "Despite his own wounds, my cousin fled in a waiting coach with my blessing. I gave him my forgiveness before he left, as a dying man should, but I recovered. Unfortunately, when we made enquiries, thinking to contact him, he had already sailed, or so we were told." He heaved a sigh. "Such a pity. We've heard nothing of him since, apart from the letter we got in August, giving me power of attorney. We could not tell from that where the letter had come from. I do not even know where he perished, but it seems likely his wound eventually got the better of him, or he encountered some other incident we know nothing of."

He caught Dorothea's attention for a fleeting moment before passing on, his gaze encompassing everyone in the room. Truly, he was astonishingly handsome. His turquoise eyes attracted her attention first, but after that, the pure line of his straight nose and the clear outline of his firm chin and strong forehead. Naturally he wore the fashionable wig, as did most men present, but his seemed snowier than the others.

Looking at him, and his control of the room, she could barely believe that he had gone through a fortune in the last few years. He seemed intelligent, poised, and perfect. But he was not.

"Miss Rowland," he said suddenly, breaking through the people surrounding him and heading straight for her. "You have a comment to make?"

What had he seen in her? Had she frowned? No, but perhaps that fleeting glance had shown him more than she wanted to display. She gathered her senses, brought herself back down to earth. Next to her, Dorothea's sister-in-law, Ann, remained perfectly still, as if sitting for her portrait. "Only that I could be referring to you as 'your lordship' before the week is out."

Would that be enough to deflect him? She could not give her mission away now. He must not know she had severe doubts about his accession to the title.

One corner of his mouth turned up in a half smile. The gesture looked practiced to her. Why should she be surprised, when society itself was full of poses and rehearsed remarks? "You flatter me. I daresay the process will take a week or two at the least, not a few days. Is that not so, Sir James?"

Sir James, who had not looked her way since their first mutual recognition on entering the room, glanced at her and nodded. "Indeed, I'm afraid the wheels of administering an unusual occurrence can take time to roll. We are unused to such events. However, I am certain the matter will be concluded to everyone's satisfaction."

Beside him, an audible "humph" came from Lord Evington. The man had been a close friend of the late marquess, or the missing marquess, or whatever they were going to call Benedict when he was declared officially dead. He had been present at the duel that had started this whole affair. "What will you do if he turns up alive after all?" he asked.

Of course Lord Evington would not want his friend to be dead. "That is why we make the process so thorough," Sir James said. "I am here to ensure justice is served."

Lord Evington nodded. "I will abide by the decision, naturally." He slanted a glance at Sir James. "I would have a word with you, sir."

"Indeed, and so you should, to ensure everything is done properly." At last Mr. Thorpe turned away from her. Dorothea fought against breathing a sigh of relief and revealing her own thoughts. She found his attention deeply unsettling, especially so close. "I, too, want the matter decided beyond dispute."

As it would be. Once the Crown decided on Louis Thorpe as the new marquess, the decision would be hard to revoke. If the missing man turned up, he'd have to challenge the decision in court and create a precedent in the law. The Crown could even rule not to recognize him, because a title *holder* was just that. She couldn't recall a time outside the Civil War where a title had been removed from a living person and awarded to someone else. What a mess. Enough to wish that the matter was clear now, as Mr. Thorpe desired. But she wanted justice done and needed to ensure Angela was compensated for the heavy debts Mr. Thorpe had run up. No wonder he was looking triumphant, the very set of his head as if he proudly wore a crown. Or to be more precise, a coronet.

"It will be decided soon," Mr. Thorpe said confidently. "Keeping the estate in limbo like this is not good management. Honoria and I will be making our bow at court before too long as the Marquess and Marchioness of Belstead."

A new voice came from the doorway. "I believe the saying is 'over my dead body.'"

Chapter 4

Louis had a pinch of snuff in his fingers, and that, together with his open snuffbox, tumbled to the floor. Fine brown powder spilled everywhere, but nobody took notice.

Lord Steeping strode forward, flinging up a hand, palm out, as if that would stop the man standing in the doorway. "Who are you, sir, to interrupt us so rudely? Are you a guest here?" He turned to Louis, an expectant sneer on his arrogant face.

"No, sir, I'm not a guest." The man turned his full attention to his cousin. "Tell them, Louis. Who am I?"

Dorothea watched the tall, powerful, travel-stained man as his gaze swept the room. Shock arced through her. He wasn't dead? Ben didn't have a twin, so surely it couldn't be anyone else. He'd grown broader in the shoulder, and his face was not as smooth as it had once been, but for all that, it couldn't be anyone else. Those emotions she had considered dead, had fought to kill, returned in full force.

As she rose to her feet, she caught his attention. He halted, staring at her, eyes widening. Dorothea did not think to look away. The fraught few seconds lasted a lifetime, and then his gaze swept on, taking in the guests dressed in their finery.

She knew him, as did most of the people in this room. Benedict Thorpe, more properly known as the Earl of Brocklebank, only son and heir of the late Marquess of Belstead, firmed his square chin and gave his whole attention to his cousin. "Well?"

He was certainly arrogant enough for a marquess. He always had been.

The footman had completely forgotten his duties and stood gaping at the door.

Louis raised his quizzing glass to his eye. "I do not think I have the pleasure of knowing you."

"No, Louis, that will not wash. Do not pretend not to know me, it's only been seven years. I'm back to claim what is mine."

Schultz had come up behind Benedict and addressed Louis. "Mr. Thorpe, sir, I would have announced Lord Brocklebank's arrival, but he moves faster than I do."

Mr. Thorpe held up a hand. "Stop. We have no proof that this rapscallion is Lord Brocklebank, much less the new marquess. Do you admit every ruffian who comes to the door claiming to be a dead man?" He glared at Schultz, who met his gaze directly.

The butler bowed. "Only when he is his lordship, sir. I have known his lordship since he was in short clothes, and I am seeing him now." He pivoted on his heel and addressed the newcomer. "My lord, your room is ready."

Dorothea forced herself to breathe.

Lord Brocklebank glanced at the butler and nodded, flashing him a smile that did terrible things to Dorothea's heart.

"Sir, you may have the appearance of my late cousin, but I have evidence that he died," Mr. Thorpe said, lifting his chin, so he could glare down his nose at the disheveled man standing at the door.

"Then your evidence is wrong," his lordship snapped. "Because here I am, not dead."

He had changed, but not so much that nobody could recognize him. The young Lord Brocklebank had drawn all eyes. But back then he'd had a slender, elegant figure, and he'd laughed all the time. Too much, she'd thought sometimes. He worked his way through society frantically, as if avoiding reality, seeking out distractions like a dying man who had a week to live. As if his proposed betrothal to Dorothea and their marriage would end his fun. This man was far more powerfully built than the Lord Brocklebank she remembered, but the voice was the same, rumbling and low, the air of command unmistakable.

Dorothea had long reconciled herself to be unremarked, ignored, but now it irked her. She wanted to be the person he turned to. The desire delved deep into her, to the parts of her body she did her best to ignore. He had once, however briefly and reluctantly, been hers.

He was not dead. She repeated the words to herself, trying to come to terms with them. *He is not dead.* She had to change "was" to "is" and learn to cope with it, just as she had coped with his—probable—death.

Sir James cleared his throat. "If I may introduce myself, I am Sir James Hunstone, here on behalf of the Crown to settle the question of the title.

Am I correct in assuming you are claiming to be Lord Brocklebank, who was last heard of seven years ago this month?"

The man inclined his head. "You are indeed correct. But I do not claim to be him. I *am* him, although I have gone by the name of Benjamin Thorpe for the last seven years."

"Then may I suggest you continue with that name for a few days longer?" Sir James might be formal, but nobody would gainsay him.

After staring at Sir James for a few moments, Ben nodded. His chest moved as he took several deep breaths. "Very well. But this matter must receive your immediate attention."

"I intend for it to do so, sir. However, this unexpected development puts a different cast on the affair. You will allow me a day or two to question the household and gather more information."

"Yes, of course. And in the meantime, I'll go to my room and change for dinner. I shouldn't be above twenty minutes."

Thorpe spoke, his voice trembling, though whether with anger or fear was not clear. "How do I know you will not steal what you can and leave? Or murder us all in our beds?"

Slowly, Benedict Thorpe turned his head. "Because you do. You know me, Louis."

Thorpe gasped and closed his eyes. No one had stepped forward to support his claim that the intruder was an impostor.

With a sigh, Mrs. Thorpe, who had expected to become the marchioness before the year was out, put the back of her hand to her forehead and collapsed in a graceful faint.

A very well-timed faint. Dorothea admired her timing. Very graceful, too.

Her husband caught her, lifting her against him before glaring at his cousin as if to accuse him of causing the dramatic reaction. "You see what you've done?"

Benedict—not Benjamin, why had he used that name?—studied the woman cradled in Louis Thorpe's arms. "She always did enjoy being the center of attention."

"You should have warned us you were coming."

Benedict gave a slight shrug. "What would you have me do? Send a letter and wait for your invitation to my own house? I think not."

Standing by the fireplace, Major Thorpe watched, no expression on his austere features.

The arrogance, the assumption that Benedict would be instantly accepted, astonished her, until Dorothea, naturally observant, spotted a tiny twitch by the side of his left eyebrow. He was not as relaxed as he at first appeared.

He glanced at Honoria. Did his lips curve, did his eyes soften when he looked at her? Dorothea thought so. "Please offer Mrs. Thorpe my best wishes if she recovers before I return."

And he turned on his heel and left, followed by Lord Evington, who had always been his friend.

A low voice at her side told Dorothea that Sir James had taken advantage of the confusion to move closer to her. "Goodness me," he said softly, so only she could hear. "If you are free at ten tomorrow, I would appreciate your opinion." He didn't have to say where. She already knew.

"Indeed, sir. What a shock! Had you any idea that this would happen?"

Sir James grimaced. "None at all. The new guest certainly made an entrance, did he not?"

"He is the marquess."

"That," said the Lord Chancellor's representative firmly, "remains to be seen. We can assume nothing yet, not until I have ratified the title and written my recommendations. If he carries any title at all, it's Lord Brocklebank."

"Surely that is merely a formality?" Lady Steeping pursued. "Oh, it is he, no doubt. Even under the mud of the road I recognized him. He set London on its ear when he appeared at the balls after his grand tour." She glanced at Mrs. Thorpe. "Everyone said he would win the heart of Mrs. Thorpe, but of course Mr. Thorpe beat him to it."

Dorothea didn't know whether to be glad or sad that Lady Steeping hadn't remembered Ben's brief connection with her. On the one hand, she didn't want to be pitied, but on the other, it evidently meant more to her than it did to anyone else.

Mr. Thorpe tenderly carried his wife over to the sofa and laid her on it. Even in a faint the lady was graciously lovely, the silk of her pink gown billowing around her like a protective cocoon. Major Thorpe stood with his hand on the back of the sofa, as if guarding her, but his gaze strayed to Dorothea. He nodded, unsmiling.

Sir James added his mite. "It is not unknown for someone who greatly resembles a missing person to attempt to claim their inheritance."

"Then you think he is an impostor!" Mr. Thorpe's color returned, and his eyes sparkled. He seemed positively energized by Sir James's words.

Sir James stared down his long, patrician nose at Mr. Thorpe. "No, sir, that would be foolish. However, proofs must be obtained."

"Is not recognition enough?" Dorothea's brother demanded. "We all know him."

"Or you think you do." Sir James lifted a hand. "I wish to be absolutely sure this is the missing marquess. I will set about obtaining signed statements from those people who recognize him, how and from when. You may call him whatever you wish, but to call him Lord Brocklebank is to accept that he is without doubt the missing heir."

The man was nothing if not meticulous. Fussy, even.

"Oh." Mrs. Thorpe came to with a graceful wave of her white hand. Her husband helped her to sit up, as she protested apologies. Not a hair out of place, as if she'd fainted in some kind of gossamer tomb. "I am so sorry, I must apologize. Such a vulgar response!"

Someone handed her a brimming glass of red wine. She took a sip, then another larger gulp.

"Think nothing of it, dear lady," Sir James said. "Such a shock would make the most straitlaced of women fall down in a dead faint."

Dorothea liked that, but from the approving murmurs, she assumed she was the only person to collect Sir James's deeper meaning, that Mrs. Thorpe was not at all straitlaced. Or perhaps she was imagining it. It wouldn't be the first time.

People were talking in small groups, fans wafting or covering faces so words could not be read on their lips. Dorothea remained by the fireplace with her brother and sister-in-law as Sir James drifted away.

"Is he who I think he is?" Ann asked her.

"Yes," Dorothea answered. Ann had not met Ben in person. "It's Benedict Thorpe, all right. Lord Brocklebank as ever was, whatever Sir James says."

Laurence lowered his voice, "I thought Mr. Thorpe would be the first to faint. He went white as chalk when Benedict appeared. Despite his accusations, he knew his cousin on sight."

"Did you see Louis's brother?" Ann murmured. "He is completely frozen. One cannot discern what he is thinking."

Dorothea must write to Angela posthaste. She was staying at a house about fifty miles away, so the message would not reach her for a few days. Perhaps Laurence would let her borrow one of the grooms he'd brought to convey the message as quickly as possible. But she would not talk to him about that now. Better to leave it until later.

Her mind spun with questions. So much to think about. Where had Benedict been? Why had he not returned before now, or even contacted anyone? Had he discovered that his cousin had put forward a claim to have him declared dead?

She voiced none of them aloud. Some would become evident in time, and others...she'd talk to Sir James about those.

Mrs. Thorpe had recovered her composure by the time the marquess— Lord Brocklebank—returned, about fifteen minutes later. Behind him, Lord

Evington stood like a guard, although from the size of the newcomer's frame, he needed nobody to protect him.

He presented a formidable sight, now he had washed off the mud and changed into something more suitable. He wore a wine-red coat of broadcloth with plain gold buttons, and a waistcoat of cream silk striped with a paler shade. His embroidery was limited to the edges of the waistcoat, his buttonholes, and the pocket flaps. Very plain for a society outfit, but the embroidery was gold twill, which made up for the severity somewhat. A gold ring adorned the smallest finger of his left hand. Apart from that, and the gold buckles at his knees and on his shoes, he wore no jewelry. Interestingly, he wore his own dark hair unpowdered. He hadn't done that before. The style was catching on with the more daring set, but the simplicity of his appearance indicated he had little time for fashion.

For all that, he was every inch an aristocrat.

Benedict Thorpe had put on muscle. His broad shoulders were only the start of a magnificent body, finished with a pair of well-shaped calves and ankles. Whatever Ben had done in his long absence, he had not wasted time on indulgences. His complexion was darker than fashion dictated, indicating hours spent in the open air, and his skin was weathered, roughness apparent on his cheeks and forehead.

He crossed the floor and bowed to Mrs. Thorpe, where she sat, pale faced, on the best sofa. "My apologies for causing you any distress, madam." When she held out her hand, he bent over it, but not far enough to turn the courtly gesture into a romantic one. "Schultz has advised me that he has added the extra place at the dinner table." He moved away, leaving her hand hovering in midair. "I requested that he remove the places at the top and bottom of the table. Tonight, we are rudderless until the representative of the Crown makes a decision about the estate." He bowed to Sir James, who inclined his head in response. "I assume nothing, and since I've been known as Mr. Thorpe since I left the country, I'm quite happy to continue in that for a few days more."

Cleverly done. Benedict had given Sir James the courtesy of ratifying his claim. And he had reduced Louis to the same stature as himself. That negated any advantage Louis had by being the acknowledged heir presumptive to the marquessate for the last seven years.

Louis Thorpe's low growl could be heard by everyone in the hushed room, but he said nothing.

By custom, the marquess, or Mr. Thorpe, as he must be called for the time being, should lead the highest-ranking lady into dinner, but he made his way over to where Dorothea now sat by her sister-in-law. "Since we are to go into dinner with a lack of ceremony, I would like to request the honor of escorting you, Miss Rowland."

Dorothea tried not to gape and failed. She closed her mouth with a snap and accepted him by rising to her feet and placing her hand on his arm in the approved manner. Her hand met firm muscle, discernible despite the coat sleeve and shirt between them. Ben was so much—more than he'd been before. But she would not forget the way he had abandoned her. Nothing had been confirmed, nothing formally agreed upon, but society, and her family, had an understanding. She had been devastated when he pursued Honoria.

Her response to him now, an instinctive wanting, angered her. Had she lost all pride?

Louis hastily rose and performed a similar office for his wife. Since he was closer to the door, he led the company out. Small recompense, someone murmured as they passed.

"Is something the matter?" Benedict asked her.

"No. Why do you ask?"

He glanced down at her hand. "You appear to be trembling."

"Really?" She followed his gaze. "How perceptive of you."

The rumble in his throat signified his amusement—or did it? Not a muscle moved on his features when she glanced at him. Perhaps he was just clearing his throat. "It's good to see you again, Dorothea." As if he'd said nothing of significance, he continued, "I have to compliment you on your presence of mind, ma'am. I saw you exchange a few words with Sir James."

"I've known Sir James for a while," she said mendaciously.

Ben shot her a considering look. "Society is a morass of mutual acquaintances," he said smoothly as they entered the dining room. "The interconnections are staggering. I will have to relearn much of what I have forgotten, but I daresay a number of helpful people will put me in the way of it."

They would indeed. Dorothea allowed him to help her sit before he took his place next to her.

His presence overwhelmed her. He radiated confidence, strength, and yes, nobility. Everyone looked at him, even though he had refused to take his rightful place at the head of the table. Nobody would have mistaken him for anything but a man who understood his world and how to control it. But he seemed at ease. His poses were not studied, but natural, although grace prevailed. While he was no longer the laughing youth who'd lit up London's ballrooms, he'd gained something. If she had to put it into one word, she'd call it power.

She was experiencing a strong set of emotions, few that she could put a name to. Turmoil filled her, her powerful reaction to his return mingling with horror that they'd been about to declare him dead. And Ben, the man, had effortlessly evoked the memories of the young girl she'd put away years ago, together with the dreams she'd had back then. She would not allow them to return. That way led to heartbreak and loss. She would never open herself to anyone ever again, least of all the man by her side.

The table was already set. A plethora of dishes adorned the white linen, the porcelain the finest Chelsea, the hand-painted scenes of the estate lavishly adorned with gilding. Benedict glanced down at his plate. "This is new," he commented mildly.

"It's all the rage," his cousin said, raising his quizzing glass to examine, not his plate or the tureens, but the man sitting next to Dorothea. "I commissioned this set some time ago. Took the ruffians a year to make it. They sent an artist to make views of this estate and the one in Devonshire. They made quite a fuss, but I do think the result is pleasing."

"Yes," Benedict said. "And very expensive, I have no doubt."

A faint chill settled over the table. Nobody discussed expense, not in that way. "But worth it," Mrs. Thorpe remarked. She had quite recovered from her earlier fainting spell. Color had gathered in her cheeks once more, and the customary light smile that attractively tilted her lips was firmly back in place. "Who counts the cost when the result is so delightful?"

"I do," he said crisply. He lifted the lid from the nearest dish and offered Dorothea a helping of the contents.

She barely suppressed her shudder. The porcelain might be lovely, but what lay within was the stuff of nightmares. Her nightmares, at any rate. "Thank you, but no," she murmured. "I am not particularly hungry."

He glanced at her. "I recall you are not partial to white sauce."

He'd remembered that? Some people loved the stuff, but Dorothea was not one of them. All those years ago, when they'd attended a dinner and she had eaten very little, he'd noticed, and discreetly arranged for the fish in white sauce to be exchanged with something else. If he did that now, his attention would be commented on, and that was the last thing she wanted.

The dish had no steam rising from it. It must be cold, and a skin was forming on the surface of the food. She wished she had not taken this place, and was thankful, once he had lifted the lid of the other dish, to discover something more palatable. But the mixed vegetables, while acceptable, were also cold.

He sighed, and exchanged a glance with her, while their neighbors helped themselves to dishes. Guests were expected to make their meal out of whatever was nearest to them on the table. Besides, there would be other courses, and a dish of creamed potatoes stood nearby.

Dorothea took a deep draft of admittedly excellent wine to fortify herself for the ordeal ahead. This meal could hardly be anything else. Tensions ran high, not the most pleasant atmosphere for a meal of any kind.

After a few mouthfuls, Benedict sat back, holding his wineglass delicately between his fingers. The facets caught the light from the candelabra that were ranked down the center of the table. Above them the chandelier added more sparkle, its crystal drops polished to a high sheen.

"You have not enquired about the dowager," Louis pointed out, leaning over to snag a dish of beef.

"No, I have not," Ben agreed. He glanced across the table at his friend, Lord Evington, who gave him a discreet nod, presumably permission to reveal their continued friendship, as if nobody had seen it before. "Hal kept me informed of events. I asked the butler, who told me my mother keeps early hours. I will pay my respects as soon as she is well enough to receive me."

The dowager saw nobody these days, after falling ill with a condition not properly explained. She lived quietly and never went out in public. Rumor was that she was mad, or incapable, but the stories varied, so nobody knew for sure. The guests didn't expect to see her during this visit. With Louis in charge, she might be a prisoner, but his disinterested nod did not speak of someone keeping a woman under lock and key. "I'm sure she'll appreciate it." He narrowed his eyes. "If you are the person you claim to be."

Benedict's dark, winged brows rose slightly. "You do not object."

"No, why should I? She enjoys visitors. But do not stay too long, or she will tire." Louis returned to his meal, seemingly unaffected by the conversation.

Ben picked at his food. For such a large man he surely needed more than he had consumed. Perhaps thinking of his mother did not agree with his stomach.

The servants returned and took the dishes away before bringing in the second course. More tableware from the state service arrived in the footmen's white-gloved hands. Benedict lifted a finger and at once a footman appeared at his elbow. He murmured something and the footman lifted the dish he'd just set before them, went around the table and placed it in front of Ben's cousin. Louis glanced up at him, his eyes sparking with an unspoken challenge.

Ignoring his cousin, Benedict lifted the lids on the two dishes nearer to them when the footmen stood back. "We have a dish of lamb chops and one of glazed vegetables. No white sauce in sight. Oh, wait..." The dishes served to Louis were smothered in it.

Dorothea suppressed her smile. Benedict was a perceptive man. Louis picked up his wineglass and leaned back in his chair, his mouth in a mulish pout.

"Neither of us was fond of food covered in white sauce," Benedict continued. "Once my parents made us eat a pint each when we sent the dishes back from the schoolroom untouched. With nothing to make it interesting. I was—" he broke off, and grinned. "Never mind. It isn't a subject suitable for the table."

So Louis had the dishes served to his cousin, knowing he disliked it. That was either spiteful, or some kind of test.

"I still don't like white sauce," Benedict said conversationally, smiling. "I have learned to tolerate it, though."

Louis beckoned to the footman behind him, who obligingly refilled his glass.

"I have not lost my memories of what I left behind," Benedict said.

Farther down the table Sir James shifted in his chair and exchanged a glance with Dorothea.

"I have heard of cases of men with a remarkable resemblance to a claimant," Louis said. "I believe it is the custom to test the person."

A tendon in Benedict's throat tightened, but to all intents and purposes he remained relaxed. He lifted his knife and fork, and prepared to tuck in to a much more appetizing plateful. Dorothea had beaten him to it. "I believe it is," Benedict said now. "I am at the disposal of Sir James. I will do anything he wishes to establish my credibility." Smoothly deflecting the trouble brewing across the table, he addressed Sir James. "I believe people here recognize me and I must have certain memories, is that correct?"

Sir James breathed in deeply. "I believe in cases in dispute, that is the procedure."

Benedict's childhood memory was not accidental.

"I regret we must insist." Louis had regained some of his calmness. His voice had lowered to a normal tone, and his lips were not so tight. "The inheritance is considerable, and we must be sure the right person receives it."

"Of course," Benedict replied, and returned to his meal. The tinkle of fork against porcelain recommenced, and people conversed again.

"Did you say you planned a duck hunt for later in our visit?" someone asked Louis, his voice too bright, too obviously intent on changing the subject.

"Indeed. I had thought the gentlemen could leave the ladies to their tea and gossip for a day, unless they wish to come with us."

Dorothea choked on a quite delicious morsel of lamb. Immediately Benedict turned to her, picking up his glass of water and offering it to her. She held up her hand, warding him off. "Truly I am fine, sir. Thank you for your concern."

She caught the amused glint in his eye. Tea and gossip indeed! She had taken on a nobler cause, and something infinitely more interesting. She was positively glad Louis would not have a sniff of the marquessate. Not that she would dream of being so rag-mannered as to say so, but nobody could read her thoughts.

However, that would mean the absence of the male contingent for most of the day, when they were gone. She could run wild over the house, or rather, concentrate her research. A sense of relief swept over her. And she must write that letter to Angela. Perhaps she would do it tonight.

"Do you still hunt?" Lady Steeping asked Benedict.

"Sometimes." He paused, narrowing his eyes, assessing the company. A small nod, and then he added, "The quarry is somewhat larger and more dangerous in the colonies."

A hush fell over the company, and then, as if they had taken a collective breath, they came back at him. "What were you doing there?"

Benedict turned a cool, gray stare on him. "Making a living." But why had he not come back once he discovered he hadn't killed his cousin? Why would he stay away?

"You took ship for the colonies, then?" Louis asked.

"I did. I made landfall in Boston and obtained a position there."

The collective indrawn breath told what the assembled company thought of that. Dorothea looked at Lady Steeping, a lady in late middle age who had been an arbiter of correct behavior since her marriage twenty years before. Dorothea had wondered what she was doing at this gathering, but now she knew. Her gaze passed over the occupants of the table. The guests, at initial glance a motley crew, a very mixed collection, had all been chosen carefully. They were here to ratify Louis's accession to the title, and to spread the news as efficiently and fast as possible. Also, to lend their blessing to the occasion.

But it wasn't turning out that way.

"You were in Trade?" Lady Steeping asked, quiet outrage in every note. Dorothea hadn't realized that word contained quite so many syllables, and all with their separate intonation.

Benedict seemed totally oblivious to the polite consternation he had caused by his dramatic appearance and subsequent confession. However, Dorothea would wager her best aquamarine necklace that he was fully aware of it. "Indeed. Although I fled in a panic, the journey led to a most interesting adventure. I proved that I do not need the wealth I was to inherit. I had very little when I sailed, but I managed to make a decent fist of my career in the colonies." He sounded proud of his achievements. He should be.

"Where you went by the name of Benjamin Thorpe," Louis said.

Calling himself Benjamin instead of Benedict was a mistake. Perhaps his real name was Benjamin, after all. He did not appear perturbed, but Dorothea didn't know him well enough to be sure. However, no muscle twitched in his jaw in that telltale flick. "When I arrived, I said my name was Ben—you remember how everyone called me that? In my first position the man recorded my name as Benjamin, and I decided to stay with it."

That explained the change of name. It was entirely plausible that he would continue using the name people had assumed, rather than his real name. The use would help to disguise him, should someone recognize it.

Dorothea took a mouthful of lamb chop, savoring the food while watching the scene carefully and keeping her conclusions to herself. Benedict had moved the discussion on the names to his advantage, but not decisively so.

"What did you do in the colonies?" Ann said eagerly, giving voice to the question everyone wanted to ask.

He dealt her a bone-melting smile. "I worked for a ship owner. Clerked for him. Eventually I had a ship of my own."

"You were a captain?"

He shook his head. "I left that to the people with the best expertise to accomplish it." Then he turned his attention back to his plate. "I engaged in other pursuits."

So the Marquess of Belstead had been in trade, and he hadn't gained those muscles sitting at a desk scratching columns of figures with a pen. Goodness! But he was not encouraging any more questions. When Lady Steeping asked him what life was like in Boston he said, "Tolerably good for a working man."

He turned the answer to every question after that into a vague statement, not allowing the company to prize any more information from him. Eventually they tired of asking. Dorothea was certain he said only what he meant to say and no more. The man had learned much in his years away. The impulsive, arrogant youth with a short temper had gone, replaced by a man of considered temperament and confidence born from achievement rather than status.

"And I married."

Shock jolted Dorothea into choking. Solicitously Ben poured a glass of wine for her and waited until she'd dabbed her watering eyes and swallowed. She avoided his gaze when she accepted the wine and sipped carefully, allowing others to ask the questions.

"Where is your wife now?" Louis demanded.

"I lost her," he said softly. "Mary died in childbirth three years ago, together with our son."

Condolences followed in short order. The murmurs made Benedict visibly uncomfortable. He avoided meeting people's gazes, unusual for a man as direct as Ben. He stared at the tablecloth. "She was lively and kind and beautiful," he said. "I will miss her."

"And your unborn baby," Ann said softly. "I'm so sorry."

"Thank you. The child was not unborn. He breathed. But he was severely damaged inside, or so the midwife said." He picked up his glass and took a deep gulp of the liquid, then gave a shaky smile. "I beg your pardon; I did not mean to make anyone upset."

"Dear sir, we are sorry you had to go through that experience, and you are not the only person here today who has suffered a loss like that," Lady Steeping said, sympathetic for once.

Such were the vagaries of childbirth that many people had indeed gone through a similar ordeal. However, each tragedy was separate. "The doctor said the baby was too big for her," Benedict explained, his features totally impassive. "She was such a little thing."

Was it only Dorothea who saw he was deeply affected by his loss? He masked his expression so effectively he must have done it before. He must have loved his late wife very much to feel the loss so deeply.

Even now, she wished that woman was her. Mary had been the recipient of Ben's love, something Dorothea had never laid claim to, much though she wished she had.

Quiet conversation resumed. Ben ensured she had a generous helping of the apple pie that fortunately lay close to hand before the servants took the dishes away once more. After they removed the dinner and the candelabra from the center of the table, the servants reverently placed an exquisite Meissen dessert service on the polished mahogany surface. Figures of monkeys playing various instruments, and a set of dishes and plates containing sweets and fruit.

Benedict picked up a monkey playing the clarinet, his touch delicate, although his hands were large and showed evidence of work. Not calluses, of course not, a gentleman would never allow those, but his nails lacked the polish a valet would add to them, and the cuticles were ragged and thick. When Dorothea imagined male hands on her body, these were the ones she wanted. Strong, definitively masculine, rather than a pair of hands with polished, manicured nails and soft, pale skin.

Her weakness, but many women secretly dreamed of such. How else to explain the number of affairs ladies had with their footmen and gardeners? Hastily, she concentrated on the peach on her plate, fumbling for the fruit knife a footman had placed next to it.

"My mother bought this set," Benedict said. "She loved it. I am glad to see it still in service. She used to allow me to play with it, although my father would have it that I broke everything I touched." He skimmed the line of the black clarinet and put the monkey precisely back in place.

Dorothea tucked the knife under the skin of the peach.

"Allow me, dear lady," Benedict said softly, removing the knife from her grasp. Deftly he skinned the fruit, leaving as thin a line of peel as she had ever seen. As he quartered it, stoned it and sliced it into neat sections, people chatted of society affairs and other matters. Not a polite thing to do, but he had unnerved them by his command of the situation and his free admission that he had worked for his living. With those hands that were currently placing neat, perfect slices of succulent peach on her plate.

She lifted a piece to her mouth, and he watched her do it, his gray eyes set on her actions. Under the fine silk of her evening gown, Dorothea's body changed, warming, her skin growing sensitive and the place between her legs swelling and heating.

He could do that with one look? Turning his attention to her alone?

This man was dangerous. Far too much for her, even today. But Dorothea wanted to play with fire. He was clever, he was thoughtful, and he was turning this conversation exactly the way he wanted it. And she recognized her own bias. She'd loved him once, and if she did not take care, she'd find herself bound all over again.

Treasures like this dessert set, rather than the overdecorated, self-aware dinner service that had preceded it, the jewels Mrs. Thorpe made free with, needed saving, preserved from the carelessness that sought to destroy it all. And the power and wealth behind it that was helping to make the country a force to be reckoned with.

And why should she deny her attraction to Benedict? She'd wager every woman in the room felt that devastating allure he was turning on her now. Why, she wasn't sure, but it couldn't be because of her. She was nothing in this company, an older, unmarried spinster. Men could be cruel sometimes and more than once she'd been the recipient of it.

She ate another slice, forcing a pleasant smile, doing her best to hide her reaction. Why would he want to win her approval, seek to control her response to him? Did he know about Angela's commission?

That was the only answer. What else could it be?

Chapter 5

Reacquainting himself with the house he'd grown up in had proved a pleasure and a heartache in equal measure. But the worst and best had been visiting his mother. She was really ill, but to do Louis credit, he'd ensured she was as well as possible. Members of staff were assigned for her sole use, including a companion nurse. She had the seclusion she needed, and the comfort she was accustomed to.

But seeing her in that condition made him terribly unhappy.

Gazing out of the window on his way to his room, he saw two little girls romping in the sunshine. Pretty children, one three, and one seven years old, according to Hal's letter.

The nurse accompanying them smiled when Louis joined them. In no time at all he'd stripped off his coat and joined them on the grass, giving the older girl a ride on his back, and laughing as the baby flopped down on her well-padded bottom.

So they weren't abandoned, as Ben had been. His father had always been a distant figure, ensuring only that his heir had the education he needed. His mother was little better, but at least he'd seen her once a day, at least when they'd been in the same house. His cousins were his companions, but no more siblings came to join him. Ben was the one and only.

Would his son have had Ben's eyes, or Mary's? Been a placid boy, or a joyful, mischievous one?

Instead, the tiny child had drawn one breath before expiring. When the midwife had moved to take him away, Ben had stopped her, and gazed down into the face of his son, memorizing every feature, every pink fold, before saying goodbye.

There would always be a space in his heart for the boy. Even if he had other children, and he must if he was to cut Louis out, they would not take the place of his firstborn.

Ben made his way downstairs, thinking of escaping to the garden. There was a grotto where he used to go when he wanted solitude as a boy. That would be welcome now. At the back of the hall there were several rooms which led indirectly to the outside of the house, avoiding the huge back hall that was as grand as the front one. If he used one of those passages, he could avoid the guests, who seemed to be everywhere.

A door opened before him and a woman emerged.

"Oh!" Flushing, Dorothea dropped a small curtsy and made to hurry past him.

He caught her arm, not to hold her, but enough to make her pause. "No, stay. I was heading outside. Would you come for a walk with me?"

She glanced down at herself. "Without gloves or a hat?"

"I might allow you those." For the first time that day he smiled, and enjoyed her answering warmth. "I'd like to speak to you, if you don't mind."

"All right. I'll see you on the terrace in ten minutes."

Ben didn't know if she would come, but she did, charmingly arrayed in a simple straw hat and with the promised kid gloves on her hands, gloves that had seen more than one wearing. He liked that. The honesty appealed to him, as a more elaborate toilette would not. She approached him with long strides that matched his. He recalled what pleasure he'd found in a woman who could keep up with him. And a woman he did not have to bend double to kiss.

Still, shame filled him, as it had over the years when he'd thought of her. He was about to do what he should have a long time ago, but he'd been feckless and selfish then, far too unthinking of others. He'd learned some harsh lessons since.

Outside, the day had fulfilled its promise and the sun blazed down. "This summer has been an odd one," she remarked as they descended the stone steps to the garden. "The ground is still soft from the rain yesterday. It's been like that all summer."

"So you'd prefer to avoid the earth," he said.

Stopping, she lifted her ankle-length skirt to reveal a pair of sturdy half boots. "I can stand a little dampness."

He laughed, the sound surprising him, his mood lightening. "But not too much. No swamps, I promise you."

Her hat was broad brimmed, her gown a pretty cotton print with flowers rampaging around the hem. A favored gown, showing signs of wear and laundering, but not shabby. Dorothea had never indulged in the extravagances of fashion, although she was far from impoverished. She had a refreshing practicality he should have appreciated more when he'd had the chance. But the marriage between them had been arranged by their parents in a way both were used to. They liked one another, got along splendidly, but when Honoria had appeared on the scene, he'd left her without a backward glance.

Now he couldn't remember why. True, Honoria was dazzlingly beautiful, but Dorothea had a quiet loveliness that would last longer because it emanated from within. Since he'd been away, she'd grown into the woman she should be. She bore herself with grace rather than her previous habit of stooping, ashamed of her height. Her style of dress suited her, not too fussy. Her simple hairstyle, her fair locks drawn up into a knot at the back of her head, revealed a purity of feature he had not noticed before.

He led her to the edge of the rose garden, where a path wound up toward the grotto. She walked by his side like an equal. He didn't offer her the support of his arm. She didn't need it. "I'm surprised to find you here," he began.

"Ah, yes." Flicking open her fan, she plied it vigorously, but he'd taken care to walk in the shade. "My brother was invited, so he brought his wife and myself."

"You act as her companion?" He hated that he'd driven her to such a fate. Being a shadow, an ignored spare woman, part of society as an unpaid servant.

"Good gracious, no! I do help Ann when I can, because she is such a sweet woman. However, I am in control of my own fortune, and have been since May, when I turned thirty."

"So you did." The notion shocked him. She looked like the young woman he'd known seven years ago, as if no time had passed at all. "I thought you would be married by now. Have men here no taste at all?"

"You didn't have any," she returned with asperity.

That was new. The Dorothea he had known had been unsure of herself, but this woman had more about her. Perhaps it had always been there. If it had, he'd been a fool to miss it, because he liked this aspect of her very much. He grinned. "Perhaps I did not, especially where you were concerned. In fact, I'm sure of it."

They were out of sight of the house, sheltered by an overgrown bush of some kind. He stopped and took her hands in his. She gripped his fingers firmly and met his eyes with a directness he admired. "Dorothea, I owe you an apology. Many of them."

She opened her mouth, but he wouldn't let her speak. Not yet.

"I am deeply sorry for the way I treated you. Although the betrothal arrangements had only just begun, you deserved better from me. I should have told you I meant to pursue Honoria, instead of leaving you to find out for yourself."

"Actually, it was my brother," she said. "He told me. He would have confronted you, but I ordered him not to." She slipped her fingers away from his, and he missed her touch immediately. "As you say, the negotiations weren't far advanced."

"But I asked your father for permission to address you. I should have had the courtesy to ask you to release me. I was carried away, imagining myself in love."

She began to walk again. "I know. I saw your face the first time you set eyes on her. I would have asked you to release me once I saw that in any case. There was no harm done. At least, not much."

Was that pride, or was she telling the truth? Did she care nothing for him? He had thought otherwise. Their first kiss—their only kiss—had been soft and sweet, but he recalled it with an intensity that overshadowed many kisses he'd shared with other women. It had held a poignancy that he wondered about at the time, but put down to her inexperience. Seven years ago he'd been a fool. And a cad. He'd learned a lot since then.

"Not much?" he prompted.

"No. I fancied myself—fond of you, and the match would have been more than excellent. Marrying into the Thorpe family was a triumph, or so we thought." She smiled wryly. "Too good to be true, as it turned out."

"No, don't say that." Grabbing her hands, he spun her to face him again. Despite his determination to treat her carefully, he could not bear her talking that way. "You are good enough for anyone, Dorothea. Better, even. You deserve the best, and I am certainly not that."

"You seem to be the only man who thinks so." She pulled away, holding up her hand to still his protests, and gave a light, shaky laugh. "Indeed, I have come to see the advantage in a life as a single woman. I will live as independently as I may, and I have found other occupations, things to fill my time. I am an old maid, a spinster—oh, I have heard them all, and the words have ceased to hurt me. Instead, I revel in them. I am a single woman and I have the world in front of me. I have enough to allow me to choose my own future. If marriage is not for me, then I have plenty of other interests. Do not spare me a thought, my lord. I am content."

She left him strangely dissatisfied. He'd thought that once he'd apologized, the matter would be closed, but she had left him with a deeper understanding of what he had done to her. That went beyond an apology. Society knew they had been discussing marriage, and then he'd spurned her, leaving her to face the hidden ridicule, the whispering behind fans at balls. If she was not good enough for Benedict Thorpe, perhaps she was good enough for nobody.

He should at least have allowed her to reject him firmly and publicly, but he had not. Instead, he'd left the wound to fester, and however sorry he was, he couldn't undo that.

* * * *

Sir James took his time verifying Ben's claim. If Dorothea had not seen him at work, then she'd have imagined he was delaying on purpose, but the man was a fusspot, his attention to detail complete. He intended to take depositions from everyone who remembered Ben, including herself. Dorothea kept her statement brief, explaining the failed betrothal as her brother had done at the time, a discussion in its early stages that did not amount to anything. But she was firm in her identification of Ben. This was the missing marquess.

After their uncomfortable discussion in the garden, she'd expected Ben to avoid her, but instead, he sought her out. During the following days he always seemed to be in the vicinity when she went outside to take the air. A heavy downpour had delayed the much-anticipated duck hunt, and when she'd gone upstairs to walk in the long gallery, he'd been there too. Afterward, he spent time with her and her sister-in-law in the library, helping them to discover the scandalous novels hidden behind the sermons. The shelves were deep, able to conceal a multitude of sins. He teased out her laughter and told her amusing stories of his time in the colonies. But he rarely mentioned his wife, which Dorothea wondered at. Perhaps he was merely being tactful.

She liked him. That was the trouble, because she'd imagined that after so long, any lingering feelings she might have for him would have died. Unfortunately, they had not, even though Ben had changed. He had lost his air of superiority and that casual carelessness so many in society possessed.

The other guests remained too, Ben assuring them they were most welcome. They took to calling him "my lord" instead of "Mr. Thorpe," which made Louis set his jaw, but nobody remarked on it. Ben did not comment on the title one way or another.

After a pleasant and brief Sunday service in the house's private chapel, she managed to exchange a few words with Sir James on the way upstairs to breakfast. "Have you made your decision?" she asked. Surely, he'd taken enough time.

"I have made up my mind, but in order to satisfy the House of Lords and make a ruling nobody will question, I need ample proof."

Ah, that made sense. "I see. So you are collecting all the statements you can?"

"Indeed. I wish to fill in every hole in the narrative. I have sent enquiries to the docks in London. The records will confirm the ship Mr. Thorpe took. I have sent enquiries to the colonies, but I do not expect to receive the replies inside of three months. But they can be filed with the others when they finally arrive."

Sir James was being courted assiduously by Louis and his wife Honoria, while Benedict was all but ignoring the man. Dorothea couldn't understand him. Didn't he want the marquessate?

"My other problem," said Sir James as they strolled along the wide corridor, deliberately lagging behind the others, "is that Mr. Louis Thorpe and his wife have already started their nursery. With two children already, both daughters, unfortunately, they could easily produce a son. Sadly, Mr. Benedict Thorpe is decidedly single. If he remains so, then the inheritance will pass to Mr. Louis Thorpe's son, when he has one. For that reason I would prefer a cordial relationship to exist between the cousins. I thought to give them a little time to settle to the idea. A child born to the title or brought up in the knowledge that he will one day inherit will always prove a better candidate than one thrust into the part or drawn away from his regular circle in order to learn the business."

Dorothea thought of several men who had unexpectedly inherited wealth or a great title and made a huge success of it. But she kept her thoughts to herself, since they were approaching the breakfast room.

Polite chatter covered what they'd said. But they did not see Benedict, which was strange because he had sat behind her in the chapel and quit the place before she did. However, she thought nothing of it until he glanced at her and sent her a wicked grin before taking his seat opposite her. He shook out his napkin and spread it on his lap before the footman could do it for him. That was typical of the man.

Breakfast was an informal meal and a substantial one, the sideboards positively groaning with food. The guests helped themselves or asked a servant to fetch what they required. Then they sat at an empty space at the table, instead of using order of preference as they did at dinner. So Ben was free to sit close to her if he wished.

He fixed his gaze on Sir James, who was sitting next to Dorothea. "I am sensible, sir, that I will have to start my family." He grimaced. "I am perfectly content to marry again in the service of the estate."

So he'd overheard Sir James. Dorothea sucked in a deep breath, trying to prevent by sheer willpower the flush rising to her cheeks. Because really, she shouldn't be taking an interest at all. And that Sir James confided in her made it look like she was in cahoots with him. Which in a way, she was, but nobody except Sir James knew why. Angela would not be pleased if Dorothea used her name in such a public place, so she remained quiet. The bank prided itself on its discretion and would be put out if its name was involved in this title dispute, or if Angela took sides. She hadn't even told Ben she was acting for Angela. Why, she was not quite sure.

Being a banker was a tricky balancing act at times. Dorothea wished she could have the running of such an enterprise. A large estate like this one, for instance, would challenge anyone to run it properly. Mrs. Thorpe appeared to care for little except her own pleasures, but Dorothea would take far more of an interest in the running of the estate.

Not that she would ever be in that position.

Louis glared at his cousin. "I am making my own enquiries," he said. "I cannot understand why you stayed away so long without a word."

Ben only shrugged.

"Could you have made Benedict's acquaintance, then done away with him and taken his place?"

Lord Steeping snorted. "Hardly likely, is it?"

If Louis had his quizzing glass about his person, he would have used it on his lordship. But today, he wasn't wearing it. "I have read of more than one instance. True, this man has a passing resemblance to my cousin, but that could be coincidence. And if he knew Benedict, he could have learned many of the stories he is reciting now."

Sir James exchanged a glance with Dorothea, his brow slightly raised. Yes, if he could possibly do it, Louis would challenge Ben in court. That would deplete Ben's resources and keep him busy for years to come. So the thorough investigation was necessary.

Ben stretched lazily, and smiled, not a jot of strain in his features. "Why would I do such a thing?"

Pointedly, Louis glanced around the room. "The estate is a great one with a considerable income."

Much reduced by Louis's demands on the resources, but nobody mentioned that.

"From what I have seen, it needs a deal of work to bring it up to scratch," Ben replied. "I have enough. I am content, and unlike the Thorpe holdings, what I have is in good heart." He glanced at Louis, fixing him with a dark stare. "Do you visit your daughters every day? I would like to make their acquaintance. After all, we are related, and I do not want to be a stranger to them."

Louis snorted. "As to how often I visit them, that is my concern." But he didn't answer Benedict's request.

A distraction arrived in the form of Schultz, bearing the morning post. He handed a large packet to Benedict, wrapped in waxed paper and sealed carefully in two places, so it must be something of note. He put it aside. "Business," he explained briefly. "Tedious," and turned to a smaller missive.

Conversation changed to other matters as people opened their post or took a newspaper from the butler and discussed the contents. Dorothea found a week-old copy of *The Tatler* that contained some interesting court gossip. "Do you think the peace will hold?" she asked.

"Perhaps," Sir James answered.

That distracted the company well enough. The peace talks to end the current war with the Austrians were proceeding apace, but acrimoniously.

"What do you think?" Benedict asked her.

"Neither side has what it wants. So I believe the peace will hold long enough for each side to catch its breath and regroup."

"Like a round in a boxing match!" Louis exclaimed. "Very good, Miss Rowland! Have you ever seen such a thing?"

She had to admit she had not. Officially, ladies did not attend boxing matches, but it hadn't prevented a few, more intrepid women snatching a glimpse of one. After all, the participants stripped almost bare.

"Scandalous," Benedict murmured. His discomfiture at the discussion of marriage appeared to have passed, and his eyes had regained their usual liveliness of expression.

How could she not have known? But she could not help a shameful feeling of relief that Benedict was not currently attached to any female.

Such a foolish notion. She could not think that way, even though some ladies had declared Benedict was partial to her, and they suspected a courtship was taking place. Foolish again, particularly in the light of Benedict's revelation of a few moments ago. She attended to her rapidly cooling breakfast and breathed a sigh of relief when conversation passed to more impartial topics.

After he had made a light repast, Louis got to his feet and flung down his napkin. "If you will excuse me," he said to the company at large. "I will go to ensure arrangements for tomorrow's duck hunt are well under way. The ground is finally firm enough to take our trampling and the birds are plump and waiting for us."

Ah yes. The gentlemen were looking forward to tomorrow's senseless slaughter. Perhaps murdering innocent ducks by the dozen would help them to feel more like men.

Chapter 6

Ben woke to his valet moving silently around the room. Rougier had arrived along with the bulk of Ben's luggage earlier in the week. He had not employed a valet for a while, but he had stopped at the best registry office in London to find one appropriate to his new position. The man certainly understood what he was about. His wardrobe had been unpacked, ironed, and bestowed in the old clothespress with expediency. Ben couldn't remember when he'd had a closer shave than the one Rougier had given him yesterday.

He watched the man reverently laying out his hunting outfit. The coat had certainly seen better days, but it was probably more suited to the day's activity than a fashionable garment. Rougier treated it like spun gold.

Ben gazed at the familiar walls. Strange to be back in this place. The same paintings, mostly landscapes of the estate, hung on the walls, and the small bookcase was filled with the tomes he was studying before his visit to London that fateful year. They were a mixture of scurrilous novels and volumes on mathematics and calculus. His fascination with numbers had worked well for him in the colonies. The novels, not so much, but he still read them.

As a boy, when he'd been moved here from the nursery wing, he'd open the window on summer nights and listen to the events going on down below. Sometimes he would hear talk, when his father's political friends gathered to discuss the affairs of the day. Murmurings on the balmy summer breeze. Or music, when his parents were entertaining, the tinkle of the harpsichord, the thin whine of the violin.

Or arguments. Not many, but they did happen. Nobody's childhood was completely free of sadness. Ben had been fortunate, and he'd considered himself blessed. Until he went abroad on his Grand Tour and ran wild, coming home to repeat his behavior in London. Why not? Heir to a great title, possessor of a substantial estate, what could go wrong? And he was to marry soon, he'd discovered. Dorothea Rowland was pleasant, but he resented the arrangements being taken out of his hands, and he'd used Dorothea shamefully as a result. He had not told her that he didn't want to marry her, but left it to her brother to do so.

It was not Dorothea he had resented, but the decisions being made for him, as if he'd have no say in who he would spend the rest of his life with. However, until he'd met Honoria, he had gone along with the plans, not seeing anyone else he preferred, as if the female population of London was ready to prostrate themselves at his feet.

At the time he'd been more self-centered, more feckless, but now he knew how much she deserved the apology he'd given to her. However, he'd found much more than a woman he owed reparation to.

The chilly morning on Hampstead Heath had shown him another side of life. After the duel, Hal had shoved him into the waiting carriage and they'd rushed to the docks, where Hal loaded him onto the first ship carrying passengers leaving on the next tide. If he'd been in his right mind, he'd have written the letters he later had to send from the colonies, but he wasn't. He'd been at sea before the shock had worn off. A week after he'd reached Boston, a letter from Hal had arrived at the local receiving office to tell him that Louis lived; his wound not as serious as they'd assumed.

He'd made his decision to cut ties with his home then, and only recently had he come to regret it.

He glanced at the table by the window, where he'd laid out the proofs he was planning to show Sir James. Eventually. The document he'd received yesterday had sealed the case for him. That would reassure the damned man.

Sir James had spent quite some time in the servants' quarters. Since only the butler was left from his day, Ben would be forced to make an excursion or two into the village, where more people remembered him. He had made a private visit there and greeted the old ones, glad to see them again, but the state of their houses had saddened him. Louis had a lot to answer for. And very soon, he would.

Flinging back the covers, Ben swung out of bed. The valet hurried across to lift the hot water can and pour a generous libation into the porcelain basin resting on the substantial washstand. They had changed the pottery since his time here. This set had blue transfers of happy villagers. Perhaps the original had been too scratched or damaged. Staring into the mirror, Ben cracked his jaw in a mighty yawn before picking up the cake of ivory soap and dipping his hands into the water. Beside him, Rougier ran the razor expertly along the strop.

"I have laid out your hunting dress, my lord, but you might wish to consider ordering a new one if you desire to make a mark in London." He had a pretty French accent. Too pretty. Ben didn't entirely trust it.

"You are French?" Without warning, Ben switched his language. "Vous ne vouliez pas chercher un emploi en France?" After all, Paris was the center of the fashionable world. Some valets feigned an accent in order to increase their worth to the less-discerning master.

The valet answered fluidly in the same language. "My father is French, but my mother is English. I was brought up speaking both tongues. My father came here to work in the house of the Duke of Richmond and my mother was a housemaid there."

"What do they do now?" Ben couldn't imagine the superior Duke of Richmond employing a married couple. The man was a stickler for the proprieties.

"They own a shop selling optical instruments in the City of London," Rougier said.

Ben switched back to English. "I may visit it some time. Remind me when we're in Town." He used to watch the stars through the telescope he'd inadvertently left in Boston.

While he sat back and allowed himself the luxury of having someone else shave him, Ben went over the events of last night. After a good night's sleep, he was better prepared to ruminate on events here.

What did Dorothea Rowland have to do with Sir James and his investigation? He'd caught her glancing at Sir James once or twice. When he'd come upon her in the passage at the back of the house, he could have sworn he'd spotted Sir James turning a corner ahead. There was something going on, and it wasn't of a romantic nature.

Now he'd had a glimpse of the state of affairs at home, he was determined his cousin would not benefit from the inheritance. His stop in London had included a visit to an old friend, a lawyer who could give him a frank opinion about Louis and what he'd been up to—leaving Ben with the impression that he shouldn't have stayed away so long. He still planned to return to Boston, but only when he'd arranged matters here to his satisfaction and put a responsible, trustworthy manager in place.

Did he dare consider Dorothea for that position? There would never be love between them, not least because Ben had hardened his heart against it, but there was still liking. She could bear his children, and he would trust her with the management of the estate. Surely that would be better than living as a spinster. And it might help to assuage his conscience, to give her the position she should have had years ago.

Going down to breakfast, he found mostly gentlemen, with two intrepid ladies who were looking forward to the duck hunt. Either that, or they were determined on a different kind of hunt, one where being part of a minority would work to their advantage.

Although his future was far from clear to them, they flirted gently with him and the other men in the room, but Ben took little notice. He had no mind to engage in another love match. One had been enough.

Fortunately, he wouldn't be the target of the matchmaking mothers, not until his claim had been resolved. He would either take up the reins and do what he could to mend Louis's depredations before going home to Boston, or he'd walk away, knowing he'd done his best. In that case, he wouldn't be looking back. If he went now, he would leave a mess behind him, so he was duty bound to stay until Sir James had made his decision. But he was sorely tempted to try to persuade the man to find in his cousin's favor.

Damnation, what a coil!

Today could provide a welcome distraction. Much laughter surrounded his cousin, and although the hostility was not voiced aloud, it was a potent presence. Hal entered and cast a glance over the room before helping himself to food and coming to sit by Ben. "An interesting division of forces," he commented, shaking out his napkin.

"It has not gone unnoticed," Ben responded dryly. He lifted his coffee cup to his lips and took a reflective sip. Whatever else the domestic staff got wrong, they made an excellent cup of coffee. He'd come to respect the power of coffee in the morning since his sojourn abroad. "But I'd rather face them than give the gossips free rein."

"Hmm." Hal forked up a tender morsel of pork chop and examined it as if interrogating a wrongdoer. "I'm not sure I would do that. Let them talk, what does it matter?" He popped the meat into his mouth and ate it, closing his eyes as he chewed. "My, that is good," he said when he finished. Catching Ben's amused gaze, he grinned. "What? I am half starved. I swear I barely ate a thing at dinner last night."

"A complete lie." Ben marveled that he was still so easy with Hal. When they'd met again here at Cressbrook House, they had melded as if they'd last seen one another the day before, instead of after a seven-year separation. True, they had corresponded often, but that was not the same as day-to-day contact. They'd led separate lives, done different things.

Ben admitted, if only to himself, that his ordeal would have been ten times worse without Hal. His friend had urged him to return, but Ben had chosen not to. Despite that, they had been linked in more than friendship. They were business colleagues too, jointly engaging in ventures that had proved profitable for them both. And all that time, Hal had acceded to Ben's wishes and not told anyone where he was, or even that he was alive.

Hence the current pickle, but Ben had to concede the fault was entirely his.

"Did you do much hunting in the colonies?" Louis called across to him. The breakfast room was set up with several round tables to encourage informality. It also worked to separate factions, apparently. Ben's side of the room was sparsely inhabited, but he had no doubt that once he started winning the battle, many would come over to his side. "Your outfit appears well-worn."

"Enough," Ben answered, preferring not to go into details.

Louis got to his feet and shot Ben a triumphant glance. "If you are ready, ladies and gentlemen, we should make a start. The beaters are waiting outside."

As any good host would, he led the way. Ben was not amused, but he kept the easy smile fixed to his face, even though he seethed inside.

Outside, the day was dawning, the sky a light peachy color. "A good sign," Louis remarked.

Several men stood holding weapons. Louis took two, and handed one to Ben, keeping his gaze. The last time they'd both been holding a weapon and facing each other had been on Hampstead Heath, over seven years ago.

"Well met, cousin," he murmured, as he had then when they'd been standing back to back on the Heath. A startled look shocked his cousin's eyes wider.

As before, he said nothing, but turned away to join his friends. William glanced at Ben as Louis said something to him.

They set out on foot over the dew-sprinkled grass toward the flat lake at the edge of the estate, where they would spend the rest of the day.

Every time someone shot him a speculative glance, Ben smiled blandly at them. They must think he was devoid of intelligence. All well and good, since he preferred to be underestimated. Lord Steeping, a smooth-looking man wearing a brand new country coat in a shade more orange than russet, drifted to his side. "I have to say, Thorpe, that I admire any man who can make a new life for himself, however humble."

Ben appreciated the sentiment. Unfortunately, he had to work on the humble part. However, he seemed to be doing fine now. "Thank you. Working with my own hands, growing calluses and making profits, suited me well."

Steeping blanched. The man actually lost the color in his cheeks. "Why did you not tell everyone who you were?"

Ben refrained from rolling his eyes. "Because I had behaved disgracefully. I knew Louis was alive, and I thought they were better without me. A new life, I thought." That reason sufficed. He'd been determined to leave his old life behind, to wash his hands of everything that had gone before and start again.

For the first time in his life, Ben had been free to follow his inclinations. With the heir to the estate after him alive, Ben had felt free to explore and enjoy life. Louis had wanted the inheritance more than he had, so why not let him handle the responsibility?

"I spent a year in the wilderness. I was hunting bear." A slight exaggeration, since the bear had hunted him, but the result of the encounter was the same thing.

Several people turned their heads, showing him how many were eavesdropping. "Bear?" Lord Steeping perked up, his sharp features gaining a keener edge.

"Black bear. Very large, very dangerous. Unfortunately, they can climb trees, should the mood take them. And a mother bear guarding her cubs is one of the most dangerous creatures in nature."

He wasn't lying. He wasn't afraid to admit that the only time he'd confronted a bear, he was scared for his life. But he had never gone seeking them; he'd confronted one on his travels. Still, it made for a good story, and he wasn't ready to divulge the whole. Let them think him a moderately successful man, rather than a wealthy one. Let them believe he wanted the title for what it brought, rather than rescuing it. Allowing them to underestimate him would have better results.

But he had killed the bear. "It took more than one shot. The damn thing wouldn't stay down. The first bullet did no more than madden the creature. It chased me in fury, and I was never so close to dying. They have huge paws with long, thick claws that can strike you down with one blow. And they move fast. I had no choice but to turn and fire before it was on me. Luckily, the second shot slowed it down. The next felled it, but it took two more before it ceased to breathe." And yet he would have preferred to leave it alive.

"How many people were with you?" Lord Sandigate asked, his gray eyes, so like his sister Dorothea's, sparkling.

"One, but he was half a mile back on the road. I'd gone foraging."

"For nuts?"

"For wood." For a fire, ironically to keep the wild creatures away.

"Then where did all the bullets come from?"

He laughed at the ridiculous question. "Have you seen engravings of pirates? They have six or more pistols stuck into their belts. I had the requisite half dozen, and a rifle." After confronting the bear, he'd had to retrace his steps, picking up his discarded weapons. Loaded a couple in case he met another creature. But bears were not sociable animals, so he did not believe he'd meet a second. Fortunately, he'd been right.

Now he had the company in the palm of his hand. The women were staring at him openmouthed, admiration in their gazes. Better still, his cousin was distinctly annoyed. Although he was smiling, he had a spark in his blue eyes that didn't indicate amusement.

Ben understood Louis so well. He had the advantage there, too, because Louis had not changed, while he had. He felt twenty years older, not seven, such had been his experiences since he'd set sail for the colonies.

About half the house party had decided to rise early and attend the duck hunt. There wouldn't be many ducks left when they finished, and since this was the season for hunting birds, Louis would have more expeditions planned. Ben preferred to hunt purely to eat, but he was better off here to quell the inevitable gossip than at the house.

The weapon Louis had given him was a shotgun, adequate, but not particularly fine. It didn't have the chased stock and silver mounts sported by Louis's weapon. As long as it worked, he had no particular opinion on it. It had been loaded, too, something Ben especially disliked. He preferred to make sure of that himself. The only other time he'd allowed someone else to load his gun was on Hampstead Heath, when the rules of the duel demanded that the seconds oversaw the loading of the weapons.

He gritted his teeth. Old history. Now he had to concentrate on preventing Louis ruining the estate. He would not allow it. Justice would be done.

Hal kept up with him, stride for stride. "Do you think anyone truly imagines you are not who you claim to be?"

"They want to believe I am not."

"You have changed, but not that much." Hal's boots swished through the wet grass, thicker now they were walking across open fields. "People know you. You have not returned hideously scarred or with anything else that would prevent identification."

Recognition wasn't enough. "Nevertheless, we will go through the right channels. I want Sir James's decision to be without doubt." He said no more, because people were walking close to them. But he did not want to give Louis any opportunity of bringing a case to court. That could waste thousands of pounds and drag on for years. In that time the estate could be completely ruined. Without effective managers for the minerals, the farming produce, and the investments associated with the estate, it would fall apart. Even worse, the court could allow Louis to continue to manage the estate.

Rather than that, he would subject himself to any process Sir James thought fit. Then the man would make his recommendation and the title and estates would be his.

"Of course," Hal answered. He would understand. Instead, he moved to another topic. "Rather fine, Miss Rowland. I wonder how I have not noticed before."

"I thought so," Ben said, recalling Dorothea's fine eyes, and the way her breasts swelled invitingly over the low neckline of her dinner gown.

Hastily, he turned his mind elsewhere. To the hunt. The lake had come into sight, together with the collection of flat-bottomed boats set aside for their use. At the edge of the lake was a canal, constructed by his father. Trees and weeds overflowed the wide stretch of water to entice the birds to roost there. While Ben's father had introduced the birds to the estate, these days they were carefully conserved and nurtured by the gamekeepers. Only for people to come along and shoot them.

A sense of being hunted had not left Ben since he'd woken up. Uneasiness crawled under his skin, of something not quite right with this morning. He would get over it, except that this sense had never let him down before. When everything appeared right, sometimes only his sense alerted him to something being wrong. Though he had not the least idea what it was.

Usually he would set his staff to double-check everything. They would invariably find something. Either that, or an external event, like a drop in the price of the goods they were selling, would happen. Today, he had nobody but himself.

But he would rather face his enemy, if there was one, than wait for him to strike. If he kept Louis in his sights, he'd be prepared, and now he was a better shot than he had been, and a better hunter, too.

He hefted his shotgun, reassuring himself with its solid weight. He'd lingered behind the rest, waiting to assess the lay of the land. Soon they'd take to the flat-bottomed boats and set off along the wide river to where the ducks were. The birds had been bred for this, their special day.

Men waited with dogs to retrieve the fowl as the guests caught them. The animals were straining at their leashes, eager to start their jobs. Their sleek, well-fed bodies told Ben where some of the estate's income had been expended. On amusements. What else?

A flash of fire alerted him and without thinking he dropped to the ground, dragging Hal after him. His friend cried out as the retort rocketed through the still air. Morning dew soaked them, a flock of birds rose up with a clap of wings, and the dogs set up a volley of barking.

Someone had fired their weapon, and not at the ducks. At him.

Chapter 7

On her way down to breakfast, Sir James fell into step next to Dorothea, so they took a detour to the small parlor. "I will not keep you long," he said, holding a chair for her. The furniture in this room was mismatched, some pieces old, the upholstery worn. She took the seat, the best on offer, an overstuffed chair with worn plush cushions.

"Thank you. Was there something in particular?"

"I am still a little way from declaring him the missing marquess. I have interviewed the domestics, but I would like something more."

"What more do you need to declare him the missing marquess?"

He paced to the fireplace. "Documentary evidence that links the man we know now to the man we knew then. Recognition can be challenged, as can memories. And Louis Thorpe won't hesitate to seize any weak spot in the chain."

"I see." Dorothea concentrated on staring at her hands. For some reason, thinking of Benedict Thorpe made her grow uncomfortably hot.

"The fact that he used a different version of his name also speaks against him."

"Why?" She jerked up her head. "That seems foolish."

"Because it might be his real name," Sir James said softly. "Someone called Benjamin Thorpe who had a passing resemblance to Benedict Thorpe might decide to use those facts to gain more than they were entitled to."

Where she had been warm before, Dorothea suddenly felt chilled. "That's ridiculous!"

Sir James's ascetic face turned still and cold. "Young lady, I am here to adjudicate. I cannot appear biased. As the evidence stands, nothing is clear. I need something that will provide a link between the man here today and the one who left England seven years ago."

"I thought there was no question."

Sir James shrugged and spread his hands wide in a gesture of helplessness. "I merely adjudicate. I will be as fair as I can, given the evidence I have. I must present a solid report to the Lord Chancellor, or there will be court cases aplenty."

He was right. If he found for Benedict with only anecdotal evidence, Louis wouldn't accept the decision. "What about his mother? Would her evidence tip the scales in his favor?"

Sir James gave a tiny shake of his head. "The lady lives completely isolated. She is well cared for, but either her mind or her body or both have gone. If her body, then I will seek an interview when she is ready."

They were talking about somebody's life here. The impact of their discussion hit her amidships, completely without warning. "What we're doing is of the utmost importance, isn't it? It affects lives."

Sir James turned a look of deep understanding on her, studying her gravely. "Yes, it is. That is why it's important to get this decision right. Once I have given Lord Hardwicke my recommendations, the House of Lords will accept it, then the findings will be sent to the King, and he will accept them."

"And when I tell Miss Childers, she will make her decisions about finance." He nodded.

She did not like Louis, but if she was instrumental in denying him the title he'd been borrowing on for years, what would he do then? How would he and his wife, and the two children upstairs in the nursery, survive?

A long court case could ruin the estate and both parties. Sir James was right. The evidence had to be concrete. Not just hearsay.

She bade the Crown officer good day and went downstairs to breakfast in a much more thoughtful frame of mind.

A footman directed her to the small dining room, although "small" was not the word she would use to describe it. Spacious, sunny, the expansive windows opened on to the magnificent gardens at the back of the house. The modern furniture, lighter in style than that of a generation ago, added to the airy feel. A long sideboard groaned under a large selection of viands.

The gossip was all about Benedict and Louis.

Mrs. Thorpe was making a good breakfast, seemingly unperturbed by the momentous events of the night before. She could be turned out of doors by the end of the week, but she was not in the least concerned, or so any impartial observer would believe. She was wearing a beautiful heavy satin French sacque in cream, embroidered with spring flowers, her natural fair hair on seemingly negligent, but actually carefully arranged, display.

Dorothea's fairer, cooler shade of blond was dull in comparison. But she was used to not showing to advantage next to society beauties, so she settled to her breakfast in a reasonable frame of mind. More thoughtful, to be sure, and with a new resolve to impartiality, not to allow personalities to sway her opinions. But she did want to find something that would prove Benedict the true marquess. His kindness to her last night put her at the center of events instead of constantly on the fringes.

Mrs. Thorpe was holding court. She announced, rather than conversed, expressing her distaste with the current situation. "After all, who knows who the man is? He walked into the house as if he owned it, although he does not, and tried to overwhelm everyone with his presence."

"Admittedly, he has a considerable bearing," someone commented. Ann exchanged a glance with Dorothea, and a slight smile quirked her lips. Dorothea said nothing, but she did not have to. Everyone had remarked his attention to her. For once, she was having to cope with being the center of attention, and much to her surprise, she didn't enjoy it. She did not comment. What was the point?

"That does not mean he is who he says he is. At first, he claimed to be Benjamin Thorpe, not Benedict. There must be plenty of Benjamin Thorpes in the world, but none of them belong here," Mrs. Thorpe continued.

Murmurs of agreement followed. "But if he is not the missing marquess, he has a remarkable resemblance to him," Lady Steeping put in. "And he knows details of the house and the family."

"You remember him?" Mrs. Thorpe said icily.

"Naturally I do," the woman said warmly. With a half smile on her face, she carefully chose three chips of sugar and added them to her tea. "He turned society on its head back in his day." Obviously referring to the duel, she glanced up.

"Hmm." Mrs. Thorpe was fortunate that her name had not been definitively connected with the notorious duel. "But he left, and now we have this person to contend with. He doesn't dress well and he has the air of a fortune hunter, a man taking advantage of a situation. Shame on him for doing so. I cannot wait for the day when we may turn him out of doors."

"Why don't you do it now?" someone asked.

"Because he will only go to London and cause trouble there. Rather than that, Sir James may make his decision here and now, as quickly as may be."

A tiny snort from Dorothea's right told her that her sister-in-law was fighting her reaction. Dorothea made short work of her breakfast and excused herself.

She would take a walk in the gardens, but she needed to change her shoes for sturdier ones. The blue satin slippers she had on wouldn't last very long outside. Dew lay heavy on the ground, only just dissipating, mist over the fields showing where the growing heat of the sun was dissipating it.

Upstairs, a maid scurried away from her, a full bucket in her hands. They must have just completed service in her corridor. That meant she would be alone for a while, something she appreciated after the fraught atmosphere of breakfast.

A flood of light poured into the corridor from a room whose door was usually closed. The maid must have left it open. Dorothea leaned in to redress the error.

And paused.

That coat hanging outside the clothespress—Ben had worn it last night at dinner. A scent lingered in the air, one she recognized. The faint aroma of sandalwood combined with a masculinity that infiltrated her. It seeped through her skin until she knew she would never rid herself of it. When she closed the door, she was inside the room, not outside.

Ben was occupying a chamber similar to her own, but it had more personality, as if someone lived here all the time. The bed, draped in dark blue cloth, was neatly made, the coverlet smartly in place, but still, he had slept there last night. His body had warmed those sheets.

Papers were strewn on the desk by the window. Several guests walked among the flowers, along the paths that wended between them. To one side, the maze's green box hedges showed streaks where it was becoming overgrown. Time to gossip and mend the world with words.

Dorothea turned her attention to the papers. Prying did not come naturally to her, but if she could find proof, she could help bring this unfortunate situation to a conclusion. Then Angela would have her answer, and Dorothea could put her mind to assessing what exactly Ben meant to her, this new, more thoughtful man she actually liked.

Letters from Ben's friend Lord Evington were stacked in a neat pile, the creases and soiled outers showing how far they had traveled. Halfway across the world, carried on small ships that were tossed on the waves like toy boats on a pond. Dorothea took care to precisely replace the one she had picked up. The letter only carried tidings of Louis's request to have his cousin declared dead so he could inherit the title. But it was evidence that at least one person had been in constant contact with him.

Another pile was official letters from a lawyer's office. They detailed ships, cargoes, prices. She added up one column, rapidly running down the figures.

Surely, she had miscalculated. The total was a staggering amount. Whoever owned that ship must be a wealthy man. And the owner—Mr. Benjamin Thorpe.

The letter proved nothing except that Ben was wealthier than people were assuming. Quickly, she rifled through the rest of the documents in that pile. Ben Thorpe was wealthy indeed.

So why was he eager to claim the marquessate? The possessions were much depleted since Louis had made hay with them. Did Ben need money? From what she'd just read, she doubted it.

He had crossed an ocean to get here. Only one possibility remained. Ben cared about his inheritance. He had a connection with the title that made it impossible for him to turn his back on the estate.

Before, he had never cared. His dazzling presence had lit up London society like a crystal chandelier, but he'd skimmed over every encounter, never expressed a care for the estate. Only that it was his by right.

Had his seven years away brought him a new appreciation of what he was and what he could be? Certainly, his absence had turned him into the kind of man to be relied on, one that Dorothea could admire as well as...like.

The other word, the evocative, romantic one, she would not use. Dared not, in case voicing it became an expression of the truth. And while she found him deeply attractive, she honestly could not tell what she felt, never having been troubled by romance before, nor even expecting it.

Another stack of papers lay between the two she had just examined. She would take a quick look at them, then make her escape while this side of the house was still quiet.

As she reached for them, a commotion from the corridor outside startled her. She spun around, her skirts catching on the edge of the letters. They tumbled to the floor in a flurry, and she grabbed at them wildly, panic rising to tighten her throat and send her heart into overtime.

Ben entered, flinging the door open so it bounced off the guard preventing it hitting the wall. Reflexively he caught the rebound on the edge of his foot, but paid it no more notice than that.

He was not alone. Benedict had his arm around Lord Evington's shoulders, almost carrying him. His friend's hat was gone, and he was reeling like a drunk man.

As he turned, bringing Evington's body into full view, Dorothea gasped in shock. Evington's red coat had initially hidden the blood that stained it, but a flood, darker than the coat, had soaked the whole of that side. A kerchief was tightly bound around his arm just above the elbow, but for all the attempts to staunch the flow, the blood still came.

Two men followed closely behind, then a maid, her arms full of cloths and towels. A man dressed more plainly carried a can of hot water and more cloths. He ignored Dorothea completely and headed to the bed. Dragging the coverlet out of the way, he draped a rough blanket over the sheets, folding it expertly so it formed a thick pad.

Ben took one glance at her and jerked his head, a peremptory demand that she should come to him. "Do you faint at the sight of blood?"

"If I did, I'd be flat on the floor by now," she snapped, only belatedly realizing that a dead faint would have served her purpose better than standing staring.

More people came in. Louis shot a poisonous glare at her, then followed the others to the bed. By the time Ben had laid Hal down on it, a crowd had gathered. Dorothea ignored them and obeyed Ben's unspoken command, drawing closer.

Benedict had a wicked hunting knife in his hand. He used it to slit the side of Lord Evington's sleeve, the fabric giving way like butter. As he sliced through the binding over the wound in his arm, a fresh gush of blood started up. Several shrieks from the ladies alerted him to the presence of the crowd. He spared a glance at his valet. "Get rid of them all, Rougier." His steely glare pierced her with intent. "Except for her. Dorothea stays."

He flung off his coat, leaving him in shirtsleeves and waistcoat.

She did not question his decision, but hurried to the bedside. As the valet ushered everyone from the room, his way of herding them efficient enough to rouse Dorothea to admiration, she turned her attention to Lord Evington. "What happened?"

"A stray bullet," Benedict said shortly.

Lord Evington spoke, his voice thready. "That was no accident, and you know it."

Dorothea froze. *No accident?*

"Hush! We'll talk about that later," his friend commanded, until the soft closing of the door indicated the valet had carried out his master's order. "Let's see to you first."

Rougier came to stand next to the bed, several clean cloths draped over his arm. A bowl of hot water lay on the nightstand.

"No," his lordship said. "If this kills me, I want the perpetrator brought to justice. Promise me, Benedict!"

"Of course I promise." He pitched his voice a touch higher. Dorothea flicked a glance at him. A deep frown carved furrows into his forehead and his mouth was set in a grim line.

"Thank you." Lord Evington actually smiled, though the expression was more of a rictus than a true smile. Still, few people could show such insouciance in the face of death. While he wasn't injured in a vital organ, the bleeding could kill him if somebody didn't do something about it. The binding over the wound had staunched the flow, but it was bleeding freely again.

Ben laid the wound bare, sliced the fabric away.

"This is a bullet wound. I expected pellets from a shotgun," she said. Ducks were hunted with shotguns, not pistols or rifles, but this was a bullet wound, and as such, potentially more serious than being peppered with shot.

"Many of us had other weapons. Pistols and a couple of rifles. But yes, predominantly we had shotguns," Ben murmured.

Lord Evington groaned and clenched his teeth. "Shotguns for ducks, pistols for men," he managed to gasp out.

Had somebody deliberately aimed at him, then?

Without asking, Dorothea snatched a cloth, one long enough to wrap around his lordship's upper arm. She made a slipknot, tightening it until Lord Evington winced and cried out, a sharp sound that echoed around the room. She glanced up, meeting Benedict's hard glare.

Sweat beaded his forehead, trickling into the creases formed by his frown. "How did you learn to do that?"

"I helped a maid who'd cut her arm on a kitchen knife." With domestic staff falling to the ground around her, Dorothea had seen what to do. To her, the action seemed intuitive, to cut off circulation to the vein providing the blood to the wound. "The artery is intact." Or the blood would have pumped out bright red and put an end to his existence long before they'd reached the house. As it was, Lord Evington would be weak for a few days while he recovered and made up the loss. If he did not take an infection—but she would do her best to prevent that.

Benedict reached out an imperious hand and his valet put a dampened cloth into it. He set about cleaning the wound.

A fair amount of thread and cloth had to be removed from the mess before they could assess the wound. They might have to go digging for the bullet. Shuddering, Dorothea took another cloth and started working from the other end, below the slipknot. Camaraderie born of necessity settled around Ben, Dorothea, and the valet as they worked.

The bleeding was slowing down now that the man was horizontal, and eventually the ligature gave results.

By that time several bloodied, crumpled cloths filled the pot Rougier had put on the floor. Dorothea had little room to move, but enough to do her task effectively. She kept the rags wet until the flow eased, then held a fresh cloth over the arm.

Lord Evington stared at the wound, his blue eyes heavy. He winced as Benedict passed another damp cloth over it.

Benedict sighed, a short "Ah!" of relief once they could see the spot properly. "He's carved a groove along your skin, but the bullet has gone. A pity, that."

Evington snorted. "Such a shame you can't cut the bullet out."

Ben gave a grunt that turned into a laugh. "You'll have an interesting scar to show the ladies. Shall I call your man?"

By now, Evington had rallied a little, no longer crying in pain but watching their progress as best he could. "God, no. Mayster faints if he nicks me when he's shaving me, but nobody is as good with starch as he is."

Benedict huffed a laugh. "We're not talking about fashion now. You'll be fine if the wound is dressed regularly." His voice lightened with relief.

They worked together until they had cleaned the wound and dressed it, wrapping a fresh bandage around the entirety of Lord Evington's upper arm. By that time his lordship was breathing heavily, the shock of the incident evidently getting the better of him. "Thank you. Apart from the loss of blood, I believe I will do." He smiled at Dorothea. "I shall count you my angel."

"Nobody has ever called me that before." Straightening, suppressing her groan as her back protested, she dropped the last bloody rag in the bowl.

"They should. You have the face of an angel."

Ben glanced at his valet and nodded. "Thank you for your help. Please take the mess away and ensure there is nobody lingering outside. Let them know that Lord Evington is recovering, if they ask, and close the door behind you."

"Of course, my lord." Rougier gathered the stained cloths, poured the contents of the basin into the water can, and left the room.

Dorothea grunted, drawing Ben's gaze. His attention lingered on her while she answered his lordship. "Believe me, my lord, I am anything but an angel. I happened to be here, and I knew what to do."

"That reminds me..." Lord Evington smiled. "I apologize for interrupting your tryst."

"Tryst?" She shrieked the word, shock reverberating through her. "There was no tryst," she said, quieter now, but her stomach plummeted. "It was nothing."

"I beg to differ," Ben broke in. "Everyone saw you as we came in. They will not forget that you were here first."

"Oh, so now this incident is about me?" How could they turn this on her? Indignation roared through her. "After all I've done, you can't find some excuse?"

"Unfortunately, there is none. They will gossip. Will you allow it?" his lordship said, turning shrewd eyes on Ben. "You know what's at stake."

"I do," he said grimly. "Sir James is a stickler for correct behavior."

Oh, so she had compromised herself now? Because she'd wanted to help an injured man? Words failed her. Of course Sir James, with his pernickety way of speaking and his insistence on the rules, would condemn her. But she would still do her best for Angela. "I...I..." She wet her lips.

Ben reached across and urged her chin up, closing her mouth. "Yes, we will talk," he said, far too gently for her liking. Menace thrummed behind his words. "And soon."

Lord Evington looked from Dorothea to Ben's closed features and back again.

"Oh! Oh no, I was merely passing by, and the door was open..." Unwilling to tell an outright lie, she stopped. "Perhaps we should," she added lamely.

Ben nodded, as if the matter was settled, and turned back to his friend, leaving Dorothea in turmoil. "Are you sure you feel quite well? Brandy?"

"Not yet. If I drink strong spirits now, I will fall asleep directly. I want to talk to you first." He glanced at Dorothea, then continued. "I believe I can trust you, ma'am."

"Yes, of course."

"Though why you should think so I'm not sure," Ben added dryly. Obviously, he had not forgotten the circumstance of Dorothea's being here first.

"Oh, you know..." Lord Evington began to raise his hands but winced and stopped. "Someone shot at you, Ben."

"I know."

Dorothea swallowed. "Are you sure this was deliberate?"

Ben gave her a terse nod. "It did not have the outcome they wished. But for the time being, outside this room we will call it an accident, if you will."

Reluctantly, she followed Lord Evington's example and agreed. "For now."

"I want them to think I don't suspect anyone," Ben added.

"But you do?" she demanded. "Did you expect this to happen?"

"No. But it did, and it was no accident."

Evington's voice was faint, but sure. "Ben, we have to come to the inevitable conclusion. I merely got in the way. Someone wanted to hurt you."

Ben nodded. "But I will not have my friends brought to account for this. I had no intention of drawing you in. God, the man must be desperate."

"You mean your cousin Louis Thorpe shot at you?" she said, unable to stay quiet. Shock turned to anger. "He would go that far?"

Two pairs of eyes met hers, two intent gazes, one gray, one brown. "Of course he would," his lordship said. "Didn't you understand that?"

"Did you see him?" Ben demanded. "Would you bear witness to it?"

Regretfully, Lord Evington shook his head, the short strands of his brown hair catching on the white pillow, now smudged with mud and splashes of blood. "I saw the flash, and it certainly came from where Louis was standing, but I cannot be sure who fired the shot. A lot of people were standing around waiting for the boats to be ready."

Ben sighed. Dorothea's attention fixed to his chest. Lord, he must be big under that waistcoat.

Someone had shot at Lord Evington. An accident? Folding her shaking hands together, she stood back while Ben leaned over his friend. "Speak," Ben said. "I'll make sure nothing is said outside this room." He shot Dorothea another glance. She nodded, lips pressed tight together.

Evington gave Ben a resigned glance. "Very well. Merely that I had a thought. This is a relatively minor wound, and yet it bled a great deal."

Ben fixed him with an intent stare. "Go on."

"Louis's wound after the duel was not so great, as matters turned out. Perhaps the messy wound persuaded him to let certain people think he was hurt much worse than he was. The surgeon who attended him would have been easily bribed."

"For what purpose?" Ben demanded.

"To force your hand. To make you leave the country or give yourself up. Any outcome would be to his advantage."

Paralyzed with horror, Dorothea listened.

"Dueling is against the law, and you made the challenge," Evington said, his words slower than usual. "Honor demanded that he meet it. But he provoked you to it. If you had been taken up, the authorities would have taken a dim view. And so would your father."

Ben growled. "Damn, you're right of course. He recovered quickly, did he not?"

Evington nodded. "As fast as I will. This hurts like the devil, but I saw the wound for myself. It will heal well, if properly treated. I should be up and about in a day or two. Louis lay sequestered in his lodgings for a week, until he was certain you were on the way out of the country and you were not coming back."

Someone wanted Ben out of the way, so had forced the duel? How could that be? Questions crowded into Dorothea's mind. What was going on here?

Getting to his feet, Ben pressed his friend's hand. "We'll leave you in peace. Sleep, and I'll have a man put outside the room. Do not think of going to your own until you feel better."

"I would appreciate an hour or two."

"Gentlemanly behavior!" Dorothea snorted.

Lord Evington turned an amused glance on her. "I beg your pardon, ma'am?"

"You must be in *agony*." Coming out from her place at the head of the bed, she forced Ben to step back. She shook out her skirts, now sadly crumpled and bloodstained, likely ruined. A small price to pay. "You should rest as long as you need."

With a sigh, Evington closed his eyes. Far too perceptive, those eyes. "I fear you are right. I'm exhausted. Send my man to me in an hour, if you please. I'll repair to my own room and leave Rougier to make what he can of the mess."

"Take all the time you need," Ben murmured. "I owe you more than I can say. Would you like to exchange rooms?"

His eyes still shut, Evington answered him. "No. My chamber is much better appointed than this one."

Ben gave a rough laugh. "I had this room when I was a boy after I left the nursery. I spent years here. I never found it lacking."

"No, you wouldn't. It's time you gave some consideration to the appearance you cut in the world, dear boy."

Ben held out his hand in an imperious gesture. Without thinking, Dorothea crossed to him and put her own hand in his. It closed around her, locking her fast. "Come. We'll repair to your room and have that talk."

"But sir!" Real shock made her tremble.

"Come, you can hardly be missish now." He towed her across the room, grabbing the stack of papers she hadn't had time to examine before pulling her toward the door. "I'm sure you want to see these."

Chapter 8

Ben took Dorothea to her door, and opened it wide. With a sigh, she walked inside and left the door ajar. Invited or not, he followed her inside and closed the door.

The room was empty. Too empty. Only the most necessary furniture lay within. There was no rug on the floor to cushion her bare feet, nor elaborate drapes around the old-fashioned four-poster bed to keep out the drafts at night. The sight appalled him, especially when they could have put her somewhere else. The room he was now using, for example. "Why did they put you here?"

She shrugged. "I'm hardly the most prestigious guest. But the covers are warm, and the room is quiet."

"There's quiet, and then there's spartan. We have plenty of well-appointed chambers."

"Please, don't concern yourself." Her voice was frosty.

"Ah, but I do. I will see about this. You do not belong here."

Although the room was spacious and filled with light from windows on two sides, he couldn't like it, and with a jolt he remembered why. "This used to belong to my tutor. I ran the poor man ragged. He was a tyrant."

"I see." She kept her head turned away from him, ostensibly staring out the window to the gardens beyond. A pulse throbbed at the base of her neck, making him wonder what she tasted like there. What she tasted like everywhere. Good Lord, he hadn't thought of a woman in those terms since Mary had died. Putting aside the sensuous life he had once reveled in had come easily to him, and since his wife's death he had not had another woman. But now, here he was. His libido roared back to life. Most inconvenient.

Except this time, only one woman occupied his thoughts.

In the distance, heat shimmered over the fields beyond the formal gardens. When she turned back to him, her eyes were hard, a shell covering whatever lay beneath. He wanted to discover that secret part of her, and he vowed he would.

He took a step toward her. She held her ground, so he took another, and another, until they were only inches apart. "What were you doing in my room?" he asked, keeping his voice soft and intimate.

This close, she couldn't hide her reactions from him. Her eyes darkened as her pupils widened. "Sir James wants absolute proof," she answered.

"Of my identity? Why do you care?"

He narrowed his eyes, examining her wary expression, and the way her pulse throbbed in her throat like a little bird's.

"I wanted to help." She swept the tip of her tongue across her lower lip. That little action wasn't helping Ben control himself. "My room is close to yours, so I thought I'd just look—"

"Did you indeed? Are you related to Sir James? Or is there another reason you want to know?" A suspicion crossed his mind. "Who has sent you?" Was she, after all, in league with his cousin? Had he allowed his groin to lead, rather than his head?

He waited. Would he have to do the elaborate dance of denial and confession? That would take far too much time.

She glanced at the papers in his free hand. "Because I—oh, Lord!" She tucked her fingers inside the front of her gown and pulled something out as he tossed the papers on a nearby table. A pin, about an inch and a half long, fashioned from silver. She held it up, so he could see the entwined letters.

"SSL? Is that a relative?" What had a piece of jewelry to do with this?

"No." She pushed the pin through her gown once more, this time proudly on display. "It's the Society for Single Ladies. A club I belong to. Miss Angela Childers set it up."

He knew that name. "The lady banker?"

He recalled Angela Childers vividly. While the City held a few independent businesswomen, none were as important as Angela Childers. Brilliant, beautiful, and single.

"Yes, Angela." Dorothea lifted her chin. "She set up a club for single ladies, the overlooked and the less fortunate, widows and spinsters. Ostensibly we are a literary society. We read improving sermons and lectures."

"Truly?" He had not thought Dorothea Rowland the kind of woman to devote herself to sermons. She had a lively mind. A shame to waste it on dull-as-ditchwater tomes like that.

She laughed, short and hard. "No. No doubt in time our mission will be known, but for now, it is much easier for us to move about unnoticed."

"You make yourselves sound like spies."

She shook her head vigorously, loosening her hairstyle. A ringlet of pale moonlight tumbled onto her shoulder, making her at once more desirable. He urgently wanted to see the rest of it. His body thrummed to life, and while he did his best to ignore the urge, it remained, underlining their conversation.

"Angela, in her capacity as head of the bank, sometimes needs to know more about a situation, but does not want to draw attention to herself. We, the members of the SSL, act as her agents." She lifted her chin proudly. "*Paid* agents."

"Fascinating," he drawled. He guessed where this was going, although he wouldn't spare her the explanation. "Go on." He'd use the extra time to place this information into his plans and assimilate what she'd just told him.

"Your cousin has borrowed a great deal of money against the expectation of inheriting. You may not know that rumors were racing around London that Louis had done away with you. Or at the very least that you died of the wounds you sustained in the duel. Angela wished to ascertain the truth of these. She didn't want to incur his displeasure, in case he did become the marquess, but she doesn't want to lend him any more funds."

He frowned. "She sent you into danger?"

She laughed harshly. "At a house party? I don't think so. I have written to her to inform her that you are still alive, and it is a matter of time before you are declared the marquess. But Sir James wants documentary proof. The Chancellor insists on it."

He grunted. "Lord Hardwicke has always been a stickler for paperwork. He was Chancellor when I left, and I daresay he'll be Chancellor until he dies."

He kept his eyes on hers. She was nervous, her lovely eyes wide, but not afraid. He liked that. "And so you came to my room this morning when you thought I would be at the hunt." That was the part he didn't like.

"Yes." She swallowed. "I should not have pried, I know, but the maid left the door open. It was the act of an instant to walk inside. And then you arrived." She bit her lip. He focused his attention on it until she let it slide back into place. The plump, pink flesh tempted him far too much.

"So I did." He recalled the scene, and the help she'd rendered. Honoria would have fainted. Lovely as she was, his cousin's wife did not have the presence of mind of this woman. Or the common sense. "Before the events of this morning, I had intended to wait awhile."

"To what purpose?" She raised a hand, then let it fall, rustling the silk of her gown. Ben found the sound strangely alluring. For once in his life, he was having difficulty concentrating on the point of discussion. "I see. To discern friend from foe."

Ah, she was sharp. "Precisely. To assess the lay of the land before I made my move. But I will not have my friends put in danger. If Louis is that desperate, then this must end." Unfolding his arms, he lifted the papers in his hand. "These are the proof of my claim. You should have looked at this pile first."

"What are they?"

"You will trust me to summarize for you?"

She nodded.

Gratification suffused him. It should not, but her approval meant more than he cared to admit. If Angela Childers was involved, that explained a lot. Miss Childers had a mind as sharp as a newly stropped razor, and she would have had her eye on the sums his cousin was borrowing. She'd want to secure her investment and ensure it could be repaid. If Louis was not the marquess, then she would cut his line of credit.

"These are the letters Hal wrote to me while I was away, and he has lent me some of my replies to add to the stack. They have a continuity no claimant could achieve. And they have all the proofs of transport on the outside—the seals, the franks, the declarations, all that. I also have affidavits written by my representatives in London, and the lawyers connected with the estate."

He drew a sheet out. "And this...this is a letter from the King, assuring anyone interested that I am the true Marquess of Belstead." He allowed a small smile to curve his lips. "I had time to attend court while I was in London arranging to come here. Fortunately, the King saw me with little delay, probably eager for the small gift I brought for him from the colonies."

"A gift?"

"Snuff." He shrugged. "A small token of my loyalty. He has a penchant for snuff made from tobacco harvested on a particular estate in Virginia. Over the last few years, I have made certain he got it. When I visited him at court last week, I brought his usual supply myself. He recognized me, although he evinced surprise that I was *that* Thorpe."

"He knew you were alive?"

"Not until I presented myself before him," he admitted. The company his father-in-law had owned had dealt with the British royal family for years. Ben had ensured the King got what he wanted and established a chain of supply personally. He'd even fought and killed a bear in its cause, knowing the favor would pay off one day. And it had, magnificently. "The King expressed his appreciation, as well as revealing his disappointment in Louis and his wasteful, immoral ways." He grinned. "That helped him in his decision. And Louis's adherence to and friendship with the Prince of Wales."

After a sharp laugh, she clapped her hand over her mouth, as the sound reverberated around the room. "Yes, he is, he does! I mean, he is forever at Carlton House dancing attendance on the prince. And the King hates the prince, does he not?"

"Cordially. As his father hated him. A family tradition, you might say. His majesty never hesitates to do his son a bad turn. Putting paid to the ambitions of one of Frederick's friends will do nicely."

A reluctant smile flickered over her lips. "That was clever."

He swept a brief bow. "Thank you." Agitation still disturbed him, and the remnants of his fear and fury. Fear his best friend would die. Fury that anyone would attempt it. And now, attraction for this woman, far more than he'd felt before. Her new boldness delighted him, and she had grown into her looks. Whether she realized it or not, Dorothea was beautiful. Where she'd been coltish, grace and elegance had taken its place.

"But the king's letter will be enough." He glanced at the documents. She could have stolen it, or anyone else for that matter. Leaving it in the open was criminally careless. Not something he could usually be accused of.

He would not make such a mistake again.

"And you... Of course they would." He moved closer. She backed away, her hands clenched by her sides. "You are my ally, are you not?"

Her back connected with the wall. He kept coming until he stood before her. He slapped his hands against the painted plaster on either side of her head and leaned in. Tipping her chin, she stared up at him. Beautiful eyes he could get lost in. The soft gray had a darker outline, defining her irises. As he watched, the pupils widened, letting more of her soul free.

Taking a hand from the cold, unfeeling wall, he grazed the tip of her chin with his crooked forefinger. "Lovely," he murmured.

This time she did not gainsay him, only swallowed and blinked. Her mouth dropped open slightly. She had elegant lips, carefully shaped and full. Eminently kissable. And it had been a long time since he'd kissed a woman. Months. Maybe longer.

The memories of others faded, became mere dreams as he gazed at the one before him, the heat of her body warming him. Lowering his head the fraction of an inch that it took, he brushed his lips over hers in the briefest of kisses. Instead of lifting away, as he'd meant to do, he hesitated, and returned for more.

A blaze of instant fire took him, shocked him into deepening the kiss. What he'd meant as a mere tease, a demonstration of his power, turned into something else entirely. He pressed closer, heat searing him, his awareness of her body wrapping around him like a protective sheath.

He wanted everything she would give him.

* * * *

Dorothea opened her mouth and let him in. She could do nothing else. His power, so carefully harnessed, swept through her and put her in his thrall. If he'd forced her, she'd have broken away immediately, but he didn't.

He persuaded, and that was worse. Offered her just enough to make her pursue him, to become an eager participant. Had a kiss ever proved so seductive, so irresistible? She had kissed men before, but not like this. She recalled hard lips on hers, or young, eager ones, clumsy and unpracticed. Nothing like this. Never had she known the power of a mere kiss before.

When he touched her lips with the tip of his tongue, she almost swooned from the intimacy. But she was no schoolroom miss. She was made of stronger stuff. Dorothea looped her arm around the back of his neck, the velvet of his hair ribbon grazing her skin. The enticing fabric of his shirt barely concealed the powerful muscles beneath. If he had not bent to her, she wouldn't have been able to reach his arm, such was the width of his shoulders and his height. That alone fascinated her, that he had to bend to her instead of reaching up.

He dipped his tongue into her mouth and she clutched at him, grabbing his waistcoat and pulling the top few buttons undone. He groaned into her mouth. Eagerly she swallowed the sound and came back for more. Her fichu loosened, whether from her frantic need or his hands she didn't know. Nor did she care. He could rip it off her if he liked.

Drawing away, he gasped, "I did not mean—" but she pulled him back, using her arm to haul him against her. So there were advantages in being tall, after all. A shorter woman wouldn't have had the leverage. Triumph soared through her when he responded, dragging her even closer to press her breasts against the firm wall of his chest. It brought her some ease but not nearly enough. She needed more. She wanted skin.

Working her hand between them, she found his waistcoat buttons and tugged them through the buttonholes. He did not stop her and, emboldened, she carried on, until she could flatten her hand on his chest. Now only his shirt lay between her and her desire. If she didn't have him now, she'd never have the chance again. He was rough around the edges but still a gentleman, and he'd keep away from her. Voracious, unfulfilled, she pressed her lips to his, afraid that if he came to his senses and recalled who she was and what she looked like, he'd move away. If he did that, she would die. Or something inside her would. She'd never felt desire like this before, and she wanted more. Now.

He responded, pulling her close and dragging her fichu up and away. Her breasts swelled, threatening to burst out of her stays and shift. If only they would!

Tracing his finger across the top of her breasts, following the line of her stays, brought tingling awareness to her skin, deliciously sensual.

A click behind them heralded the entrance of—someone, and the scandalized cry brought her back to earth. "Unhand her, sir!"

If ever a brother was de trop, this was the time. Ann's shocked, high-pitched cry was broken off.

Ben spun around, pushing her behind him as if to shield her, and standing tall. "Yes?"

If anyone doubted his aristocratic pedigree, they should hear and see him now.

His arrogance made her giggle, half nervous, half shocked. Bending, she retrieved her fichu and tossed the light square of white linen across her shoulders, shielding what should never have been exposed. Hastily she gathered the precious papers, which she'd let fall when she'd lost her senses to his kiss.

"May I ask what you are doing in my sister's bedroom?" Laurence demanded, every inch the proper guardian.

"I must apologize, Lord Sandigate," Ben said smoothly. "I had private business with Dorothea, and we got somewhat—carried away."

She did not bother wondering how and why she could have done this; she knew perfectly well. The man had overwhelmed her senses from the moment she'd laid eyes on him. She would do it again. And, resenting his protection of her, she emerged, smoothing her skirts and holding the papers with hands that barely trembled. "And really, Laurence, what business is it of yours?"

Laurence lifted his sandy brows and met her gaze directly. "I am your protector, my dear. My duty is to ensure your safety."

"I am perfectly fine! And I am all of thirty years old." Closing her eyes, she huffed a sigh. Every time she said that, her heart plummeted.

But when she took a step to cross the room and join her brother, Ben curled his fingers around her arm, preventing her from moving. "I regret my behavior, but not the reason why. I have been courting your sister, my lord, but decided to delay any formal approach until the title had been declared."

"And this is the result?" From the chilly tone in his voice, Laurence was not mollified.

"Entirely my fault. I would make amends."

Laurence nodded. "Accepted. We will discuss settlements."

After exchanging an appalled look with Ann, Dorothea shook off Ben's restraining hand. "I am here, and I will speak for myself." Any embarrassment had been dissipated by the arrogance of the men. "I am long past the age where I need to apply to my guardian to make my decisions for me. I have no guardian." She turned a glare on her brother. "What I do, I do for myself, in full knowledge." Her breath came in short gasps, her fury taking even that from her. "I will not be forced, sir. I will make up my own mind."

Triumph soared through her. With her acceptance of work from Angela, she had done more than found something useful to do with her time. She was herself, and she had people who believed in her. "I have my inheritance now, and I control my own fate. I would like you all to leave." After handing the papers to Ben, she turned her back pointedly.

They left. Even Ben.

* * * *

Ben refused to discuss Dorothea with Lord Sandigate and his wife. "If you will leave the matter to me, I will resolve it. I have made my desires clear, and I will continue to do so. Even if Sir James finds against me, which he will not, I have more than enough to make Dorothea happy."

Fine words. After replacing the papers on the table, he sent a note to Sir James, requesting a meeting as soon as he could arrange it.

Lying on his bed, his hands tucked under his head, he allowed himself to think.

Her outburst had made a few things clear. She would make her own decisions, she said, and he respected that. She obviously had enough money to ensure her future, but he could offer her much more.

If he married her, he could trust her with the affairs of the estate. He could get her with child, and if the baby was born well and alive, return to Boston. She would not want that; society was much smaller, and restricted.

At home, Dorothea would be a marchioness, a woman with an assured place in the world. He could give her that.

And he wanted her.

This woman had life, so real and vital to him that he still felt the warmth of her skin under his hands. That one brief touch he'd stolen of the soft skin of her upper breasts had made him yearn for more, and yet more. To have her under him, his body in hers, his mouth worshiping her skin.

Sitting up, Ben swung his legs off the bed, crossed the room to the washstand, and stripped off his waistcoat and shirt. Dinner would be soon, and Rougier would be up directly. He might as well make a start.

Life wouldn't wait for him. Facing imminent death across twenty yards had taught him that.

Chapter 9

The last person she wanted to see was walking toward Dorothea along the wide corridor of the main floor. She'd dressed quickly and missed breakfast, opting for a light repast in her room and planning a day outdoors.

She wasn't running away, of course not. But she needed time to think and work out what she would do. Her instincts told her to run to Ben, to claim more of what he gave her yesterday afternoon, but her common sense warned her to stop. She needed space, and a chance to regroup, to rebuild that façade she'd relied on for years.

She couldn't avoid him; no rooms were open and going back would be positively rude. She could not see how to escape him, so with a sense of helplessness, she stopped and waited for him to come to her. Between the wide windows, the heavy, dusty upholstery gave her no exodus.

His gaze followed hers. "This house needs more domestics. Or servants who do their jobs better." His attention returned to her. "And I need someone to help me do it." He continued before she had time to reply, "I see you're dressed for the outdoors. May I join you?"

She could hardly say she intended to discover the most out-of-the-way pavilion and stay there. "Of course." She even managed a smile.

"I'll behave myself; I promise." That would have been fine except he added, "Unless you don't want me to."

Best to pretend she hadn't heard that last remark, but her ears heated, and she'd wager they'd turned pink. At least the flush hadn't spread to the rest of her face.

Fortunately, the day was a fine one, so they could not expect to be alone. Leaving the house by a side door, they walked toward the rose gardens at the back of the house.

She quickened her pace, her feet crunching on the gravel. He easily kept up with her. "I would apologize for the incidents of yesterday, but I cannot find it in myself to be sorry," he said.

She kept her gaze fixed ahead. She would not head for the far reaches of the park, as she'd planned, but the main gardens. A formal arrangement held little interest, but the flowers were pretty and the paths dry and in full view of the house. He could not misbehave here, and she wouldn't be tempted to let him. "Most women would consider what you did a grave insult."

He chuckled, a low rumble deep in his throat. Impossibly attractive. "Unless they responded. My dear, you were pure fire."

Whipping her head around, she stared at him, shocked. She knew how she'd behaved, but she never thought he'd refer to it. "You are not a gentleman, sir."

"My title says otherwise," he replied. "What I am is honest, and I admit a gentleman is not always so. We deserve to discuss this matter with no bark on it."

"I thought I made my position clear. I am a single woman and like to remain one."

The way she'd responded to his kiss worried her, frightened her a little. He was too close for her comfort, but moving away wouldn't help. He'd only come closer.

"You were caught in the moment, as was I. What would have happened, I wonder, if your brother had not come upon us?"

He wouldn't let her look away, but kept her gaze. She stopped, lest she trip and fall, or make a fool of herself some other way. "I do not know. I have no experience of that kind of situation." She shrugged. "I am not sought after, sir."

Turning her head, she continued ambling along the paths, seeing nothing. The scent of newly cut grass stung her nose, invading her senses.

"It's my belief that you've hidden your true nature for too long. I fear I might have had something to do with that. I'd be sorry, except I mean to make up for that in every way possible." His response made her shiver in anticipation, her reaction involuntary.

"Honesty, you said, sir. Let us keep to that."

"I am completely honest. I can't help what other men think. They are all fools if they can't see what's in front of their eyes. I want you, Dorothea, for my wife, and I intend to renew my courtship of you."

"Too late for that." He'd destroyed any attempt at propriety yesterday. "Why would you want me?"

"You are an intelligent woman. I like you. And our arrangement would give you a much better future than any you could expect."

"You're so sure of that? An independent existence would suit me well. I have enough to ensure my future. I will buy an annuity and a comfortable house and be perfectly happy." Defiantly she held her head high, refusing to give way.

His derisory snort did not need words, but he said them anyway. "You deserve more than that. Your intelligence, your beauty demands you have the position you deserve."

Again, she stopped and faced him. "You strike me as a man who likes his own way in everything. I doubt you'd welcome my interference."

"I regret I have given you the wrong impression."

In the distance, two women engaged in a stroll blatantly watched them. Dorothea chose to ignore them, but they were a warning to her, not to allow her emotions to override her behavior. Her brother had read her a lecture yesterday, one she had deserved. Her behavior had not shown the restraint and hauteur required of a lady. Perhaps she was not a lady, after all. Her instincts certainly hadn't been those of a lady.

"How can that be, sir? You are a man of decisive behavior, used to running your own affairs. Do you require a housekeeper, you will find plenty eager to serve you, especially when Sir James declares you the marquess."

"You believe he will, then?"

He was toying with her. "After what you showed me yesterday, the decision is a foregone conclusion." She shifted away from him. His attention made her uncomfortable.

"Thank you. We must wait on events. But you know better than anyone else in this house that I am wealthier than most people think. Even without the title and lands I can keep a wife and family in luxury."

"I have never yearned for luxury."

"I am aware. Your mind is set on higher things, is it not?"

Despite her determination, his statement sent a riot of pleasure through her, especially when he followed his words with a sultry smile, hinting at intimacy—blatantly promising it. "You would have influence over politicians, servants, clerics—and me."

"Oh!"

Her cheeks were blazing. She turned away and groped in her pocket for her fan. He moved closer, but not too close, so the observers could not object to it. "Honesty, Dorothea. Let's deal with one another plainly."

Ignoring her discomfiture as best she could, she met his gaze boldly. "Yes. Let's."

Turning again, she walked down the path and into the maze, a series of knee-high box hedges. If they tired of seeking the center, they could step over the hedges—at least, that was the theory. But like everything else in this house, the hedges weren't kept properly. Twigs stuck out, and the ground was festooned with dead wood that the gardeners should have long since collected.

He kept pace with her, the paths wide enough to walk two abreast. Behind them, the house reared up, half a dozen stories of grandiose magnificence. She turned, and the house was before her, the blank windows holding who knew how many secrets. Behind one, at the opposite end of the house to the one holding her room, someone moved, a whisper across the glass.

His attention went to it sharply, then he deliberately turned his head, to gaze at her instead. "I need a wife. I want you to fulfill the role."

He would not be deterred, except, perhaps, by one thing. "You know I am thirty years old. I might be barren."

"You are a brave woman to face that possibility." He moved his hand, which he'd been holding loosely by his side, but returned it without touching her. Nevertheless, the intent remained. "You are not. I am certain of it."

"You can tell by looking?"

"No." His gaze remained steady. "I'm willing to take that risk, if you are. I can't think of anyone I'd rather have by my side on this adventure. And it will be an adventure, that I can promise you."

She walked again, trying to discern the path to the center of the maze, where a bench was set. Inside, she was a mess, her previous resolve shattered. Adventure? Yes, please, but the rest, she wasn't so sure. "At least you haven't told me you love me beyond bearing, or that you are passionately devoted to me." She injected as much venom as she could into her words.

"I might do that yet," he said. "Would it persuade you?"

"Not if it weren't the truth. And perhaps not even then."

* * * *

Maybe he shouldn't have laughed, but Dorothea delighted Ben. Her insistence on straight talking and honesty was rare in her sex. A declaration of passionate love would not work with her, so he hadn't even considered it. The sunlight struck her hair, turning it a shade of delicate, rare, pale gold that had far more value to him than a flashy yellow. She wore a broad-brimmed bergère hat, which she could have used to avoid his gaze, but she had not.

They could forge a partnership like no other.

He'd never sought out a lady who preferred to stay in the shadows. In his previous London career, the dazzlers, the beauties, the society darlings had attracted him. They flirted, laughed, nothing serious, everything fashionable, all the look-at-me people. He'd changed more than he'd realized. Because this quiet, intelligent, elegant woman drew him more than the lovelies, and he desperately wanted her to marry him.

No, not desperately, of course not. She wasn't the only woman of substance in London. But it was this one he wanted. Better not to question his decision, but to get on with it. She would take some persuading.

"The longest-lasting unions have a deep affection that grows over the years." Marriages based on passion rarely worked for very long, and he was tired of short-term solutions.

She met his gaze straight on, her eyes silver in the sunlight. "Did you love your first wife?"

"Yes." When he'd first met her, Mary had enchanted him. She was so pretty, so dainty, that he had been certain he had fallen in love with her, but that emotion had not lasted long. "Besides, what does that have to do with anything? Love, or what passes for it, is a fleeting emotion. I value friendship and affection much more."

Dorothea remained absolutely still, but a shadow crossed her eyes as the light dimmed. A cloud must have covered the sun. "I see. Thank you for your honesty. I will need time."

Disappointed, he asked, "How much?"

She waved a hand and glanced down, away from him. "All I need. If that isn't enough for you, then maybe you should look elsewhere."

"I apologize. Of course, take as much time as you need." Although quicker would be better. Her brother wouldn't wait forever. In fact, he was expecting an announcement today, but he could fob off the viscount for a little while yet.

She looked up again, her mouth flat. "Sir James said he would like the new marquess to have an assured line, did he not?"

Ah, yes, straight to the point. Despite not wanting her to recall it, he was pleased that she did, because it displayed her presence of mind. And, yes, honesty. "He did. Louis, any son he might have, and then William are eligible."

"So you don't really need me."

Put like that, no, he didn't. But he wanted her. "The idea of taking a girl fresh from the schoolroom makes me shudder. I can't imagine we would have much in common."

"Some schoolroom chits are up to the task. After all, most are trained from childhood."

He shook his head. "No. And to have them making a play for me." He let her see his shudder this time. "No."

The horror of stepping into a fashionable ballroom and feeling the target on his back. He had no intention of subjecting himself to that ever again. The giggling, the fan-wafting—no.

"Madam, I would be honored if you would consider my request. Shall we now turn to enjoying the day, and speak of other matters?"

"Yes." Her smile had an edge of relief to it. If he was a man aware of his own consequence, he might have taken offense at that. However, her reaction merely amused him. "What do you consider a suitable topic of discussion? Your friend's injury? How is he today?"

Recalling his visit to Hal earlier that day, Ben grinned. "A couple of strong footmen transferred him to his own room. This morning he is decidedly bored, and consequently naggy. That's a good sign."

"I'm glad. So he will make a complete recovery?"

He nodded. "Barring infection. His man is taking good care of him. It is only a graze." He glanced at the hedges. "We've been this way before, have we not? Don't I recognize that hole in the greenery?"

She glanced at it and sighed. "Indeed. A shame the hedges have grown too high to step over. We should try to find our way out."

"Indeed. I can hardly wait to have jurisdiction over this estate. Everything is merely adequate. Except for the extravagances my cousin has invested in for his own aggrandizement."

"If you cared so much, why did you not return earlier?"

Her tart remark edged too close to home. Because—because he was hurt, because he was finally done with fashion, because he had made mistakes he couldn't easily resolve. He'd faced all those uncomfortable truths and dealt with them. In many ways, he was not the same person who had fled the country nearly seven years ago. He chose not to tell her any of those reasons.

"I had a new life, one I created myself. It owed nothing to anyone else. I needed to stay away to build that up. If Louis had managed the estate well, I daresay I would have stayed away. But he did not, and here I am."

They had found their way out of the maze, except for one hedge, which had grown uncomfortably high. He chose the temporary shelter to stop her questions in the most effective way he knew. Turning quickly, he drew her to him, his hands firmly around her waist. She stumbled and fell against his chest, but before she had a chance to recover her balance, he'd stolen a kiss.

The touch of her lips energized him, gave him ideas that should certainly not be occurring to him here and now. He dared not linger, but savored the kiss, then lifted his lips, enjoying her expression of stunned amazement. In those few seconds, when he had taken her unawares, she'd revealed something. The way she'd clutched his shoulders and opened her mouth under his told him so much. She wanted him. Whether she wanted him as desperately as he did her remained to be seen.

But he had experience on his side. She was an innocent.

He would use any weapon he had to win this war, because he wanted her too badly to lose.

Chapter 10

Shaken by the swift kiss, Dorothea did her best to regain her composure. "You are a rake, then."

Ben seemed untouched by his move, except for a slight flush high on his cheekbones. "Only with you, my sweet."

With exaggerated courtesy he extended his arm, tacitly inviting her to lean on him. Either she spurned him or risked a stumble. She accepted his support with a murmured word of thanks.

Under the fabric, his arm was as hard as iron. Ah, so he wasn't unaffected. That was tension. Knowing the attraction was not only on her side reassured her a little. She let the endearment pass, or rather, put it in her personal treasury of memories.

They strolled back in the direction of the house. The honey-colored stone reared above them, the windows glinting in the summer sunshine. A fine building, one that deserved better than it was getting. The far right of the upper stories was where Ben's mother was rumored to live. Nothing had been heard or seen of her, bar a few shadowy movements, like the one she'd witnessed earlier. "Why do you not just ask your mother to identify you? After all, nobody can gainsay a mother."

Unexpectedly his arm tightened, clamping her hand against his side. "I am due to pay my daily visit. Won't you accompany me?"

The mild words did belie the strength he was using to hold her to him. "Of course," she murmured. "Unless it would disturb her."

"I doubt that." The bitterness in his voice surprised Dorothea. No rumors of a break in the relationship with his mother had appeared, and so likely they didn't exist. Not even Louis had said anything about Lady

Belstead. One would have thought he would use her evidence, unless he was afraid of a positive identification.

Entering the house, Ben handed his cocked hat to a footman and waited until she had divested herself of her straw bergère and gloves. The day being fine, she had not bothered with a shawl or cloak. He waited until she checked her appearance in the mirror and patted a strand of hair back into place. She wore her hair in the regulation high knot and covered it with a small lace-edged cap. Everything was as it should be.

Turning, she caught him gazing at her as if he really saw her. Unused to that reaction, Dorothea's throat tightened, and she looked away, swallowing. Usually, nobody noticed her,. Here, though, Ben had brought her into the center of the gathering. If she rejected his proposal, she might become the subject of unpleasant gossip, but it wouldn't last for long. Being found in his room when he was not there wasn't the end of the world. She could recover from that.

But not her reaction to him. Every time his brawny shoulders hove into view her heart missed a beat. Any woman would behave the same way. Of course they would.

He gestured for her to climb the broad, carpet-covered stone steps. She mounted the curved staircase to the first floor, then to the next, where he indicated she should walk to her right, to the only door that lay in front of them. A footman stood on guard, one she had never noticed before. He bowed to Ben and opened the door for him to walk through.

A quiet room met them. The curtains were half drawn over the windows, dimming the bright summer day. Furniture was arranged deliberately and formally. The pieces were old, giving the room an air of stateliness absent in other parts of the house. Perhaps Lady Belstead preferred it that way. A hush, a quiet reverence hung over them.

Tension tightened her nerves and the hairs on the back of her neck rose to attention, prickling her skin. "Come," he said softly. "My mother will be in her boudoir at this hour. Or in bed."

In bed? "Then should we go?"

He shook his head. "She receives people in her bed sometimes."

Some people saw visitors in their bedrooms, but in bed? She did not think so. But she said nothing as he led the way to a door at the other end of the quiet room. After tapping on the woodwork, he pushed it open. "Mama?"

He held the door for her.

This room was as dimly lit as the one before it, but as she entered, a wall of heat hit her. The fire was lit and blazing in the hearth. Before it, in a high-backed chair that resembled a throne, sat a woman. The marchioness. Technically, since Ben had been married, the dowager.

Dorothea had seen the lady before in very different circumstances, but not like this, not so intimate. She sank into the required curtsy.

"Mama, this is Miss Dorothea Rowland, the sister of the Viscount Sandigate."

Why did he introduce her like that, when they'd met before? As if this was the first time?

"Mama?" the marchioness said in a thready voice.

Ben sighed.

A woman entered the room, a personal maid. Hatchet-faced, she wore a plain green gown, a lacy apron over the front, the kind ladies wore as fashion rather than for any practical reason. Dorothea rose from her curtsy, since nobody took notice of it.

"My lord." The woman dropped a brief curtsy before going to her mistress's side. "Her ladyship is having a quiet day."

"Good morning, Miss Sullivan. I thought Mama would like to meet my bride-to-be," Ben said calmly.

Before Dorothea could protest, the marchioness broke in. "Tom! Where have you been? I have been wanting to say something to you this age."

A significant pause ensued, before he said, "No, Mama, it's Ben. Your son, not your husband."

"Please don't contradict her, my lord," the maid put in. "It will distress her. She is not in the best of moods today."

Ben nodded. "Very well." He addressed his mother once more. "We find you in good health, ma'am?"

Obviously not. The marchioness thought Ben was his father? Why would she think that? Dorothea stepped back, her heart thumping too fast. Something was very wrong here. She'd imagined the marchioness frail, in poor health, but the illness was in her mind.

"I am well," the marchioness said, sounding every inch the bored aristocrat. But her eyes, so much like her son's, bore a distant look. She did not rest her attention on anything for long, her gaze darting from one thing to another. "I want to talk to you about our son, Tom. You ignore Benedict, when he does everything he can to bring the title into disrepute. We must deal with him, Tom. Soon."

Ben sighed and closed his eyes. "Yes, Amelia. We will handle him."

He turned and held out his hand to Dorothea. Silently, without demur, she took it and let him lead her from the room.

The marchioness shouted after them. "Come back! I mean it, Tom! You will not ignore me again; I will kill myself first!"

Dorothea stopped. Ben did not. If she had not begun to walk again, he would have dragged her. His hand held hers too tightly for her to free herself. As they left, the woman behind them screamed out her late husband's name, followed by a torrent of abuse, using language that would have made a sailor blush. This was terrible, horrible. The marchioness was undoubtedly mad.

At the door to the suite, Dorothea glanced back, catching sight of the scene. The maid was attending to her mistress, holding her hands, soothing her in quiet tones as the woman's cries died down to a faint whimper. The tantrum was over, leaving a broken woman.

They walked out of the apartments before Dorothea realized that tears were pouring down her face.

Ben took her to a small antechamber nearby. He closed the door, but she was too distressed to cavil. Nor did she object when Ben took her into his arms and held her until her shaking stopped and the tears dried. When he gave her his handkerchief, she dabbed at her face.

Ben spoke softly. "I'm sorry. I should have sent word before we visited. Her volatility is increasing."

"What is wrong with her? Is she mad?"

When she pulled away, he released her, but indicated a small sofa set under the window. She took a seat and he joined her, laying his arm across the back of the sofa in a protective gesture she appreciated. Not too familiar, but enough to offer her comfort. Really, she should be giving it to him. When she returned his handkerchief, he thrust it in his coat pocket.

"No, she is not mad. Not precisely. It is more accurate to say she is senile." Removing his arm, he leaned forward, resting his elbows on his knees. "It started before I left, but that was no more than bouts of forgetfulness. Occasionally she called me by my father's name, but people put it down to absentmindedness. Nobody thought much about it."

"I'm so sorry."

"You see why neither Louis nor I want to bring her into our dispute. She lives quietly, and we put it about that she is ill, that is all, nothing specific. But she is fit and healthy and she could live for years. Those apartments have a private stairwell that leads into a small courtyard. There's a garden, where she spends much of her time. She is happy, except for the few occasions when she knows she is missing something important, or when, as you just saw, she becomes distressed or loses her temper."

His voice was steady. Too steady, as if he was holding his emotions in check.

"Yes, I saw that. She seemed puzzled, even when she called you by your father's name."

He nodded and kept his head bowed. "I should not have put you through that, but yesterday she was in a good mood. She even recognized me without anyone prompting her."

They remained silent for a few moments. "I have never met anyone with that...condition."

"Neither have I. I'm told my father's grandmother was the same, but she was eighty when she grew too forgetful to be on her own. My mother is sixty, far too soon for senility. It is much more than that. Nobody can explain what caused it, or how we can stop it. Louis sought medical advice, and they bled her and fastened her in restraints. Louis sent them away. I can be grateful to him for that, at least."

"Oh, the poor lady!"

Turning back to her, he laid his hand over hers, but the look in his eyes, the bleakness, told her he needed the comfort more than she did. She clasped his hand. "Thank you for trusting me. Obviously, you have kept your mother's condition from society, and I will respect that."

"I know you will. Thank you for coming with me."

"You must find visiting her very hard. I would, if I were in the same situation."

"I do. But I see her every day, while I'm here. When I distress her, as happened today, I leave. That is the only thing that calms her down. Martha, her maid, takes care of her, and Wright, the footman at the door, is employed for her use alone. She has a maid assigned to her rooms, and nobody else is allowed in."

Before they'd entered those apartments, Dorothea had doubted his ability to feel any depth of emotion since his return. He'd expended it all before he left. But no, he merely pushed his emotions under his calm exterior.

Her heart went out to mother and son. "I am so sorry."

Abruptly he got to his feet. "We should go. I appreciate your discretion and your sympathy. For the most part, she is happy. Apart from today. It is only the people around her who are distressed on her behalf."

Chapter 11

After leaving Dorothea at the door of her chamber, Ben took a long walk in the grounds. He ranged way beyond the formal park and up to the model farm, which was supposed to act as an experimental facility, displaying the best of modern innovations and testing them out for viability. He found a run-down, dilapidated house and a few starving animals living in filth.

So many small and large abandonments infuriated him. Good management would mend all of them. He would have his work cut out for him, but with Dorothea by his side, he could achieve it. His planned one-year stay might have to change to two, but he could run his shipping business from here. He had hand-selected a number of trustworthy, competent managers. Although, he would miss it. The company he'd inherited through his late wife had been the seed that formed the basis of what he'd built.

Returning to the house, he came in by the side door into the modest black-and-white tiled hall used by the staff and people returning from the stables. One of the quieter entrances that he knew better than the grand halls at the front and back of the house. His mother had discovered them too. She wouldn't know them now.

As always, he forcibly turned his thoughts away from the memory of the woman upstairs, who lived, but had lost everything that made her his mother. Visiting her distressed him, but at least Louis had ensured she was properly taken care of, and he had not used her to justify his depredations on the estate.

Receiving the letters from Hal that outlined the slow deterioration of his mother's mind had almost broken him. Of both his parents, he'd been closest to her, but now she didn't even recognize him. It seemed a symbol of what he was going through now, with his own cousin denying him. Of course, Louis knew who he was, but rejecting his identity had not drawn him closer to the cousin he'd grown up with, only the resentful man he'd become.

He asked a footman to have his valet sent up so he could change for dinner, and climbed the staircase. He turned away. His rooms were on the other side of the house, where, his mother had said, she couldn't hear the noise which gave her a headache. She had constantly complained of his boisterousness, claiming he kept her awake at night. So Ben, with Louis and William when they'd been visiting, had taken to the outdoors, a place of constant amusement and wonder.

And somewhere they could forget who they were, and how they were to behave, away from the rules they were supposed to live by.

A woman turned the corner, periwinkle silk skirts rustling, fine lace at her elbows. Honoria.

Ben prepared to nod and walk past, but she dropped a curtsy, which was foolish, but she did it anyway. He had to stop and return the courtesy. "Mrs. Thorpe."

"Oh, dear me, Ben, we were never so formal. Why start now?" Flicking out her fan, she waved it before her face. "The day is far too warm for formality." She peered over the top of her fan at him in a way he well remembered. "We missed you, Ben."

He refrained from snorting and masked his reaction of incredulity. "Indeed. So much that you want to take my title from me?"

She shrugged and closed her fan with a snap. "We're alone now. I believe you. I know you too well. More muscle and a rougher complexion does not change the man you are. I remember some things very well." She met his gaze. "Like your kiss."

He lifted his head. At some point she'd moved closer to him, giving their encounter an unwelcome sense of intimacy. "Why did you do it, Honoria? Why did you set Louis and me against each other?"

It had hurt, that they fought over a woman, Honoria especially. Unknown to either of the men, she had flirted with both, made promises to both. Agreed to Ben's marriage proposal when she was already involved with Louis. Hedging her bets, one might say. Neither man knew she had promised herself to the other, and when the affair had come to a head, they had exploded.

"I wanted you." She moved closer. Ben fought his instinct to step back. "You know that. But with you gone, what could I do? My reputation was tarnished. I could not repudiate Louis."

"Are you saying you did not love him?"

"How could I? I had already given my heart to you."

She was lying. Why would she bother with Louis if she did not love him? Ben had been the prize, the one all the ladies had set their sights on. He was the heir to a great title, Louis merely the cousin. Or had she meant to make him jealous?

One reason made sense of it all. Was she already with child when Ben had proposed to her?

With a seductive rustle of silk, she moved closer. Her golden hair was curled becomingly, a lock drifting across the soft skin of her shoulder when she moved. Every inch of her was designed to entice.

And yet Ben was not enticed.

Honoria loved Honoria, and she would do her very best to ensure the well-being of her first and only love. Leading the cousins on had fed her sense of importance, had given her a triumph she could trumpet to her friends. She probably wanted Ben as a husband and Louis as a lover. That had not worked out for her.

Such a pity.

"To both of us." The night he'd discovered that, in the middle of a prestigious coffeehouse, he'd nearly caused a riot by drawing his sword and demanding that Louis fight him then and there. They had been drinking, laughing, the world at their feet. Then split apart, because of this woman.

Honoria was the spark that had lit the fuse.

Still outrageously beautiful, despite giving birth to two children, Honoria might have stopped time. Only by close scrutiny could Ben detect the clever powdering of her face and reddening of her cheeks. The current fashion was for artifice, but here in the country, people attended to à la mode less than they did in the fevered atmosphere of town. However, Honoria still used it.

Unable to stop himself, Ben lifted his hand, crooked his index finger and ran the back of it along her soft cheek. A light skim of powder dusted the tip. "You don't need this, Honoria. You are still as beautiful as ever."

She glanced down, avoiding his gaze, before flicking her eyelids up to meet his eyes once more. The unerringly flirtatious gesture reminded him of the arrow she'd left in his heart. He would never forget it—or her treachery.

"I have learned more since we parted." Her voice, low and intimate, should have sent shivers of desire through him. It always had. Even the sight of her on his return to this house had stirred him. But not now. Something had changed. Unaware of his thoughts, she continued in the same tone. "I am a mother; I have children to protect."

"If you have a son, he could be the next marquess," he pointed out.

"Yes, he could. And I could be a marchioness, even if Louis is refused the title."

She said that last part so softly he couldn't believe he'd heard her properly. "Are you unhappy with Louis?"

Turning her head away, Honoria did not answer for a few, fraught seconds. "No, of course not."

When she turned back to him, he caught the glimmer of tears in her eyes. "But I did not love him the same way I loved you. Losing you broke my heart."

He'd heard enough. Whether she was telling the truth or not didn't interest him in the least. But if she thought she had any chance with him after what she'd done, she must be living in a different world from him.

However, telling her outright seemed pointless. She would probably not listen. She skillfully avoided inconvenient truths. But he would make one thing clear. "Honoria, the night I asked you to marry me, you said I'd made you the happiest woman in the world. But you'd already given yourself to Louis. Hadn't you?"

She stared at him, unmoving.

"You were already with child, were you not? Little Helen is seven years old. Do you think I can't do simple arithmetic?"

No reaction. Just a stony stare.

"Did you try to seduce me that night to persuade me I was responsible for the child Louis had fathered? To win the greater prize?"

When Hal had written to him about the birth of Honoria and Louis's first child, the chains tying him to his lost love had fallen away. At the time he'd thought she had fallen into bed with Louis very quickly, but she had not. She was already there.

Tears in her heavenly blue eyes, Honoria lifted her face to his. "It was always you, Ben. I succumbed to Louis in a moment of madness. I went to him because I thought you would not have me after that awful argument we had, and he took advantage of that."

Ben couldn't remember an argument. If there had been one, it would have been slight. No, she had wanted to keep the two of them dangling, forming her court. Ladies of fashion collected admirers, and the more they had, the more successful they were considered, but few went to the lengths Honoria had taken.

He wondered about that seduction. Had she appealed to Louis, claimed an argument Ben could not remember? Knowing she had Ben in hand, she could have allowed herself to be seduced by Louis.

Would she have enjoyed foisting Louis's child off on Ben? Those kinds of games engendered a disgust in him, and he would never have suspected her of playing like that before he left the country. But now he knew Honoria could give an actress lessons.

She continued, her lovely eyes glistening with tears. "But then there was that terrible duel, and I couldn't reach you. I would have gone with you, if I could. You must know that."

He had severe doubts about that. "I know nothing of the kind."

None of her wiles touched him. Only disgust that she should consider him such an easy target and that she had fooled him before. He had learned much, and come to his senses. Thank the lord, he remained in the same frame of mind. Honoria had no hooks in him now, and if she'd lodged an arrow in him, it had long rotted away, leaving no trace behind.

"Madam, while you remain the wife of my cousin and heir, you may visit this house, but I would advise you to look to your own estates now. I am here, and I will become the next marquess."

"You're so sure?" A smile touched the corners of her pale pink lips. "Do you have no doubts?"

"None at all."

But her expression was knowing. "I might know something that would interest you. It might affect your inheritance of the title."

Another ploy, no doubt. Ben had no interest in what she had to say.

He stepped back, bowed, and walked away.

He was done with her, but he would not tell Louis of her attempts to win him. Even though Louis had his faults, he would never have sent his wife to seduce Ben. No, Honoria was playing her own game. What precisely she hoped to gain he wasn't sure. Perhaps she wanted to draw him back into her net. Perhaps she wanted to bear the next heir to the title. If Ben thought there was any possibility of her next child being his, he might prefer not to marry at all, but to let her child inherit his title. The answer to that was easy. He would not have an affair with her.

If Louis was borrowing heavily, she would want those debts paid. Perhaps she would offer to earn their price in bed.

Tomorrow Ben would see Sir James and confirm his accession to the title. Enough of this nonsense. Time he moved on and accepted his lot. And found himself a partner to cut out Louis and his designing wife.

Dorothea would make him a fine marchioness. When he thought of her, arousal stirred in his groin. Entirely absent where Honoria was concerned, his interest was most definitely piqued. She would bear him a fine child, too. When he'd touched her, he'd discovered a firm body beneath the plain fabrics, her skin silky, begging for his touch. Oh yes, he wanted her, and before too long she would discover it.

But he would make a child within the sanctity of marriage. Nobody would ever call his heir a seven-month baby, even though they could say that about Louis's older daughter.

* * * *

She had not meant to witness that tender moment. On her way to her room, Dorothea had crossed the large corridor leading from the east wing, and she'd seen Ben touch Mrs. Thorpe's cheek. They were so close. Kissing distance.

He had wanted her once. Perhaps he wanted her still. He'd told her she was as beautiful as ever.

The expression in his eyes had disturbed her. He would never look at her with that utter devotion. The intensity of his gaze had rocked her because he'd never regarded her in that way.

He didn't talk much about Mary, his wife, but that in itself demonstrated that he found discussing her painful. He'd been devoted to her, fallen deeply in love, and her death had torn him apart. That one word when she'd asked him if he'd loved Mary, that "yes," had pierced her to the heart.

The rare times he talked about her, it was in hushed, reverent tones, with a sorrow she couldn't deny. Dorothea had never caused a man to love her, and nobody ever would. It suited Ben to have her, that was all, and when Laurence had found them together in her room, he'd reacted in the only way he could.

Dorothea had always been second best, disregarded. She had responded to his flattering attention. She should have known better. How many times did she have to be hurt before she learned that she was not made for love? He'd offered her affection and friendship, but not love.

She could accept his offer and live in this lovely house, even bear his children if God willed it. But she must always remain on guard, knowing she could never win his love. Hold herself apart lest he dealt her the cruelest cut of all.

Finally reaching the safety of her room, Dorothea slipped inside and closed the door, leaning her back against it. They had not seen her, at least, he had not. Mrs. Thorpe had glanced around and maybe caught sight of her, but that didn't matter. She would hardly take note of her lowliest guest.

How could she ever have imagined that Ben wanted her for herself? She would write to Angela and tell her the whole. Nothing but the truth. Her fee had been agreed upon, and Angela would pay it into Dorothea's new account. Money of her own, a life of her own, to do as she wished. Because she could not marry him and then watch him walk away, back to Boston and the life he had there, which would never include her.

Perhaps she would find a companion among the ladies of the SSL, share an establishment. Ladies did that all the time, if they had the means. Why should she care what people said? She would continue to sit at the sides of the ballrooms, but she would be her own woman and make her own choices, trivial though they might be.

Buying her own home and living quietly was her answer. And now she had the means to do it, together with an interesting way of earning a little more money. Because seeing Ben with the woman he'd fought for had clarified a few things. If she stayed, she would fall in love with him. And she couldn't do that because he would never fall for her in return.

Tears rolled down her face as she forced herself to own the truth. No romantic fantasies for her, only hard, cold facts. From now on she'd put a guard on her senses, and she would make her refusal clear to Ben.

* * * *

"Will you accept?"

Another stroll in the garden the following day brought Dorothea into contact with her sister-in-law. She had been agitatedly pacing along the paths she'd strolled with Ben the day before. "Accept what? Oh, that."

"Yes, 'oh, that,'" Ann said with a grin. "The marriage proposal. I will not give you my opinion unless you ask for it."

Dorothea clasped her hands tightly together. "I won't accept his offer. I'm not made to be a marchioness. I shall take my portion and buy a small house somewhere. Sussex, I thought. I may find someone to live with. I have a few friends in mind. Retire into the country, not too far from London, and continue to work for Childers's Bank when the fancy takes me."

Ann wrinkled her nose. "Are you serious? You'd turn down a great future for that?"

"But I would be on my own, you see. I could do as I pleased." Even when she said it aloud, the idea didn't appeal. In the last twenty-four hours, her enthusiasm for becoming a spinster of the world had palled. She would have to obtain guides and companions for everything.

"You can do that as the Marchioness of Belstead." Ann gave a most unladylike grin. "And anything else you want. What is unacceptable in a single lady of moderate fortune is completely unexceptionable for a marchioness and an arbiter of fashion." Turning serious, Ann touched her arm. "Don't wring your hands, dear. People will know you're concerned."

"He's with Sir James," she said. "Showing him the evidence. It seems conclusive, but still..."

"And you're worried about him?"

Yes, she was, but nothing would bring her to admit it. "Sir James is a man of habit. He belongs to the establishment and the status quo. Although Benedict is undoubtedly the last marquess's son, I'm concerned, yes. This house is beautiful, the estate is still substantial despite what Mr. Thorpe has done. It deserves a better curator."

Ann shot a knowing smile at Dorothea. "I think you have answered your own question. You would love to restore this estate, to oversee its recovery. Would you not?"

Dorothea didn't have to give her answer, but Ann's words made her understand. Yes, she wanted to take on this task. But more than that, she craved its master far too much for her peace of mind. And that consideration still gave her pause.

"And Mr. Benedict Thorpe, lately Lord Brocklebank, and soon to be the Marquess of Belstead. Do you want him, too?"

"I wouldn't know what to do with him," she said lightly.

"But he knows what to do with you. At dinner he can hardly take his eyes off you. He doesn't even try to hide it."

They were gossiping. Of course they were. But what she'd seen yesterday would not leave her mind, and she would do well to remember it. He had never looked at her with that intensity.

* * * *

The first person Ben thought of was Dorothea. Although his mind was spinning after his interview with Sir James, he wanted the stability of the woman he'd proposed to. The woman he was already thinking of as his wife in all but name.

He found her coming into the house in the company of her sister-in-law. After she'd doffed her hat and gloves, she glanced up the stone staircase, past the wall paintings of paradise, straight into his eyes.

He smiled. She smiled back, bringing intimacy to this huge space. They were in the south entrance, which to him sounded vaguely obscene, but that was what his ancestors had called it. The walls and ceiling were painted in what the artist considered an image of paradise. He wasn't looking at that now.

She started up the stairs. He met her halfway and took her hands. "Will you talk with me?"

She pulled her hands away. "I'm talking to you now."

"Come."

He took her back up the stairs and into the last room in the state enfilade, the state bedroom. He closed the door behind him.

Two exquisite cabinets stood to either side of the great bed, the cupboard fronts and myriad doors behind them decorated in pietra dura, semiprecious stones set into the rich wood of the frame. He ran his finger over the top part of the cupboard as he always had since he was a boy, relishing the total smoothness under his skin, appreciating the skill of the unknown artist.

Before she could speak, he drew her close and kissed her, needing to hold her, to take something of her before she could speak. After his encounter with Honoria yesterday, he wanted her more than ever. He'd gone to her room and stood outside the door like a loon before deciding not to show her his vulnerability, his need of her.

His lips met hers and he drank her in. Waiting for a push against his chest, he braced himself, but no shove came. Instead, with a small sigh of surrender, she slid her arms around his waist and nestled in.

Relief surged through him. With a touch of his tongue, he opened her mouth and plunged inside. Her taste roused him even more, and he drew her closer, roaming over her body with the flats of his hands, instinctively searching for skin.

When he dragged her fichu free, he found soft, silky warmth. Not nearly enough, but some. Tucking his finger under the neckline of her gown, he ran it down, desperately seeking a way in. A pin fell free. Then another. He groaned into her mouth and received an answer of a sort. She pressed closer, her upper breast crushing against his palm.

Reaching up, she tugged at his neckcloth. A loose knot lay between her hands and his throat. It stood no chance. She pulled at it, it fell to the floor, and she curled a hand around his neck, pulling him back down to her.

He wasn't about to refuse that invitation. His cock pressed against his underwear and the front of his breeches, but all he could find was fabric. Although she wore a hoop, it was a small one, little more than two modest cages on her hips, holding the fabric of her gown away from her body. He could lift those skirts. Underneath lay heaven.

The surge of emotion, mingled relief, delight, and most of all, desire, overwhelmed what little sense he had left. He pulled at her gown until the front came free and he could slide it off her shoulders.

The fabric fell to her feet in a *whoosh* of silk. Now more of her was available to him. But tapes and ribbons and hooks still lay between him and what he sought. He rid himself of his coat, letting it fall to join her gown.

Drawing back, he looked at what he'd done. Her skin gleamed, pearly in the slanting sunlight, and her cheeks were adorably flushed. Her stays and shift were all that lay between him and paradise now. Somehow the tapes of her hoops and pockets had gone, and her outer petticoat. He wanted more. He wanted it all. "Dorothea?"

She looked up at him, eyes bright. "Yes," she said, her voice a mere breath. "Ben, yes. Make love to me."

Chapter 12

Dorothea's common sense vanished with that first kiss, her determination melting away as if it had never been. He'd given her the same look as he'd bestowed on Mrs. Thorpe yesterday, and she wanted that so much, his burning, desirous gaze, richly deep, all his attention trained on her. Once, just once she wanted this, to revisit the dream before she thrust it away forever. She could not resist him, God help her.

"Now, here, just this once, I want you."

"Then you shall have me," he promised, and bent to pick her up.

Dorothea gasped, both at his strength and the ease at which he lifted her. He made her feel small and delicate. He carried her to the bed, up the two steps to the platform that held the draped monstrosity where nobody ever slept. All the time he gazed at her in the same way he'd looked at Honoria. Or perhaps not. She wanted to know his gaze was for her alone. Oh, how much she wanted to know that!

When he swept back the crimson gold-embroidered bed cover, a cloud of dust flew up. She buried her head against his chest to stifle her cough, but stayed there because he smelled so good. He laid her down. "We have sheets."

"I don't care." Spreading her hands, she felt the smooth linen beneath her. "Does someone sleep here?"

That would be unusual for a state bedroom.

"We will." Leaning down, he planted his hands either side of her. "I want you, Dorothea. I will do my best to ensure you are safe, but the way I feel now, I can't be sure."

"Safe?" She laughed. "I stopped being safe when I took off my clothes."

His smile turned warmer. "Then let's be totally reckless and rid ourselves of the rest."

Her feet dangled over the side of the bed, so he started with those. Unfastening the buckles of her sturdy leather walking shoes, he let them drop to the floor. Her stockings came next, after he pushed his hand up her skirt to where her garters were knotted just above her knees. The cool air felt delicious and she wriggled her toes. His low chuckle announced his pleasure.

Pulling her up, he tackled her stays.

"You know your way around a lady's clothes," she commented, sighing in relief when the laces loosened.

"I do."

He came around to the front of her and watched her slide the shoulder straps down, then pull the garment over her head, leaving the tapes still laced. She wore the thinnest of linen shifts, but she did not try to hide the shadows of her nipples where they grazed the fabric.

Bending his head, he took a plump tip into his mouth and sucked.

Dorothea clapped her hand over her lips, biting down to prevent her shriek escaping. Someone could hear, but that added to her anticipation, her sense of daring. Thrills of pleasure coursed through her from where his mouth anointed her skin, her nipple becoming unbearably sensitive. Bringing his other hand up, he played, tweaking and teasing until Dorothea thought she might die of it.

She squirmed, restless for more. When he pulled away and gazed at his handiwork, then up at her face, his eyes were dark, sultry and heavy-lidded, his lips reddened. "You look adorable."

Nobody had ever called her that before.

He made quick work of the rest of her clothes, her remaining petticoats and her shift, then leaned over her, blatantly scanning her body. The pale hair at the apex of her legs, the shocking dampness gathering there, then up, to where he'd turned her nipples into sharp points of need, and her breasts to plump cushions. Her skin was flushed all over.

If she lost everything else, she would have this moment of complete abandon, when nothing outside this room mattered.

Reaching out, she unfastened the first in the long line of buttons on his waistcoat. Fortunately, he'd left the garment open just below the waist, but even then there were twelve small buttons before she could get to the inner garments.

He did nothing, but watched her, his gaze blatantly ogling her in a way that covered her skin with a sensitive prickling. Tiny invisible needles made her unable to keep still. Even though her hands shook, she completed her task, then found the buttons at the wrists of his shirt, and tackled them, too.

Glancing at his breeches, and the fall of six buttons, she sucked in a breath and went for them.

He caught her wrist before she reached his waistband. "No, sweetheart. I want you too much. Let me do the rest."

He stood on the bed platform, swiftly divesting himself of the remainder of his clothes until he stood before her, naked as the day he was born.

My, was he beautiful! His broad chest gave way to narrow hips, the frame to what reared between his legs. His member was long and thick, the head red. As she watched, drops of clear liquid oozed from the tiny opening at the tip. Although she was familiar with the male anatomy, she had not seen a man in this state of arousal before, and it gave her a moment of doubt.

But she had come this far. With determination, she reached her arms up, inviting him to take her.

With a smile that promised much, he came down to her, and kissed her briefly. "This is madness," he murmured against her lips, "but I want it too much to stop."

Then he deepened the kiss.

Dorothea opened her mouth, eagerly seeking his tongue, finding it and stroking it. His broad hands caressed her flanks, reaching her hips. He held her as if she was no more than a feather of a girl, instead of the substantial woman she knew herself to be. But he was larger than her. Much larger.

His erection swelled against her stomach, as if seeking entry there, driving hard as he lost himself in the kiss. Dorothea wanted more, and now, restlessness leading to desperate need, although for what, she wasn't sure. She had only a hazy idea of what would happen now.

Rhythmically, he pushed against her, thrust that part of him into the softness of her stomach again and again. He changed the angle of his kiss, moaning into her mouth. She sucked air in through her nose and pulled him against her, her grasp clumsy but determined.

This was all so thrilling, the most intense experience of her life. She'd be a fool to turn it down in favor of some social niceties. The rest, the implications of this, she pushed forcibly to the back of her mind. She'd worry about all of that later. *Not now, not now.*

He jerked away from her, finishing the kiss so fast her head spun. His body rigid, he pushed against the bed and reared up. Teeth clenched, he sucked in air in a hiss.

Hot liquid spurted against her stomach.

Dorothea held on to him, gripping his lower arms, his muscles bulging against them like cast iron.

Ben closed his eyes and groaned. "Dieu, I'm sorry!"

Dorothea shook her head. "That's all right."

She tried hard to quell her disappointment. She might be relatively innocent, but she knew that after *that* happened, they would be doing nothing else. The veiled references in the literature she'd read made that clear.

He opened his eyes. "No, it's not. But it's probably for the best."

Of course, if he'd come inside her, she could have fallen pregnant. Naturally she didn't want that. Of course she didn't.

Rolling off her, Ben took a corner of the sheet and tugged it free, using the fabric to wipe up the mess on her stomach. "I've never done that before," he said. "But then, I've never wanted anyone with that kind of desperation before." After examining his handiwork, he dropped a quick kiss on her navel. "You must be sure to wash before you dress."

"What kind of creature do you think I am?" she demanded indignantly. Her nurse had taught her about cleanliness and godliness. However cold the morning might be, she always stripped out of her nightwear and washed before dressing. Although for once she was tempted to keep the memento he had bestowed on her. *Foolish.*

He rolled over next to her, supporting himself on his propped elbows. "Do you want me to answer that? Well, I will, anyway. I think you are the kind of gorgeous woman I would be proud to call my wife."

When she would have answered, he touched his forefinger to her lips. "No, not yet. I want to finish what we started."

Dorothea widened her eyes. "I thought we had finished."

"Nowhere near." He glanced down her body. "I have to take care of you now."

Leaning up, he kissed her. His hair, now loose from its tidy bow, fell across her cheek. It caressed her with its silkiness as he took control of her mouth, dipping his tongue inside with lazy sensuality. Finishing the kiss, he opened his eyes and gazed into hers. He was smiling. "If you don't come by the time we leave this bed, you might not invite me back. I have every intention of persuading you to let me join you again. We've only just begun, sweetheart." His breath heated her lips, and she reached up for another kiss, but he had gone.

Smoothing her hair back from her face and carelessly flicking his own behind his shoulders, Ben kissed her earlobe. Who knew that such a tender nuzzle could cause her senses to riot? And when he took the lobe between his teeth and nipped, she nearly came off the bed.

"You're so responsive, my beauty."

Slowly, he moved down her body, taking his time touching and nipping. Tracing her nipple with his tongue, then sucking it in and subjecting it to delicious torture made her squirm, as every part of her body responded to him. She was to come? What did that mean? Like when she touched herself in bed occasionally? Although she had never brought herself up so far. She had to stop before whatever it was happened. Her body had moved toward—something—but she'd always been too sensitive to continue, and afraid to do it on her own. Everything she had learned was from the literature she had read and the odd erotic print that had escaped notice in the library of her childhood home.

This was so far from her experience that she didn't know what to do. When she squirmed, trying to get away, he held her hips steady and murmured to her, soothing sounds that ended in, "Trust me. I'll take care of you."

She did. She tried to still under his hands. The touch of his body sent her wild, and while she had been bold before, the hiatus had brought her doubts and fears crowding back. But she watched him, met his steady gaze and calmed.

He went even slower, stroking and exploring her until he grazed the sensitive skin at the top of her thighs.

"Open your legs, sweetheart. Let me in."

What could he do? When she did as he bade her, he lifted up and settled between her legs. Slipping his hands under her knees, he urged her to lift them, so her legs could widen, and the soles of her feet were flat on the bed. She was exposed to him as she had been to nobody before.

Propriety had gone, probably forever. Even his gaze made her moan in suppressed excitement.

He bent his head. Before Dorothea could make sense of his intentions, he'd drawn that peak of flesh into his mouth, the one she had touched before and then abandoned. He would hurt her. But he did not. His tongue was so much gentler than her fingers, and he knew what to do, how to arouse her. When the familiar tingling intensified, he gripped her thighs, holding her steady while he worked on her. When she arched her back in involuntary response, he released one leg and instead played his finger around her opening, circling it, driving her mad. She didn't know what to do, how to push this intensity into a response, the one he must be searching for.

His actions grew in intensity, his sucking harder, drawing her into his mouth completely. He made a sound, and it resonated through her body.

And she broke.

Gasping, faltering cries escaping her lips, Dorothea turned her head and crammed the back of her hand against her mouth. Her body jerked as waves of acute pleasure, thrills of delight coursed through every inch of her, from the tips of her toes to the top of her head and everywhere between.

This was what the poets had written about, this single moment out of time when everything stopped except the sheer sensation soaring through her.

Dorothea lost her mind.

* * * *

She came to curl in Ben's arms, her head resting on his shoulder. They were still in the state bed, and he'd dragged the sheet over them. Startled, she sat up.

"How long have I been asleep?"

"Barely ten minutes." He tugged her back down. "But we will have to go soon, before someone discovers us. I want an answer to my question."

"Which one?"

He kissed her forehead. "You know. Dorothea Rowland, will you marry me?"

Her heart plummeted as she gave him the answer she must. "No."

With a convulsive move, he sat up and leaned over her. "What?"

"I said no."

Back in her own mind now, she stuck to her answer. She could love him so easily, if she didn't already. Before, when they had nearly become betrothed, she'd been dazzled by the glory that was Lord Brocklebank, but she liked this man, Ben Thorpe, so much better.

But he didn't love her. He'd had a youthful passion for Honoria, then married a woman he still missed. His love belonged to Mary, and Dorothea wouldn't share.

"No," she repeated. "I won't marry you. I don't have to give you a reason."

Confusion warred with anger in his eyes, but he didn't make her afraid. "Dorothea, even if Sir James finds against me—which he will not—I have more than enough to ensure you live in luxury for the rest of your days. Is it Boston? Are you afraid to go so far away?"

"Of course not." Indignant, she pushed him off her and sat up, letting the sheets fall away from her body. Before he could prevent it, she climbed out of the bed and reached for her shift. "No, Ben. But I have the means to live as I wish, and the will to do it." Angela had given her more than a fee when she'd asked Dorothea to help with this case. She'd given Dorothea confidence. To have someone who trusted her with a business matter, which it was for Angela, meant so much to her. Would she give that up? In a heartbeat, if Ben loved her. But passion and desire didn't equal love.

"So you wish to be a single lady for the rest of your life?" Anger simmered under his words.

"I had thought that was to be my fate, and it's not so bad after all." Long years of loneliness, being despised as someone who couldn't attract a husband; yes, she could tackle that, and make a place for herself. She had a choice. But she couldn't articulate what she really wanted. She gathered the thoughts in her mind, and finally faced him, all but naked. And unashamed.

"I want a man who will devote his life to me, who will love and cherish me, but not overwhelm me. I want a husband who will put me above him. I've waited this long, so I might as well go for the ultimate prize. And I'm not looking at him now."

Now she didn't feel naked; she felt bare, exposed. She hurried into her stays, but when she reached around for her stay-tapes, he came up behind her and helped her tighten them, fastening them expertly. He'd probably done that before, for some other woman. His wife, most likely.

"I meant what I said." He kissed her bare shoulder. "I might not be able to give you everything you want. I doubt any man could. But I'd have a partner in you. Someone I can trust to manage the estate while I'm away. You'd have complete power to run Cressbrook as you wished."

"Away?" She turned around, and to avoid his gaze, bent and picked up her pockets. She tied them around her waist. "Where are you going?"

"Boston. I can't abandon my business. I have to visit from time to time." He slipped his arms into his waistcoat and fastened a few buttons.

"You see?" In the act of tying her pocket around her waist, Dorothea paused and turned to face him. "That's it, isn't it? You want a competent manager you can trust, not a wife. I was right to refuse you."

She hustled into her clothes as quickly as she could, inwardly cursing her decision to wear a hoop that held the fabric away from her body on this hot day. It made the process more elaborate. They dressed in silence, and when Dorothea glanced toward the rumpled bed, he said, "I'll take care of that."

"Good." Her steps firm, Dorothea walked away, not giving way to tears until she was in the safety of her bedroom.

Chapter 13

To say Dorothea's answer stunned Ben would be to make a huge understatement.

She'd given herself with such sweetness, her passion matching his, that he had assumed it was only a matter of time before she was permanently in his bed. He looked forward to that with a hunger he'd never felt before. Women fell into his arms, if he wanted them, and Dorothea had done just that. He'd enjoyed every minute of their lovemaking, so much that he had come long before he was ready. Now he wanted to experience the ultimate intimacy with her, but if she would not marry him, that had to be denied.

He let Rougier prepare him for dinner in silence, answering the valet's questions with monosyllables.

She wanted respect? Devotion? Then he'd show it to her. But not love. After Mary's death—before it—he'd seen what love could do to a person. Any illusion that he'd been under that he was in love with her had died when she had turned love into a weapon. He'd told Dorothea the truth, that he had considered himself in love with Mary when he'd met her, but he hadn't told her the rest. Perhaps he should. Love was not for him. He would not contemplate it. Refused to.

He went down to the drawing room in the worst of moods, but with renewed determination.

At the bottom of the stairs he encountered Major Thorpe. "I understand an announcement will be made tonight," William said.

"Indeed." Ben nodded coolly and made to walk on.

The major fell into step with him. "I'm glad of a quiet word with you. I have to admit I am relieved that you will become the next marquess. You understand I could not betray my brother, but I refuse to support him in his extravagances. I cannot approve of what he has done to the estate."

Ben regarded him steadily. The man was a good officer, by all accounts, who would make general before he was done. While he respected William's loyalty to his brother, Ben appreciated the quiet words. "I see. Thank you."

The major returned his gaze. "I will not embarrass my brother in public by saying so."

He stood back to give Ben room to enter the room first.

He sent Hal a small nod and smile. Hal, who appeared perfectly recovered from his injury and had dressed in royal purple for dinner tonight, smiled back. Dorothea stood with Hal, watching Ben warily. He had bridges to mend there.

A hush fell over the room as Ben stood alone, framed by the doorway. Louis glared at him, and Honoria, from her seat on the best sofa, opened her eyes wide and tilted her head to one side, a slight smile playing on her lips.

Before Ben could speak, Sir James joined him. "May I be the first to greet the seventh Marquess of Belstead?"

His bow was precisely correct for a marquess. Ben had to admire the gesture. He gave the responding bow, much shallower, more a nod of his head. "Thank you."

As he turned to address the other people in the room, he noted Louis had gone completely white. Had Sir James not informed him? "I produced the required proof this afternoon. I regret having kept you in suspense, but the King works at his own pace, not ours."

"The King?" Louis almost spat the word. "Did you pay him a great deal to ratify your claim?"

Ben refused to take offense. "Nothing. He recognized me spontaneously."

Although he had promised to ensure the King had his regular supply of snuff sent posthaste. That did not count, because he would have done that in any case.

"I don't believe you." Louis touched his wife's shoulder before stepping forward. The rest of the people in the room stood stock-still, a collection of bejeweled exquisites, all hanging on their every word. "You are an impostor. You cannot be my cousin. I have made enquiries about you and I have reason to believe you are a cousin, a distant one, the son of a man who left for the colonies fifty years ago."

That was interesting. If he had relatives over the ocean, Ben had not met them. "Prove it. I am who I said I was from the beginning. You know me, Louis. I can even tell you how you got the scar on your upper arm. How you howled when you fell out of that tree!"

A small scar, barely noticeable, but he remembered the incident. He could even point out the tree.

Louis shook his head, his lips contorted into a sneer. "Anything else?"

"If you insist. How about the day you hid in the state rooms and broke that Chelsea vase? My mother may not remember it, but I do. And the time you told my father that I had run the length of the long gallery, when he had expressly forbidden us to do so? And yet you were the one who did the running. I got my own back though, do you remember?" Memories flooded into his mind, any number of them. "I can go on."

"Pray do not." Louis gave an exquisite shudder. "Very well."

Louis bowed. It was surrender, but when he rose from the obeisance, he was glaring. "I will not give up. You tried to kill me seven years ago, and so I will say."

He wanted to drag that up again? "We were both foolish, acting on impulse."

"Out of love," Louis said, sparing his wife a fond look.

Ben shrugged. "Passion, certainly."

He sent Dorothea a particularly warm smile before he led the company in to dinner, but she didn't respond with anything but a slight nod. Then she turned away, taking Sir James's arm.

Louis was on the brink of an explosion, for sure. He glowered, and he was breathing deeply, the diamond buttons on his waistcoat glittering every time he took a gasp of air. If Ben did not distract him, he would explode. His wife sat completely still. A portrait painter would have found her position perfect: *Lady Belstead in Her Drawing Room*. Except she was not Lady Belstead, and never like to be so.

He would not exchange Dorothea for anyone in that room, including Honoria. While Honoria's beauty still dazzled, Dorothea had much more substance. He would win her over. Anything else didn't bear thinking about.

"I believe the head of the table is now decided," Sir James said with utmost satisfaction as they entered the dining room.

"I will leave this house first thing in the morning," Louis announced. "I have business to attend to."

Like putting his own house in order and talking to his creditors. Including Dorothea's sponsor. "I will ensure a carriage is available for you," Ben said and received a glare for his pains. He felt particularly vicious. When Sir James had made his declaration, he had wanted Dorothea by his side.

* * * *

After a restless night, Ben rose and dressed. His valet entered just as he'd finished shaving and made himself busy finding a coat and waistcoat. "We should work on expanding your wardrobe, my lord."

"Indeed." He supposed he should, although the necessity did not concern him. Not compared to being at outs with Dorothea and discovering who was trying to kill him. With Louis gone, the house should be a safer place, at any rate.

"Would it be too forward of me to offer my congratulations?"

Ben put the razor down on the side of the washstand. "No, it would not, and thank you. Rougier, we will get along much better if you leave the subservience to others. I don't know what your previous master was like, but I very much prefer simple politeness. And in private, 'sir' will do. You may 'my lord' me all you like outside this room, but I prefer informality in the privacy of the bedchamber."

Now the man did smile, and the expression transformed his features. "Yes, sir."

Ben sensed they would get along. "As to my wardrobe, we will have to go to London at some point to attend court, and we will both need suitable costumes. When I visited before, it was informally. The presentations are a bore."

After allowing Rougier to help him with his coat, Ben headed outside. Footmen bowed and Schultz congratulated him, adding that they were all delighted he had been ratified as the marquess at last. He asked for the inventories to be sent down to the armaments room. They should be up to date, but he would wager they were not.

Becoming the marquess meant he had a lot of work ahead of him. But he would take a walk before he locked himself away.

The day was fresh, and since the hour was early—the clock struck seven as he walked through the hall—still refreshing. It would no doubt get much hotter later, but dew was heavy on the grass, and the birds were still doing their best to wake everybody. The house slumbered, curtains and blinds covering most of the windows. He glanced up at the state rooms, in particular the bedroom where he'd spent such a wonderful hour with Dorothea yesterday.

The sound of horses snorting and harness rattling alerted him to the fact that he had walked around to the stables, even though he did not plan to ride anywhere that day. The stables were in excellent order, as he'd discovered when he'd gone there the day after his arrival to check on the horse he'd ridden here.

"Hold his head!"

He knew that voice too well, but he refused to go back now.

Louis, dressed for the road, turned, a sneer on his finely cut lips. "Come to ensure I don't make off with the family silver?"

Ben kept his expression neutral. "Haven't you already done that?"

Louis's face darkened. "You have no idea what it takes to live up to the position of marquess, do you? You've spent the last seven years turning yourself into the perfect merchant. You will ruin the title and the family name." He stepped closer, ignoring the groom standing by the horses' heads. He'd had the traveling carriage harnessed, with the marquess's crest on the doors.

"You'll have to wait and see," Ben said mildly. "I saw the recognition in your eyes when I walked in the door that first day. Even marked as I was by the filth of the road, you knew me."

"I thought a ghost had walked in." Louis bit his lip. "I truly believed you had perished. The marquessate was mine. All I had to do was bide my time."

"I need not have gone at all. You were not badly hurt in the duel, were you? You used that injury to drive me away."

Shrugging, Louis walked off. "I will be back. You are not the marquess, you know. You never were."

"I have been the marquess since the death of my father. I merely allowed the formalities to take place."

"I know better." He paused by the door of the carriage. "I have left my wife here for the time being. Honoria is deeply distressed. I would ask you to care for her while I am away. But no more, or as God is my witness, I will come for you."

He didn't know how off the mark he was. But by leaving his wife here, Louis was retaining his foothold in the house.

Ben would see about that. Except—his bedroom was awfully convenient to Dorothea's. Perhaps he would use Honoria as a reason for not moving to the marquess's apartments and putting the house between them. And he would like them renovated. Yes, that would suit him well.

"Since I have to thank you for taking good care of my mother, I will keep your wife safe for you, but I will not touch her in any way. You have my word on it. I assume you'll be taking up residence in the house that belonged to your father?"

Louis had inherited a tidy estate from his father. He would not starve.

Ben glanced at the traveling vehicle. "You will have to take another carriage, Louis. Either that, or paint over the marquess's coronet. We wouldn't want to give people the wrong impression, would we?"

Oh yes, he would. But Ben was wise to his cousin's tactics now. He had not considered he would do that, but he would take care that Louis did not encroach any further.

Louis scowled. "I never noticed. We can cover up the coronet."

The carriage had flaps that could be used to conceal the symbol if the owner wanted to travel incognito. Ben did not believe him for a minute. As soon as he was out of sight, Louis would remove those flaps. He would travel through the country and allow people to think he was the marquess.

He nodded to the groom. "Find another vehicle. One without the coronet."

Anger simmered inside him because Louis had assumed he could take the best traveling carriage in the coach house, and that he could use the coronet. And most of all, Ben would be foolish enough to let him.

As he turned on his heel and walked away, he was gratified to hear, "Yes, my lord," from the groom.

He stopped by the last stall in the row, where the men used to congregate to eat their meals and exchange news. Pushing the door, he went in.

Silence fell over the low conversation that had been taking place. "Good morning," he said mildly.

"Good morning, my lord." Three men scrambled to their feet and dusted themselves off, performing hasty bows. None were in livery, he was glad to see. Otherwise, he'd have to tax Louis with that, too.

"I merely want to make it clear to all of you that there is only one marquess. And that is me. Please refer everything to me from now on. I'll be making new appointments and reviewing all positions in the house. I'm pleased to find the stables in a reasonable condition. But do not allow anyone to make free with the stock or the carriages without my permission. Is that clear?"

"Yes, my lord."

Satisfied, he walked out and over the cobbles. Louis had left the stables, perhaps realizing he would have to wait at least another half hour before he could leave. Ben had no wish for his company. Whatever the man was up to now, it wouldn't be good. Louis was eaten up by revenge, and perhaps fear, if he'd built up too many debts to pay. No doubt Ben would hear about them before long, but if Louis expected Ben to mildly pay off what Louis owed, he'd have to think again.

He still had some time before going to the muniments room, where he planned to spend most of the day working through the inventory and accounts. However, as he rounded the corner on his way back to the main gardens, he caught sight of Dorothea leaving the south entrance at the top of the broad stone staircase to the gardens. She wore an ankle-length russet gown and sturdy outdoor shoes. To his eyes she appeared delightful. Perhaps she would allow him to apologize to her now.

"Good morning!"

She gave a sound, a tiny squeal, and turned to face him as he climbed the stairs up to her. She had evidently not seen him. "Oh, good morning!"

She backed up as he approached her, but he walked forward until he was a bare foot away. Catching her hand, he lifted it to his lips but at the last minute flipped it over and kissed her palm. As he rose, he curled her fingers, enjoying her surprise and incipient arousal. She could not deny what he saw in her eyes. That faint tinge of color on her earlobes would spread to her cheekbones, over her face and down to her breasts. The flush and its accompanying heat was an invitation for him to tease and rouse.

Tonight he would not keep away from her. "Dorothea, will you walk with me? Allow me to talk to you?"

She swallowed, as if he'd said something far more intimate. "I don't think we have anything further to say to each other."

He glanced up as a grinding sound came from above.

Just in time to see a large stone cherub toppling over the edge of the roof right above their heads.

Chapter 14

One moment he was talking to her, the next Dorothea was flat on her back, a pot of flowers crushed beneath her. Shards poked into her, her breath completely gone from her body. A heavy weight was holding her down. Her ears rang.

As she gasped for air, Ben raised himself on his elbows, his face white. "Are you all right?"

She sucked in more air. "I think so. What happened?"

"One of those infernal statues fell off the roof." The lines bracketing his mouth deepened, and his lips tightened. "Or was pushed."

"Pushed?" He thought someone had thrown a statue at him? At them?

Abruptly he lifted himself away from her and shook off the fragments of stone that had landed on him. Then he bent to pick her up before she could scramble to her feet. "We'll talk about it inside. I'm taking you to your room and then I'll find out what this is all about."

He went in through the side door she'd just used, maneuvering her through as if she weighed the merest trifle, which was far from the case.

Her mind still whirling from the speed of events, she clutched at him. A maid gaped as they passed her, but she was past caring about appearances.

"I want you safe before I find out if the incident was deliberate or an accident. This house is in a precarious state. If the statues are ready to fall from their perches, I'll have them all taken down."

She grabbed his coat front. "I want you safe, too. Put me down. I'm fine."

"Are you sure?"

She nodded.

Slowly he lowered her to her feet but kept his hands on her waist. Dorothea wasn't used to men who could pick her up at a moment's notice. "Goodness."

Taking a step back, she shook out her skirts. "Is this house a complete death trap?"

"I didn't think so. But we shall see. Stay in your room."

She answered that simply enough. "You can whistle for that," she said, disregarding her manners. "No. Do you believe me to be so craven? Good Lord, I could be murdered there just as easily. In any case, I doubt they were aiming for me, if anyone was responsible for the—incident, rather than it being an accident. Now we need to hurry."

Still flustered from him holding her so close, she turned away. Uncaring of propriety—Lord knew it was far too late for that—she picked up her skirts and headed up the stairs. Four more floors to the roof, but there was no helping it, so she put her best foot forward, although she slowed down somewhat once the flush of embarrassment faded from her cheeks. Nevertheless, her legs were aching when she reached the top.

"This way." Annoyingly, Ben did not seem a bit out of breath. He unlatched a small door hidden in an alcove, revealing yet another set of stairs. The air was distinctly cooler here, and as she climbed the steep staircase, a breeze made itself known, gusting around her, although the day wasn't cold. The opposite, in fact.

When she pushed open the small door at the top of the stairs, she couldn't resist a sigh of pleasure, as a balmy breeze swept around her. Despite the modest hoops keeping the bulk of her skirt fabric off her body, she was still warmer than she would like.

As she stepped out onto the flat roof, Ben caught her arm. "Be careful."

Startled, she stared at him. "It's perfectly safe, except, perhaps, for the statues. Look, you can see where they've been repairing the lead." She pointed to a new patch on the sloping part. Below it, a broad walkway gave plenty of room to stroll, even for a lady in a hooped skirt.

Up here on the leads, the broad expanses gave a wonderful view of the countryside for miles around. Another time she would have lingered to enjoy the view, but she had other business.

"Except for a possible assassin."

Oh, yes, that. "But if there is one, he doesn't want me. I plan to come up here another day, just to enjoy the views and the breeze." If there was an assassin at all.

Because his fingers were loosely circling her wrist, she felt his fine tremor, so slight she wouldn't have noticed it by sight alone. "I would advise you not to consider it, until we discover what is happening here."

She touched the parapet. It was a plain wall, fronted by the honeyed stone that formed the façade of the house. Up here, the bones of the structure were more evident, a few old timbers visible, and signs of the older building that the new one covered. Like a hidden secret. "This is firm enough. It doesn't seem to be crumbling."

"We need to go around the corner to the south front," he said, steering her away from the parapet.

She gave him a curious stare. "Are you unnerved by heights?"

"Not generally, no, although I do have concerns for you up here." His jaw was set firmly. "Come."

When she would have moved closer to the edge, he gripped her elbow and drew her away. The space between the parapet and the slope of the roof lessened at the corner, but there was still plenty of room. His hold on her tightened. She didn't try to move away.

The shock of the near miss was having an effect on her overwrought senses. She had not slept much last night, and now realization pierced her like a spear of doom. She had rejected him too late to prevent him disturbing her dreams and her plans. What he offered, the control of a large estate and a position in society few could rival, made her plans pale in comparison. When Ann had learned Dorothea had rejected Ben, she had berated her for a fool. Although, Dorothea did not tell her of the circumstances in which Ben had proposed. Giving up an opportunity like that was more than foolish, it was downright insane. Dorothea had never seen her sister-in-law so agitated.

Could she bear the pain of separation? Ben would be absent for years at a time if he traveled between the colonies and Britain. But unlike most people in this house, she knew how large his holdings were. They had to be attended to. That would leave Dorothea on her own for long stretches. Perhaps she had been cowardly yesterday, backing off too hastily.

The crashing statue and the realization that she might have nothing of him from now on had brought several topics into sharper focus.

But she would not blame Ben if he chose to accept her rejection as final. He could move on and find someone else. They'd be queuing up to get their hands on him now.

Around the corner, the site of the problem was obvious. Statues were erected at regular intervals along the parapet, but one was missing, as obvious as an absent tooth. Dorothea quickened her pace until she reached the empty plinth. The area was wider here, a good couple of yards. Slipping out of Ben's hold, Dorothea went to examine it.

The stone was weathered, pockmarks denting the rough surface. But there was something... Dorothea bent closer to examine it.

"It was a cherub," he said.

"Pardon?"

"The statue that fell. A cupid. My grandfather had these put up when he renovated the south front. The statues are supposed to be the Virtues, with cherubs between them."

He did not come to join her. "See this," she said, pointing out what she'd found.

Footsteps approached them from the other direction.

"Major Thorpe!"

William and two menservants hurried to where they stood. "I saw the thing fall past my window. Was anybody hurt?"

Dorothea peered over the edge. Servants were clearing up the mess below. "Only a cherub."

The major let out a long sigh of relief. "Thank God! Where is my brother?"

"On his way to London by now, I assume," Ben said coolly. "This is probably nothing but an unfortunate accident."

Dorothea bridled. "How can you say that? Besides, there is some evidence here it was anything but accidental." She addressed the footmen. "Go around the whole roof and see if you can find something that could be used as a lever. A metal implement, a crowbar perhaps."

One of the men bowed and hurried away.

Dorothea nodded, and turned back to her discovery. "Look at these marks. Someone has made deep grooves in the stone, and they are fresh. There are scratches, too, someone trying to push something under the statue."

William came closer, and touched the stone, his fingers grazing hers. "You're right. Someone was up here recently. We passed nobody on the stair." He glanced at her, his eyes cold. "There are four staircases leading up here, one for each corner of the building, and two narrower places of access, more ladders than steps."

"So anybody could have come and gone without being seen." She sighed. "We saw nobody, either."

Ben was standing as far away from the edge as possible. "I ordered the carriage for Louis changed. He took the wrong one, so there would have been a delay." He closed his mouth with a sharp snap of teeth and glanced at the remaining footman. "Not a word."

"N-no, my lord." The man paled. "I swear."

If Ben's words got into the servants' hall, only one person could have carried them there.

Ben jerked his head and the footman scurried away.

Fresh marks scored a garish white in the weathered stone, and there was only one way they could have been made.

The statue was toppled deliberately.

Which meant... "Either the person who did this did not care if their attempt was discovered, or it was an impulsive act done on the spur of the moment," she commented.

The old stone was porous. A few scrapes and scuffs would have taken care of the marks, at least to a casual observer. And yet, there they were, deep, fresh grooves with no attempt at concealment.

As she spoke, a rumbling sound came from the side of the building and headed toward the front of the house. Wheels on gravel. The second carriage had been harnessed and Louis was on his way.

The three exchanged meaningful looks. No need for anyone to comment. Louis flew into rages and made impulsive decisions he might later come to regret.

"You should bring him back," William said into the heavy silence.

Ben shook his head. "That will achieve nothing."

"What if he flees the country?"

As you did. Nobody said it, but they might as well have. Retribution for what Louis had made Ben do seven years ago. And serve him right. He would doubtless have to flee before long, once his creditors had caught up with him.

Ben only shrugged, his broad shoulders a potent reminder of his physical strength. "He is welcome to do that, if he wishes. At least I'll know he will not continue to oppose me." He turned his head to meet her gaze. "We can do no more here. If Davies finds the crowbar, or whatever it was, I will let you know. Be that as it may, the attempt to push a statue onto my head was deliberate. Bear in mind that we do not know who did this thing. And even if we discover who did it, the person could be an agent of the real perpetrator."

The major groaned and closed his eyes, leaning against the parapet, seemingly at ease. "You are right. But if that is true, if someone did this at Louis's bidding, then the act was planned in advance."

"That's unlikely." Both men glared at her, but undaunted, she continued to speak. "Nobody could know Ben would come out of the house or would stand in precisely that spot."

The major's eyes widened. "Did you not arrange to meet for a morning walk?"

Ben shook his head. "Although had I thought to do it, I would have asked her. No."

He was right. This act was impulsive, something done quickly, taking advantage of a circumstance.

Major Thorpe pinched the bridge of his nose, then opened his eyes and met Ben's steady regard. "If I can aid you in any way, please do not hesitate to come to me. I have long been disturbed by my brother's behavior, but I could do little about it, being abroad with the army. I had planned to return."

Dorothea moved to Ben's side and hooked her arm through his, to support him. He'd gone quite pale. He began to walk back to the corner of the roof, breathing steadily. Too steadily. But Dorothea said nothing until they had descended the narrow staircase and once more stood in the corridor by the servants' quarters.

"Come with me," he said, and instead of continuing toward the family wing, opened a small door to one side.

Light filtered through dusty dormer windows onto a storage area. Furniture was ranked neatly against the wall opposite, covered with Holland sheets, giving the place an eerie quality.

Dorothea shivered, and as if acting automatically, Ben drew her into his arms. Resting her head against his broad chest, she wasn't sure which of them was more agitated.

She'd nearly lost him.

It had taken a stone cherub to show her how much he meant to her. Far too much, for sure, but she couldn't help that now. The thought of never seeing him again caused a suffocating sensation in her chest, as if she'd forgotten to breathe.

But she'd spurned him. He wouldn't ask her again.

His heart thumped under her ear, the slight quiver it delivered a welcome reminder that he was still alive. "Thank you," he said. "You were right. I hate heights. I have controlled the reaction, but I still detest it."

"We all have something. Hmm. Do you think it was Louis?"

His arm curled around her back in a protective gesture she liked too much. "Probably. Or Honoria."

When she lifted her head, gazing at him in astonishment, he smiled down at her and dropped a hard kiss against her lips. "What, you think her incapable of doing that? My dear, I have learned just how self-centered Honoria can be. She is unscrupulous..." He paused. "But she never knew anything else. She was indulged as a child, and she grew into an accredited beauty. Everyone loved her."

"Including you."

"I thought I did, but I learned otherwise soon enough."

"Because of your wife."

He touched her chin, tilted it up so she had to meet his steady gaze. "My *first* wife." He wouldn't let her look away. "She was my past. I want you to be my future."

Although hearing that thrilled her, Dorothea reminded herself not to become carried away. "You could have anyone you want."

"I choose you," he said. Still no sign of doubt in those gray eyes. "This time, Dorothea, say yes. This is not our parents making a convenient arrangement. Only we decide this time."

What else could she say? When that statue had smashed so close to him, so had her willpower. She couldn't bear to lose him, because she loved him. So much. She gave a sigh of surrender. "Yes."

"Just like that?" Tenderly, he turned her head, gazing down into her eyes.

"Just like that. Yes, Benedict Thorpe, I will marry you."

He reached for her hand, playing with her fingers, gazing down at her face with soft but unmistakable desire.

Wonder infused her. She had said yes to being his wife, but he was giving her more. She would be a marchioness, a grande dame in the fullness of time, even a matriarch if God was good to her and gave her children.

Before she could speak, he kissed her. Cupping the back of her head, he sealed their promises with a kiss to remember.

Eventually, after an untold length of time, he lifted his head. His gaze had softened, and he was smiling, his lips fuller than usual. "We'll tell the others at dinner tonight. Then we may put up the banns and marry in three weeks' time."

"Three weeks?" The words came out in a squeak.

"Yes, why wait?" He grinned at her. "Sir James said he would prefer my marriage to be soon. The King wants an assured line. His majesty also informed me of that fact while I was in London."

"Naturally," she said softly. "But Ben, I'm thirty. I might never give you a child, and you need a son. You'd be better off with a younger woman."

He clutched her tighter. "I don't want a younger woman. I want you. You'll help me make sense of this madness."

But he deserved to have a chance to change his mind. "If you find a younger woman, one who would make a better marchioness, then you must tell me. Promise?"

"Promise. But I doubt I'll find anyone better in three weeks. Or three years, come to that. Or thirty."

He growled low and kissed her again. That seemed a suitable conclusion to their discussion.

Chapter 15

They announced their engagement to Schultz and let the butler do the rest. Before the hour was out, everybody knew Dorothea had accepted Ben's proposal of marriage.

For the remainder of the day, Dorothea kept busy helping guests depart. Today marked the end of the visit Louis had invited them to. They would be eager to spread the word about the shocking events at Cressbrook House.

When Ben extended an invitation as a matter of courtesy, several guests opted to remain. Dorothea's brother and sister-in-law remained, as did Lord Evington and Major Thorpe, Lord and Lady Norman, and to Dorothea's surprise, Lord and Lady Steeping.

"I want to ensure poor Lady Honoria is all right," she confided in Dorothea as they were standing in the great front hall. Her voice echoed around the vast space. "None of this is her fault, and she is deeply distressed. I will try to persuade her down to dinner tonight."

Then for all her faults, the gossiping and the snide comments, Lady Steeping was a true friend. She'd chosen to stay with the distressed Lady Honoria rather than rush to the next country home on her summer visiting list to create gossip. Dorothea had to appreciate that.

"His lordship said we should eat informally," she warned her.

Lady Steeping trilled a laugh, and Dorothea tried to suppress her wince at the high-pitched sound. Standing too close to this woman was painful. No wonder her husband kept his distance. "Oh, not too informally, I trust! I would hate for standards to slip! Such a pity Mr. Thorpe went off like that, just as his wife needed him, but he was ever so. No doubt he has gone ahead to prepare his estate for her. He inherited Thorpe Park from his father, you know, but he has neglected it in favor of caring for this estate."

Dorothea turned to the stairs. "I believe Lord Belstead means to make matters easier for Lady Honoria to deal with her change of circumstances."

Lady Steeping placed her hand on her slender bosom and heaved a sigh. "If only that were so! But the poor lady is completely distraught. Everything she thought to be true has betrayed her. She grew up at the heart of society, expected by all to have a great future with an important man, but now, this. She expected her husband to enter Parliament once he inherited the title he has been caretaker of for the past seven years. The application to the Chancellor was intended to be a formality, but it has turned out to be anything but. One must feel for her, dear Miss Rowland." Her expectant smile emphasized her expectation that Dorothea would cause no trouble.

Dorothea seethed.

"I do believe that Mrs. Thorpe could be a great help to you," her ladyship went on, oblivious to Dorothea's growing anger. "If you go ahead with this impulsive marriage, which I do wish you would reconsider, you will need a great deal of assistance. This house will not run itself. Mrs. Thorpe has managed it with great success for the past seven years."

Dorothea had had enough of staying silent. All her adult life she'd smiled while bleeding inside from another scratch inflicted by someone who thought they were better than her, more beautiful, the best height, wealthier. The heat of anger seethed inside her, as it had done so many times before. But she would not remain politely silent, or agree with this cat smiling sweetly at her, waiting for her response.

No more. She lifted her chin, heedless of the fact that Lady Steeping had to crane her neck to meet her eyes. "Unfortunately, Mrs. Thorpe has retired to her room, perhaps until her husband returns." She paused, leaving the words "if he ever does" unsaid. She did not need to say them.

Lady Steeping, who had been drifting away, turned her head and gave Dorothea her full attention.

Dorothea smiled sweetly. "If she decides to join us, however, she will be most welcome. My betrothed has asked me to help him at this difficult time, and of course I will do everything I can to be of service."

The Dorothea of years gone by might have said that, but not in the tone Dorothea used now. Did Lady Steeping think she sat in the corners of ballrooms and learned nothing? Or maybe she hadn't thought at all about the forgotten and unwanted.

Time for the single ladies to shine, for Dorothea Rowland to become the woman she was meant to be. Whether she married Ben or not, she would make the most of what she had now, grasp it with both hands. Why shouldn't she be the great lady? "While matters are so confused, I will act as the hostess of this house, because the marquess would have it so. He has much to arrange. I doubt you have noticed that this house has fallen into rack and ruin. There is much to do."

After one shocked glance at her, as if the bird had bitten the cat, Lady Steeping turned in a circle, arms spread. The costly lace at her elbows fell in a graceful stream. "I see no rack and ruin."

Dorothea was ready for her. "Dust lies on every surface, and the china is in sore need of a bath. The chandeliers have not been cleaned this age." She raised a brow. "Or is this normal for you?"

Lady Steeping made a sound like "Humph," a sort of feminine grunt. "No doubt Mrs. Thorpe has had much to think about. I'd say they kept the seat warm for his lordship to come home. Especially when we all thought he had died. Unfortunately, nobody could trace his body."

"Because he had not died." No need to continue. Her ladyship understood Dorothea's point, and she would no doubt relay the message to Mrs. Thorpe. The throne had changed hands, from the regent to the king, so to speak.

"I cannot imagine why he did not come home."

"I can." Dorothea didn't care to elaborate this time, but she had her suspicions. Ben had found a new life in Boston that suited him better. It was so simple. He'd decided to stay dead. But what had brought him back? He'd told her Lord Evington had kept in touch with him. Was it his wife? Had he wanted to leave that part of his life behind?

Sadness touched her, as it always did when she thought of poor Mary and her dead baby. Their loss must have broken Ben's heart. So perhaps that had made up his mind for him. She would share none of that with Lady Steeping, who, after shooting Dorothea a poisonous glare, headed for the stairs.

Dorothea did not accompany her. Instead, she made her way to the small study she'd discovered in the ground-floor corridor close to the hall and collected a pad and pencil. The shafts of graphite had recently come into fashion and, bound with twine to prevent the mess coming off on the hands, were proving a useful instrument. She had her small wax tablets, tucked into her pocket before she left her room, but she needed something more substantial for what she planned to do.

A full list of requirements and tasks to be done, starting with this floor. Worn furniture, cracked glass, broken ornaments, clocks that hadn't been wound recently, and everywhere a fine film of dust, except in the rooms used by the family. She would transcribe the lists later and show them to Ben and to Schultz. There was work to do.

If Dorothea went through with this absurd but welcome betrothal, she would have plenty to do.

Absorbed in her work, she lost all sense of time until Ben found her. She was poring over a collection of hideous china animals huddled together in a crooked cabinet in an anteroom on the other side of the hall when she heard, "There you are!" making her fumble with the creature she was currently holding.

It smashed to the floor. "There! Now I'll never know if it was meant to be a sheep or a rabbit."

"It was so bad?" He came to where she stood, staring at the shattered piece. "I remember those. My grandmother bought them from a peddler. How odd to find them here. I played with them when I was a boy. Rather roughly." He picked up another figure, this one unmistakably human, though it was difficult to determine its sex. "This is the shepherd, and you dropped one of his flock."

"I'm so sorry. I didn't know they meant so much to you."

"They didn't." He put the shepherd back. "I only remember them, that's all. Fairings bought on a whim. They should go." He glanced around the room. "The fact that this chamber is exactly as I remember disturbs me somewhat. It should have been cleaned out years ago."

Broken chairs were stacked in a corner, and a rickety table stood under a window. "This was once a fine anteroom, made to display treasures, or so I was told when I was a boy."

"It will be so again, if you want it," she said, picking up her list.

"What have you here?" He didn't take the paper from her but peered over her shoulder. This close, the heat of his body seared through her and the scent of sandalwood and male eased into her senses. "Oho, I see you mean to be thorough."

"Someone has to be. I was merely making preliminary notes. I must speak to the housekeeper soon."

"Yes, you must. I believe old Mrs. Bush died, or retired. I remember her from my father's time." He paused. "My memories are not fond ones. I believe she gave my father some—comfort at times."

"You mean she shared his bed?" Dorothea didn't care for polite euphemisms.

Thankfully, he did not seem concerned by her frankness. "Exactly, but she wouldn't have shared it for long. Only enough time for him to take what he wanted from her. He was not a faithful husband, and my mother was fully aware of that." He touched her shoulder. "I will be. You need have no fears on that score."

Honestly, she had not considered the matter until he'd brought it up, which was foolish of her. Every gentleman had a mistress. Some wives considered the mistresses useful, especially the ones who did not care for the carnal side of marriage.

Dorothea suspected she would not be one of those.

"I came to find you because we are to see the vicar today. I want the banns read this Sunday."

She bit her lip. "What about a bishop's license?"

They would not have to have the banns read. At the back of her mind, Dorothea still did not believe the marriage would happen. Not that she doubted him, but herself. A bishop's license would mean fewer people knew about their proposed marriage. And the breakup.

"I am not ashamed. Are you?"

She shook her head, using the excuse of finding the case for her pencil to not look at him.

"Dorothea?" The soft tone made her look up. He crooked a finger under her chin and brought her close for a soft, sweet kiss.

"Go and collect a hat and gloves. I'll order the carriage put to."

* * * *

Having located her hat and gloves, Dorothea hurried outside. Ben waited with the carriage. To her relief, he had an ordinary-looking gig, not a grander vehicle. With a smile, she placed her sensibly shod foot on the iron step and climbed up onto the wooden seat next to him.

Ben set the single horse into motion. "You can use one of these?" he asked as they rolled down the drive at a steady pace, careful to avoid the rabbit holes.

"Yes. We have one at home. I have been using it for years."

"Then I will ensure this one is at your disposal, as well as the grander vehicles. I confess that I didn't order the carriage or anything more elaborate, so that we could have a chance to be alone. We don't need footmen or grooms with this." He smiled when he looked at her, warming her all the way through. "We need to discuss the little problem of this morning."

"Never say that. Someone tried to kill you, Ben, and you are taking it in the most infuriating manner."

He swung around the bend, bringing the village into sight. Cressbrook House was nestled between two hills, the rolling green giving an impression of lushness.

"Infuriating?" His lips tilted in a grin. "My dear, I've faced a bear and survived. I fought a duel and I'm still here."

"You can fall over a doorstep and break your neck," she observed, having heard of that very thing happening to a neighbor.

"Should you wish it?"

Her vehement, "No indeed!" raised a chuckle from him.

"I am glad. You are sure I am the target of the attack?"

"Who else? Not I, to be sure." Who would want to kill her? She had no great fortune, or anything else to mark her out as special.

He tightened the reins, slowing the horse, who was gathering speed going downhill. Dorothea admired his skill, the neat way he held the reins and the smooth anticipation of the obstacles on the rutted road.

"Who knows about your investigation on behalf of Miss Childers?"

"Only you, Sir James, and Laurence. Sir James left for London to present his decision to Lord Hardwicke, my brother is hardly likely to try to kill me, and you were with me at the time."

"Thank you for that."

"You're welcome." Her dry tone matched his, and they shared a moment of amusement. Sharing the same sense of humor would go a long way to ensure a happy union. Goodness, she was thinking of it as a fact now. Perhaps she should, since he seemed intent on the marriage. Reality was sinking in, and she could finally accept with equanimity that she was about to beat the field and marry the marquess.

They traveled in silence to the outskirts of the village, a substantial settlement of its type. This close, the houses lost their appearance of picturesque quaintness. Holes gaped in roofs, and walls crumbled, moss overgrowing structures.

"So we can say that Mrs. Thorpe, the major, and Mr. Thorpe were not in sight of anyone else when it happened. Mrs. Thorpe could not have done this on her own, the major was abed, and that leaves Louis Thorpe or someone unknown. The other guests were accounted for. I asked Schultz."

His nostrils flared. "I suspect my cousin Louis."

"But Mr. Thorpe was downstairs at the stables. We saw the coach leave."

"He could have run up to the roof, levered the cupid off the plinth, and returned downstairs. I know, I timed it myself."

Shocked, she swiveled to stare at him. "You did?" The image of him racing up and down stairs in his shirtsleeves quickened her heartbeat. All that honed muscle put to use.

He nodded. "He wanted me gone all those years ago, went so far as to exaggerate his injury to rid himself of me. He considered himself the marquess in all but name. Who else would have made such a reckless attempt?"

She sighed. "You are right." But she would not give up her list, or the record she had made of the people present today. Not servants, because the act was an impulsive one. It had to be, considering their proximity at the time. Too much time would have to pass for someone to give the order to a servant. She had come out of the house, Ben had come to join her, then the statue had tumbled.

"But why would Mr. Thorpe run up to the roof in the first place?"

"Ah." A dull flush spread over his cheeks. "I wish I had not promised the truth now."

"Oh?" Her stomach tightened. What had he done?

He sighed. "Honoria accosted me this morning. Her attempt to win me back, I think."

"I saw you together. Why would she do that?"

He shrugged. "Because she likes to collect men, whether she does anything with them or not. Some women collect porcelain figurines; Honoria collects men." Hastily he added, "She did not succeed."

"You don't have to tell me that." He'd already given her his opinions on fidelity. However he felt about Honoria now, he would never trespass on his cousin's ground.

"She was flirting, using her skills on me. If Louis caught sight of that, he would know what she was about, and maybe he would want to go to a place where he could watch unobserved."

How terrible to have a spouse one had to watch all the time! But yes, that would give Louis a reason to run up to the roof.

"He had the opportunity because I made him change the carriage he took, from one with a crest to a plain one. That in itself would be enough to rile him." Ben flicked the whip over the horse's head. "He used to go up to the roof often when we were boys. He knew I was not fond of heights, so he was always sure he could be on his own."

That answered her question. The way Ben told it, the act was inevitable. Louis went up to the roof, saw Ben flirting with his wife, or to be more exact, his wife flirting with Ben, and decided to take advantage of his position.

Ben glanced about him as they drove around the village green to reach the church at the far end. "The sooner I can begin on renovations, the better. I own this village, and my family built the church. I will not have it fall apart. But until the title is confirmed I cannot touch the entailed funds, such as they are. I am minded to use my own fortune. I've sent for a man of business I can trust, and he can help me record what needs doing."

Thinking like a businessman, every item in its proper department.

"What are you smiling at?" His voice had softened as he drew the horse to a stop.

"You," she said, just as quietly, but she would not elaborate on her words. Because she dared not.

Having no experience with falling in love made her doubt herself. She might merely be falling in like with him. Lust, certainly. A measure of both could lead to deeper emotions, but what was she supposed to feel? She had nothing to compare it with, no way of assessing. For the first time in years, Dorothea didn't know what to think.

* * * *

Going home, Ben let Dorothea drive. She suspected he wanted to see her skill with the ribbons, but a gig with one horse wasn't much of a test. Still, she had to admit the road leading to the house gates was an adequate trial.

"I thought that went well," he said.

"Yes." The vicar was a pleasant man, and at least the vicarage was in good heart. He promised to have the banns up, complimented them fulsomely, and expressed the desire that he would see Ben and Dorothea at church regularly. "He didn't seem too enthused when I talked to him about the repairs."

Ben grunted. "He's probably heard it before. My cousin is good at promises, not so good at fulfillment."

Dorothea recalled some of Angela's comments. He'd borrowed far too much from the bank and only made a few payments. If he reneged completely, would Ben, as head of the family, be responsible? She didn't think so, but she would ask Angela in her next letter.

"So, my dear, we will be man and wife in twenty-three days' time, because I mean to make good on the banns as soon as possible." He folded his arms, leaning back as well as he could in the confined space, showing a remarkable trust in her driving. If she tipped the gig over, or sank into a rabbit hole, he would be sent head over heels. She redoubled her efforts to drive carefully, despite his alarming words.

Yes, they would. A wife. "Indeed," she managed, and kept her tone cool, although she had to make an effort to do so. "I should write some letters."

"You should indeed," he said, amused. "So should I. I assume you've written to Miss Childers, and the guests just departed will spread the word efficiently. After all, that was why Louis invited them. He planned for them to spread the word of his accession to the title. Fortunately, events did not go that way." He paused while they rolled along. "Should you object to walking the distance to the village tomorrow? It cannot be more than a mile."

On the Sabbath people who could walk were expected to do so, and the mile to the village would not be difficult. The weather had cooled today, giving some much-needed relief from the heat of the last week. A walk would be pleasant.

"I expected to do so," she answered. "I doubt the vicar would consider either of us unable to travel on foot."

Usually the vicar walked to the house to take service in the chapel after morning service in the village. However, since they wanted to hear the reading of the banns, they would have to attend the church. "I wonder if Mr. Thorpe would have done so."

"If it suited him."

That brought them back to the events of the morning. Neither spoke of it, since they had discussed it already, but the reminder cast a pall over Dorothea's thoughts.

"You know your brother requested to change chambers, now the prime guest rooms are available?"

"Really?" That didn't sound like them. Unless there was a problem with the room they occupied. Perhaps the window rattled or something. "I thought them fine."

"They are. However, they are somewhat distant from the other chambers we are using. Though that is not the reason either. I suspect they were being tactful."

Heat rose to her cheeks. "What do you mean?"

The gates to the estate came into sight. Dorothea concentrated on those, and the sharp turn she would have to make.

He chose that point to say, "It means we're the only people sleeping in that part of the house. I send Rougier away at night, so unless your maid sleeps with you, there are just the two of us in that passage."

Dorothea caught her breath on a gasp. At least he waited until she'd negotiated the curve, and they were heading up the drive. Unfortunately, its state was no better than the road, but the quick beating of her heart wasn't because of that.

"My dear," he said in a softer tone, "I have been burning for you. Knowing you are so near but so unattainable has driven me mad, especially considering what I already know about your delectable body."

She tried to speak, but it came out a strangled squeak. But how could she deny that she wanted him too? The notion would never have crossed her mind before, but with her new, daring approach to life, it had. More than once she had considered her bed a vast, empty space that needed a companion. She'd almost considered asking for a maid, but now she was glad she had not.

"I don't have a maid. I share one with my sister-in-law, and as I dress simply, I do not always need her help." She clamped her mouth shut, afraid she was about to babble.

"Forgive me." Ben sounded completely calm. "I did not mean to upset you. But if I were to try your door tonight, and find it open, I might come inside and pay you a midnight visit. But *only* if it is open, of course."

Her heart was beating frantically and her mind whirling. Dorothea barely managed to take the horse and gig around the house to the stables. When Ben came to her and lifted her down, his hands around her waist, she trembled under his touch. She prayed he would not notice, since her stays were not insubstantial, but her fingers shook when she put them on his sleeves for balance. She stepped back quickly, as soon as he had released her.

He lifted her gloved hand to his lips. "Please don't distress yourself, Dorothea. It is merely a suggestion, that is all. I can easily wait three weeks." He laughed harshly. "Well, perhaps not easily."

Chapter 16

Dinner was tediously long, but at least Dorothea had been able to order a simpler repast, since many of the guests had left. They talked of politics, the weather, anything but the events of that day, as if somehow a tumbling cherub was something to be embarrassed about. Ben sat at the head of the table now, and Dorothea took her place next to him. Taking the hostess's position at the foot of the table would have been premature. At Ben's request, Lady Steeping fulfilled that honor.

After dinner there was tea and gossip. Someone played a sonata on the harpsichord, and Dorothea nodded and smiled, God knew at what. However, the ladies ended their evening early, some to walk in the garden before the sun went down, and others to attend to private business, letters and suchlike. Dorothea went upstairs before the gentlemen had quit the dining room.

The maid came to help her undress, and then all she could do was wait. Agony. She shot the bolts on her bedroom door and then slid them back at least twice before she made her final decision.

Dorothea was sitting at her dressing table when a soft knock sounded on the door. She licked her lips, which had turned unaccountably dry, and whispered, "Come in."

The latch lifted, and Ben entered her room. Dorothea's heart rose to her throat. She was in the process of unfastening the nighttime braids Ann's maid had insisted on doing for her.

Smiling, he walked over to her. His knee-length ultramarine silk banyan revealed bare legs. Those calves needed no padding. She kept her gaze fixed on his lower half, discomfited.

He stopped beside her chair. "It's only me," he said, gentle as a whisper. "If you want me to leave, I'll go."

She choked out a laugh. "That's the trouble. I don't. But I've never been in this situation before."

"Count this as the first of many nights." He gripped the back of her chair, his knuckles turning white.

He knew she would be cautious, but after all, couples anticipated their marriage frequently. Didn't they? At any rate, a fair number of first children in society were born early. It was just— "I never expected to find this happening to me. Not in these circumstances."

"What do you mean? Dorothea, look at me. I can't tell what you are thinking if you don't."

Drawing a deep breath, she lifted her chin and looked up. He'd shaved, and he wore his hair loose. It hung either side of his face like a silken curtain, but somehow, the hair made him appear more masculine, almost a barbarian. He was smiling.

She stared.

"Sweetheart, I want you. What we did before was only a beginning."

Her lips formed an O. His eyes darkened.

He held out his hand, palm up. Lines were engraved into the surface, his long, strong fingers curled slightly. But the nails were neatly trimmed and polished, despite the scars that nicked his fingers, signs of the physical work he'd done.

Tentatively, she reached out and laid her hand in his. His fingers closed around hers, and he urged her to her feet. She let him draw her into his body, a hard wall of heat and muscle. "By the way, there's a footman stationed at the end of this passage."

"Why did you put a man there?"

"Because I don't want you disturbed."

"Who will disturb me?"

He watched her, his expression grave. "I don't know, and that's what worries me. You could have been the target, and Louis has plenty of people willing to do his bidding."

She shook her head, her remaining braid hitting her cheek. "Who would want to attack me?"

"Anyone not desirous of our marriage. Anyone who found out you are acting as Angela Childers's agent."

"Nobody here can know that." And she hadn't said yes until after the cupid's fall. But everybody knew now.

"You wrote to her, did you not?"

The words fell between them like small bombs, sputtering in her mind. Yes, somebody could have seen the address and come to certain conclusions.

Word about the SSL was slowly spreading. They were certainly making no secret of it. "So you think I'm in danger, too?"

"You were the one who established that it was not an accident. So yes. I want you safe, but I don't want you to retreat. Your work makes you happy, and I love watching you blossom." He released her hand and caught her braid, deftly unwinding it from the neat plait.

So he was protecting her, so she could continue with her work for Angela. He didn't want her in danger. The words felt like balm to her soul. Nobody had thought that much about her before, not even her brother. He'd have told her to withdraw from the SSL.

He released her hair and folded his hand over hers again, drawing her close enough to loop his arm around her waist. "Someone put you in danger. I will *not* allow it."

"Goodness!" She widened her eyes, gazing up at him in surprise. "You should reject me, then, tell everyone that we are not marrying after all."

He lifted her fingers to his mouth and kissed them, one by one. "I thought of asking you to keep our agreement secret, but I didn't want to. You are mine, Dorothea." Without raising his voice, he forced understanding into her.

"I'm hardly likely to fall out of your arms into anyone else's," she said tartly.

"I won't risk it. You are perfect for me, and once I've uncovered a treasure, I don't let go of it."

No one had called her a treasure before. She rather liked it. His proximity was making her dizzy, or perhaps that was his evident desire for her.

When he nudged up her chin and fastened his mouth to hers, Dorothea stopped thinking at all.

Instead, she curled her arm around his neck, as if afraid he would pull away, and held on. Their previous encounter had only made her eager for more. When he licked into her mouth, she met his tongue, flirted with it, sucked it and moaned, although she wasn't aware of the last part until she'd done it. He groaned back.

The vibrations traveled down her throat into the deepest part of her. That place between her legs tingled and seemed to swell, making her want to rub her thighs together to bring herself easement.

She wanted him. If he stopped now, she might just die.

He held her steady, drew her closer so she could lean her head on his shoulder, and gave her a series of kisses. Each one was deeper and more lascivious, until she was clutching his robe with her free hand, afraid she'd fall to the floor if he released her.

He caressed her waist, then up, shaping her body, until he cupped her breast and stroked his thumb over her nipple. Even through the layers of robe and night rail, he sent shivers through her.

Drawing his mouth away from hers, he gazed down at her, his eyes slumberous and heated, the silver darkened to the color of the sky in a storm. He layered tiny kisses on her face, slowly moving from her lips to her ear, pausing to play with her earlobe, giving it a playful tug with his teeth. Down her throat he went, carelessly nudging her robe aside to reach the base of her neck and the little hollow there, which proved extraordinarily sensitive. Her body rose to him, every part of her yearning for his touch.

If they never married—and after today she understood that was a remote possibility—she would have this. And she would die if she didn't know what a man and woman could do together. She murmured his name, the long version and the familiar. "Benedict. Ben..."

"Dorothea, sweetheart," he murmured against her skin, then straightened.

Deftly he unfastened the clasps of her robe, untied the sash around her waist that held it together. It gaped free, but she didn't attempt to grab it. She did the opposite, shrugging the silk off her shoulders so it slid down her body. She dropped her arms to let it fall the rest of the way, into a pool of green.

And stood there, in a night rail thin enough for him to see the shape of her body through it. Her hair tumbled over her shoulders and halfway down her back. Irresistible.

Ben picked up a strand and wound it around his finger. "Heavenly. It's spun moonlight." He glanced up at her face, his expression warm. "Do you trust me?"

She didn't have to think about that. "Yes."

He nodded and reached for the remaining buttons on her last garment, unfastening the buttons at the cuffs and the single one left of the three at her neck. He'd already undone the other two. Once more he slid his hands down her body, but this time he gathered the fabric, and lifted it.

Obligingly, Dorothea raised her arms and let him whisk off her night rail. When she'd shaken the hair out of her eyes, what she saw rocked her. His expression was almost worshipful. For her?

Yes, for her. While she had always considered herself clumsy, a giantess among the ethereal loveliness of the society ladies, Ben made her feel beautiful. She would stand here all night, as long as he kept looking at her like that.

"You're so lovely, Dorothea. Either men were blind, or you strove to hide your beauty." A smile tilted the corners of his mouth. "No more, I promise you. I want everyone to see what a treasure they missed, the one they can't have. Because you're mine."

Slowly, he undid the frogged toggles at the top of his elaborate banyan, dragging the robe off carelessly.

He wore nothing underneath.

Broad shoulders gave way to a strong chest framed by a pair of arms that looked as if they lifted tree trunks on a regular basis. Dark hair, darker than on his head, was sprinkled by a generous hand around his nipples, curving down to a thicker line that led down and down.

Dorothea did not avoid the rest of his body. She let her gaze follow the line of hair, punctuated by the indent of his navel and farther down, to the impressive erection rearing from the nest of hair at his groin. The thick stalk of muscle reared above, crowned by a plump head, the purplish head shiny and straining.

As she watched, a bead of moisture leaked from the tip in a crystalline promise.

With a gasp, she jerked up her chin and met his gaze. "You had better like what you see," he rumbled, his voice even deeper than usual, "because you will be seeing that for a long time to come."

He encircled her waist, his fingers hot on her skin, and lifted her. He planted her firmly on her back on the crisp white sheets that a maid had exposed before Dorothea returned from the tedious sojourn in the drawing room after dinner.

This was anything but dull, and the way he was looking at her as he came down to join her thrilled every inch of her body. He lay by her side, propped up on one elbow, unashamedly studying her. And God help her, she loved it.

Tentatively at first, she spread her palm over his chest, the hair tickling her in a new stimulation. "This is..." She faltered, trying to find the right word. Everything she thought of was inadequate.

"Different? Delightful? Thrilling?" he suggested. "Or terrifying, unpleasant, and distasteful?"

"Oh, definitely the first set." New textures caressed her palm as she moved it over his muscled chest. "Who in their right mind would use the second set?"

"Many people do. Some men, when they're discussing the necessity of making an heir, and I've heard some women feel that way."

"Nobody ever said it to you?"

He shook his head, his chestnut hair glinting red when it caught the candlelight. The branch of candles on the dressing table, two pairs in the sconces either side of the bed and set in holders on the headboard revealed every muscle, each delicious dip and swell of his body. "Ladies don't talk about such things in front of men. At least not in front of me."

Why did that not surprise her? Ben was nothing short of magnificent. She stroked over his nipples, the flat muscles beneath twitching at her touch. "Were you like this when you left England?"

"No." He took her nipple between his fingers, gently tweaking until she shivered. This restraint was another kind of excitement, but the anticipation was almost too much. "Honest toil gave me the body of a working man."

She burst into shocked laughter. "Who on earth said that? You're splendid."

His eyes darkened. "Thank you. I've heard it a few times, especially from our departed guests. They meant it as an insult, but I took it as a compliment. Honest toil beats sleek muscles honed in the fencing salon."

As she slid her hand up to test the breadth of his shoulders, she purred in pleasure.

He traced a line down her body with one finger, lingering at her navel, then leaned over her. "Better now?"

He'd given her time to accustom herself to this blatant nakedness, displaying her body in this way. She wished she could be bolder, but she had never considered herself anything but too big to be admired. But he was admiring her now, openly doing so.

When he kissed her, he brought her nipples in proximity to his chest, but delicately, so they brushed the furred surface. Until she tilted her head and opened her lips to him.

They flung themselves back into the storm, their mouths melding, exploring, as he levered himself over her. Dorothea opened her legs to accommodate him, as if her body was merely relearning a forgotten skill. His member, hard and insistent, pressed against her belly, the damp kiss of the tip anointing her skin.

"I want you so much," he said after he'd barely separated their lips. "But I'll keep you safe."

His protection made her feel safer, but more than that, knowing she was wanted gave her strength. He did not seek to shield her from every feather in the wind but gave her the freedom she yearned for.

So they were to wait for the ultimate act until their wedding night? Not if she could help it. Last time they were together he'd drawn back from completing the act. This time he would not.

Lifting her legs, she clamped her thighs around his hips, blatantly opening herself and holding him in place. "I want you too. Please, Ben. Give me everything."

A pause until he raised his head and met her anxious gaze. She nodded, once. He smiled, and the taut lines at the corners of his mouth eased.

After a swift, teasing kiss on her lips, he moved down, cupping her breast and bending to lick first one nipple, then the other, where he lingered to nip and tease. She caressed his shoulders, letting the muscles shape under her hands, relishing so much man. But when she pushed, he resisted. Glancing up at her, he gave her a wicked smile. "You'll get your turn. But I want to do what I've been longing to do since the dinner on your first night here."

"What's that?"

"Wait and see."

His caresses were driving her to madness, and when he slipped his fingers between her legs, urging them apart, she opened them even farther. He took possession with one long lick, tasting her from opening to the little bud she occasionally teased when she was alone and needy.

People thought spinsters had no urges, because nobody had woken them to the possibilities of sharing their bodies. People were wrong.

Shivers passed through her. If she was standing, she might be shuddering, but her fever was of the best kind, arousing and urging her to do what she wanted. She'd thrown propriety and commonsense to the winds the minute he'd lifted the latch and come in—no, before that, when she hadn't locked her door. And she'd never been so glad of disregarding the conventions.

Ben lavished her with licks and strokes. He slid his hands from her knees to her hips and up, grazing her breasts before gliding back down, heating every inch of her with his touch. The harder skin delivered a gentle abrasion that only served to drive her further up toward the peak she'd only ever known with him.

The sounds he was making, the soft slurping, should embarrass her, but they didn't. She adored every single one, and the way he gripped her hips, surely he'd leave bruises. But she'd love them too, visible signs of his arousal that she could enjoy for days to come. Even that thought didn't strike her as perverse. Ben was blowing every idea she'd gleaned completely out of the water.

He brought his fingers into play, releasing her hip to slide them under her, tracing her entrance, circling around and around before slipping the tip of one inside her. Gently he pushed, easing her wider. Nobody had ever done that, not even herself. When she'd tried while experimenting with her body, wanting to know it better than anyone, pressing had hurt, so she'd stopped, fearing she was doing something wrong. But she trusted Ben. He would take her where she needed to go, and every minute, every second, her arousal grew.

She wasn't aware of shifting until he firmed his hold, but she was close, her body rising to a peak.

Then he stopped.

Dorothea wailed in protest, but he released her hips and pushed on the mattress, bringing himself up to her. His eyes were bright, his lips wet. Wet with *her*.

"Ready?"

Ready? She'd show him ready. "Why did you stop!"

A low chuckle rumbled through his chest as he reached down and guided his erection to where she needed him most. When he grazed the place he'd been sucking just a moment ago, she whimpered, so sensitive now, but he didn't stop there. He gave one long sigh as he notched the fat head against her body. It felt much larger now. The soft skin with that hard core fascinated her.

He was gazing at her, his eyes silver steel. "I stopped because I want to feel you come apart when I'm inside you."

Nobody had ever said anything like that to her before. The breath caught in her throat, and she reached for him. She grasped his shoulders, cupping them. "Do it."

He took her in a series of shallow thrusts, each one lodging him more securely inside her. The sense of tension, of something about to break, made her tighten her muscles.

"Lift your legs high. Open yourself up." He touched his lips to hers.

She clamped her thighs to his sides and rested her heels on his backside. The muscles there tightened when he pushed. Then, without warning, he pulled almost out and plunged, driving in deep.

If he hadn't kissed her, her yell would have been heard on the other side of the building, but he swallowed her cry of shock. She clung to him, riding the waves of pain. Why did it hurt so much? Would it be like this every time?

He lifted away, catching her gaze once more. "Don't close your eyes. Look at me!"

She did as he bade her without thinking. She hadn't realized she'd closed her eyes until he ordered her to open them. The pain was already receding, ebbing away as she watched him. "Is it always like this?"

"Hell, no!" He sent a rough laugh around the room. "You feel so good, sweetheart. I've broken through. That's the only time you will feel pain with me." He brushed a strand of hair away from her forehead, where it had stuck to her sweat. "How is it now?"

He kept completely still inside her. She felt stuffed, full to bursting, but when he moved a tiny bit, he slid quite easily. That surprised her. "Better. It doesn't hurt when you—do that."

She received another kiss. "Good. It will feel better, I promise."

He pulled out further, and drove back in, touching a spot inside that sent delightful shudders up her spine to the top of her head. "Oh!"

A low growl told her he liked her response, but that wasn't why she'd done it.

Dorothea stopped thinking when he repeated his action, and then again and again. She found if she pressed her shoulders against the mattress, enabling her to move her hips to meet him, the sensation returned, stronger this time. "More!"

When he did as she bade him, she sucked in a deep breath of cool air, and then they were in the dance, working together. He came down, she pushed up, and the sounds of their lovemaking filled the room, the heady scents winding around them, like nothing she'd ever smelled before. Thick musk with an edge of tartness, sour apples and caramel.

Their bodies connected harder, with a slap of flesh every time he came down to her, or she ground up to him. They fit together so well they could have been one person. That spot inside her was going insane, apparently spreading until it encompassed every part of her, until nothing mattered except this room, this bed, this act.

Heat and sensation spiraled up until she froze, her back arched, and choked out his name. Her body tightened around him, clenching in rhythmic waves, drowning her in pure, undiluted Ben.

He cried out and clenched his sharp, white teeth as he groaned, and his shaft pulsed inside her, heat and wet warmth spilling out to bathe her thighs.

* * * *

He hadn't meant to do that, to take her virginity, until they married, although he'd had no intention of staying away from her. That didn't last long.

They could enjoy what they'd shared the other night, everything right up to complete penetration. But he could not regret it. Not when she gave him such bliss. He was shaken to the core. As he slid off her, he pulled her close. Dorothea draped a leg over his thighs and snuggled into his arms. This was where she should be. This felt right.

Why would he ever regret doing something so good?

They weren't married, but they would be. He might even consider bringing the wedding forward, obtaining a special license from London.

No, that would mean leaving her here for a week or more while he traveled there and back. He wouldn't go while she was in potential danger. Louis had left, but his agents, in the form of servants and family, were still here.

Her steady breathing puffed over his chest, and he reached down and idly scratched. She chuckled. "Such a man."

"Guilty." Turning his head, he kissed her sweaty forehead. She'd worked hard for her orgasm, and he'd done everything he could to take her there. Not like before. This would be a bedding to remember, for her as well. Except when he'd hurt her.

That was the second time he'd taken a virgin. With Mary, they had barely noticed, so this time had shocked him as much as it had Dorothea. Strange, considering Mary's delicacy versus the statuesque Dorothea.

He'd nearly pulled out, but her determination had driven him on. That and her magical body. Voluptuous, her touch urging him on, the heat and liquid warmth of her body pulling him in. But he couldn't quite define what had driven him to madness. He'd lost himself in her, completely.

"Tired," she mumbled against his shoulder. "Meant to talk, but..."

"We'll have plenty of time for that. I'll have to go to my own room, but I'll wait until you sleep."

The grumble she made pulled him in further. He kissed her forehead. "Sleep now, sweetheart."

Chapter 17

The sharp gasp woke Dorothea. She sat up. A man stood in the doorway of her room. Her involuntary squeak as she dived beneath the covers woke her lover.

The male groan next to her shocked her into dropping the sheet she'd pulled up to cover herself. Her thoughts froze.

"Oh, Lord." He sat up to join her and flipped a hand at the man. "I want discretion, Rougier."

The tall, thin man bowed. "I will ensure you are not disturbed, sir, madam. I beg your pardon. Considering recent events, I was concerned for my lord's safety so I came to find him."

He left the room, closing the door quietly behind him.

Dorothea turned on Ben. "Why didn't you order him not to tell anyone?"

"It would make no difference. If he spoke about this in the servants' hall, that disobedience would undermine what authority I have in this house. He was probably curious as well as concerned. After all, his employment depends on my being alive. Consider this a test. If he speaks, he's gone. If he doesn't, he stays." He tugged her back down, the light in his eyes kindling. She had completely forgotten that she was naked, but she recalled it now. "The staff here belong to Louis, apart from the ones the guests have brought with them. If Rougier does tell anyone, I'll dismiss him without a character. I did not have to say that—he will understand."

"Except Schultz." The butler had been here long enough to remember Ben.

"Except Schultz, and a few others. This house should hold fifty servants, including gardeners. It did in my father's day, but there are only twenty now." He stirred, rubbing against her, and she came to life. Eagerly, she reached up for his kiss, and he gave it.

"Good morning, sweetheart. I'm sorry I didn't leave when I said I would. I honestly meant to go."

"But you're tired."

"And I wanted to care for you. Yes, I was tired, too. However, here I am and here I'll stay."

"What?" She was startled enough to pull back.

"Why hide it? That would be ridiculous now. I don't want to go around hugger-mugger, ruffling up an unused bed."

Heat tinged the tips of her ears. "I don't know..."

"It happens more often than people care to admit, anticipating the wedding." He pulled her back. "Now sleep, and I swear that this time I'll get up. I'll order you tea, toast, and a bath. You'll ache a little after what we did last night."

"We shouldn't have." What was she thinking? She buried her face against the strong column of his neck, unable to cope with the events of last night and this morning.

"Yes, we should. You were magnificent, sweetheart. We will marry the Monday after the banns have been called. Do you hear me?"

She nodded. "We have to go to church."

"Yes, we do. And it's usual to walk."

Oh Lord, yes it was. He was right, she did feel uncomfortable in the place between her legs.

"Of course," she said, as if the prospect did not concern her in the least. But she couldn't deny she felt stiff. And how was she to sit for hours in church, knowing the congregation knew what she'd been doing?

A flash of recognition crossed her troubled mind. That was why couples had a honeymoon after their marriage, or one of the reasons at any rate. So the wife could accustom herself to her new status, to people knowing she shared her bed with a man.

Except she wasn't married. But lying here, in his arms, she couldn't be sorry, only regret others would know. "Is that why Laurence and Ann moved rooms? They didn't have a rattling window at all, did they?"

"I haven't checked." He stroked her back, as if soothing a disturbed cat. "But yes, I believe they wanted to give us some privacy."

The truth lay between them, unspoken. They were not married, and someone was trying to kill Ben. But in that case, Dorothea could only be glad she had taken this opportunity. To have never experienced the pleasures of Ben's lovemaking would have been a tragedy.

He was right. She wouldn't regret it.

He rolled up onto one elbow, depositing her gently on her back. "I know what you're thinking. Today, I'm writing a new will. You will be the beneficiary of all the property I can give to you, and I'll leave it with the trustees of Childers's Bank. That way you'll have complete control over it."

She clutched his shoulders, forcing him to meet her gaze. "You can't do that!"

"Yes, I can. The title is more difficult, but I have enough independent income to assure your security. And in case you aren't perfectly sure, we could have made a child last night."

"But you won't take risks looking for who pushed the cherub and who aimed a shot at you?" She didn't want to contemplate the would-be assassin succeeding. She refused to consider it. Surely fate wouldn't be so cruel? She couldn't lose him now.

Despite what he said last night, she doubted anyone would want to kill her, but she had not protested too much, because she'd wanted him to stay.

"I can't go that far, but I will promise you I won't take stupid risks. We'll find whoever is doing this, if we haven't already."

She stroked his chest, loving that she had the right to do so. "But we know, don't we?"

Catching her hand, he stopped her caresses and put his hand over hers. His heart beat against her palm. "It's Louis. I just need to prove it. If I set a guard around him and have him watched, he can do little harm." He lifted her hand to his mouth and kissed it. "And I've signed and helped compose enough legal documents to ensure this one will stand up to rigorous questioning. It's only insurance, sweetheart, to guarantee you are acknowledged. This is my fortune and I can leave it where I may. I choose you."

Put like that, she could only accept he meant it. One way or another, she would be a wealthy woman. But without Ben?

She would be a very impoverished wealthy woman.

* * * *

Every morning since she'd arrived at Cressbrook, Dorothea had taken a short stroll in the garden to blow away the cobwebs of the night. A habitual early riser, she usually had the area to herself, and so disappointment filled her when she spied a woman approaching her. Lady Honoria, wearing a broad-brimmed hat and bearing a parasol, had an easy smile. Her signature golden locks were tucked away under a lace and linen cap, which was why Dorothea had not recognized her immediately.

"Good morning." She shook back the ruffles of her elbow-length sleeves and shielded her eyes as she looked up. "A pleasant day, but it promises to scorch later. I thought I'd have my constitutional before it becomes hot. Much more pleasant to spend time in the coolest part of the house when the sun is at its height."

"Indeed." A politeness that meant nothing, but Dorothea could trade pleasantries until the sun went down, if she needed to. "A strange summer, with the sun and showers, but I daresay the gardeners are pleased."

This woman could be behind the attacks on Ben. She could even have committed one of them. While aware, Dorothea refused to back down.

"I daresay," Lady Honoria said without much interest. "Do you mean to keep the gardens as they are?"

They strolled along the paths, the scent of the late roses swirling around them. Not many blooms were left now, but there were always the stubborn few overblown blossoms. The plants could use some pruning, but Louis and Lady Honoria had severely reduced the number of gardeners available to tend the sprawling park and gardens. "We will do what is required."

"You only needed to add 'God willing' and you'd have been the perfect marchioness to follow the Puritan Anne. You know they were staunch supporters of Oliver Cromwell and his herd of commoners?"

"I've read some history of the family, yes," Dorothea answered cautiously. The marquess of a hundred years ago had made a considerable fortune for the family, most of which Louis had spent in a way his ancestor would not have appreciated.

"We cannot have the title spoiled in such a way again, don't you agree?"

Ah, so that was where she was going. "What way would that be?"

The breeze strengthened to a gusty wind, and Lady Honoria had to grab her hat. The straw flapped up and threatened to fly away, despite the broad pink satin bow securing it to her head. "Oh, dealing with tradesmen. The title can never go into trade."

Ben was in trade.

"My grandmother was," Dorothea reminded her. Not that Lady Honoria needed reminding. No doubt she'd researched Dorothea's family.

"Perhaps, since dear Benedict was engaged in trade for the last seven years, that was what appealed to him in you." Lady Honoria spared Dorothea a haughty smile. "You must see that a title as venerable as Belstead cannot succumb to a common streak. The third marquess was an aberration, but at least he was wellborn."

"Every aristocratic family owes its origins to a man who got his hands dirty." Dorothea shouldn't get so riled, but anger simmered under an exterior she was struggling to keep calm. "Whether he pored over account books or fought in a war, that is usually how titles begin. And unless there is investment, there can be no great house."

Although she'd planned to say much more, Dorothea clamped her mouth shut. What was the point? She would never win such an argument against a woman like Lady Honoria Thorpe, a duke's daughter, no less, and fully aware of it every moment of the day.

"Oh, you are so naïve, bless you!"

Dorothea gritted her teeth.

Lady Honoria sailed on. "You know, of course, that the—unpleasantness was over me. They both wanted me, though only one could have me."

"Hence the duel. Yes, I know that."

Lady Honoria winced at her blunt speaking. "Indeed, although ladies are supposed to be unaware."

"We'd have to be stupid not to know about duels. It's one thing to be vague for the newspapers, but another to be genuinely ignorant of such a deplorable event."

Lady Honoria preened, rippling her shoulders. "At the time, they were the two most eligible bachelors in London. But such a tragedy, that Benedict ran off. He should have stayed, then none of this would have happened."

"None of what?" Why should she allow Lady Honoria to wriggle off the hook? She was evidently building up to something, so Dorothea was determined to make her as honest as possible. "We are the only people here. Don't be afraid to speak the truth."

"Goodness, you're quite formidable! I understand why Ben is attracted to you. You're a novelty next to the women he usually pursues." Lady Honoria pursed her lips. "But then, you would have seen him in London, would you not? You must be aware that he prefers the delicate, gentle female. You're a novelty. He will soon tire of you." She laid her hand on Dorothea's arm in a confiding way, and leaned in, lowering her voice. "Naturally you are aware of his first wife. I never met the poor woman, but I understand she was gentle and sweet, and tiny."

Staring down at Honoria was no compensation for Dorothea, whose heart sank to the soles of her sturdy shoes. Ben had made her feel like a beautiful woman, so why did this example of femininity make her feel large and clumsy?

She let the feeling wash through her; then it was gone. The memories of constant humiliation and cruelty had their numbing effect, until she grew older and truly didn't care. Now she could use the other's reaction against her.

Learning to cover the response didn't mean it didn't still happen. Dorothea didn't want to run and hide from the cruelty of others, but by now, the unnecessary unkindness made her angry. These days she didn't care—truly, and if she'd needed proof it stood next to her, in the exquisitely beautiful Lady Honoria. Let her say what she would. This time Dorothea would listen.

After this—no more. "But he has promised to marry me," she prompted.

That was enough to start Lady Honoria off again. "Expediency. Benedict is a gentleman. Look how he fought an affair of honor and chose to keep my name out of the encounter. He is also a man who appreciates beauty. If I were single again..." She looked away and sighed. "But I cannot even think of that while my dear Louis is with us. However, be warned, if the worst ever happens, I might choose to demand of Ben what he asked of me seven years ago." She smiled brightly at Dorothea. "You saw us together that morning. You must know how he feels about me. His passion for me has never faded."

If Ben had not been so frank with her, Dorothea might have taken her at her word. As it was, she knew better. But Honoria had not done.

"He will not marry you, my dear, he is merely taking his pleasure in you, in default of me. Once I succumb, I will be all he needs. You should find a different man to marry. A bishop would appreciate your strength and your Puritan style. You'll need more than that to hold Benedict."

Seemingly unaware of Dorothea's stiffening, Honoria still kept hold of her arm. "Forgive me, my dear, but you did bid me speak freely. I am still enamored of him. Who would not be? Do not blame either of us if fate draws us together."

Dorothea had heard enough. She pulled her arm away. "You mistake me. If fate draws you together, it will be against my will, and be warned, I will demand satisfaction."

A smile quirked the woman's lips. "Satisfaction? You would fight a duel for him?"

Dorothea shrugged. "I shared my brother's fencing lessons. I believe I can give a good enough account of myself." Their parents had thought the lessons would help Dorothea become graceful. A shame that had not happened, but at least she'd gained a measure of poise and inner strength.

So Lady Honoria wanted what she'd always hankered for—both men at her feet. And she had the arrogance to assume she would get it.

She would have to climb over Dorothea's dead body first.

Chapter 18

"I wondered where you'd got to." Coming into the library, Ben leaned over Dorothea and gave her a kiss, which she returned with enthusiasm. During the two weeks since their first night together, they had slept in the same bed. Ben had overwhelmed her with passion, trying to give her all the confidence she needed to take the lead, to initiate what she wanted. But his attempts were far from altruistic. He had taken as much as he had given. In Dorothea, he had found his partner, his friend, his—

No, not that.

And nobody knew. Rougier had kept his silence and his position. He was dealing with Ben's nightly absence from his room, and despite Ben's brave words to Dorothea, the empty bed was getting ruffled.

"I'm going through these." She indicated the books. Since this was the main estate, copies of all the household accounts for all the properties Ben owned as the marquess were kept here. "The muniments room was cold, so I had a footman bring them up."

He knew what she meant. The muniments room was below ground level, in a part of the building that never seemed to get the sun. The precious papers that went back for centuries were well protected from the damp and cold, but the person occupying the room was not. He would see to having everything moved somewhere else and to hell with tradition.

He glanced at the carefully scripted columns of figures. "All these?"

Numbers fascinated him. Rapidly, he assessed what she was studying and heaved a sigh. "They're not good, are they?"

"No." She indicated an open folder, containing receipts and notes. "And they've not been kept up to date. These are the last month's notes, and they haven't been entered into the accounts yet."

"Do you suspect wrongdoing?" Had someone been embezzling?

"Not precisely. Carelessness, certainly. But Schultz is watching, or so he tells me."

Pulling out the chair next to her, he took a seat at the broad table that ran down the center of the library. This used to be the dining table when feasts had been held in the great hall, in the days of knights and ladies. The library was very old. Although thanks to Louis it had a veneer of fashion, it held ancient, handwritten books as well as modern volumes covered in tooled leather and the Belstead arms.

Bookcases interspersed the wide windows, which were covered with blinds to protect the precious volumes. The long table allowed large books to be spread out.

"There's much extravagance here, and worse."

"What's worse?"

"Dreadful waste. The cook is certainly making the best of her perquisites." Precious tea leaves and leftovers could be sold at the kitchen door.

Ben studied the figures. "I see. Do you think Louis knew?"

"I think he didn't care. As long as everything went his way. You should be glad that there are only twenty members of staff. Any more would have been even more wasteful. Why didn't he fill the house with liveried servants and pomp and grandeur?"

That was a good question, but Ben believed he had the answer. "Most of the servants are upper servants. He stinted where nobody could see it—in the kitchen, the garden, and the home farm. I've already made plans for those."

The burden of the estate had proved so much worse than he'd imagined. A large property, left to molder for years, had provided so much work, far more than he'd expected.

But he had Dorothea to help. She pointed at a few figures, and he bent to examine them. "I find several things puzzling here. This, for instance, the wine that never arrived. That's Schultz's purview, but I doubt he would do this."

"The wine that never arrived?" he queried.

"I checked. Discreetly, of course, but I took inventory and the wine never arrived. And that," She pointed to a large consignment of tea. "That didn't arrive either. Not even smuggled." The payment for smuggled goods would naturally take a different path.

"So Louis may have been embezzling."

She sighed. "It might not be Louis, but it looks that way."

"It's his writing." Ben pointed to the crossed *t*'s. "I recognize it. Now we're here, that will not be happening again."

He touched her chin, and she turned her head, ready to receive his kiss, which he gave eagerly.

As well as warming his bed at night, she helped him more than he could have expected, or had any right to. He'd changed his will, copying it twice and having it witnessed by Schultz and Rougier, who was turning out to be a good hire.

Rougier had even personally stripped Dorothea's bed after Ben's first night with her and disposed of the sheets before Ben had time to ask him to do so. He didn't want anyone gloating over something that should remain private. Not that he'd told Dorothea of it, although he would have if she'd asked him. When he questioned the valet, Rougier had confessed that he'd put the sheets in the fire. Ben gave him a bonus.

Dorothea and Ben were forming a partnership, and every day he told himself he couldn't be happier with that. Each night he pleasured her, and showed her how to please him in return, something she did with delight. But after the first few days, he'd taken an emotional step back. He would not allow her to express more than liking and happiness. Anything else would make their relationship too complicated, and he had no intention of going there again. Physical pleasure was part of what he wanted with her, but he needed to know that she could cope with this estate and the others on her own. He still intended to return to Boston for extended periods of time, and he would not be taking her with him. He needed her steady presence and intelligence here, to run the extensive Belstead lands in his absence.

Mary still haunted him. Her utter devotion, his loss of temper when she clung so close, her subsequent unhappiness, one might even call it grief, when she discovered he was avoiding her. He could not allow that to happen again. Dorothea was ten times stronger than Mary, but he wouldn't cause her such unhappiness. He'd cut his own arm off first.

Love could not become a factor between them. Friendship and mutual passion, for certain. He intended to remain faithful to her, because he despised people who did not keep their promises. Long periods of abstinence would not cause him problems. He'd gone for long periods without physical satisfaction before, except for what he could do with his own hand. He would continue in that vein if he had to.

Dorothea had acceded with the tact he admired in her. But he would have to stay longer, if only to clear up the mess she was competently handling. He couldn't let her deal with all that alone, especially if she did fall pregnant with his child. He would stay to see his baby born, of course he would. Then he'd make his first visit to Boston as brief as he could; no more than a year, including the travel time.

But to stay longer? That wasn't possible.

And he would ensure Louis never came near her again.

With a sigh, Dorothea straightened and flexed her shoulders, easing her hands over her back. "I will walk in the gardens for an hour."

Regretfully, Ben indicated the windows. "It's raining. You'll drown."

The weather had broken, and early September had brought squally showers. While the gardens drank up the rain, the remaining guests, immured indoors, were getting restless. The roads had immediately become mired in mud and the drive leading to the house was almost impassable.

"It will ease in a week or so."

"After the wedding," he reminded her softly.

"Yes. After that."

Barely a week away now.

"Ben..." She took her lower lip between her teeth.

"Hmm?" He gave her his complete attention.

A frown pleated her brow. "I—I should probably go back to my own bed tonight."

"Why?" He wouldn't force her, but he'd become accustomed to having her with him, to waking up to her sweet smile.

She swallowed. "I can tell you that I'm not—not enceinte."

Ah. "Your courses have started?"

She nodded.

That was why she'd stretched. Not just from long hours bent over account books, but the cramps that went with her condition. His jaw muscles, which had tightened in anticipation of her rejection, relaxed. "I see. But there is no reason to spend time apart, unless you'd be more comfortable that way. Come to bed in your night rail and let me warm you."

"How did you know I get chilly when..." Her voice faded. "Oh, I see."

Yes, this was not his first marriage. However, he had rarely shared a bed with Mary and never spent a whole night with her. She didn't like him in bed with her all the time; she'd said she was afraid he'd squash her and not notice. Although the fear was silly, he'd complied, and while they didn't stay apart, distance had begun to grow from that moment on.

At this stage of his relationship with Dorothea, he didn't want that to happen. "I won't force you." He took her hand, chafing it between his. It was cold. "But I'd like to help. Please join me."

She jerked a nod. "All right."

For such a private woman, that was a great leap forward. He rewarded her with a kiss.

* * * *

Every day Ben pushed her a little more, persuaded her to step out of her comfortable ways of thinking.

That had to be good. He treated her with care and consideration and, slowly, Dorothea was releasing her idea of living as a single lady. Her inevitable fate, she'd thought, but one she'd been determined to make the most of.

When he kissed her, she tingled all over, and when he spoke to her he really listened. She wasn't used to that.

As their lips separated and an intimate smile warmed his face, the sound of carriage wheels came from outside.

Dorothea frowned. "Who on earth is traveling in this weather?" She went to the window and peered out. "I can't see properly, but it's a traveling carriage for sure. Visitors?" She turned. "Who are we expecting?"

He was standing by the door. "We'd better go and find out."

Downstairs, the hall was busy. Footmen were hauling a trunk across the space, and two men were divesting themselves of their outer clothing.

Louis was back, and he'd brought Sir James with him.

Pasting a smile to her face, she took Ben's arm and they went down to greet them.

Louis, dressed in his usual finery, this time a scarlet riding habit, had a smile to match hers. "Ah, here you are. I do trust you have not turned my wife out of doors?"

"Of course not." Ben frowned. "Why would I do that? She, and you, are welcome here for as long as you wish."

No, they're not. Dorothea fought to retain her smile, although she had to fix it in place. "Of course."

"Very gracious, I'm sure."

"You may use the marquess's apartments as long as you wish," Ben said.

Sir James was not looking happy. He shook his head slightly, although Dorothea didn't know what he meant by that. "We have decided," she said, "to make our apartments in another part of the house."

"Just as well." Louis's smile turned cold. "Since you won't be the marquess after all." Louis glanced at Dorothea. "Just as well," he drawled, "since my marchioness is a better example of the kind than yours. If you intend to marry her, that is. After all, you don't have to produce an heir any longer."

Dorothea gripped Ben's arm hard. She did not want him to respond to that blatant attempt at provocation. "We will marry," Ben answered, his voice like ice. "We do not need your approval."

"Not even as head of the family? However, we may choose not to acknowledge the more disreputable element."

Beside her, Ben straightened. The atmosphere between the cousins froze. "Care to explain that?"

"Gentlemen." At last, Sir James came forward, although he had to walk around Louis to do so. "Should we not take this to a private place?"

Ben raised a dark brow. "It would be more civilized."

They were interrupted by a voice from above. "Louis, oh Louis! Oh, I have missed you! You have no idea how tedious this place is without company!"

Showing little sign of her recent indisposition, Lady Honoria, gloriously attired in pale yellow silk, hurried down the stairs, trailing her hand elegantly along the banister. She stopped a foot away from them, eyes wide. "Is there something amiss?"

"Not for us." Louis bent over his wife's hand. "But for Mr. Thorpe here, perhaps so. I am not even sure he is entitled to use our name."

Sir James sighed. "That has yet to be ascertained."

"Really?"

"The yellow parlor," Dorothea murmured. She would not stand in the hall yelling their business for everyone to hear. Her stomach tightened, and she felt ill. Something was seriously amiss here.

Pulling away from Ben, she led the way. For a few seconds she wasn't sure the others would follow, but eventually she heard the echoes of their footsteps behind her. She had that much authority then, at least.

The yellow parlor was a family room set behind the hall, close to that other chamber where Ben had found her before. But she didn't want to use that. These were rooms that belonged to the original Tudor structure, and they had lower ceilings. Dorothea liked the dark-paneled, simply furnished austerity, but she would wager her best pearls that Louis and Lady Honoria disliked them. A good reason for choosing them, because she had a feeling Ben needed all the help he could get. He was on the edge of losing his temper, especially from Louis's blatant attempt to rile him. She needed him to stay calm.

"Do I offer you my felicitations?" Louis asked. "Otherwise, I have to insist that Miss Rowland leave us."

"Next Monday," Ben said shortly, holding a high-backed chair for Dorothea, the best this small room had to offer. She accepted it. "We had the banns called the week you left."

"Unfortunate," Louis said. "You might wish to think again, Miss Rowland."

Dorothea said nothing, since the question was evidently another jab at Ben.

After helping his wife to a chair, then taking a seat himself, Louis dug into the pocket of his riding coat and brought out an oilcloth-covered parcel. He unwrapped it, revealing a sheet of paper. "It appears your parents married in haste, my dear cousin," he drawled. "They wed in London."

"Yes, they did," Ben said.

"And you were born a mere seven months later?"

Ben nodded. "Within the sanctity of marriage."

Slowly, as if sorrowful, Louis shook his head. "Except they were not married at all. The cleric who performed the office was an impostor. I have the proof." He tapped the paper. "I have the original safely at the solicitor's office, but I thought you might like to see what I have found. This is a true copy. Discovering it took quite the search, but eventually I tracked it down to a small church in an unfashionable parish." His lip turned. "A *very* unfashionable parish."

Ben clutched the back of Dorothea's chair, shifting it a fraction.

"Proof?" Dorothea said icily. "Marriages can be irregular but still legal."

"Not when the person performing the ceremony was not a recognized cleric. Handfasting is all very well for the peasants, but our kind need something more legal. The man who married your parents, Ben, saw a quick way of making money, so he posed as a vicar. But he was never ordained, and I have proof of that."

Dorothea's stomach plummeted. Ben had done much to control his temper in the last seven years, but Louis was pushing him to another confrontation.

Louis leaned back and stretched his booted feet before him. "Which of course means that I'm the Marquess of Belstead."

Dorothea's chair vibrated with the intensity of Ben's grip on it.

"That is for me to determine." Sir James stepped between the two men and shot a sharp glare at Dorothea. "I am the arbiter of this question. While the marriage you investigated was indeed invalid, probably conducted in too much haste, I found the records we have at the office. They give another date for the wedding of the last marquess, a month after the first. I want to investigate that discrepancy."

Louis waved away the statement. "I have never found any proof of that. And the current marchioness is hardly in a position to confirm it. She is quite mad."

"Not mad," Ben corrected him firmly. "My mother is not without her wits. They wander sometimes, that is all." He moved from behind Dorothea's chair, pausing to snatch up the paper. "I will look at this."

Dorothea rose, relieved Ben was leaving the scene. If he stayed, Louis would doubtless provoke him to display his anger. Nobody got to him like his cousin. Louis got under Ben's skin and poked fine needles into every sore spot. Ben's rugged face was pale with fury, and the flat line of his mouth would have made a weaker woman tremble with fear.

He did not look back, but she followed him anyway, hearing a low feminine laugh as she did so. "Fortunately, I stayed in the marchioness's chambers," Lady Honoria said, loud enough for Dorothea to hear.

She didn't care. Not very much, anyway. Ben stormed up the stairs, forcing Dorothea to lift her skirts as she scrambled after him. At the top, he turned, the very image of a powerful lord.

Even if he wasn't.

"Why do you follow me?" he demanded. "You should be running away."

She didn't reply until she joined him. She folded her arms and glared at him. "Why? Are you planning to hurt me?"

"No, of course not."

"Well, then."

He spun around and stalked to another room, the cabinet, it was called, because of the magnificent Italian cabinet of curiosities that it contained. This room was a sharp contrast to the one downstairs, the furniture gilded, delicate, exquisite, and French. At least it was clear of dust. The extra ten maids Dorothea had engaged last week had worked hard to eliminate that annoyance.

"How would your family feel about you marrying a bastard?"

She flinched. That name, so ugly, didn't describe Ben, in any sense of the word. "You're giving up?"

His upper lip turned in a sneer. "Giving up what? This place? The debts? I'm well rid of it."

When he swallowed, Dorothea recognized his pain. This house, the title, was his father's legacy to him. Ben wouldn't want to give that up. "You would disgrace your mother? Have her labeled a sinful woman by the whole of society? How do you think she will take to being called Miss..." She didn't know Ben's mother's maiden name.

"Bassington. I suppose I am a Bassington, too. Not that they would accept me any more than the Thorpes." A wealth of pain lay in his voice, held back by sheer self-will.

How could she abandon him now? How could he think that of her? "You're a Thorpe, and the Marquess of Belstead until Sir James decides otherwise. We must find the record of that other marriage."

Emitting a choked laugh, Ben turned and strode to the window, resting his clenched fists on the ledge. "I never heard of it before."

She softened her voice. "What is the story of your parents' marriage? Please tell me."

"How much do you know?"

Were there tears in his voice? Although he rarely mentioned his parents, he visited his mother every day, and she knew the disappointment he'd caused his father was a great sorrow to him. He had never said anything, but Ben was a man of honor, and when he spoke of his father, it was with reverence.

She recalled the stories, old ones, but still occasionally spoken of. "Your mother was on the brink of betrothal to another man, one she disliked. Your father came to her in her bedroom, took a brass ring from the curtain, and they eloped. Surely that is enough."

"Not if the priest was not a priest at all."

Tired of talking to his back, she went to the window and tugged at his sleeve. "Look at me, Ben. Tell me the whole."

He had his eyes tightly shut, but he opened them and turned to her. She'd never seen such a bleak expression on his features before. This wasn't the grief she'd witnessed after he'd seen his mother for the first time in seven years. This was despair. But he spoke steadily.

Dorothea faltered. He'd locked himself away. That was how he'd coped with his cousin and taken the news that his parents had not married. "I should have stayed dead. Because then Louis could have gone on his merry way wrecking the estate, and he would not have dug up this old scandal. My mother has lucid days, but once she hears this, she will retreat completely." He swallowed, his Adam's apple bobbing. "There is so little left of the woman she was. Louis will turn her out of doors or have her locked away."

"Why, when he has cared for her since you left?"

Ben's eyes sparked in fury, but Dorothea refused to retreat. That anger wasn't for her. "Because once both parties are dead, a marriage cannot be questioned. The legality or otherwise dies with them. Louis knew this was a possibility. He's always known. Otherwise he wouldn't have thought to look for the records. He may have always had them in reserve. I don't know and I'm damned if I'm going to ask him." He pulled the document out of his pocket and thrust it at her. "This was his insurance. If I returned, he had this. That was what he meant when he left. But once Sir James has verified his claim to the title, he'll have no more use for Mama."

He was right. Louis would cast the marchioness off like a broken shoe. "You will care for her." She knew that for a certainty.

A stream of thin sunlight shone through the window onto a spot on the floor. The rain had stopped.

"Yes, of course, but once people call her Miss Bassington, and she understands that she is no longer the marchioness, she will lose what is left of her mind. I cannot bear that. I've brought enough sorrow to her; I can't give her any more."

She nodded. "Then we will speak to her."

"We? Dorothea, you can't want me now."

Dorothea bridled. That was the outside of enough. "Do you think I would abandon you because of this?"

"Your family will suffer, not just you."

"Do you think they will care for that?" She knew her brother, once he heard the story, wouldn't advise her to abandon him. What a cowardly thing to do!

When she took a step forward, he retreated. "Dorothea, I have done enough damage to you. I have taken your innocence—"

Dorothea laughed, shocked by the suggestion. "No, you gave me great pleasure. Why would I regret that? And never, ever call it damage. You did no such thing. You completed me, you showed me what I had missed, what I would miss without you."

Before meeting Ben she'd been happy with her lot, or at least content. She'd planned her future. After thirty, as she always thought of it, she'd have become a true spinster. She'd even ordered spinsterish garments. They hadn't left her clothespress since Ben had first taken her to his bed, and she'd rid herself of them as soon as she could.

"Sweetheart, you're not expecting. If you were, we would have to marry."

"We still do." She put up her chin. "Not because I'm no longer a virgin, but because I...we...we *work* together. We are a team, you and I. You even said so yourself, yesterday, just after we..."

She wasn't ashamed of what they'd done, but to articulate it would be to say the word she must not utter. *Love.* The prospect of losing this man terrified her far more than losing the title, or even bearing his child out of wedlock, come to that. She loved him. But if she told him now, she would only add to his burdens. He'd feel obliged, and if—when—they married, it would not be from an obligation. God forbid that should happen.

"Yes, I remember." He gazed at her. "But Dorothea, you deserve better."

This time her laugh was bitter, mocking. "You mean a comfortable little house in Bath, with a modest group of servants and a companion for respectability? That kind of better?"

He reached out, touched her SSL pin on her bodice. She always wore it now, but nobody had asked her about it. Nevertheless, she was still proud of it. "What about this?"

"I can work for the SSL much better as a marchioness. Or the wife of a wealthy ship owner, whichever you turn out to be." She would not give him up. Absolutely refused to do it. "I would not be a single lady, but I could act as their friend."

"My fierce Dorothea," he murmured. He slid his hand to her shoulder. "I have no right to drag you into this mess. You have no idea..."

"Yes, I do."

He let his gaze roam over her, murmuring to himself. "Yes, we could do that. I'm someone else in the colonies, and nobody cares if I am a bastard or not. Only how rich I am."

Oh, thank God, he was beginning to reason again. She'd thought that despair would last, that he might give up the fight. "Yes."

"Would you really come with me? Boston is a civilized city, with many similarities to life here, but not as..." He sought for a word but gave up. "I cannot ask you to leave everything."

"There's only my brother and sister-in-law. I wouldn't miss anything else."

Naturally she would, but she wasn't about to tell him that. Her friends, the comfort of life with people she knew, the countryside, her family home...any number of things, but with Ben she could do something new.

And she'd be with the man she loved.

Oh Lord, yes. She loved him. She'd never stopped. Her youthful passion had returned threefold when he'd returned, as if it was only dormant. Then, with the added attention and the unwanted spike of danger, her emotions had become deeply involved. She couldn't untangle herself from him now. It would kill her to try.

Although he didn't love her. She suspected he'd fallen deeply for Mary, and her loss had killed the desire in him to get as close to anyone ever again. She couldn't compete with a dead woman. But he was fond of her, and he respected her. That would *have* to be enough.

Ben's regard was worth so much more than another man's adoration.

"So you'd leave," she said dully.

"For good," he confirmed. "After I've ensured my mother is comfortable and cared for. I might have to move her out of this place, the home she's known all her life, but I'll do my best to help her."

For good. Yes, although the notion filled her with fear and regret, Dorothea would go with him.

If he saw any hesitation in her, he'd leave her behind. That didn't bear thinking about. She couldn't allow this opportunity to slip through her fingers. "I'll come with you. Let the marriage arrangements stand."

He heaved a sigh. "Very well. For now."

She'd won the first battle, but there would be more ahead. Dorothea braced herself and prepared her mental armor. "I think," she said, "that you should go and see your mother, before Louis scares her half to death."

Chapter 19

Ben's visits to his mother were the best and the worst parts of his day. Sometimes she knew him; other times she mistook him for his father, and increasingly, she didn't recognize him at all. There was no way of knowing, no pattern, and that made entering her room fraught. But he persevered because of love and guilt. He had not understood how ill she was, or how rapid her deterioration would be.

He would visit her every day until he died, or she did, and that made the fight with Louis more important, not less.

Despite his forbidding her to do so, Dorothea followed him when he left for her rooms, and refused to stay behind. "I will listen, I promise," she told him. "Nothing else."

Sighing, he stopped and waited for her to catch up with him, then when she reached for his hand, he let her take it. He would not deny she comforted him and bolstered him in this time. But it was not fair to her. She had already allowed him far more than he should have taken. Now she wanted to give more.

After a soft tap on the door, he opened it and went in. As usual, the drapes were pulled halfway across the windows, but now the rain had stopped, bright sunlight streamed in.

Today his mother was sitting by the lit fire, her maid in close attendance. She turned her head and as always, instinctively, Ben expected her to welcome him. The constant disappointments crushed him, but he could not direct himself to stop expecting anything from her, other than the vague, "Who are you?"

But the light of recognition warmed him today. "Ah, Benedict. Do come in. Who is this lady?"

Shock reverberated through him. Today of all days, she knew him. As Dorothea made her curtsy, he introduced her again.

"It is right that you marry. It is time."

He'd never told her about Mary and his son. The nurse had informed him that the boy's chest moved once at birth, and that was enough to have him buried as a living being. Ben had found that a comfort in the pit of his despair after their loss. Now he merely said, "Yes, Mama. Dorothea is the daughter of Viscount Sandigate."

"A good, solid choice." The marchioness gestured to the chairs her companion had set ready in a way he remembered from his youth. The memory was so vivid, the tears rose in his throat. He'd sat in a chair very much like the one he used now, but back then his feet hadn't touched the floor. She'd read to him or have him read to her. She was not the kind of mother who had her child brought to her once a day and never visited the nursery or schoolroom.

He missed those days. If he was fortunate enough to have more children, he would treat them the same way, and talk about his mother as she was then. As she was for a brief time today.

Next to him, Dorothea sat quietly, her hands folded in her lap. But he felt her presence as if she had her arms around him, supporting him.

Today he could not afford to bask in the past. At any minute she could lose her concentration and fade into a hazy version of the woman who had run the estate so well for so long. "Mama, do you remember marrying my father?"

Her tinkling laugh filled the room. "Well, what a question to ask! Of course I do! My dear, we ran away together. Caused quite the scandal at the time." She frowned. "I feel sure I've told you this before."

When he paused, Dorothea said, "He wanted to tell me, your ladyship, but he could not remember all the details."

The gentle prompt did the trick. "Of course, you would not know everything. We married in a little church in the East End of London, the day after my father ordered me to marry old Lord Norris. He was a terrible roué, riddled with all kinds of unmentionable diseases, but he was a friend of my father's and a political ally, so Papa wanted to unite the families. And Norris needed a healthy woman to bear him sons. He had two already, both older than me."

She shuddered, but before her maid could reach her, she continued. "Thomas said we should elope, and I accepted. We went to the Fleet and found a cleric. A dirty individual, but he had been there a long time. Not at all the kind of person we should encourage, reeked of brandy. We paid his debts, which didn't amount to much, and went to the church we'd found. But he married us, and we set out for this house, to wait out the scandal." She bit her lip. "But the vicar, old Mr. Scarsdale, would not accept us as married. An irregular marriage, he said, was worse than none at all. He said he would repeat it."

"Did you do so, Mama?"

She looked around and found her maid. "I'm thirsty."

"You have your barley water, ma'am, and your tea will arrive soon."

As if by demand, the clock on the mantelpiece struck the half hour.

Lord, they were so close! "Did Mr. Scarsdale perform another ceremony, Mama?"

"Scarsdale?" Although his mother appeared the same as she was five minutes ago, her blue eyes had lost focus. She licked her lips. "Thirsty."

Her companion picked up a glass filled with cloudy liquid and held it to her lips. As she drank, she blinked, and looked around. A thread of liquid trickled out of the corner of her mouth and the maid gently dabbed it away.

Her ladyship gave her son a broad smile. "Tom, what are you doing here? I thought you were in London. Where is my maid? The girl can't keep still for five minutes. I need to discuss something with Mrs. Catchpole, would you find her for me?"

The rambling heralded the end of her lucidity. She carried on for a while, dodging from one subject to another and back again, slowly losing her senses and the thread of her discussion.

"Her ladyship will have her tea, and then she will nap," Miss Sullivan said. She got to her feet. "I will see if the tea is here. It does not always arrive when it should."

"I will make sure it gets here on time in future," Dorothea said firmly, getting to her feet, which meant Ben had to stand, too. But she was right. His mother was tired, and she was losing what concentration she had. They would discover no more from her today.

After leaving the room, he leaned against the wall and pinched the bridge of his nose. "I cannot believe my mother has come to this."

"People do," Dorothea said softly.

He expected her to launch into a story about her aunt, or cousin or some such, but she did not, although most people did that. Then he would be forced to sympathize with her, as if two tragedies made the first one better. But she did not. He was grateful to her for that. "She was sharp, bright, always interested in what went on around her. And yet she only leaves her room to walk in the gardens with Miss Sullivan when the weather is good. She was feted as one of London's greatest hostesses. She fought her way back from their scandalous marriage by sheer power of her personality. If she can suffer this, what does it say for the rest of us?"

"How old is your mother?"

He sighed and forced himself to concentrate. "Sixty-five. The same age as my father would be if he'd lived. From what I can gather from Schultz, her deterioration worsened after his death."

Turning away, he strode along the passageway, heading for the stairs, his heart heavy with grief and helplessness. He could do nothing. Nobody had an answer for senility. She should not suffer this at her age, surely, but she was, and nobody could halt it.

"I will take a walk around the gardens, if it's not too muddy. Taking tea in the drawing room does not appeal to me at the moment."

She even read his mind about that. "I will accompany you. We both need some fresh air."

Instead of them separating to find outer clothing, Schultz had cloaks, hats, and gloves ready for them, as if he'd read their minds. The staff helped them into their outerwear. Dorothea was already wearing a sensible day gown, the dark blue skirt ankle-length. She donned her sturdy black leather shoes in the hall, allowing a maid to fasten her buckles for her.

It struck Ben that he preferred Dorothea in a sensible, practical outfit than any fashionable lady in powder and delicate silk. She was far better suited to being a wife of a Boston merchant than she was a marchioness, where she would face many situations that would bore her silly. Not to mention the clothes. Dorothea dressed simply but with elegance.

But because of the change in circumstances, he had to give her the choice, and that was killing him. She might not want to leave the country, a big step by anybody's reckoning, and with events as they were, Ben doubted he would ever want to come back.

* * * *

Dorothea did not have to be a mind reader to know how agitated Ben was. He would not meet her eyes and he shut himself off, but at least he had offered to walk with her. If she pushed him too far, he would not talk to her, but the matter was growing more urgent. She would see if Sir James would speak to her.

With her arm resting on his sleeve, they strolled along the paths, which were distinctly less overgrown than they'd been when they arrived. The new gardeners were making their mark. The gravel was raked properly and the roses were neatly pruned, except the few late bloomers. Their scent wafted in the air, a faint reminder of the glory that had passed.

Ben drew a deep breath. He always did that when he was about to broach an uncomfortable subject. "So, Louis will be the next marquess after all. In that case, I will leave the country. I doubt I would ever return. My mother's memory is fading day by day, getting worse. Soon, she will not recognize me at all, but I will take advice and see if it is advisable to take her with me. Nobody needs me here, or even wants me. Society would prefer to forget me. I have a good life in Boston. I'm a respected member of society, and wealthy. Nobody there will care if I am illegitimate or not, because my reputation and standing is entirely different."

She turned her head. "I said I would go with you."

He nodded. "I remember. But the colonies are a long way away, and I doubt I would ever want to come back. You have people here who love you. Please think about what you're doing. I won't hold it against you if you decide to remain. Without me here you would be safe. Nobody would be trying to kill me anymore. They have what they want." He met her eyes frankly. She loved that about him, that Ben did not hesitate to tell the truth, however painful.

He was asking her if she wanted to leave her family for good, to travel halfway across the world with him and start an entirely new life.

Why would he even ask? She had pledged herself to him; she loved him. And as much as she loved her family and her country, the prospect of traveling with him gave her a new impetus: excitement.

She turned to face him, holding out her hands. Ben took them in his. She drew a deep breath, gathering her courage.

"Ben, I have fallen in love with you. I know you did not ask for it, and I don't expect anything in return, but I have. But I need some indication of your feelings for me."

He stared at her, his expression going flat. "Is love so important?"

Her heart plummeted down to her stomach. He didn't love her, then. "To me it is." Now she had found it, she didn't want to lose it, but if he merely tolerated her, she couldn't consider what he was asking. "I know you loved your wife. I understand, but is there any prospect that you might come to...?"

Unwilling to beg, she stopped.

He frowned. "Yes, I told you I loved Mary, didn't I?"

"You always speak of her with such reverence. I know she is in a place in your heart that I can never touch, but I would like to think that someday there might be another place, for me."

Her stomach churned. If he said no, what would she do?

He heaved a heavy sigh and looked away, as if avoiding her gaze. "I need to tell you about Mary. She was pretty, fragile, charming, tiny, a perfect catch. And she loved me. She said so, often." He swallowed, then opened his mouth again to continue.

Whatever he planned to say next was lost in the cheery greeting from his best friend. Dorothea cursed Lord Evington, but she did it silently, since Ben turned to him in what she suspected was relief.

"Hal! You decided to brave the mud, then?"

"I did." Lord Evington had declared his intention of going for a ride that morning. Apparently he had changed, since he wore clean clothes. His green coat went beautifully with the distant hills. He raised his hat. "Morning, Miss Rowland." He glanced at Ben. "Oh no, did I interrupt something? Wish me to perdition and I'll go straight there."

"Not at all," Ben said before Dorothea had a chance to say anything. "We were just planning our future. I have given Dorothea something to ponder."

"Really?" Lord Evington scowled. "I won't ask what it is. I came to tell you that that scoundrel Thorpe is raising hell in the house."

"In what way?"

Evington turned back and waved at the upper story, where someone was opening curtains, then winced and pulled his arm back to his side. He was still experiencing some discomfort, then. "He is crossing out names on your guest list and adding his own guests. He's also ordered the rooms you desired opened and cleaned to be closed up again."

"Assumptions he is not entitled to," Dorothea said. Anger rose inside her. Why would Louis want to undo all their work? Did he hate Ben that much? "I will insist the household continues to run as I have set it."

Ben smiled. "I'm sure you will. But the documents appear conclusive. I'm ready to revert to plain Mr. Thorpe once more."

Hal glared at Ben, his eyes wide, the lines at the corners of his mouth deep. "You'll give up?"

Ben lost the smile. He shrugged. "I can't argue with the facts."

"So you'll abandon all this?" Hal jutted his chin forward belligerently. "The place your ancestors built, all the people that depend on you and your estates? You know Louis will lay waste to it all. He'll spend himself to a standstill, then he'll mortgage what is left. Not only does that degrade the title, it degrades the country, too. And your family. You'll give up without a fight? This isn't just about you, Ben."

He flicked a glance at Dorothea. "You have the perfect marchioness, a woman with poise and intelligence. You'll take all this away from her, too?"

"What would fighting do?" Ben exploded then, his hands flying up from his sides. "Would that bring credit to the family name? And if I am a bastard, what then? I can do nothing about that, nothing!"

"But you might not be. That discrepancy in the dates."

"It's because he doesn't want it." In a flash, Dorothea knew what was wrong. "He never wanted the title, not after he found his own life. Making your own future, I understand that. That's what I did when I accepted Angela Childers's offer to become one of her agents."

"What?" Now she'd garnered the attention of Lord Evington. "What are you talking about?"

"This." She touched the silver pin on her shoulder. "Who sees and isn't noticed? Who is so much a part of the scenery that nobody remembers if they were there or not?" She pointed at herself. "The single lady. Miss Childers comes across many problems we can help with."

"Good God," Evington drawled. "I will never look at a poor relation the same way again."

At least she'd calmed the two men down.

"Excellent." Dorothea faced him, eye to eye. Being of a height helped, but she would have done the same had she been four feet tall. "I wouldn't, if I were you. But if you've done nothing wrong, you have nothing to fear."

After a fraught silence, his lordship threw back his head and howled with laughter. "Oh, that's rich! Perfect!" He held out his hand. When Dorothea put hers in it, he did not raise it to his lips, or bow, or some such obeisance; he shook it.

That gesture meant more to her than anything else he could have done.

"I love that. Am I to keep this to myself?"

"By no means," she said. "We discussed this at the last meeting before I left London. We want people to know where to come, who to contact. We are acting for Miss Childers, but we could help others."

"I admire that, I truly do," his lordship said.

"You would not be my friend if you did not," Ben put in. "Dorothea is a resourceful woman."

Not what she wanted him to say, but she was glad of it anyway.

His lordship gestured to Ben but spoke to Dorothea. "What will you do about this? Will you accept the situation?"

Emboldened by Lord Evington's question, she shook her head. She had been ready to give everything up. Used to sitting in the background, being overlooked, she had shaped her reactions accordingly. But she had a band of people to support her now, and the courage of her own convictions. "No." She spared Ben a glance. "I will ensure justice is done. That discrepancy of dates is significant, I'm sure of it. It was a month and a few days after the original ceremony, which does appear to have been invalid." She sent him an apologetic, wry smile, but he was watching her, a gleam in his eyes that she couldn't interpret. "Ben has asked me if I want to marry Mr. Thorpe and move to Boston with him. If I have to, then I will." The decision filled her with trepidation, but she wouldn't allow anyone to see it. That was for her alone to know. "But I will first do everything I can to ensure he is not cheated out of this."

"But I don't want it," Ben said.

"It is not yours to turn down." A title belonged to the person inheriting it. "You may choose to turn your back on it, to appoint a manager, to call yourself Mr. Thorpe. Nobody can stop you doing that. But you will be the marquess until the day of your death, and your son will inherit. If you have one," she added hastily. Because if he meant it, and he still wanted her to marry him, she would have to fulfill that duty.

"I cannot imagine you not bearing fine sons." His voice softened, he stepped toward her and took her hand. "I am honored that you chose me, Dorothea. I would be the luckiest man alive if you decided to go ahead with the marriage." He smiled. "But the choice is yours."

"I've chosen." She would stand by her promise. Not least because she loved him.

Chapter 20

The muniments room was not the finest space in the house, but it contained the family's greatest treasures. It was situated at the end of the old part of the building, down a level, in an area Ben told Dorothea had been in existence since Cressbrook House was built. Perhaps before then.

She repressed a shiver when she entered, wishing she'd kept her cloak on, or at least brought a shawl. The room was lined with stone, its windows high up and only barely exposed to the light, certainly not big enough for a person to gain entrance, not even a contortionist like one of those children thieves were said to use to gain ingress into small spaces.

A large iron safe was set into one wall, and an ancient chest was pushed next to it, forming a rudimentary seat. The large, scarred oak desk held a plethora of papers, and crudely built glass-front bookcases contained folders and documents, some of them leather bound. Two worn chairs and an oil lamp were set next to an unlit branch of candles.

"Goodness, this is secure!" Dorothea exchanged a glance with Sir James, who had followed Ben and Dorothea in.

"Family legend has it that it was used as a prison cell to hold wrongdoers before their trial," Ben said. "It's dank enough."

Collecting a tinderbox off the table, he busied himself lighting the candles, casting a warm glow over the scene. It didn't help a great deal. Dorothea touched a folder, drifted her fingers over it.

"That's my father's will," Ben said. "It's straightforward enough; it leaves everything to me."

"Does the estate have much unentailed property?" asked Sir James.

"It's about half entailed and half not. I am entitled to the unentailed part, whether I am legitimate or not, since my father's will left it to me."

"So if the title went to Louis, half the estate would be yours."

Ben nodded. "Yes, it would. I could save some of it, anyway. Unless Louis found a way to dissipate that as well. He's borrowed on the expectation, but while I was considered still alive he couldn't sell it." He touched a large tome that looked very old, the leather cracked with age. "Here's the inventory of this house. Each part of the estate has a separate list, and the estate manager is supposed to aggregate them every year and prepare a report for the marquess. I have no idea if this has been done, but Schultz assures me that a man came up from London every six months to keep the records up to date."

Sir James frowned. "I would have thought an estate this size would have a permanent person in charge of recording the inventories. A secretary, or the estate manager."

"I have someone doing something similar for my business," Ben said. "If we find what we're looking for, I will ensure that will happen again."

"Then let us pray we find something," Sir James said.

"In what circumstances would the title become Ben's?" Dorothea asked the officer.

"If we discover that his parents remarried before his birth, making the marriage valid." He lifted his hands. "I will have to report this to the Lord Chancellor, as it is his decision that counts. Unfortunately, Lord Hardwicke dislikes irregular marriages exceedingly. He is working toward an entirely new law that will make marriage a regular and more defined state. It has been his obsession for years. So to him, an irregular marriage is an illegal one."

"There is no doubt the man who wed them was a fraud?"

"None at all, I'm afraid. He was a notorious impersonator, gaining money from his transactions. Many people were caught out by his antics." Sir James sighed. "The situation is made difficult by the fact that the man was a well-known fraudster."

"What about handfasting?" Ben put in. At least he was trying. Hal's angry speech must have roused him to action. "If a couple declare themselves married, is that not enough?"

"Not in his lordship's eyes, though you could test it in court. But what is done is done. If the title is awarded to your cousin and later the decision is found to be faulty, it is unlikely he will lose the marquessate. Possession is nine-tenths of the law."

Ben heaved a sigh. "I do not want to hold this family up to recrimination and ridicule. A court case could take years and prove ruinously expensive for all."

"True," Sir James agreed.

"I would rather the decision was made quickly. For my part, I will not question it, if it goes against me. I cannot speak for my cousin's reaction, of course, but if the decision is for me, at least the title and lands will not be his to use and abuse." He plucked a bound volume off the shelf. "This is the register of the family's personal documents from this century, so the last fifty years. If there are marriage certificates, they should be here. These are not the originals, but copies, and a recording of where the originals are held."

Sir James rubbed his hands together. "Ah!"

Clearing a space on the table, Ben set the candelabrum there and placed the book below it. Together, all three looked on as he turned the pages. His grandfather's marriage and the records of the children born to him and his wife were faithfully registered there. Almost all had the original records as "In St. Edmund's," which was the parish church where Dorothea and Ben were to marry next Monday, or "At Mr. Exeter's." In most cases, both places were named.

The third marquess had a quiverful of children, but only three were boys.

"I never knew my grandfather," Ben said. "He died before I was born. My father was the marquess when I came into the world. But I had a herd of great-aunts. Still have three. They have all sent their warm regards but prefer to keep their distance. Two uncles, both of whom have died. Louis and William are Uncle Alexander's sons. My other uncle has no children, or no legitimate ones, at any rate. He is abroad, serving in the diplomatic corps. As matters stand, he is the heir after Louis."

"Ah yes, I met him once. A perspicacious man, fond of detail," Sir James said. "He is in Constantinople, is he not?"

"He is. He is not married, nor likely to be so."

Dorothea read every one of the carefully written lines. Ben's uncle had the right of it, at least where records of this nature were concerned. Detail was all-important. They outlined the story of a family, and if she'd had more time, she'd have enjoyed exploring the volumes. Her imagination filled in the gaps. The generation that had girl after girl until the precious boy came along, then had two more. Their poor mother must have been exhausted by that time. "I have heard some women can have children like shelling peas. I have never met one."

Ben touched her shoulder. "A man should not demand that of a woman."

"Perhaps he did not. She could have been the one to insist."

He sighed. "You're right. They were both formidable people, by all accounts. My grandmother lived to see me born, but I don't remember her. By all accounts, she was not a fond mama. More the kind that had her children brought to her once a day so she might quiz them on what she considered important."

Dorothea could imagine what that was. Her parents had been the other kind, the ones who did not abandon their children to servants. She remembered her father as a kind and loving man, who had taught his children the standards they strove to live up to.

Ben turned the page. The left-hand side contained the accounts of Ben's grandfather's death, and his will with the bequests to the servants, good causes and...

After that—nothing. The facing page was blank.

"Shouldn't your parents' marriage be here? The settlement and your birth?"

"They should."

Ben ran a finger down the center of the book, sucked in a sharp breath and drew his finger away. A streak of blood marred the flesh. Dorothea found her handkerchief and passed it to him in silence.

"Someone cut out the page," she said numbly.

"Indeed." Sir James examined the book for himself, more carefully than Ben had done, and came away without a paper cut. "That means there is a need to examine this issue. It also means this book was tampered with recently, or the paper wouldn't have been sharp enough to nick you."

Ben shot a quizzical glance at him, but Dorothea understood. "If the records confirmed Louis's story, there would have been no need to remove them."

"I don't have to ask you if you removed them, do I?" Sir James asked Ben.

At least the officer understood who he was dealing with. "No, you do not. I came back because I had to. I am not a poor man, and if I inherit the title, it would be more of an inconvenience than otherwise. You have, I take it, investigated my business?"

Sir James nodded. "Naturally."

"What do we do now?" Dorothea asked.

"We must continue to investigate. Discover who has taken this sheet, and if the originals are safe."

"I doubt that." Ben closed the book with extravagant care and stared down at the leather cover, which had his coat of arms stamped on it. With the tip of his finger, he traced the lines of the stag that formed one of the supporters. "Louis went down to London, where our man of business holds copies. And if he has not visited the vicar in the village, who holds the parish records, I'd be shocked. He has systematically destroyed any rebuttal we might have."

"What do we do now?" Dorothea wondered. "Apart from hunting for the records."

"I will consider that." Sir James took one last look at the book, then walked toward the door. "Currently, I intend to order a pot of tea and a fire in my room. I'm chilled to the bone."

Ben watched him leave. "It appears I might be the marquess after all. I would have preferred to draw a line under the matter, one way or another." Reaching out, he drew her close, and Dorothea went as if she belonged there. Which she did.

"I won't hold you to our arrangement," he murmured, his lips against her hair, "but I am looking forward to showing you Boston one day. I think you will like it."

* * * *

Upstairs, the house was in a bustle. Footmen were hauling traveling trunks across the hall, and people stood gossiping. At least eight, by Dorothea's swift count.

"Mr. Thorpe is planning a ball to celebrate his accession to the title. Mrs. Thorpe is quite revitalized."

"I'll wager she is," Ben said grimly. He took Dorothea upstairs, where, fortunately, nobody had been placed in what they were beginning to regard as their part of the house.

An hour later, Dorothea entered the drawing room to a slight hush. She had expected that. People would be talking about her. She even caught a few pitying glances sent her way. Assuming an air of quiet dignity did not come naturally to her any longer. But she did her best, and went to join her brother and sister-in-law where they stood by the fire.

"You look in fine fettle tonight," Ann remarked.

Dorothea glanced down at her clothing. As usual, she was plainly dressed, but her deep blue gown was in the latest fashion, with its smaller hoop and delicate pattern, and her white damask petticoat was a recent purchase. Still, she'd worn them before.

Her luggage had arrived today. Because of her expected marriage, she had sent for her belongings. The contents of her wardrobe had arrived, and the maid Ben had assigned to her had spent the afternoon unpacking them. Soon her books would come. She looked forward to that.

A strong perfume wafted over her. "Dear Miss Rowland, do you intend to go ahead with your planned ceremony?" Lady Steeping waved her fan, which only sent a stronger gust of the sickly aroma in Dorothea's direction. "After all, circumstances have changed."

Dorothea didn't hesitate in her reply. "But the man I promised to marry has not changed. And isn't that the most important consideration?"

Most people in the room would have said no, and cited standing and wealth, but she dared them to articulate it.

Lady Steeping favored her with an amused titter. "Some might say so. However, the man is only part of the bargain. I must say he is a bear of a man, if one likes that kind of thing, and he's been most gracious in his conduct. That does make me think better of him."

Considering what Ben had said to Lady Steeping the other day, her words surprised Dorothea. Perhaps they were for someone else's benefit. Sir James stood on the other side of the room while Louis Thorpe talked to him, or rather, talked *at* him. What was he saying? What had Sir James told him?

"Thank you."

Conversation started up again and passed on to town gossip, which Dorothea would not deny she had missed. She would miss it all the more if she went to Boston. However, they probably had their own society gossip. She could not imagine a situation where people would not listen avidly to other people's business.

Ben entered, a lady by his side and the Earl of Marston, commonly known as Mars, on the other. Marston's dark good looks were balanced by his modest fortune. Few people knew how hard he was working to restore the depredations made on his estate by the previous holder. Dorothea only knew because Mars had a tendre for Angela Childers, and so she'd seen more of him than many people.

Dorothea was delighted to see them both. Surging forward and knocking everyone out of the way would not have been acceptable. Therefore, she had to wait for them to make their way over to where she stood.

Ben smiled at her, an intimate caress that warmed her. Then he set himself to work his way past the guests, all of whom craved a word or two with him.

Eventually, Dorothea could embrace her friend. "Angela! I am so happy to see you!"

Angela, as beautiful and fashionable as ever, returned the hug warmly. "After your last letter I could hardly stay away, could I?"

Ignoring Louis's glare, Angela flicked open her fan with careless elegance and plied it gently, the brilliants set into the pattern flashing in the sunlight. At this time of year sunset wouldn't occur for three hours or so yet, and the curtains remained open.

As always, Angela displayed her considerable wealth in the subtlest of ways. But everyone knew the fine pearls around her neck were not fish scale and glass beads, and the diamonds in her hair owed nothing to the glassmaker. She wore them with careless elegance, but nobody would miss the message. Although she had one foot in the City of London and the other in Mayfair, she belonged equally in both places.

After she had made her curtsy to Lord Marston, Ben bent over Dorothea's hand, his lips grazing her skin and raising the inevitable thrill along her nerves in response. "Did I do well to bring her to you?"

"Did you know she was coming?"

He rumbled a laugh. "Not until she arrived in the wake of Sir James and Louis."

"She threw the Duke of Devonshire's house into complete disarray," Lord Marston added. He was as tall as Ben, and as powerfully built, but in Dorothea's eyes, not nearly so handsome. "I offered to escort her."

Angela threw him a roguish glance. "I thought better to allow that than to have you trailing behind."

Marston raised a dark brow. "Like a pathetic puppy?"

"I can think of many people who would appear that way, but not you." Angela raised a laugh with that comment.

"Why the haste?" Dorothea asked her.

"How could I stay away from your wedding?" Angela demanded.

Her exquisite presence had created quite a stir. Louis was definitely not pleased to see her, but he was making his way across the room to her when Schultz entered and announced that dinner was served.

Formality dictated the order people processed in to the dining room, and where they sat. Since two claimants to the marquessate were present, there was some hesitation. "I suggest that we use our current status," Louis said. "You are the superior by age, cousin, so you may go in first."

His wife smirked.

Dorothea went in with Ben, who had merely nodded his agreement. That put him in a dilemma. Did he claim the head of the table, or leave it for Louis? To do the first would be to assume his claim, but not to do it would cede the ground to his cousin.

His solution was to accept the head, which he was almost bound to do. But he gave Dorothea the place by his side, instead of at the bottom of the table, which the marchioness would automatically assume. She left that to Lady Honoria, who took it reluctantly.

Honor was served.

Angela sat opposite, on Ben's other side. The chatter was lively, everyone avoiding the fraught topic they had all arrived to witness, until Lady Steeping stepped in where angels, and Angela, refused to tread.

"So, Sir James, do you intend to keep us all in suspense about your decision? Will you bestow the title on Louis Thorpe, or his cousin?"

Conversation stilled. Lady Steeping lifted her glass of white wine and fixed her bright blue gaze on Sir James. "Indeed, you really must tell us, sir! Surely now the marriage of poor Mr. Benedict Thorpe's parents has been declared invalid, the decision is made for you?"

Sir James took his time replying. He put his knife and fork crossways on the plate. Louis had ordered the most elaborate set to be pressed into service again. The gold gleamed balefully, and Dorothea could not help reflecting on what she would have done with the money Louis had frittered away on it. The green drawing room needed new drapes, for one thing. Louis was all show, no substance.

"Not at all," Sir James said. "There is a discrepancy in the dates of the wedding, enough to indicate that another wedding might have taken place. I cannot discount that possibility."

A low murmur started up.

Sir James glanced around the table, pausing at Ben, and then Louis. "Naturally, I will inform the parties concerned when I have made my decision, but I am only discerning the truth and listing the evidence. It is only a recommendation. The King has expressed his interest in the affair, but the title must be awarded according to the rules set down in the letters patent. His opinion is only peripheral."

"What is his majesty's opinion?" Lady Steeping leaned forward, bringing her ruffled bodice perilously close to the sauce boat set before her plate.

"I cannot possibly betray the King's confidence."

Sir James first gave Louis his attention, then Ben. He smiled at Ben. That was enough. Dorothea didn't care what the King wanted, or even why Sir James hadn't mentioned it before, but that look gave Ben the advantage, and she was glad.

Sir James sipped his wine and put the glass back in its spot. "Some would say the suspicion of a second marriage was enough. Others would recall that handfasting is sometimes sufficient to seal a bargain. At the Royal Exchange, thousands are contracted on a mere handshake."

The gentle sound of silver on porcelain accompanied the discussion. Lord Steeping laughed. He was a hearty man who cared little for nuance. "If you believe that, why not say so, man? For God's sake, is this a game to you?"

"Besides," Louis put in quietly, sparing Ben a glance. "My cousin has become a prosperous merchant. He has a tidy business to return to. Perhaps we should allow him to do that. I have to admit I do admire your achievements, but the colonies are so far away. No doubt you are well respected in your little community."

"No doubt," Ben answered, unruffled. "But I do not intend to abandon what I have built in the last seven years, whatever the outcome of this dispute."

"That is up to you." Louis's smile was smooth. "It can hardly affect what is happening over here."

Ben raised a black brow. "Do you think so? Louis, do you remember selling the merchant traders my father used to own?"

"I do. They were not raising the profit I expected."

More likely, the ships were an easy way of making money.

"Six fine ships, newly refurbished. They came at a good time for me, since I had put some of my fleet into dry dock for repairs. And the price was so good, how could I refuse to buy them?"

"*You* bought them? But the price was—"

Ben stopped Louis mentioning the amount. "A bargain. Almost enough for me to believe you knew I was behind the sale, but of course, you could not. That was before my father-in-law passed away and I took sole control of the company."

Louis's jaw dropped. "You own Foulson's Shipping?"

"I do."

"How can that be?"

Ben smiled. "A combination of hard work and marrying the owner's daughter." He glanced at Dorothea, checking with her before he said anything further. She gave him a brief nod, agreeing to him revealing more. "The bargain was to both our advantages. I was not anxious to make my presence known, since I had every intention of leaving my mistakes behind and starting anew."

"Good Lord!" Lord Steeping had a reputation for intemperate language, but if he had not made an exclamation, someone else might have done. "You see reports of that company every day in the newspapers! You own that, sir? Why, then, do you want the marquessate?"

The implication was, after Louis had laid the title to waste.

"Honor," Ben said simply. "If I am to inherit the title from my father, then I will not abandon my duty."

"Glad to hear it, sir. One must always put one's country first."

As if half the people sitting at the table tonight didn't think of themselves before country, or how they could benefit from their service. Dorothea sipped her wine and allowed the footman to remove her plate. The servants quietly set about clearing the course in preparation for the next one.

"I do plan to change the company name," Ben said. "Now my father-in-law and my wife are no more, I am the sole owner. Thorpe and Foulson has a good ring to it."

"It does, sir. But you would not need the company, surely, once you inherit."

Ben merely lifted his brow and leaned back to give the footman access to the tureen at his elbow. Gossip would carry the news of Ben's wealth, and soon everyone would know. The villagers would prefer Ben in charge, surely, considering the state of their cottages. Ben was turning the tide in his favor. If Sir James could find for him, he would do so.

But Sir James was a fussbudget, and he would work to ensure the correct decision was made. By which, he would mean not the person who could do the most for the title and estate, but the one who had it by right. Which currently appeared to be the person who wanted to take it apart.

Chapter 21

A bloodcurdling scream woke Dorothea from a deep slumber. Ben's arms tightened around her, and he cursed. "What in all Hades was that?"

Light was seeping in through the crack between the curtains as Ben pulled his watch from underneath his pillow. "It's a quarter past seven. Has a maid dropped a chamber pot?"

His prosaic suggestion helped to calm Dorothea, who was not used to being woken up like that. After a night when Ben had collected her from her room and deposited her firmly in his bed, she was feeling cherished. She wasn't sure what to do with the emotion.

Nobody cherished her. As she was still in the throes of her monthly courses, she'd assumed Ben would prefer not to be with her and had prepared for bed in her own room. Bundled up like a baby, wrapped in layers of cloth and her night rail on top, she'd protested in vain. "You need warmth, and I intend to provide it. Besides, I find that I sleep better with you."

Now, her fuddled senses scattered, she was prepared for the worst. The house tumbling down at the very least. She never woke well.

Scrambling out of bed, she threw on her robe, tying the belt hastily and reaching for the buttons. She shoved her feet into her soft shoes and went to the door, but Ben, attired in that jaw-dropping dark blue banyan, arrived before her and opened it. "If I say run, you run back here and bolt the door. Understand?"

He had a pistol in his hand.

"What? You think there's trouble?"

He gave a mirthless laugh. "With all that's been happening recently? At the instant I say it, come back here, do you understand?" He glared at her fiercely.

Oh. "Yes," she said meekly, although other circumstances would have had her answering differently. "Do you have another pistol?"

"Not loaded, no."

"Pity."

He eyed her with consideration. "I'll make sure there are two available next time. If there is a next time."

He went first, waving her behind him. Amused by his masculine assertion of control, especially if it turned out a maid *had* dropped a chamber pot, she followed him. He would feel safer if she was behind him. Perhaps he needed to protect her, who knew? Men had the most foolish notions sometimes.

More people were about, including Hal, and farther along, William Thorpe. As they turned into the main corridor on this floor, other guests were hurrying in the same direction. And then they heard another scream.

Her brother emerged from his new bedroom, glanced at her, then Ben, and flicked his gaze up in an exasperated expression, but he said nothing. He, too, carried a pistol. Lady Steeping and her husband emerged, then Lord Marston, then Sir James. "What on earth is happening?"

Everyone was in undress, either nightclothes or a loose robe. Dorothea marked the people they met and when they joined the group, because she might have to remember later. Her heart was pounding against her chest by now; something was badly wrong, she sensed it.

Angela joined them and handed Dorothea a loaded weapon. Dorothea breathed her thanks.

As they approached the suite occupied by Louis and Lady Honoria, the door was flung open and Lady Honoria's maid raced out, straight into Ben's arms. He set the woman aside without speaking, and, grim-faced, strode into the room.

Nobody waited for an invitation.

The boudoir, which seemed perfectly in order, led into the bedroom that traditionally belonged to the marquess. Ben was first through, followed closely by Hal and William. After a cry of "Good God!" Ben came back to the door, but Dorothea would have none of it. She met his gaze, challenging him to keep her out.

"The ladies should not see this," he said, his voice shaking. His eyes were wide, and they had the blank look that signified he'd cut off his emotional side.

Dorothea swallowed. Whatever lay inside was not pleasant. But she was not so feeble. She opened her mouth to say so, but Angela forestalled her. "I am not just a lady, I'm his banker. Let us through."

"Very well, but only you two, and Sir James." Raising his gaze, he addressed the others, lifting his voice over the unearthly wailing coming from inside the room. "It appears that Mr. Thorpe has perished. There is no danger here. Not any longer. Please return to your rooms and allow us to deal with the situation."

"I will call the maids to have tea and coffee served in the breakfast room," Lady Steeping declared. Strident she might be, but Dorothea blessed her practicality.

The guests filtered out, their voices raised in speculation.

She exchanged a look with Angela. Louis was dead? No doubt Ben would expect them to deal with what was obviously a hysterical Lady Honoria. Had the poor lady woken to find her husband dead beside her?

The bed formed the centerpiece of the room, draped dramatically in crimson brocade, the Thorpe coat of arms emblazoned on the headboard. The setting was almost theatrical, as was the woman slumped on the counterpane over the body of her dead husband.

Who had perished not from any natural cause, but because of the dagger inserted between his ribs.

* * * *

Blood soaked the bed, the once-pristine sheets drenched in gore. The dagger stuck up, a dramatic counterpoint to the grief-stricken widow in her pale lemon banyan. Honoria's loose golden hair flowed over the lower part of her husband's body.

Like a beautiful depiction of grief, Dorothea thought irreverently. But she could not help the notions that popped into her mind unbidden.

"Dear God, the children," Angela murmured. She moved forward, careful to keep her skirts out of the way, and touched Lady Honoria's shoulder. "Come, my dear." Dorothea followed her lead, but walked around the bed, taking note of the scene. Ashamed that she didn't feel anything but shock.

"Who is the lord lieutenant of the county?" Sir James demanded. "And the local magistrate? He must be sent for."

Ben answered him. "We will send word. Nothing can be done now. We must comfort Lady Honoria and ensure the room is secured."

At the sound of her name, Lady Honoria flung Angela's hand away, got to her feet, and threw herself at Ben. He had no option but to catch her, even if only to stop her falling to the floor. Her sobs began anew, this time into his shoulder, and words arrived. "I came in and there he was.

H-he w-was s-so angry tonight! B-but alive, and now he's deaaaad! Take me away, Ben, I can't bear this! I was in the next room, the m-murderer c-could have come for me! Who did this? Please, Ben, I want to go!"

With his arms full of Lady Honoria, Ben couldn't shrug, but the slight tightening of his mouth gave away his exasperation.

If not for the situation, Dorothea would have smiled. But she could not say she liked the way Ben swept Lady Honoria up and carried her in the direction of her bedroom. He used no effort at all, but at least her hysterical screaming had quieted to convulsive sobbing. Dorothea couldn't deny she would react the same way if she ever found Ben in that condition.

Putting her clenched fist to her mouth, she took a few deep breaths, now Ben was not here to see her weakness. He would have sent her straight back to bed, and that would never do. The room reeked of blood, the distinctive sweet metallic tang hitting the back of her throat every time she inhaled. She breathed shallowly and went closer.

Sir James was standing by the bed, staring down sorrowfully at Louis. His eyes were open wide, no doubt in shock, and his cherry-red lips were partially open, revealing a glimpse of sharp white teeth. Even in death he was handsome. He had cropped dark hair with chestnut highlights, the same as Ben's, but while Ben wore his own hair, Louis had always worn a wig. The short strands revealed a tendency to curl. She forced herself to take note of everything, in case it was needed later. Poor Louis!

"They say that if we look into a dead man's eyes, we can see the last sight he had in this world," Sir James said. "I have no faith in superstition, but you are welcome to look, if you wish."

Dorothea shuddered. "No. How could this happen?"

"Not suicide," Sir James said. "Why would he do such a thing? And in any case, suicides are disgraced. They can lose their property and their right to be buried in consecrated ground. So I think we can assume this is murder."

"Undoubtedly," William Thorpe said.

"I'm sorry, Major." Sir James lifted his gaze to meet William's sorrowful one.

William's eyes were the same blue as his brother's, but they were alive, filled with emotion. He heaved a great sigh. "I am sorry too."

"Did you hear anything? Isn't your room close by?" Dorothea asked.

William glanced behind him to where Lord Evington stood. "We were playing cards until late. Louis seemed fine when he left us."

His lordship nodded, confirming William's words.

Angela straightened. "What time did you last see your brother, Major?"

"Three o'clock. We played for small stakes, but Louis wanted to raise them."

"Did he?" Sir James enquired.

William shook his head. "Neither I nor Evington have the taste for deep play. We told him we would leave if he wanted to do that. It was a way of passing the time, that was all."

"Indeed." Hal moved closer to Dorothea. "We can do nothing here. We should leave this room as it is, for the magistrate to see. Dear lady, would you allow me to take you back to your room?"

Instinctively, Dorothea wanted to protest at leaving Lady Honoria with Ben, but that was foolish. He didn't care for his lost love. At least, she didn't think so.

Steadier now, she nevertheless accepted the support of Hal's arm when he offered it. It felt wrong because it wasn't Ben.

"I believe that's my duty."

Ben stood in the doorway. "I called a maid for Honoria, one with a sturdier temperament than her usual woman. We should retire and dress. I believe Lady Steeping has arranged for hot drinks in the breakfast room, and if anyone requires stronger sustenance, that is freely available. I suggest we meet in the breakfast room when we are ready." He addressed Sir James. "I will send for the magistrate immediately. We must put ourselves in his hands."

"And let a puffed-up squire take control of the affair?" William went to the bed and put his hand over Louis's face. It was his right to close his brother's eyes for the last time. As a soldier, he'd most likely done that before, but never to one of his own. Nevertheless, his hand was steady as he performed the office. "I thank you, no. He will be informed. That is all."

"He will do what he needs to do, and nobody will interfere with that." Ben was clear.

As if Ben hadn't spoken, William said, "I will work with my brother's valet and ensure he is made decent. Nobody should see him this way. I grieve that so many people did so." He glared at Sir James, as if daring the man to gainsay him.

Sir James spread his hands in a gesture of surrender. "Very well."

Ben sighed. "I'd rather the officials saw the scene, but he is your brother, and you have the right."

When Dorothea would have protested, Angela held out her hand by her side, palm down, in a signal to keep quiet. Dorothea took her unspoken advice. William was not convulsed in hysterics like Lady Honoria, but his grief was no less palpable. Performing this office for his brother did seem right.

Hal went to the door and opened it. The sound of quiet sobbing came from the other room in this suite, and the murmuring of another woman, presumably the maid. This part of the house was shrouded in sorrow.

Lady Honoria's maid would have carried the news down to the servants' hall. They would have been awake for an hour or two, preparing breakfast and laying fires in the unoccupied rooms. There was no keeping this news quiet.

Only one woman would be oblivious to the shocking events of the morning, and she was in a suite not far away from here. Ben's mother.

Silently, everyone filed out of the room, and Ben locked it, handing the key to William. Sir James gave him the others, tacitly acknowledging his right to claim them. William thanked him quietly. "I want my brother to have every honor. He should be buried as the Marquess of Belstead."

Sir James sighed. "I'm sorry, but that is not possible. He will be buried with all honors, but he was not the marquess when he died, and he cannot claim the title in death."

"I see." William turned around, the sheen of tears in his eyes. He went back inside the room.

Instinct urged Dorothea to go after him, to offer him some comfort. Ben pulled her back. "Give him some solitude," he murmured in her ear. "Let him mourn in peace."

Slowly the five people remaining walked back the way they'd come. Hal bade them a subdued farewell outside his room. "Unfortunately, he cannot even be buried as the heir. He was never that, because you were alive."

Ben nodded.

They had reached Sir James's room. "Does it not occur to you that if you declared your decision, we would all be less fraught?" Ben asked him.

Sir James frowned. "I had not thought of it that way. Allow me to consider it."

He went inside his room.

"He does nothing but think," Ben muttered as they made their way to Angela's room. "I wish he would just say something. We can't hare off after missing papers and also discover who murdered my cousin."

"But we should," Angela said. "I have held Mr. Thorpe's debts for too long. His debts of honor might die with him, but not the ones he has with my bank. If he is not the marquess, then he is a debtor I must deal with. I fear foreclosure will be in the widow's future. There is little I can do about that now. If I allow his widow to renege on the debts, the City will not take it well."

She bade them a quiet good morning and entered her room which, Dorothea noticed, was exceedingly fine, as if Louis had wanted to keep her sweet. He probably had.

Back in their corridor, she made to walk on, but Ben asked her into his room for a moment. She entered, assuming he wanted to talk about Louis's murder. His murder! "I can't believe he's dead. Only last night he was saying—"

Ben pulled her into his arms and kissed her, then released her and stepped back. "I've never known fear before. But I'm afraid they might come for you."

She frowned up at him in surprise. "Pardon me?"

"Someone tried to kill me twice now. I thought it was Louis, but now he's been murdered. I'd assumed it was Louis, but now I'm not so sure." Turning, he strode to the window and flung back the drapes. The household was in turmoil, and the maids hadn't yet been up. Digging his fingers into his thick hair, Ben sent it into wild disarray. "I was concerned when the cherub dropped from the roof. But now we know what lengths the murderer will go to, and I can't bear to think of you in such danger."

He cared that much about her? Or was this all a subterfuge? Her experience with men at this level of intimacy was limited to one. She was in the dark. "Why do you say that?"

"It could be anyone, and now he has committed murder."

"You think the incidents are linked?"

"I'm sure of it. And because of that, the perpetrator is a man. Only two women came on that duck hunt, and neither of them were in the right position to fire the shot."

"I hate to mention it, but I must." She hesitated, finding the right words. "Could Honoria be involved?"

His eyes widened. "Truly?"

She swallowed. "She did tell me that if you were both single..."

He said nothing for a moment. Then he said, "I think it unlikely. She would have needed an accomplice for the duck hunt, and there is nobody I know she would have that kind of control over. But I will bear it in mind."

Relieved, she took a deep breath. Because of their previous connection, she'd been concerned that he might react badly. But he no longer had Honoria on a pedestal, and she'd had to mention it.

"I'm thinking about sending you away, so you can be safe."

He was mad. He had to be. "Safe? How safe? Do you mean to force me to the other side of the house? Or even away from Cressbrook completely? Is that what you want?"

"No, God help me!" He spun around to face her. "I need to take care of you, Dorothea. I've never felt this strongly before or been so afraid."

"You've faced bears." She folded her hands tightly in front of her. "How can this be the first time you're afraid?"

He tore out the velvet ribbon confining his hair and tossed it aside, the better to run his fingers through his already disordered locks. "I had no time to think when I confronted the bear. Now I've done nothing *but* think."

"But we can still marry?" Her throat was relaxing, and she took a couple of deep breaths.

"The marriage will still take place, but in private. We'll cancel the wedding breakfast." They had planned a large celebration to include their neighbors and tenants, but that couldn't happen now. "You deserve better." His tone was gruff, and he wouldn't meet her eyes, but paced around the room restlessly. "But I will have you."

"I want that, too," she said.

He jerked his head around and met her gaze. Even from four feet away she saw the pain in those steel-gray eyes. The frown between his brows was graven deep. "Even if we end up going to Boston?"

She smiled. "I've never met a bear."

"There are bears and natives. Not all the people who originally occupied the colonies are friendly. They attack at will, destroy, rape, and steal people, who are rarely seen again. The settlements are small, even Boston and the other larger cities. Nothing like London exists there. No palaces, no kings."

She would not be deterred. He would have to admit that he didn't want her if he wished to persuade her to walk away from him. She could not do it. Once she knew him, inside and out, she recognized the man she was meant to be with for the rest of her life. It was this man or no one, because nobody else would come up to the standard he'd set. But she would not say that now. She refused to beg. "It sounds interesting."

He sighed and his mouth flattened, deepening the lines either side of it. "After church, we must make arrangements for the funeral."

And to think, she'd have been happy with her cottage by the sea and the elderly companion.

Who was she fooling? Not herself, not any longer. If she had to do that, she would, and she'd make the best of it. But want it? No, not any more.

Chapter 22

Waking in his own bed, Ben tucked his hands behind his head and stared at the ceiling. Although he and Dorothea spent every night together, after that first night he'd ensured they were in their own beds by dawn. He didn't want to embarrass her again, but he could not keep away from her either.

Had she realized that he could be the prime suspect in the murder of Louis? One would think he had the most to gain—that is, if he wanted the title. The death of Louis left his brother as the other potential marquess. But William wanted to return to his army career. He would gain promotion to colonel, and end as a general. If he had to deal with the duties of restoring a depleted estate, he could not concentrate on the military. It would suit him to have Ben as the marquess, so his motives were far less compelling.

Would Dorothea take to life in the colonies?

Dorothea had no idea what it was like. It could be tedious in the extreme, and the dowagers over there expected a finicky standard of behavior she would not like. And if they decided not to accept her, then she would be on her own, and miserable. Expulsion from the achingly small community would leave her truly isolated.

He had every faith in her, but she deserved better. And if he did not inherit the marquessate, he saw no point in staying in England. He could not effectively run his business from London, not without a great deal of expense and rearrangement.

But all that was excuses. He wanted Dorothea badly, but he didn't deserve her. Not after Mary.

Rougier entered with Ben's clothes for the day draped reverently over his arm and a tray holding coffee and bread and butter in the other hand. Ben tried to make sense of his whirling thoughts.

Up to now, his business, the fleet he'd built ship by ship until he was wealthy enough to buy the six belonging to the Cressbrook estate, had meant more to him than anything else. More than his name, more than Mary.

More than Dorothea? More than the tiny body of his son, who had taken one breath in this cruel world?

That he couldn't answer. He refused to. Deliberately, he turned his thoughts away. Instead, he sat up. "What are they discussing downstairs?"

Rougier gave him a jaded look from under heavy lids. "They talk of the death incessantly, sir. Some wild stories are already circulating."

He could understand that. It wasn't every day the potential heir to a marquessate was found stabbed to death in his bed. The sight of that body, still for the first time in restless Louis's life, had brought back memories Ben hadn't realized he was still carrying with him.

As Rougier shaved him, Ben went through the recollections of his childhood. Infrequent visits to his parents, long sessions with his tutor, and a lot of time spent with his cousins running about the estate and swimming in the ornamental lake. They'd been severely punished for that. His father had not spared the whip. That had been the only time his father had personally handled their punishment. Only later did Ben understand why, when his father had taken pains to explain it to him. If the three boys had drowned, the title would have died. There were no other heirs.

Not that the three boys would have been lost, or that their mothers would mourn. No grief, just the perpetuation of the title. The blasted title could go hang. Ben had made his mind up that very day. What if Louis had decided that too, and set about laying waste to the estate?

No, he had not done that. Ben tilted his head so Rougier could gain access to his throat with the cut-throat razor. Without a second's thought, he'd allowed someone he'd known for a matter of weeks access to a vulnerable part of his body with a deadly weapon.

Strange, that.

Enough. Time to face the world. Speculation was useless.

On his way down to breakfast, Miss Childers waylaid him. "Do you have time to meet me and my man of business?"

"Your manager is here?" He didn't remember meeting him.

"He's staying at the inn in the village."

That offended Ben. "I'll order Schultz to have a room prepared for him. Pray tell him to have his things sent up. How could you imagine I would allow him to stay elsewhere?" If it crossed his mind that he was behaving like a marquess, he quelled it.

"That's very kind of you. I didn't like to impose, considering only I was invited."

"Nonsense."

"Well, if you meet us after breakfast, you may tell him yourself."

"I will be there."

Seeing Dorothea so unhappy and trying so valiantly to hide it struck Ben to the heart. However, he said nothing, merely helped her to sit and took a place further down the table, since the ones either side of her were already occupied. The guests were avidly waiting on events. Being well-bred, they began by discussing affairs in London with their friends, aided by the newspapers that had arrived from the village.

Lady Steeping expressed her sympathy and offered, "As a dear friend of your father, I will do everything in my power to help you through this terrible time."

Was she such a good friend? Ben had no idea, but perhaps she planned to use the ploy to get more information.

Her husband, as usual, made a good meal and spoke little. He'd helped himself to a newspaper from the pile by the table. Louis had them delivered every day, but most were a week old, having been brought up from London.

Few people did more than glance at the printed sheets. They all wanted to watch the ensuing show. They had the best seats in the house.

William appeared, dressed in somber black, and reported that Lady Honoria was in bed, heavily sedated, since she had gone into strong hysterics once more. The guests expressed their sorrow.

Lady Steeping's comments brought the subject around to the inevitable discussion of Louis's death. Everyone commiserated with Ben. "To come back to this!" one lady exclaimed. "How dreadful for you!"

"I didn't exactly expect it," he said. Few people had connected the stray bullet and the cherub falling from the sky, but it would not be long until they did, especially with this new development. "Yes indeed," he said gravely. "Despite our recent disputes, Louis and I grew up together—and William, of course. I will always remember those days fondly."

Further down the table, William murmured his agreement.

Leave, Ben thought, but did not say it aloud. When someone died, wasn't it polite to give the family some privacy? But the guests here would not leave until the whole grisly business was over with. Goodness, if they left, they might miss another murder, and that would never do.

William sighed. "Truly, I am still confused by the whole business. Who could have done such a thing, and why?"

"Ah," Lady Steeping said. "That is the question. We must ask ourselves who has the most to gain?"

From his seat next to Lady Steeping, Sir James abandoned his food and picked up his tea, leaning back with an attentive expression on his face. "Mr. William Thorpe will inherit his father's property, of course."

So they were to discuss this now.

"I had not considered the matter," William said. "But my brother has never denied me the use of Thorpe Park. It is a modest estate, however, and I had not planned to spend much time there. I have my career." He sighed heavily. "I fear I might have to sell out, or at least request a leave of absence. The War Office had intimated my promotion to colonel was due, but I might have to forgo it."

"But why sell out, William?" Ben couldn't help saying.

"Because Honoria might need me. And the other matter. The inheritance. I do not at all wish to give up my career, but if Sir James finds for me, then I fear I must."

Ben had adored Honoria once, and she had responded with equal fervor, but for the first time in his life he knew what passion was.

Dorothea.

In bed, she met his demands with enthusiasm and made her own. Their friendship had deepened, and their connection was becoming too strong to deny. He had given her the opportunity to withdraw. As a man of honor he could do nothing else. But when she'd comprehensively rejected his suggestion they part, relief had filled him to such an extent he'd sagged under the power of it.

But he might have to force her to take a step away from him. He knew what was coming next, and with the inevitability of a stone cherub plummeting to the terrace, he waited for it.

"Then there is Mr. *Benedict* Thorpe." Lady Steeping, taking the position of the grand inquisitor, turned to him.

"So there is," he agreed, not in the least surprised by the supposition or the person saying it.

"But if he is not—eligible for the marquessate, surely he has nothing to gain?" Dorothea's brother put in.

Good old Laurence. Of course that was the obvious point. "I was preparing to return to Boston," Ben added.

"I have not completed my study or my recommendations," Sir James said.

"But the documents Mr. Thorpe uncovered!" Lady Steeping exclaimed.

William's entire attention went to Sir James. Would becoming the Marquess of Belstead compensate for losing a successful army career?

He had always loved any form of combat. He would find precious little in the toadies at court. Ben doubted he wanted the poisoned chalice. Without Ben's wealth, the marquessate was sadly depleted and could well prove more of a burden than anything else.

Sir James gave her his full attention. "The documents are only one factor in my decision. There are others I must consider."

"Surely if the marriage was not valid, Mr. Thorpe is not—eligible."

Or legitimate, her ladyship implied. The pause was enough to transmit that. The guests would be writing letters as fast as they could get quill to paper when they returned to their rooms. Ben would have preferred a more discreet transmission of what came as news to him, as well as to everyone else. He'd all but discounted himself from the succession.

"Not necessarily." Sir James turned, letting his gaze scan his avid audience. Not a head nodded, nor a jewel flashed. Stillness infected them all. "A marriage is a combination of factors. We may wish things to be different, but marriage is an irregular procedure. Naturally, most people prefer to make their union as regular as possible, but sometimes we have to piece together the various factors to make the whole."

Close to Ben, Dorothea's brother growled. "I have joined Lord Hardwicke's efforts to pursue an act of Parliament to once and for all clearly define what is marriage and what is not. We are making progress."

Ben was grateful for the way he made general something that had been specific.

"But in this case, the original marriage was suspect," Lady Steeping persisted, bringing the conversation right back to the particular. Damn the woman. Could she not leave the subject alone? They should be mourning Louis, not pouncing on the identity of the next marquess.

"Suspect, perhaps, but not necessarily invalid," Sir James responded smoothly. "My recommendations will be accepted by the Chancellor, and subsequently the King, so I must be exceedingly careful. Even now, when matters have taken such a grave turn."

At Dorothea's discreet signal, the footmen began to clear the table. Nobody would eat any more. "I ordered a simple repast for dinner tonight," she said. "I didn't think a feast was appropriate."

"Very wise," a few people agreed.

The company relaxed a little. More coffee and tea were brought in. A few people helped themselves to the contents of the fruit bowls. The sharp little knives flashed when they caught the light.

Dorothea accepted a fresh dish of tea. She had remained silent, and was too pale-faced for Ben's liking. He would put a footman on guard outside her room tonight and insist her maid sleep with her, if she did not wish to come to him. He would take the greatest care of her, especially with a murderer on the loose.

"So murdering Mr. Louis Thorpe is to Mr. Benedict Thorpe's advantage," Lord Marston said thoughtfully. Annoyingly, he had pared an apple keeping the peel in one piece, his thick, strong boxer's fingers deft and sure. "Where were you last night, Mr. Thorpe?"

"Sleeping," he replied.

"I see," Lady Steeping said. She pursed her lips. "Then you could have gone to Louis's room to discuss the inheritance with him and fought. After all, we have ample evidence that this has happened before. Do we not?" She offered a cold, tight smile.

The trial by houseguests was not going well for Ben. If he wasn't careful, he could find himself tried and condemned before the magistrate arrived. The man had sent word he would be there as soon as possible this morning. He couldn't have conducted a better inquisition than Lady Steeping. Marston had only vocalized what everyone was now thinking, thanks to her ladyship.

Even Sir James avoided meeting his eyes. They would condemn him because of the duel? Of course they would. "It is one thing to fight in an affair of honor. Another to kill someone in a fit of rage." Plebeian, he'd call it, but since they already regarded him as having one foot in trade, he doubted that attitude would fly.

"You do have a fearsome temper," Lord Marston put in. Built like a bruiser, nevertheless his lordship had a keen sense of what was going on all around him. He would appear sleepy, but he was taking everything in.

Hal opened his mouth. His face was red with fury. "Ben is a man of honor, and he always has been. Do you really think him capable of an act like this?"

"As matters stand," Lord Steeping said, examining his fingertips as if his manicure was as important as the trial-by-supposition, "We must consider Mr. Benedict Thorpe the prime suspect in this matter. Nobody has a better motive, or a prior history of animosity with Mr. Louis Thorpe. Indeed, I would say the matter was an easy case. We should consider confining Mr. Thorpe to his rooms until we know more."

Ben swallowed. Accused like this, he would be tarred and feathered whether the law agreed with the guests or not. The speed with which they'd sprung to this conclusion left him reeling. They had probably been discussing the topic all night in the room where coffee had been arranged for them. If they chose to waylay him like this, then his future was in their hands—and they knew it. They could destroy his reputation if they gossiped.

William wouldn't meet his gaze now. As Ben scanned the company, his mouth compressed into a tight line, gazes flitted away. They would cut him; his credit would be destroyed and everything he'd built would crumble into dust.

Lord Marston leaned back in his chair and watched, as if at the theater. He had said little, but as a supporter of Miss Childers, who was not present this morning, he would have an opinion.

Dorothea's clear, pure voice chimed into the silence as everyone considered who would be the one to lay hands on him. "He could not have done this awful thing. He was with me."

She couldn't have created a greater sensation if she'd stripped naked. Ben groaned and pressed his hand to his head, shock rocking him, while the others perked up considerably, all staring with a mixture of fascination and opprobrium.

"She doesn't know what she's saying—"

Dorothea broke into Ben's attempts at ameliorating her claim. "She does and she did." She pursed her lips. "I dislike having my private business brought into the public arena." She fixed Lady Steeping with a glare every bit as fulminating as Ben's own. "Intensely. But I cannot see injustice done."

Lady Steeping tittered, her face the picture of shock, eyes wide, jaw dropped. "I see. You were awake all night?"

"No, but I would have noticed had he left the bed. In fact, when he rose to use the necessary, I woke at once. He went into the powder room. He returned in five minutes, nowhere near enough time to go to the other end of the house, pick a fight with Louis, stab him and return to bed. In any case, I might have noticed the blood, don't you think? Whoever killed Louis did not come out of his bedroom unmarked."

He couldn't stop her now. Ben watched her, half fascinated, half appalled at the way she was so comprehensively ruining her reputation.

"It must have been someone else. Must it not?" Challenge sparkled in her eyes. "Though how you thought a man the size of Benedict could walk through the house unnoticed is a mystery to me. Servants are everywhere now. I increased their number when it seemed likely that I would become the marchioness. Lady Belstead sleeps poorly and has people running around after her half the night. And I ordered a footman to spend the night outside her room, since I did not want her disturbed any further. Anyone going from our part of the house to Louis's must pass her ladyship's apartments, unless they use the servants' corridors. In which case, they'd be bound to meet someone else."

Piqued and repiqued. Ben wasn't much of a card player, but that seemed the appropriate term for what she had just done. Cleared his name promptly and emphatically at the cost of her own. Nobody would suspect him now.

Lady Steeping sniffed. "Well, after all, your marriage was arranged for tomorrow, though I hardly expect that to go ahead now. You should have taken more care, Miss Rowland, and not jumped in too quickly. Did Mr. Thorpe seduce you? I'm sure nobody would blame you for that."

Here was a woman desperately hunting for gossip. Her ladyship lived on it, more than the half-eaten breakfast she'd carelessly pushed aside. Ben was gratified to see a spot of sauce on her lace elbow ruffles. Petty, but he wouldn't deny his enjoyment in retribution coming so quickly.

Except that they would cast blame, not least her ladyship. Yes, couples did anticipate their wedding night sometimes, but nobody spoke of it so boldly.

"On the contrary," he said. "We will go ahead with the ceremony, although it will be a completely private affair."

William watched them curiously. "I had no idea," he said, although he probably had. At least one person hadn't forgotten his manners.

"I was with him *all night*." Dorothea lifted her chin, daring someone to take up the baton Lady Steeping had run with.

More stirring. Would they leave the room, give her the cut direct? In that case, he'd stay with her. And ruin himself.

But nobody did. After a short, stunned, silence, Lord Steeping cleared his throat. "Then, unless we wish to doubt the word of a lady, we need to look elsewhere for the murderer."

Ben tried not to show his relief too much. The mob was an effective way of trying and condemning a person before they got anywhere near a jury. Only when the crisis had passed was he aware that he was much more concerned for Dorothea than for himself. He'd have defended her to the death.

Chapter 23

The interview with the magistrate and constable was much less of a trial. They arrived at the house, full of themselves and their purpose, viewed the now tidy bedroom where the terrible events had taken place, and asked a few less-than-probing questions. Ben did not correct them when they called him "your lordship." In fact, the reminder of the courtesy title he had used for most of his life came as somewhat of a relief. "Mr. Thorpe" still gave him the urge to look over his shoulder to see if Louis was there. Unfortunately, he would never be there again.

Not in this life.

Afterward, Dorothea suggested he should visit Honoria. "Only if you come with me," he said, but she declined.

"Lady Honoria doesn't like me." She laid her hand on his arm. "She will get no comfort from seeing you with me."

Once she'd recovered from the shock of her husband's death, would Honoria come back for Ben? Would she make a play for him now?

Dorothea hated the uncertainty gnawing at her insides, but she would face her fears. She had to learn to trust Ben to do the right thing. He'd asserted it; now he should be given the opportunity to prove it.

"You trust me to talk with her alone?" He did not want to cause Dorothea any distress.

She forced a smile. "Of course. She will be mourning Louis. She may need you to talk about the times you were happy together. Please give her my deepest sympathy, if that seems appropriate to you. But give her a chance to speak freely."

"Very well." He kissed her forehead. They were standing in the middle of one of the main passageways, and he relished the freedom to display his affection for her and not worry about anyone discovering them. Tomorrow they would marry. That was the only certainty he could count on at the moment.

He entered the quiet, nay, *hushed* apartment belonging to the marchioness. Would it ever belong to Dorothea?

Her maid, the superior Remington, who had been with Honoria since she left the schoolroom, glided forward. She was dressed richly but somberly, no doubt in one of Honoria's castoffs, something the lady's maid was entitled to. The dark shade of green hinted at the mood. The curtains were all closed, and candles burned in the wall sconces, casting a shadowy, eerie light over the room.

Honoria sat by the fire, watching the flames. She leaned her elbow on one arm of her high-backed chair. As Ben entered, she turned her head and met his gaze with sorrowful eyes that brimmed with tears. She wore unrelieved black, even the lace at her elbows and neck the color of mourning. Her golden hair, coiled in a simple but elegant style under a small black linen cap, showed to advantage against the somber shade. Her face, arms, and hands were the only contrast to the deep mourning. The scene resembled a painting by Rembrandt.

She lifted a black-trimmed handkerchief to her eyes, touching the inner corners, but keeping her attention on him. "Benedict, so good of you to visit." She glanced past Ben to the maid and waved her away with an impatient gesture. "Do take a seat."

Without much choice, Ben sat in the chair opposite Honoria. Probably the one Louis had used. "I'm so sorry, Honoria. Would you like me to arrange for the vicar to visit?"

Honoria graciously inclined her head. "I would prefer a bishop or higher to conduct Louis's funeral service." Her plump lips quivered, but no tears fell. "I can scarcely believe it. I am a widow."

"So you are."

"I never imagined I'd be brought so low. Just yesterday, we were—never mind."

He thought of the nursery wing. He would go up directly after this sad visit. "You have informed your children?"

Her eyes widened. "I saw them briefly last night. I had them brought down to me, but I did my duty."

"I'm surprised you aren't with them."

At even that mild comment, she fired up. "I cannot let them see their mother in such distress. I can hardly hold back my tears. They are upstairs with their nurse, and she is comforting them as best she can."

In her situation he would have remained with them, but they were not his children, and Honoria must bring them up the way she saw fit. "Of course." Although the realization of how confused they must feel filled him with sadness. "The magistrate wishes to see you. A pompous ass, but I can ensure his interview is as brief as possible."

"I cannot see him. As I recall, he is a vulgar little man. We had him to dinner once. You know the estate entertains all the local gentry close to quarter days." She gave a delicate shudder. "But we did it, for the sake of peace."

Peace? Had Honoria and Louis been at odds with the gentry, then? That would explain the magistrate's antipathy. Ben had sensed it from the moment the man had entered the room to speak to him. A full twenty minutes had passed before the man had relaxed a little, mostly due to Dorothea's careful treatment of him, giving him the best chair and ensuring he had generous helpings of brandy.

"We should have had boys," Honoria said suddenly. "Then the estate would have a clear heir. As it is..." She shrugged.

"There is William."

"He will never marry." Honoria flicked her handkerchief in a dismissive gesture. "Oh, he has his women, but he does not wish to marry."

Ben thought so, too, but if William had to do his duty, he would. "If he understands what is expected of him, he will oblige." Even if Ben had to pay him to do it, although William showed no indication of needing money. He would find a way, and he wouldn't burden Dorothea.

"You must do it." Honoria fixed her gaze on him. "I regret that your ceremony tomorrow must be canceled."

Ben opened his mouth to tell her his plans, but then thought better of it. She could make a fuss and try to force him to put it off. "Why do you say that?"

"Because of the mourning and funeral arrangements, of course. Nothing must detract from Louis's passing."

And it would not. Having a lavish ceremony and wedding breakfast would be the worst of bad taste. But marry he would. "We must discover who did this awful thing, Honoria."

Her mouth tightened, and she swallowed, as if fighting back tears. "I know. I will be brave. Pray let the magistrate know that I will see him once we have made the arrangements for the funeral. But I wish you to be with me. Ben, I cannot bear it without you. Be by my side, my love."

Those two words, "my love," were not said fondly, or with a remembrance of what had once lain between them. No, she said them almost unconsciously, as if used to saying them.

Ben's soul filled with horror. She could not imagine—he'd made his situation clear. "I will ensure that either William or myself will be with you when you see the magistrate, and the vicar. But Dorothea can accompany you for at least one of those meetings." He would ask her. She had offered to help, and that would keep a suitable distance between Honoria and himself.

"Thank you. But I want you, Benedict. I always did."

Ben listened, appalled. Her husband's body was barely cold, but he did not mistake the way she looked at him now. With barely veiled desire, her eyes sultry, her lips slightly parted. "Lady Dorothea is hardly the kind of person to endear you to Sir James. You must know that. But we could solve this terrible problem for good and all. If you married me, we would unite the two branches of the family and put an end to the dispute."

How could she even *think* such a thing, much less say it?

Another suspicion crossed his mind. Had Honoria wanted Louis dead? He already knew she would say anything to get her own way. Dorothea had mentioned her as a possible suspect for the murder. Perhaps she was right.

If they had argued, surely someone would have heard them. Slipping a knife between Louis's ribs in the dead of night was not an act Ben would associate with Honoria, but he would not discount it. Whoever had killed him, either they had done it when Louis was in a sound sleep, or it was someone he trusted, because there were no defensive cuts on his hands and arms, no sign of him fighting back.

She sighed and touched her handkerchief to her eyes again. "I adored my darling Louis. But I adore you, too, Ben. I always have. My dilemma was that I could never choose between you. First one, then the other. Now only you are left. I have to think of the future for the sake of my girls. For myself, I care little."

He doubted that. He dropped another reminder into the mix to gauge her response. "Louis seemed to think I was illegitimate. A bastard."

Honoria winced, probably at his blatant use of the word, rather than the concept. "What if there was something that proved your legitimacy?"

Like the pages cut from the family record book? "How could that happen?"

"If your parents married twice. There was mention of a second wedding shortly after the first, was there not?"

So she knew. Louis had confided in her.

Only one clear answer remained. She had seen the papers, perhaps had a hand in concealing them. If she helped to hide them, then he might be able to winkle the truth out of her.

He would behave like an innocent, since that would feed her sense of superiority. "A second wedding? Are you sure?"

"Indeed I am. The neighbors frequently spoke of it."

"Oh." So he had another line to follow. Verbal corroboration. The villagers had welcomed him back, especially when he'd started renovations on their cottages instead of merely promising to do it. He could easily find some upstanding people to support the theory, but he wanted the truth, not people who would say what he wanted in order to please him. There would be no mistake this time, and with Dorothea by his side, he would accept either fate offered to him, to be Mr. Thorpe, a wealthy merchant from Boston, or the Marquess of Belstead. "Surely that means nothing?"

"It could." She gave a small, wavering smile, no doubt intending to encourage him. "I'm sure I could find someone to prove your legitimacy. Enough evidence to satisfy that prosy Sir James, at any rate."

Or bribe someone, if he agreed to marry her. Then she'd attain her longed-for goal of becoming the marchioness.

He could find his own witnesses. He was still temporarily in charge of the estate, and while Honoria might not realize it, that gave him the whip hand. So did simple acts of kindness, which he'd undertaken with no thought of reward. Without waiting for Sir James to make his decision for the second time, he'd ordered repairs to the tenants' cottages. Other improvements were on the way, like the reopening of the home farm.

He'd sent his man of business on a tour around the holdings and property belonging to the marquessate before reporting here. The account would arrive fairly soon, or at least an interim one. Had Louis squeezed the other properties dry?

"Do you know where the records of my parents' second marriage are?"

She shrugged, her pale shoulders peeking seductively through the finest of gauze fichus. "As I recall, Louis said he had them safe. That is all I remember."

"I would not like to deprive William of his birthright, if it turns out that he is the true heir."

He watched her expression tighten, and he knew he was right.

Honoria had designs to become the marchioness, but she couldn't marry her brother-in-law. Therefore, she would do all she could to defer Ben's wedding to Dorothea and claim the place for herself, while ensuring Ben got the title.

Had she ever loved Louis at all? How could she, when she was already scheming? He could not accuse her of thinking of her daughters, because she'd barely mentioned them.

He got to his feet. "I must be tiring you, Honoria. I'll leave you to rest."

When he bowed over her fingers, she clutched his hand. "Don't leave me, Ben. Please." Her desperation showed in her low, quick tones. "We can be together now. We have both suffered much over the last seven years, but finally, we can have the happy ending destiny always intended for us."

He could walk away, but she would only pursue him. Best to have this out now. He took his seat again. "We're both very different people now, Honoria." He kept his voice low and nonthreatening, although he wanted to rave at her for her deep selfishness. Had she no thought for her children, or how he must feel, losing his cousin after such a long time apart?

Obviously not.

"We're the same here." Honoria pressed a hand under her rib cage in a dramatic gesture. "We know what we've always known. We both married others, but now that is over."

"Yes, with the death of my wife and son," he reminded her.

"But you did not love her, not as you loved me. Remember our words the day we parted?"

Oh God. Yes, he did. "The words of a foolish, indulged youth who had never experienced the real world. We were both young. Can we not leave the matter there?"

A lone tear trickled down the side of her face, glistening in the low light of the candles. "Our hearts do not change. Our souls are still bound, just as you said then." She drew her hand away from her chest and reached for him.

He did not accept her invitation. "I've learned much since then. Souls are not eternally bound, and hearts do change."

"And your heir?" Her voice hardened. "You will not get an heir on Dorothea Rowland. She is thirty. Or didn't you know that? Did she keep that from you? Far too old to have a first child. Then what will you do? Rely on William to provide you with an heir? I doubt that will come to pass. He's nearly forty, and he shows no sign of settling down, even though his father arranged several good matches for him."

Ben remembered the "good matches." He wouldn't have taken any of them, either. They had been chosen primarily for the connections they could bring to the family. If William was to provide an heir, he had to have a hand in choosing his own bride. But Honoria had allowed her long-suffering, stately demeanor to slip. Accusing Dorothea of infertility was not the right way to persuade him. He played along. "You mean I should find a young girl fresh out of the schoolroom to give me a quiverful of heirs?"

"No. Who knows what some untried miss can or can't do?" Honoria shook her head. "You were never so foolish. I have proved myself, and I am four years younger than Miss Rowland. My two daughters need a father, and I need a husband." She bit her lip, the plump flesh marked as she released it. An interesting flirtation for someone assumed to be mourning her husband.

"There is a great deal of work to be done on the estate, and not much money to do it with. Your portion is gone." That had been spent during her marriage. Squandered. He put his own fortune aside. Let her think it was spoken for.

He held out the bait, waiting for her to take it.

She did not disappoint him. He knew as soon as the gleam appeared in her fathomless blue eyes, and the muscles twitched at the corners of her mouth as she suppressed her smile. "As to that, a few seasons in town should take care of the money problem. A government position, along with some judicial investment, would bring many riches. My uncle is running the triangle. You know how hard that is to get into, but I could do it. And you have a few ships, do you not?"

Ben shuddered. "Yes, but I don't engage in the slave trade." True, it was lucrative, but he had decided firmly that he would not make money by selling other people. More than once he'd been castigated for his decision, but spices, tea, porcelain, and silk worked well for him. And he could sleep at night. He'd toured an empty vessel, and he'd never get the stink of the unwashed people forced to sleep in their own mess out of the back of his throat.

"I've heard it's the most lucrative trade to be had."

He shrugged. "I daresay." He didn't want to get into an argument about it, not now.

"We need to consider how to speed up the repairs to the estate."

That angered him. "Why should you care? You won't be the marchioness." He got to his feet. "My dear, I left our connection behind years ago. I wish you well, especially at such a sad time, but I'm telling you now. Tend to your children and consider moving to your late husband's estate."

He bowed and left, ignoring her pleas to return, to talk to her, to take care of her. As he reached the door and opened it, she wailed, "But what shall I do?"

Dorothea would never ask that. She would plot her path and take it. He'd had a lucky escape.

Chapter 24

Dorothea glanced at the library door when it opened and smiled in welcome. Ben came over to the big table where Angela had spread out her books. Her man of business, Mr. Snell, awarded Ben a small bow, which he returned.

The niceties attended to, Ben turned to the books. Dorothea didn't like his expression, a frown lining his forehead, even though he smiled at her with obvious pleasure. And relief? Why would she see that?

Later, she would ask him. For now, they had other concerns. Making room for him to stand between herself and Dorothea, Angela pointed at the page. "This is the reckoning as of today for the debts incurred by your cousin against the marquessate. I would ask you not to turn the page. Some of this is confidential, even from you, but this concerns the estate you are likely to inherit, and the requests on its behalf."

"Shouldn't William be here?" he asked. "He is a potential heir, after all."

"I sent a message," Angela said. "He has not yet arrived, or sent word to us, but we do not have all day." She glanced at the clock on the mantel, a large model with a suitably impressive tick. "We must change for dinner soon. However, I wanted to show you these. If the major wishes to see the papers, they are available to him."

Three large leather-bound tomes lay open on the table, and a pile of letters was neatly stacked above them.

"If we do not have much time, then I will be guided by you, although I am tolerably familiar with account books and inventories. More than I used to be." Ben shot Dorothea a quick glance.

"This is an account of the Cressbrook estate, house, and contents," Angela said, indicating one book with the tip of her carefully manicured finger. "Louis Thorpe sent it to us with a request for a mortgage on the unentailed parts of the property, to be enacted when he inherited. Alternatively, he asked for a loan, with the estate as security."

She indicated another ledger. "This is a list of the debts Mr. Thorpe took out. These are not just the ones with us, but also with other banks. He didn't seem to be aware that we communicate with each other from time to time. When Stickland's Bank became concerned with the number of debts, the owner contacted me. We made a list, which we share."

Ben whistled through his teeth. "That's an enormous amount. What on earth did he want all that for?"

"Gambling?" Mr. Snell suggested.

"Not one of my cousin's vices," Ben said. "And as far as I know, Honoria didn't gamble either. Oh, that is, they both played at the tables, but neither wagered much above the ordinary. When we were younger, both brothers gambled large sums at the tables. It was the reason William had a commission bought for him—to get him away from the gaming hells of London. Since his return, he has shown no propensity to gamble for high stakes. Neither has Louis, recently." Ben bit his lip.

"And yet, these amounts are staggering for someone who didn't gamble," Angela pointed out.

"Indeed." Ben's frown lines deepened as he scanned the closely written columns. "He has spent money on some extravagant items, like the dinner service, but even that doesn't account for these sums."

Angela sighed. "He did not trade on the markets, either. While we aren't aware why he borrowed so much, we had, as a group, decided to lend him no more." She indicated the other ledger. "Hence the request for a mortgage. He needed to provide security for the next loan. Which we would not have granted him."

"Even if he'd become the marquess?" Ben queried.

"Even then. It was my decision. I don't want any part in breaking up a great estate. He'd had the smaller properties valued, too. If he had not perished yesterday, he would have secured his mortgage. Not with me, but there are other lenders with fewer scruples. There would have been little to pass on to the next marquess."

"So I see. I have returned just in time." He leaned forward. "There's a marked increase in the last two years. More amounts, closer together."

"That was when he dismissed half the domestic staff," Dorothea pointed out.

Had Louis hidden something? Did he have a reason for the increase in the loans?

"Perhaps," Dorothea said slowly, "he had taken all he could from the estate without inheriting it, and needed to find money elsewhere."

Angela nodded. "But why? Louis's only extravagance seems to have been his love of fine arts. He invested heavily in statues, paintings, and the like—"

"And gold-plated porcelain dinner services from China," Dorothea added.

"Indeed," Angela said. "If he carried on in the same vein, he'd have ruined the estate in a few years."

Ben's proximity gave Dorothea the most remarkable sense of safety, as if he could shelter her from the rest of the world.

Those numbers were truly shocking. Shuffling through the letters, she found the one she wanted Ben to see. He took it from her. "This is the original letter requesting a mortgage," she said. She picked up another. "And this is a note from Louis in his own hand, requesting ten thousand pounds."

Despite the elegant flourishes taught when learning to write, one thing was clear. "These aren't in the same handwriting," he said. "Did he have a secretary?"

"No, and it's not Mrs. Thorpe's writing, either," Mr. Snell put in. He lifted his gaze, and being nearly as tall as Ben, could look him in the eye. "We're not sure who wrote that. It might be a trivial matter, but we like details, and pay great attention to them." He smiled, his thin lips stretching as if unaccustomed to the practice. "I thank you for the guest room here. It's most welcome."

"Naturally, you should stay here. And I expect to see you at dinner tonight."

Mr. Snell's nostrils flared, and since he had a nose as hooked as a parrot's, that was quite a sight. Dorothea tried not to stare. "Is that wise?" Snell asked. "I am not of your company."

Ben laughed. "That's a delicate way of saying the guests here consider themselves superior. Well, I value the work of a man like you. I am not entirely free of the shop floor myself, and proud of it, too. Please don't stay away because of a few narrow-minded individuals. We won't be using much pomp, and I doubt we'll linger long over the port, in deference to my cousin."

"Then I will be delighted to attend," Snell said, and that was settled.

* * * *

Sunday came and went, much more rapidly than Dorothea had expected. Although she still shared Ben's bed, he insisted they wore their usual nightclothes, and while he kissed her, he refused to go any further. "We have gone a week without making love because of your—condition. I want to make tomorrow night as memorable as possible."

In the darkness, Dorothea's cheeks heated. Her wedding night. She'd never expected it to arrive.

And yet here she was, on her wedding day.

At dawn she went back to her own room, and rose at seven. She dressed modestly. While nobody expected them to wear deep black for mourning, and in any case, she had no such garments in her wardrobe, she did bear Louis's tragic death in mind when she found a gown of dark green, embroidered in black, with a petticoat of the same fabric. The ruffles at the hem were scalloped, adding a little touch of festivity to her appearance. The foaming white lace at her elbows and neck, together with the filmy lawn fichu, created an air of subdued festivity.

Nothing like she was feeling inside. There, she was rioting, running around the room with her hands in the air, cheering. At last, the day of days, the one none of her friends thought she would see, not to mention herself, had arrived. She could hardly drink the chocolate the maid brought to her.

Ben met her outside her room. He lifted her hands to his lips, one after the other, pressing a gentle kiss to each. "It does my heart good to see you. I can hardly wait for us to marry. Come."

"I didn't sleep much last night." She'd spent hours staring into the darkness, convincing herself this was real, that she was marrying the one man who mattered, the one she'd fallen in love with.

After the short ride to the village, Ben helped her down from the carriage and they entered the small church, which had been there since the Conquest. That stone tower had seen many changes in its long life. To their left was the window that had been pieced together from the shattered remnants Cromwell's men had left behind. There was a face here, a piece of sky there. None of it made sense, but the pools of colored light it cast on the flagged floor of the church reflected God's glory as well as it had ever done. The font stood below it, the cover attached to the chain by which it was opened when a new life came to receive its blessing.

The vicar, dressed in his green ordinary vestments, a stole draped across his shoulders, stood before the altar, smiling a welcome. Standing facing the cleric, Dorothea's brother and his wife turned to watch Dorothea and Ben walk up the aisle toward them. Angela stood by Ann's side, and next to her, Hal Evington. Angela had offered Lord Evington and Dorothea's brother and sister-in-law the use of her carriage, leaving Ben and Dorothea to make the journey alone. And to have the privacy of their own closed carriage on the way back.

Nobody else attended. But instead of feeling lonely, Dorothea loved the intimacy. Only the people she truly cared about were here. She enjoyed the traditional aspect. Most aristocrats obtained a special license and married in their own chapels. But doing it here, where generations of families, wealthy and otherwise, had plighted their troths, meant so much more. Following them filled Dorothea with humility. She was just one more bride, and she liked that.

To one side of the main body of the church lay the Cressbrook Chapel, which contained the remains of previous holders of the title. Ben's ancestors. They would witness this joining.

The service itself seemed to take no time at all. Only when Ben turned to her and pushed the gold circlet onto her finger did time stop. She gazed up at him, smiling, and he smiled back. Such a precious moment, and one she would remember forever.

After they'd signed the parish register, Ben asked if he could look through the previous pages. Dorothea knew why. But this was a new volume. The vicar spread his hands. "Unfortunately, the previous register went missing recently. I have looked for it, and no doubt I've mislaid it somewhere. This one is just as valid."

So someone had been here before them. Dorothea would not allow the tinge of disappointment to spoil her day. Tomorrow was soon enough to investigate the disappearance of the records of the second wedding between Ben's parents. For today, she'd taken a step that would change her life, one way or another.

Ben treated her tenderly. But when they were back in the carriage and they'd left the village behind, he took her in his arms and kissed her, long and sweet. Only the jolting of the vehicle broke them apart. He took her hand, grinning. "I don't seem to be able to stop smiling. Except when I'm kissing you, of course."

"Yes. That would be difficult." She seemed to have caught his condition, because she couldn't stop smiling, either.

They swung into the drive, slowly, because that was the safest way. "I don't want a fuss," she said. "With the house in turmoil, I don't wish to add something else. And perhaps cause trouble between you and Honoria."

"Cause whatever trouble you like. You are the important person in this, not her. If you wish, I'll have her moved. The marchioness's apartments should be yours."

She shook her head, concerned. "That wouldn't be fair. In any case, I'm not the marchioness. I may never be the marchioness, and I doubt Sir James would take kindly to such high-handed behavior. What has upset you?"

She read banked anger in his eyes. They darkened when he was affected by anger or passion. She tried not to think about the passion. Not yet.

He regarded her steadily. "You should know, although it's a distasteful subject. But you need this information in case she talks to you." He leaned back against the squabs and sighed, pinching the bridge of his nose. But he kept hold of her hand. That link warmed her, a physical demonstration of how close they'd become. "Yesterday Honoria suggested that we could marry, now her husband was dead."

Judging from the still, calm tones, he was deeply disturbed. The calmer he appeared, the more upset he was. Not without cause. With her husband but a day dead, the widow was thinking of moving on?

Would she feel the same if Ben had been killed? Her heart missed a beat and an echo of might-have-been filled her mind. No, of course not. She'd be mad with grief. Even if she and Ben had been on bad terms, she would not have considered the possibility of marrying again. Far too soon.

Ben continued in the same flat tones. "That way she could bear me a child, and the disputes would be solved. She also intimated that she knew about the second marriage between my parents."

Did she indeed? Dorothea didn't credit her with knowing, but using it as a ploy. If Honoria could cold-bloodedly discuss moving on so soon after the death of the husband she professed to adore, then surely, she was capable of murder.

Ben agreed with her when she said so. "But if she knew that, she was aware Louis was lying when he produced only the evidence of the first, flawed marriage." He turned to face her. "Dorothea, I'm tired of it all. I'm within an ames' ace of telling them they can do what they want with the estate and returning to Boston. Should you mind doing that?"

She couldn't reply, since the carriage had drawn up outside the front of the house, and a footman hurried to open the door and let down the steps. Just as well, because she wouldn't have known how to respond. On the one hand, she would go with Ben anyway, but on the other, leaving when the issue was unresolved itched at her.

When he had alighted, she tucked her arm through his and waited until the servant was out of hearing distance before giving him his answer. "Consider me Ruth. Whither thou goest, I will go."

Given a choice, she'd always choose Ben.

He patted her hand. "I had thought to leave you here to manage the estate while I went to Boston. If I gave you ample funds, you could oversee the restoration of the house and estate. I have complete faith in you."

Dorothea's heart sank. If he refused to take her with him, there was little she could do. Follow him? Would he take her, or send her home? Besides, a lone woman traveling across the ocean on her own was asking to be robbed and murdered.

For him, she'd do it. Not the murdered part, though. She said nothing, not knowing where to start.

"But I don't think I could bear to be apart from you for so long," he added, almost casually.

Schultz flung open both double doors to give them access. Ben's words surprised Dorothea so much she was through the doors and into the great hall before she could get her breath back.

Had he really said that? Oh, she knew he was fond of her, but not bearing separation? She felt that way, but he knew that.

He turned to her, a light in his eyes that she couldn't remember seeing before. "I love you, sweetheart."

Dorothea caught her breath. "You do?"

"Yes."

"Oh, goodness!" Heat rushed to her face when she realized he had not lowered his voice. Every servant in the hall must have heard him. One came forward to claim her hat and gloves. She gave them to him numbly. "I—I love you too."

"I remember." He smiled at her, the warmth almost too much to take. "Whatever happens next, we are together."

"Yes."

Catching her hand in his, he led her toward the back of the hall. "Tea in the small breakfast room, if you please, Schultz," he said.

By the time they'd reached the breakfast room, Dorothea had regained her senses. He'd sent her reeling with his simple, honest statement. But that was so like Ben, to tell her with no frills, only the truth.

She'd seen it in his eyes. And when the door was closed, he tugged her to him and carried on where they'd left off in the carriage.

They shared a sweet kiss that turned incendiary very quickly. He stroked her back, the heat of him burning through the layers of her clothes, even her stays. He nudged her fichu aside to caress her bare skin at her neck. "Not another night apart," he murmured.

When the door opened, she pulled back, but he wouldn't release her, keeping her attention while the maid put down the tray of tea and beat a hasty retreat. Dorothea laid her hands on his shoulders, laughing up at him. "You'll shock them to the core."

"Good. Let them gossip. That way we won't have to tell anyone we're man and wife. I'm proud to make you Mrs. Thorpe."

"What about the Marchioness of Belstead?"

"Do you care?"

She gave a slight shake of her head, a strand of hair catching in a button on his coat and coming loose from her coiffure. "You're still Ben, whatever people call you."

"Yes, I am." He twisted the hair around his finger and tickled her neck with the end, smiling when she twitched in response. "Your husband. We could probably have a better life were I not the marquess. The estate needs restoration, and the vultures are hovering, waiting to attack. With the estate comes responsibilities I thought I'd escaped. I knew what was going on. Hal kept me informed, but I chose to stay away. I blame myself for not returning when Louis began his depredations, but my life wasn't here. It was in the colonies. It could be again."

While she was apprehensive of traveling so far, knowing nobody but Ben, the knowledge that he loved her changed everything. She would go anywhere with him now. To see the light of love in his eyes, to have the right to claim him, as she had not before, that meant the world to her.

"Ben, whatever is best, that's what we'll do."

"Yes, we will." The lines at the corners of his mouth deepened, a sure sign that something had disturbed him. "But I don't want to leave my mother. Louis and Honoria told everyone she had gone senile and then run mad. So that's what Hal told me. He said she had her first attack after my father died, and she'd never recovered. So there was no reason for me to come home. She wouldn't know me if I appeared before her. Or so Louis and Honoria claimed, and since only her companion saw Mama, I had no way of discovering anything different." He closed his eyes. "I could have written to Schultz, I could have sent someone to see her, but I did not, and I will not forgive myself for that."

He twisted the strand of her hair between his fingers. She didn't pull away, but remained in his arms, nestling close. He needed her while he talked about his mother. She would speak when he had done, but she sensed that he hadn't told this to anyone before. He had to say it now, or it would become a festering sore inside him.

Ben kissed her forehead. "I was running away. I was still mourning my father when I got the news about her. My father had ordered me to leave and not return, part of the reason I never did come back. We were not close, and he chose to believe other reports, rather than Hal's. I confess he had reason. I was wild in those days."

"He should never have turned his back on his own son." Hadn't he known that at his heart Ben was a man of integrity and honor? He hadn't known his son at all.

"But he did. I loved him all the same. My mother fell ill, and Louis took care of her. He'd wronged me, but I appreciated what he was doing for her. If she was mad, as he claimed, he could have sent her to an asylum." He sighed. "But I had no idea he was keeping her alive so that he could question the marriage if he had to. Only when I returned from the dead did he have to play that card. I shouldn't have come."

This time she did pull away, wincing when the hair tugged at her scalp as it unwound from his finger. She needed that tea. "That's just nonsense. If you try to blame yourself for everything that happened, I will lose patience with you, sir." Lifting the pot, she concentrated on pouring the brew. The housekeeper had provided deep cups. She'd need every drop, since she didn't intend to turn to strong drink at this hour. "You made mistakes, but so did everyone else. We do, because we are human."

She poured a drop of milk into each dish, and picked up one by its saucer, handing it to him.

He was smiling again. At least she'd forced him out of his orgy of self-blame. "Thank you, sweetheart. Not just for the tea. You're right. Louis kept my mother's state from the world, and I believe he did her a kindness by doing so. She probably told him to keep people away from her. That would be typical of her. She hated to display her weaknesses. But I cannot leave her again."

"No, of course not. Can we take her with us?"

"I will certainly look into it. Or stay here with her. Some days she knows me. Some she doesn't. She is weakening. Her morning constitutional takes less time than it used to, her maid informed me, and she needs her cane."

"We should go to see her." Putting down her dish and saucer, Dorothea went back to him. "Tell her our news. Whether she understands or not, she has a right to know."

"You would do that? On what should be a happy day?"

"It will make the day happier if we tell her."

Chapter 25

When he told Dorothea he loved her, something settled in Ben's mind. The words coalesced all the feelings that had been churning inside him since he had asked her to marry him.

He'd never felt like this about any woman before, though he'd liked a few, loved a few. This emotion was all-encompassing. He was never happier than when she was by his side, in bed or out of it.

After a painful visit to his mother, in which she didn't know them at all, he took Dorothea up to the nursery wing where they spent a soothing half hour playing a foolish game of Speculation with the girls. Their laughter healed some of his pain and gave him a chance to think.

How could he have not known he loved her? He had not loved her when their families had been arranging their marriage, but he'd been too callow and self-centered to know what true love was back then. His overwhelming need to cherish and protect her was a result of his love, not the cause of it. No moment marked the instant he'd fallen for her, but a collection of them: when their gazes had met in perfect understanding, when they'd shared a joke or comforted one another in sorrow. And, to be honest, the first time he'd seen her naked and touched that gloriously silky skin.

Perhaps she'd become a marchioness.

He didn't want the marquessate, but he would step up to the mark if he had to. He wasn't sure how Louis could so comprehensively have laid waste to the holdings, but he had, and there it was. He would have to buy property back, redeem mortgages, and work to restore the respect that had previously gone with the title. William was perfectly capable of doing all that, although it would take him longer because he didn't have Ben's resources. Ben had no intention of breaking up what he'd built to prop up a title he had no interest in. He'd only bought the estate's fleet because it was so cheap he couldn't ignore it.

He took Dorothea to his room—their room, and closed the door, warming at the knowledge that he had the right to do so.

"What do you say to us staying in this part of the house if Sir James decides in our favor?" he asked her.

Her face lit up, and he was happy he'd given her pleasure. "I would love that. The rooms are spacious, and we could make them grand with no effort at all. There are three good rooms, which would make a bedroom each and a sitting room." Pink tinged her cheekbones. "Not that I'll be sleeping in my bedroom."

"No, you will not, unless we choose that one to make our own." He reeled her in and treated them both to a lingering kiss. For two pins he'd say to hell with the world and take her to bed. But she would not thank him for that. She had yet to come to terms with the married state, where people knew the couple were spending time together making love. She would become accustomed to it in no time at all.

When he lifted his head, that slumberous, seductive look had returned to her eyes, and her lips were reddened. She was ready for love. He was so tempted. "We could say you're indisposed," he suggested.

"I—I'm not sure."

He chuckled. "It's not fair of me to ask it of you. No, we'll go to dinner, although I can't promise we won't have an early night. And we'll be late up tomorrow."

When she buried her head against his chest, he laughed and stroked her hair, tugging at her little lace cap and dislodging a few hairpins. "I intend to spoil you. Only the best is good enough for my wife, whatever the name she goes by. Now go before I change my mind and take you to bed. I promise you, I'm hard-pressed right now to resist." When she slipped a hand between them and cupped his burgeoning erection, already painfully hard, he choked.

Covering her wicked fingers, he squeezed, relishing the sensation she never ceased to bring, making him helpless. He wanted her badly, but the knowledge that he could take her to his bed tonight and every one after that relieved his desperation a little. Enough to enable him to ease her away. "Don't forget to call for the maid to come to you."

Her laugh echoed down the corridor as his wife headed for her room. The kind of tease a wife would offer her husband, knowing he would get his revenge later, in the sweetest way.

On second thought, probably not sweet.

* * * *

Dorothea's bedroom was far from the spartan chamber it had been when she'd arrived. Every day some small change was made. Today it was the best quality linen sheets. But she had the torture of dinner before she could retire for the night. And she wouldn't be retiring alone.

The maid was waiting for her. She was adequate as a lady's maid, and she'd do well for Mrs. Thorpe. But the Marchioness of Belstead would need a maid well versed in fashion and court dress. Dorothea wasn't a Puritan, but her height dictated elegant simplicity; wear a flowered silk, and she'd be parading around like a walking sofa. Tonight, she chose dark blue, in deference to Louis, but she refused to go into full mourning. Not on her wedding day.

When she finally declared herself satisfied, she left her room to find her husband standing outside. Like her, he wore a sober color, a rich dark brown, and again like her, he had a wide black band on his left forearm. He glanced at hers. "A suitable compromise."

He took her downstairs. The warmth in his eyes nearly felled her, but she held up bravely, and they went to the drawing room.

Cressbrook House had several drawing rooms, but the grandest by far was the one in the state apartments, the line of rooms constituting the formal procession from most public to most private. Tonight they made their way to the state drawing room, with its exquisite furniture in the French style, with much gilding in evidence. Everything was in such good taste and so well made that Dorothea felt almost intimidated by it. No doubt she would grow accustomed to it in time. Louis had added to the extravagance of these rooms.

When they entered, the guests applauded lightly. Obviously, the gossips had been busy. But after they went in, one person followed them: Lady Honoria Thorpe, looking like a beautiful specter at the feast. The expression of deep sadness on her face didn't change when Sir James informed her why people were clapping. "Then I must offer my congratulations," she said stiffly.

A shiver of fear breezed across Dorothea's skin. She stood between Lady Honoria and the title, or so the lady would think.

William filled the awkward moment by taking Lady Honoria's hand and holding it warmly between his. "We must celebrate the living, as well as mourn the dead."

"I cannot help but think that the haste was uncalled for. A deferment would have been more appropriate." She glared at Ben. "As I told Mr. Thorpe when he paid me a *private* visit in my room." She glanced around at her rapt audience.

Lady Honoria's arrival balanced the numbers for dinner. If Honoria hadn't appeared, there would have been a spare single. In the past, that would have been her, the lone woman. If someone did escort her in to dinner, she'd find herself matched to a younger son or older widower, the male equivalent of the single lady, or someone looking for a match. Desperate for one, sometimes. So much so that she would have to fight them off with one hand while eating with the other and making conversation.

Those days were gone. Now she had a husband who would have to fight her off if he lingered too long. Especially tonight.

Surprisingly, William abandoned Lady Honoria in favor of Angela. He appeared smitten, gazing at her with obvious pleasure. Lord Marston, a known admirer of Angela, watched with a smile on his face. He probably knew William would have as much luck with her as everybody else.

"Such a pity my companion could not be present to hear your good news!" Angela told Dorothea.

"Why, is she not well?"

Angela heaved a sigh. "Alas, my poor Miss Helmers suffers from a variety of ailments. But she is a good woman and suits me well."

Not for the first time, Dorothea wondered if poor Miss Helmers had the constitution of an elephant and stayed away when Angela deemed it expedient. Having a companion was, she had confided in Dorothea, the worst part of remaining single.

Dorothea would not have said that.

The dining room was grand to the point of pomposity, the rectangular table running down the center a marvel of the cabinetmaker's art. The chairs set around it were more recent additions, another of Louis's extravagancies, although she had to admit they were good quality and would last a number of years.

Dorothea had instructed the servants to remove the chairs from the head and foot of the table. With Louis so lately dead, she didn't think giving anyone the chance to claim the symbolic seats was fair or respectful.

"I ordered only one course for tonight," she said, pitching her voice over the low murmur of polite conversation. "I did not consider a feast appropriate."

She received a number of approving nods and surprised looks. And one glare.

She would not apologize to Lady Honoria for anticipating her orders. The lady would be in mourning, distressed over the loss of her husband. Dorothea had done her a kindness by attending to household matters. Most of the company appeared to agree with her.

After they had taken their seats, disposed the dishes and begun their meal, conversation turned to anything except what was engaging everyone's mind that day. Until Lady Steeping, as was her wont, broke the embargo imposed by politeness. "I thought to see that dreadful little man from the village at dinner tonight. He has made a nuisance of himself all day, keeping the servants from their tasks. Has he finished here?"

"Who would that be, my dear?" her husband asked. He generally served as her prompt and chorus. And probably audience as well.

"You know, the local squire, the magistrate." She shook her head, frowning. "What was his name?"

"Renning. Mr. George Renning," Ben said. He glanced at Lady Honoria, concern in his gaze. "He will return until he has what he wants. I told him he would be welcome to join us, if he wished. He said he preferred to return home to his wife." He lifted his glass and swirled the ruby wine around until the sharply cut crystal facets glimmered in the candlelight. "He said Frenchified food did not agree with him, and he preferred good English beef."

He sent a meaningful glance at the joint of beef set in the middle of the table, which he had just carved. Very efficiently, too. "But he is a good sort of man, conscientious. I have no doubt he'll get to the bottom of the matter."

Dorothea judged they were getting too close to the painful topic of Louis's death. Hardly something to talk about over dinner. "I'm sure he will. And swiftly, too," she said.

"We must pray for a sensible conclusion," Lady Steeping said.

They had laid Louis in the chapel, or so the maid had told Dorothea while she was dressing for dinner. He would remain there until the day after tomorrow, Wednesday, when the bishop, who was Louis's uncle, would come to conduct the funeral service. Nobody had objected to Louis being interred in the family vault in the village church. The Cressbrook Chapel attracted antiquarians and historians alike, and now Louis would form one of the draws. Unfortunately, for the first few months after the interment the visitors were like to be sensation-seekers, not scholars.

"I have employed extra men for the coming week," Ben responded. "They will ensure nobody comes to the house who has no right to be here." When Lady Honoria's mouth opened, he continued smoothly, "At my expense, naturally."

Whatever the lady intended to say was muted to a simple word of thanks.

The major spoke up, his handsome face troubled, his jaw set hard. "I feel bound to continue to promote my family's claim to the estate and title. I had decided to encourage Sir James to disregard the claim and allow Benedict to accede to the title, but I fear I cannot." He knocked back the contents of his wineglass and waited for the footman to refill it. "I must continue what my brother began, in his memory."

Lady Honoria sat like a stone, but Dorothea knew her better now. She had a shrewd notion what was running through the lady's head now that her chance to become the marchioness had died. Since Louis had never been awarded the title, she couldn't call herself dowager, or a marchioness at all. She only carried her courtesy title because her father was a duke. All that knowledge flitted across her face, those huge blue eyes watching and calculating.

"I do not care who inherits now," she said, the picture of noble mourning. By the way she held her chin just so, she could have practiced her appearance before the mirror. After all, she was so very beautiful. If Dorothea had that weapon at her disposal, she had no doubt she'd use it too.

But she didn't, so there was the end of that.

Now that Dorothea had married Ben, Lady Honoria couldn't become the marchioness through him. Unless—she glanced at Ben, whose eyes had opened wide as he met her gaze. Unless Lady Honoria had killed her husband in order to get to Ben. Marriage had just put Dorothea in danger, but in the back of her mind she'd known that. It was not enough to stop her marrying him, though.

A marriage to Ben, however brief, would be completely worth it. She wanted to face the future by his side, protecting and being protected. Her conviction was total, no room for doubt.

Could she defeat Honoria? Fear clutched at her, her throat tightening, but yes. Yes, she would dare anything for Ben.

Sir James cleared his throat. "While you are discussing among yourselves, I would remind everyone the decision is in my hands. Actually, not that, either." He touched his napkin to his mouth. Until now, he'd been busy eating, letting them argue. "The decision is ultimately the King's, although he will allow the authorities to guide him in that." In other words, he would tell Parliament his decision and they would take his advice, and so would the King. So he was right the first time. The decision was his, based on what he learned here.

"Of course." Ben conceded the point. "We will do everything we can to help you in your decision. At present, certain documents are missing, and unfortunately the parish register is also absent. Corroboration one way or the other appears to be difficult to obtain."

To put it mildly. Someone had gone about ensuring any records of the second marriage between Ben's parents did not survive. The strongest suspect was Louis, and had been from the beginning, but tragically, Louis was not with them any longer.

Who would want to do that? Who had the opportunity, and the desire?

"May I make a suggestion?" Angela joined in the discussion. Giving up all pretense at eating, Lord Marston placed his silverware neatly on his plate and watched her, his dark eyes intent on her lovely face. Everyone in town knew Lord Marston pursued Angela, but he had little chance of winning her. However, a cat may look at a king.

As if oblivious of the earl's regard, Angela continued. "I have seen disputes rip families apart and create useless and expensive court cases. These kinds of cases drag on for years and benefit nobody but the lawyers. If you can agree to allow Sir James's decision to be final, I think you will all lead much more productive and lucrative lives."

"What about Lord Hardwicke?" Ben asked.

"His opinion is out of our hands, but I am confident the Lord Chancellor will accept my recommendation on the matter," Sir James put in.

The cool dose of common sense came as a relief to the argument, which was becoming more heated. A dispute over succession was ripe for the courts. Answering it could drain the estate of any value it had left, reduce the tenants to utter poverty, and create a wilderness of a lovely house like Cressbrook.

The new marquess would have years of hard work ahead of him merely to restore the house and the estate. While Ben could do it more easily, William could also achieve it, given more time to build the income back to what it had been.

Ben met William's direct gaze. "I believe we can agree to that."

Tight-lipped, William nodded.

* * * *

Dorothea had been longing for bedtime for hours. But after dinner at four, the ladies retired to the drawing room and gossiped. She chose not to take part, but sat with Angela and discussed politics. Anything but her marriage and the inheritance problem, which seemed no nearer a solution than it was when she first arrived at the house.

Or the suspicion that a murderer could be in this house. Even in this room. But nobody would touch her here, in full view of the guests.

Tomorrow she would make a last search in the library, but until then she'd put the problem to the back of her mind. And if she couldn't find anything substantial, she could say she had done her best. Sir James might as well toss a coin.

Usually someone would play something, the harpsichord or a flute, and someone else would sing. But not tonight. In deference to Lady Honoria, the lid of the harpsichord remained closed. Dorothea answered Angela's questions, and in return touched on the subject of Lord Marston.

"He is one of many admirers," Angela admitted.

"But you aren't as hard on him as you are on most of your suitors. I've seen you barely giving the time of day to them. Or rather, giving them the office. You seem to know precisely what will irritate them the most."

She flicked open her fan and struck a shy pose. "Well, I don't like to boast, but running a bank gives me an ability to better understand people. I make a study of them, that is all." She stared down at the flowers painted on her fan, traced a rose with the tip of her finger. "Doing that to Lord Marston would be like kicking a puppy."

Dorothea choked back a laugh. At least, she nearly did. "He's built like a boxer. What makes you think he would respond badly?"

She shrugged, as if careless of what she was saying. But this seemed different. Was Angela finally falling for a man? "He is more sensitive than most people suppose."

And she cared? That was passing strange. Angela refused to become attached to any man. She'd developed flirting into a fine art, knowing exactly when to withdraw, and when a man was safe enough to befriend. The passionate ones she tended to ease away from. But not Lord Marston, who made his interest obvious to anyone who cared to look. He gazed at Angela as if the sun shone out of her eyes.

"But he is not wealthy."

"No, he is not." Her sadness came through in her words. "I cannot consider him. But then, I refuse to consider anyone. I don't see how I can trust any man with my fortune. So many women are disappointed once the first flush of marriage has passed." Her lips compressed, and she gave a slight shake of her head. "That is not to say your marriage won't be a roaring success. You both know what you want."

In a month? But now was not the time. Already people were listening. The light hush around her told her that. "Of course it will. I have no idea what the future holds, but I am excited for it. Did you catch the news of Lord Abercrombie's daughter eloping with that actor?"

Her firm change of subject started up the inconsequential chatter again. Unimportant to her, but no doubt of vital importance for the gentleman's daughter. But the juicy gossip had moved attention away from Ben and herself, so that was good. No doubt as soon as the word of Louis's death got out, it would start again. Yet another reason for seeking a swift solution to the murder. If they could discover the perpetrator, then it could be presented as a complete story, and without speculation, it would die quicker.

But a murder. She would be forever associated with it. Angela was wise to insist that William and Ben accept Sir James's decision without dispute. Nobody would gain from prolonging it in the courts, except for the gossip sheets.

Lord Abercrombie's daughter, a beauty who made her debut last season, had run off with an actor. Dorothea knew no more than that, but the chatter kept the ladies busy until the gentlemen entered the room.

Ben came over to her immediately, and she made room for him on the sofa she occupied, while Angela murmured something and left them. Her brother smiled at her from across the room and lifted his tea-dish in a silent toast. Warmth enveloped her. The people she cared most about were all here.

Her husband handed her a dish of tea and although she didn't want it, she sipped it, wishing she could leave. At one point Ben leaned over and murmured, "We may make our excuses at ten. Not long now, my love," causing a rosy flush to rise to her cheeks.

His low chuckle told her he would be up to no good. She was on edge, waiting for the excuse to go upstairs without making her purpose too obvious. They would know for sure what she was doing and who she was doing it with. That made her unaccountably nervous and edgy.

Even more when he murmured in her ear, "I can't wait to get you upstairs. I don't know if I have the patience to disrobe you."

The thought of what he might do made her squirm, and not merely in embarrassment. She wanted him very much, and her body was waking to him now the hour was creeping closer. But she could hardly turn and beg a kiss from him. Or more. She wanted his hands on her. Those broad fingers had given her more pleasure than she'd ever known in her life. The fingers currently toying with his half-finished tea, turning the gilded pink porcelain around in its deep saucer, had given her bliss.

Leaning forward, she put her dish back on its saucer. She didn't want tea. Something stronger would be more welcome, but tea was an after-dinner ritual that had to be completed. Usually she enjoyed it, but today it only increased the fluttering in her stomach.

"Lady Abercrombie is threatening to disown her child," he drawled, as if he was actually interested. He gave every indication of being so, except that when Dorothea leaned back once more, he moved a little closer to her, as much as her skirts and his wide coat would allow. Close enough for his heat to transmit to her and for her to get a whiff of his essential masculine aroma, so faint it was more of an extra sense, something felt rather than experienced.

"The girl was always willful," Lady Honoria said. "During her first ball she declared she would be married before the year was out. Although I doubt her parents had this in mind." She sniffed and fumbled for her handkerchief. "I have been thinking of asking my mother to visit." She sent William a speaking look, her gaze pleading. "You would not object?"

The blatant appeal made Dorothea catch her breath. But Honoria would have nothing to gain from seeing her brother-in-law as the new marquess. She couldn't marry him, and she had only daughters, not eligible to inherit. Her portion would take care of their dowries, unless she'd spent that, too. It should have been left in trust.

"The decision might not be mine," William reminded her, uncrossing and recrossing his legs. "I doubt either of us would object."

The lines on his face tightened as he watched her. She must remind him so much of his loss. While William and Louis were never close, they were brothers. If called upon to take the place reserved for Louis, William would have to give up his army career. Just as he was on the brink of greatness, or so she'd read in the newspapers.

At ten, Angela got to her feet. "Well, the day has tired me out. Who would have thought that I would be the first to retire? But so it is. I bid you all good night." She turned to Dorothea. "My dear, I have something in particular I wish to ask you. Would you accompany me to my room?"

"Yes, of course."

Confused, and not a little alarmed, Dorothea glanced at Ben, who smiled reassuringly. "You cannot disappoint your dear friend." He stood and offered his arm to Dorothea and his other to Angela. "Please allow me."

With aplomb, he took them both out of the room. The footman closed the door for them, and they turned in the direction of Angela's room. Once they were out of sight of the drawing room, Angela released Ben's arm. "You don't have to take me any farther. I can just about remember the right way to go. Good night, my dears." She grasped Dorothea's hand. "I am truly happy for you."

"Oh! Th-thank you!"

Ben's rumbled laugh followed Angela, but he turned and walked toward their part of the house. "A wily woman, Angela Childers. I always thought so. Beautiful, but any man claiming her hand will have his work cut out keeping up with her!"

While Angela's tactic wasn't particularly subtle, at least it got them out of that drawing room. Not one person had quit the drawing room. Usually in such a gathering, people would go their own ways earlier. They'd retire to their rooms to read or gather in smaller groups to play cards or play music. Not tonight, when they'd clung together as if afraid to be the first to leave.

But then, with somebody found murdered in his bed, perhaps they felt there was safety in numbers. Who knew who might be next?

Chapter 26

"I'm sorry Angela has set her face against marriage," Dorothea said as they reached her bedroom door. "She could have anyone she wanted, but she rejects them all."

He opened the door and met her gaze. "That is her concern. She must do as she sees fit."

Standing back, he watched her enter, then followed her. Going into her room together felt like a ceremony. The doorway symbolized the start of something different; something wonderful.

He didn't touch her until they were sure the room was empty. No servant hovered to attend to them. Dorothea turned, her skirts swinging about her legs, coming up against him as he tugged her into his arms. Then his mouth was on hers in a hungry, searching kiss. She cupped his cheeks, the sensitive skin on her palms roughly abraded by his emerging beard. The reminder of his masculinity, as if she needed any, thrilled her to her core, and her body began melting for him.

Pushing his hands between them, he found the pins holding her gown to her stomacher and tugged them out, dropping them carelessly to the floor. About to protest at the wanton waste and the danger of pins to bare feet, she smiled against his mouth at her own foolishness. She felt for the buttons on his waistcoat instead.

He unhooked and unpinned with unerring accuracy until her gown was loose, falling away when he pushed it off her shoulders. She hadn't allowed the maid to do more than use the strings under the skirt to fit it to her. There were no more pins to impede the gown tumbling to the floor with a *whoosh* of fine silk. More pins followed, then her stomacher.

"Why do we wear so many clothes?" she moaned when he drew his mouth away from hers in order to locate the tapes of her corset.

"I have no idea. I would have you wear a simple gown, nothing else." His voice had deepened to a growl. He lifted his head, looked behind her. But before she could turn to see if anyone was there, he'd tucked his hands under her thighs and lifted her, taking two firm steps to the wall. When he pushed her against it, the sharp crack and sudden give of fabric told her he'd broken her hoop. This time he growled before shoving his hands under her petticoats and finding the tapes that fastened the ruined hoops around her waist. He slid his hands over her skin, claiming her. She'd have said her hoops were firmly tied, but they yielded under his hands as if giving in to the inevitable. He lifted her as they fell and kicked them aside without marking where they landed.

She'd managed to get his waistcoat undone, and now only his finely pleated linen shirt lay between her and paradise. When the bulky coat got in her way, she dragged back the sides, and he paused to rid himself of it. It joined her gown on the floor.

Desperate for skin, she fumbled with his neckcloth. Finally she wrestled the knot undone so she could get rid of it, revealing the powerful column of his throat and a tantalizing glimpse of his chest. Knowing what awaited her beneath the expanse of fabric made her longing unbearable.

He lifted her again. "Put your legs around my waist."

Dorothea was too shocked to do anything but obey. Her thighs contacted bare flesh. When had he managed to release the fall on his breeches? She didn't know, but that meant his erection was free.

"So long," she moaned. After a brief time of loving, they'd spent a week in the same bed, separated by their voluminous nightclothes and her reticence. But she'd become accustomed to having him there, even though he claimed the necessity of keeping her safe. Now she had none of that shyness. Had that been part of his plan? Because all she had now was need of having him.

At his first deep thrust, they both moaned with relief. He rested his forehead against hers. "I believe they were trying to keep us apart. I wanted you so much from the moment I put that ring on your finger. Sweetheart, this is our first time."

"As man and wife?" Her voice came out breathy, as she was barely able to control it.

"As sweethearts. As a man and woman in love. Dear God, I love you, Dorothea."

She opened her mouth to reply but could only respond physically as he kissed her again. He ate at her mouth like a starving man before pressing kisses over her face, down her throat. And then he drove inside her, giving her a completeness that made her cry out.

The paneling behind her dug into her back and shoulders when she pressed hard against it, the better to return his thrusts and to take him as far inside her as possible. The buttons of his waistcoat slid against the bare skin of her thighs, as he drove inside her with the intensity of the single-minded.

Her body tingled, every hair, every inch of skin alert and responsive. She lifted her chin, leaning her head against the wall, sucking in cool air, gathering strength. Gripping his upper arms, his muscles bulging like iron against her, she hung on and pushed back. She held her body rigid so that every time he hammered into her, the ripples consuming her gained in strength.

She came in a froth of lace, linen, and passion, crying his name as he gave one last thrust and held himself deep, giving her all he had.

Only the sound of their breathing broke the silence until the clock chimed three-quarters of an hour. They had done all this in a rush. She hadn't even noticed the half-hour chime.

Now his kiss was tender, caressing rather than demanding, loving instead of lustful. He tasted her, and she closed her eyes, the better to glory in the wild coupling they had shared. She couldn't pretend he had wanted it more than her, or that she had only obeyed her husband's desires. She had wanted this every bit as desperately as he had. And she had no need to hide it, or to pretend otherwise.

"Do I apologize?"

She laughed shakily. "Don't you dare."

His responding chuckle vibrated her breasts. He looked down. "We had best disentangle ourselves and get into that bed."

* * * *

By the time he had stripped them both and lifted her into the bed they were sharing tonight, desire had begun to take him again. She had performed some kind of magic on him, and he was content. Happy, even.

Startled, he acknowledged the emotion, one he hadn't experienced for years. Total happiness, and contentment that went far beyond what they had done. The floor was strewn with discarded clothes. He should locate the pins he'd torn out, because he didn't want her to tread on one, but he didn't seem to be able to let her go.

Ben snuggled his wife close, his arm securely around her shoulders. Dorothea lay on her side, her hand on his chest. He dropped a kiss on each fingertip before curling his hand around hers, loving the way it fit. One long leg was tucked between his, and her intimate hair tickled his flank deliciously.

"Better," he murmured, and claimed another kiss.

Dorothea tasted sweet, and he couldn't get enough of her. Especially when she responded so enthusiastically. "You are a constant delight," he told her when he drew away. Not so far that he couldn't claim another kiss.

"So are you. I love you, Ben."

"Mmm. You will have to tell me that every day, in case I forget."

"Will you?"

When she tried to pull back, he drew her closer. He didn't like the note of alarm in her voice. "No, but tell me anyway. Hearing that on your tongue is better than any poem."

"Ben, you're positively eloquent!"

"Only with you, sweetheart. Only with you."

"Oh, I didn't mean you weren't eloquent in general, just that you are— careful with words."

He liked that. "I spend them with caution. But you deserve all of them."

She nuzzled his thigh with her knee, rousing him. "Such nonsense! But I like it."

His cock stirred. "Take care, wife. I'm trying to be a gentleman."

"Don't. Be a gentleman, I mean. I want a man in my bed, pure and simple."

Giving in to temptation, he rolled on top of her. "Oh, I can promise you that."

They made love again, but this time Ben took care to enjoy her, and to ensure she did the same. He adored her caresses, when she ran her fingers through the hair on his chest, and down, lower, to take his erection in hand and guide him to her wet welcome.

And this time, when he came inside her, he was so overwhelmed he nearly fell asleep on top of her. He only rolled to one side when she pushed his shoulders. She sprawled over him and they gave in to sleep.

* * * *

When the light of dawn filtered through the curtains, Ben opened his eyes. He'd spent years waking with the sun, eager to get a full day's work done before the light faded. Today he had no intention of rising, especially with Dorothea beside him, sleep-warm and breathing gently, her breasts nudging his rib cage with every sigh from her perfect lips.

How he could have fallen in love so completely in a month confounded him. Lying there, his senses at peace for once in his life, Ben processed what would happen next. He ran each possibility through his mind until he had satisfactory endings to all of them.

Except one. If they came to the conclusion that he had killed his cousin. Dorothea could not testify for or against her husband, since legally they were one entity, one person. If she had realized that, she wouldn't have married him. And that would have been a great shame, so he'd chosen not to remind her of it.

The story had served its purpose. In any other woman he'd have suspected she did it to force him into marriage. Since he was as willing as any young groom with stars for eyes, he wouldn't have cared much if she had. Except that wasn't like Dorothea. He'd seen her face—acutely embarrassed and endearingly sweet when she'd blurted out their guilty secret. Secret no more, for they were tied together for life. And he couldn't be happier about it.

He didn't need to look at her to know she was awake. A tiny muscle in her wrist twitched as she woke. He'd noticed that before, though he doubted she knew she was doing it. Sometimes husbands should keep secrets, especially lovely ones like those.

"When did you know you loved me?" she murmured, stroking the tip of her forefinger down the center of his chest.

Ben forced himself to concentrate. "When the matter of making an heir ceased to have any importance for me."

The movement stopped. "But you must. We must."

He turned his head, smiling. "We will do what makes us happy. If we create a child, I'll be more than happy." He frowned, recalling what had happened before. That tragedy would never leave him, nor the child he had lost.

No. Not today.

He turned his mind away from the well-channeled groove he had slipped into and moved on to her original question. "William can marry. It's time he shouldered some of the family obligations. He's been running from them for most of his life. I daresay there might be somebody else, if we go back a few generations. I'll ask Sir James to advise. Of course, if he decides for William, our troubles are over." He stroked her skin, savoring the sensation, drawing a pattern on her belly. "I wish you did not have to go through the ordeal of childbirth, but I cannot refrain from making love to you. So I fear we must leave that part to fate. When it came to a choice, there was none. I'd rather live childless with you than have a quiverful of infants with someone else. But I can promise you that if we have a child, I will spend more time with it than Honoria does with her daughters." Honoria spent an hour a day with the girls, if that. He had visited them a few times in the seclusion of the nursery wing and never found Honoria there.

She sighed happily. "I would love a family. But I have you. And Boston will be a new adventure. I am sure I'll enjoy it."

"I'm sure you will, too. I'd go so far as to say I'll make sure of it."

Their kiss lasted a bit longer this time.

But he owed her an apology. "I should have waited until Sir James confirmed or denied my right to the title. Given you a more secure future. But I wanted you too badly for that. And I wanted to ensure you were safe at nights, especially after Louis—after Louis."

"I know. And if you'd waited, Honoria would have won you back."

He caught her wrist, pulling her around to meet his eyes when she would have turned away. The doubt in her face was clear to see, and he didn't like it. Before they left this bed, he'd have her completely certain of his love. Even if they couldn't be sure of anything else. "No, she would never have done that. Never. Honoria is the kind of dazzling beauty men fall for, and don't see the woman beneath. She's not for me, and I can only be thankful that I lost the duel. We would have been unhappy together. I fear she is prone to take lovers, and my wife will never do that."

That at least made her smile. "I know she will not."

But one other person lay between them, and if he did not tell her the truth, that seed of doubt inside her could grow. He wanted to kill it before it did any real damage, and he would do it now. "And Mary. Let me tell you about her."

If she thought it odd to bring another woman into their bed, she did not say. Many women would have refused to listen. He knew she was afraid, because he hadn't said much about Mary. When he talked about Mary, he was careful to put her in the best light possible. She had not deserved her death, or the way he'd treated her beforehand; a crass youth, still finding his feet in the new world, he had not given her what she deserved. He went on before he could change his mind and lock his secrets back in his heart.

"Mary was pretty, lively, and she laughed a lot. She loved flirting, but not in the determined way many women use. She was an elf."

He watched Dorothea carefully, aware he must be hurting her with his words. But she had to hear them. "Like the other men in Boston society, I was enchanted by her. But she decided on me and badgered her father into allowing the match. I had lost Honoria, and I was still sore at Louis's victory. Mary was my way into a new life. Her father was enormously rich, and she was his only heir. And she was so different that I imagined myself in love with her. Or so I persuaded myself."

There, that spark in her eyes. "I'm sorry she died and that you went through that tragedy."

"You can't be sorrier than I am. I should have known she was too delicate to bear my child. You see, Mary was tiny. Truly, under five feet and dainty with it. A fairy of a woman. By the time I married her, I knew I was not in love with her. She was all the things I told you, but she coupled that with a distinct lack of intelligence." He bit his lip and forced the truth out, the facts that shamed him. "I should have backed away, left her to another suitor, but I was blinded by the idea of revenge against Louis. I thought I would return to London in triumph and conquer all. I accomplished part of that when I bought the fleet from Louis through a third party. I was involved in other matters, other businesses, and learning everything I could. And my antipathy faded away. It just didn't matter anymore. But he did me a backhanded favor. Being forced to forge my own way in the world was the making of me."

He wouldn't let Dorothea look away. He gained strength from her steady gaze, honest and true. He could only honor her by giving her the same in return. That meant everything. "Mary could not manage a household, even the relatively modest one we had. She could never have handled Cressbrook, much less the other houses that belong to the estate. She would never have coped with the marquessate. Life was for amusement and parties and pretty clothes. I indulged her. After all, she'd brought me a great deal. But she took to coming to the office and the docks. Then she became pregnant and she was overjoyed. So was her father, who told her she had produced an heir for him at last."

Dorothea cupped his cheek, and he moved into it, using the caress to help him tell her the rest. He gathered strength from her touch.

"Mary followed me everywhere, telling me how much she loved me, insisting on being with me. When I had to work, she came to me. She *clung,* Dorothea, and I could not bear it. When Jeremiah—her father—sent me away on business I was relieved, even though it meant fighting bears and the natives. When I came home, I discovered that my wife had miscarried of our first child.

"We conceived again, although the doctor said that was unwise. But what Mary wanted, she usually got. I was as patient as I could be. This time the pregnancy went better, but she continued to cling. I was ashamed because I nearly lost patience with her so many times. She was spoiled, indulged, and she did not know what *not* being that way felt like. I had to continue as we were, but I determined to talk to her after the baby arrived. Mary behaved more like a child than a woman. I told myself she was afraid, and I consoled her, but I knew that I would never survive her dependency. When she grew larger with the child, she accused me of taking lovers. I did not."

"You don't have to tell me that." Dorothea's soft words humbled him. "You're too good."

He pushed her hair back, relishing that touch of silk against his skin. Instinctively, he wanted to avoid her gaze, and for that reason he did not. Because he wanted to see her every response. He would spare her nothing. "I lost my temper with her, I was unkind." He dropped his gaze and swallowed, but determinedly lifted his eyes again. He would see this through. "I upset her, but when I apologized, she accepted my words and returned to adoring me. I held myself back from her, didn't encourage her, because she showed signs of getting worse. She wouldn't leave me alone. I did my best. Perhaps her mind was disturbed by her condition, I told myself. I couldn't speak about it to anyone. Her father's people surrounded me. They acted as if she was fine, I thought, so it must be me. I was oversensitive, this was normal for expectant mothers. Everyone indulged her, smiled at her, thought this was usual. So I did, too."

He swallowed. Remembering this time was so hard, but harder on poor Mary. He hadn't told anyone because of what happened to her. And his guilt, which had accompanied him like a living thing, his constant companion. Until recently, it had been with him always. "I was wrong. I should have taken her in hand. Perhaps then, she might have..." He forced himself to say it. "Not died."

"No, no. How can you say that? She was tiny, you said."

He turned his head and kissed her palm. "After the doctor told her no more children, I insisted on separate bedrooms. But it did no good. I still weakened, I should have been stronger. I had a lot to do, since my father-in-law had decided to retire and allow me to conduct most of the day-to-day business. I had to win over the men he dealt with, many of whom were suspicious of me, so I worked hard, keeping long hours. Mary was with me every moment of every day."

A fine tremor shivered through her body. "I don't think that's normal. Not in anyone."

Relief poured through him. She understood. "One evening I lost my temper. She ran off in tears and later that night went into labor. We called the midwife, and later, the doctor. She didn't call for me at first. Not until she was dying." He paused, gathering his words. "I went to her, and I lied. The physician had already told me we would lose her, but I didn't tell her. I told her I loved her, that she would be fine after she'd slept. I told her our son was healthy and with his nurse. She believed me."

"And she died," she said softly. "You did the right thing, Ben. You could have done nothing to change what happened. I believe that. And I know you. You've shown me who you are, and that is the man I fell in love with. Who I will always love. A lesser man would have told her the truth to assuage his own conscience, to make himself feel better. You did not. I admire you for that, Ben."

He closed his eyes. "My father-in-law said something like that. 'Thank you for making my little girl's last moments happy ones,' he said, but I could not accept his words at the time. He died shortly after, declaring himself content. That I was a son to him."

His tears no longer shamed him. She held him while he wept for the lives that were uselessly wasted, and his inability to do anything to help them. And the old man's grief that killed him not long after. Leaving Ben to continue their legacy, alone and certain he was better off that way.

He could say no more. He was exhausted, completely worn out, but a seed of peace rested inside him. He'd made his confession, and while he still thought he'd made some serious errors, the woman he loved more than life had accepted him and what he had done.

* * * *

Hearing about her husband's first wife in her marriage bed might not be every woman's idea of a satisfactory wedding night, but Dorothea was glad he'd told her. She'd known something had been wrong with his first marriage, but it had lain in territory she couldn't breach on her own. He slept peacefully after that, as if she'd absolved him, and she followed him into slumber shortly after.

She woke up as the clock chimed eight. She was lying on her back, her husband snuggled up close to her, and they were both naked. They had left the drapes around the bed open, such was their haste to make love.

Someone had cleared up the mess they'd made. And seen them here. Her face heated with embarrassment, but she took care to lie still because she didn't want to wake him.

Every time Ben breathed, a puff of air skimmed her shoulder. Turning her head, she watched him, her big, clever husband. His brutish build hid a kind and loving nature she was selfishly glad no other woman had discovered before her. They had troubled days ahead, but together they would come through it, one way or another.

Last night had given her a power and strength she was barely aware of before. He loved her, and he trusted her with every last secret. From the stern, forbidding man who had first entered this house to this moment meant they had come a long way, but they had further to go. Telling her about Mary had taken a lot of courage. If she had not accepted him, he'd have kept quiet and never mentioned his concerns again. And their marriage could have slowly deteriorated into one that functioned well but had no heart. A working partnership would have suited her a month ago, but she'd learned so much since then, mostly about herself. He'd helped her find the woman she'd buried deep, shown her what she could be.

And Angela and the SSL. Teaching her how to be herself, how to use what she had to make her life the best possible one. Even better than she'd imagined.

She could live with the ghost of Mary. Even remember her with fondness. The woman didn't deserve what had happened to her. But if she, Dorothea, had the good fortune to give birth to a healthy child, she would find a place for the name of his first wife. Mary would be remembered.

They'd made love again, waking and reaching for each other in the kind of wordless union that acknowledged they both wanted the same thing, and they'd find it only here, with each other. Nothing could destroy their bond now. Not even death. They'd taken their time, caressing, loving with their hands before they joined their bodies. She'd taken charge, sitting astride him, her hands on his chest, and he'd gazed up at her, smiling. In the thin, silvery light of a new day, she memorized what he looked like, so open to her. No secrets left.

The door behind her opened softly, and she braced herself to face whichever servant had come in. Closing her eyes and pretending to be asleep belonged to the past.

A housemaid walked softly across the room, a large can of steaming water in her hands. It made barely a rattle as she placed it on the washstand before plucking up the used towels and replacing them with the ones laid across her arm. When she turned around, she caught Dorothea watching.

Their gazes met, and to Dorothea's utter delight, the maid blushed, from her neatly wrapped fichu up to the roots of her hair. "You can bring us some tea," Dorothea suggested.

The maid curtsied and left, closing the door a little louder than she'd opened it.

"You handled that well."

Dorothea hadn't noticed her husband's steady breathing had changed. His eyes were open, bright with amusement. "However, in future, I think we'll tell them to stay out of the room until we call for them. They can leave the fire laid and put the water can outside the door."

He raised himself up on one elbow, smiling at her. She'd never seen Ben like this, his features unshadowed, eyes sparkling. Had he been this way as a boy? Without the bunched muscles, of course.

Reveling in her right to do so, she stroked his arm, letting her palm flow down the hills and valleys of sinew and muscle and satiny skin. He made a noise suspiciously like a purr. "If you carry on doing that, the maid is going to see a lot more than one naked shoulder. But if you're game, so am I."

In a swift lunge he had her, pressing her down, kissing her passionately. She curved her hand around his neck, holding him close, responding to him. Already he'd trained her body to react to his loving. Wetness gathered in that place between her legs. She should really ask him what the names for their private places were, because the last thing she wanted was to be coy.

But he was reacting to her, his shaft rising to press between them like an unspoken promise.

With a groan, he tore himself away and swung out of bed, erection and all. He strode across the room and picked up his breeches. "I will not impose myself on you this morning, sweetheart."

"Impose?" she demanded indignantly, but she had to suppress her wince when she sat up.

He laughed, but his brow creased when he spotted her reaction. "I'll order a bath for you. For us both. The servants will probably hate us for it but let them. You need it. Soak there, my sweet, because I'm not keeping away from you any longer." After pulling up his breeches, he fastened his falls. "I'll order Rougier to bring one of my robes here tonight. And you need something sumptuous to wrap yourself in. That I can unwrap." He smiled. "There is nothing wrong with what you have, but I'd enjoy indulging myself. Ivory silk, perhaps, a shade lighter than your hair."

"Do you have plans for the day?"

"Only for a few hours. I want to conclude the business of the estate, from my brief tenure. I'll ensure a good man is put in charge until William can sell out and come back. The accounts are in as good a state as they'll ever be, but I'll ensure they're stored properly, and everything is locked. Then I'll come looking for you, so be warned, my lady. What do you have in mind?"

"Probably the library. I've left some books out there, so I'll put them away." That part of her life was over.

He came back, leaning over her. "Take a footman with you. Don't go alone. Promise me?"

She would not insult him by pretending not to understand. "You think someone may come for me?"

"Yes."

"Lady Honoria?"

He swallowed, dropping his gaze. "I cannot discount it, not until we discover who killed my cousin. I'm sorry."

She caught his wrist, his pulse throbbing reassuringly against her fingers. "You have nothing to be sorry for."

"I had no notion of her character before I came home. It is as if there is a lack in her, an inability to believe other people exist outside her head. She cares for nobody but herself. I had no idea how deeply that went until she confronted me in the corridor. I honestly believed she cared for both Louis and myself, but she does not." He lifted his chin, his gaze burning into hers. "But I am not so care-for-nothing, and I want you safe."

"And that day in the garden? She did not want you dead."

He shook his head. "We cannot be sure. I'm a means to an end, just as Louis was. Eliminate me and Louis would have the title. Eliminate him and she was free to claim me. Either way, it did not matter to her. But if she was behind that attack, then she must have an accomplice. So beware, sweetheart. Do not go anywhere on your own. Always take a witness, and someone to protect you. Promise me?"

She nodded.

He gave her a tender kiss that threatened to become something more passionate, before pulling away with a rueful laugh and taking himself off.

Leaving Dorothea feeling well and truly married.

Chapter 27

Dorothea had breakfast brought up to her, ravenously tucking into a plateful of chops, kidneys, scrambled eggs, and fried potatoes, surprised when she finished the lot. Although she didn't stint her appetite, she never overindulged. Who knew that married love was so tiring? When they'd first made love, he'd taken care with her, but last night they'd feasted on each other like barbarians. A celebration of love. May there be many more.

He was right about Boston, too. She would miss her family, but what woman had the opportunity to start a completely new life and explore new ways? The adventure had only just begun. But for now, she should concentrate on concluding this adventure. She would draw a line under it and look forward to married life with a clear conscience. With the man she loved by her side.

The gown she chose to wear was a vivid grass green with stripes of white, and flowers embroidered over the whole, thicker at the hem, tapering to her waist. She'd bought this one new this season, but who said new gowns had to be saved for special occasions? It rustled beautifully when she moved, and she enjoyed the *shush-shush* sound as she headed down the main stairs in the direction of the library. The only somber note was the band wrapped around her upper arm.

In the hall, she motioned to a footman. Ben had asked her to keep one with her for protection, and although she doubted she was in danger any longer, she would accede to his wishes. She had no desire to upset him over so small a matter.

The man followed her without speaking.

Murmuring from downstairs told her that a few people were still at breakfast. It was served at ten and cleared up an hour later. But she had eaten enough in her room. While she was not exactly shy about her changed state, she was a little on edge at meeting people. They'd *know*. She'd prefer them to leave, but failing that, she and Ben would leave instead. Last night, Ben had suggested a trip abroad, perhaps to Paris.

She met a few guests. Lady Steeping was gracious, and back to her patronizing self. "If you need a sponsor for court, pray don't hesitate to contact me."

Dorothea thanked her and continued on her way, closing the library door behind her and leaving her footman outside with orders to remain there. She leaned against the door with a sigh of relief. A little solitude would be more than welcome. No doubt she would have to be cool and collected at dinner, but that was hours away.

The books she'd consulted yesterday still lay on the table running down the center of the room. After Angela had taken her ledgers away, Dorothea had pulled out the family histories again, wondering if she'd missed something. In a better-managed household, someone would have put them away after checking with her. Instead, Dorothea would replace them on the shelves herself. In their proper places.

As she stacked the first volume of family history, the door opened to admit Sir James. He paused, smiled at the footman, and left the door open. Sir James bade her good morning, but he didn't use a name for her.

"Mrs. Thorpe," she offered.

Smiling, he wagged his finger at her. "You do not trick me that way. I have made my decision, but I will tell the two interested parties first. If your husband wants you present, I will not gainsay him."

Her husband. How good that sounded. Whether she was Mrs. Thorpe or the Marchioness of Belstead, she was married to the right man.

"Did you find any sign of a second marriage between your husband's parents?"

Ruefully she shook her head.

He sighed. "Lord Hardwicke is extremely particular about marriage. Irregular unions pain him."

So, he was telling her that she wouldn't have a title. Her heart lightened. Since she'd already made up her mind to it, the news did not come as a blow. "So William is the new marquess?"

He spread his hands helplessly.

"William will be a worthy marquess, I'm sure." She turned to put another book back on the shelf. With the decision made, she could look forward to her new life. Indecision had made her nervous. She was done with it.

Sir James strolled to the table and turned a page in the fourth volume. The family history had been compiled by the third marquess, the man who had built this house, or rather, reconstructed it from the property already in place. He'd gone on to make Belstead a prosperous and notable title. Titles had two ranks: the formal order of precedence, and the wealth and influence wielded by each title. The order was completely different. A baron, if he had the connections and the interest, could wield more power than a duke. As could a mere commoner, as Robert Walpole showed a generation ago. With the estate reckoned up, Ben could count himself at least as wealthy as the Marquess of Belstead. In the colonies they had a new world to make, with challenges aplenty.

Sir James inclined his head. "I'll go up to write the letter to his lordship, then I will call the two principals and inform them of my decision." He bowed. "If you will excuse me?"

"Of course."

He left Dorothea alone, and she got on with closing the volumes, lingering over a couple as she daydreamed about her future.

About ten minutes later, someone else came in. Dorothea looked up with a bright smile, convinced Ben had finished his task and was coming to find her. But it was his cousin.

After closing the door, William bowed, and gave her his smile. The action revealed the similarity between the brothers, and her heart ached for him.

He came around the table and took her hand, forcing her to put the book she was holding back on the table. "I believe Sir James is about to find for me." He grimaced. "I never imagined it would come to this. That I would become the marquess."

"Not even when Louis claimed the title?"

He turned away, shrugging carelessly. "It crossed my mind. But only as a passing thought." He sighed. "I was intent on my military career."

"Do you have to sell out?"

He nodded dolefully. "I must marry and start my nursery. In many ways, I envy you. You have the chance to make your own future. Mine is set out for me. I have to restore this estate and make babies."

"Do you have your eye on anyone?" she asked brightly. He would have his pick of the crop next season.

"I'll go up to London and make my selection. That's how it is done, isn't it?" He brightened. "I could court Miss Childers. She's a very beautiful woman, and healthily rich. What more could a man want?"

Dorothea laughed. "Many men have tried before you and failed. She refuses to marry."

William raised a dark brow. "*I* have not courted her yet."

She'd heard men say that before. Dorothea let the topic drop and busied herself closing the tomes. "I had thought to read through all these, but I'm not sure we'll have the time."

"You're not planning to stay?"

She shrugged, surprised how little the place meant to her. The house was lovely. Most women in her position would have been thrilled to become a marchioness, but that didn't matter next to the prospect of being with Ben and making a new life with him. "We'll probably take ship for Boston as soon as we can. It's September already, so Ben won't want to delay for long."

"Good." Deep satisfaction colored William's voice. "And you're sure you found nothing in these?"

She shook her head. "Nothing except a detailed history of the family. No additions to describe the current generation."

His eyes gleamed as he closed a book. "We'll have to see about continuing the story. How would you describe our recent problems?"

"A confusion over inheritance."

He opened one of the books she'd just closed and flicked through the pages.

Lifting the next two volumes, Dorothea went to the bookcase and slid them onto the shelf. But these proved recalcitrant; something was stopping them from resting in their proper places. She put the books on the floor and reached to the back of the dusty shelves, bracing herself for the scurry of a spider, or worse, a dead rodent blocking the space.

Instead, her fingers met paper. Excitement sparkled along her veins. Was she about to make a dazzling discovery? Ancient documents, perhaps? Carefully, so as not to tear the delicate items, she drew out the sheets. Behind them was a large leather-bound volume, tucked well back and pushed flat against the wall.

Stacking the loose papers on top of the volume, she turned to take them to the table, where the light was better.

But standing before her, preventing that, was William.

"Ah," he said regretfully. "I wish you had not found those."

* * * *

Stepping into the munitions room, Ben shivered. If he stayed, he wouldn't keep the valuable family documents here. There were better ways of ensuring their security while providing a much more comfortable working space. He'd seen a likely room with narrow windows that could have bars set in the stone sills. This dank room couldn't be good for the documents, some of them ancient, as old as the title.

He flipped open the latest ledger and frowned at the accounts. There was a pattern here, something he wasn't seeing, but he felt it. He knew something was wrong, and it had been bothering him for a while. Perhaps if he could discover his concern, he could leave with a clear conscience. He'd have done his best.

Becoming engrossed in the book before him, he traced the lines with the tip of his finger.

Yes, there it was. Ah, yes. Why in hell had he not seen this before?

Every month Louis sold something, but the dates didn't align with the recording of the purchases, the extravagant spending that had been Louis's downfall. And the debts that had been increasing in frequency in the last two years, the ones he suspected were due to gambling. There was no notation of where the debts were incurred. From what he knew of his late cousin, Louis wouldn't have been desperate enough to visit the hells. He had no need. His club and the coffeehouse provided ample ways to dissipate a fortune. But if that had happened, the debtors and the places would surely have been recorded.

And they should not be here, in the estate ledgers. They should be in the private accounts. They were in a different hand, barely noticeable in the elegant copperplate, but the pen dug deeper into the paper, and the ink was blacker. The flourish Louis customarily used wasn't there.

That was it. The different handwriting.

He was onto something. His excitement growing, Ben dragged a piece of paper to where he stood and dipped a fresh quill in the standish. He scribbled a few notes, recorded the debts separately. Looked at them for a pattern.

And he found one.

A swish of silk announced the arrival of Honoria. Ben bit off a curse. Just as he was getting somewhere.

He should have closed the door. What point was a secure room with an open door? Any room he designed would have a self-closing door at the very least, easily accomplished with levers and weights. Too late now.

Without bothering to hide his distrust of her, he stepped behind the table. "May I help you, Honoria?" He stood ready to defend himself, if it should become necessary. After all, he had not discounted Honoria from his list of suspects.

She wasn't dressed in deep, dramatic black, but her gown was plain and subdued, and she wore no paint on her face. Except for the deep shadows under her eyes, she could be the girl who had first stepped into a London ballroom, excited for her first grown-up ball. "I merely wanted to apologize."

About to ask about what in particular, he bit off his sarcastic words. They were the last thing she needed now. "There's no need."

Her shaky laugh struck him to the heart. This was the first time he'd seen the old Honoria since he'd arrived at Cressbrook House. This was the woman he'd courted and fallen for all those years ago. The society beauty with a sensitive soul, not the sophisticated woman of fashion, excelling at hiding her true self. Or the woman crazed with getting her own way. Did she have a knife somewhere about her person? Would she take the insane risk of trying to kill him now? She wouldn't have brought a pistol. The shot would bring servants running. Unless she had a plan that would involve implicating him.

Damnation, why had he not taken his own advice and brought someone with him?

He kept the table between them.

"On the contrary, there is need. I know I provoked you and Louis to fight seven years ago. Back then, I thought it was exciting. But I came down to earth quickly when I discovered the results of my flirting. I will not say which man I preferred, and in truth, I did not know. You were the future marquess, and the man my parents preferred. But Louis was the heir, and he thrilled me."

"So your heart chose him." That knowledge would have devastated him once. Not now. Perhaps he had pursued her too vigorously or made his attentions too passionate. Now, she was his cousin-in-law, and that was all.

"Yes, it did. And after he died I went out of my mind. I thought of the children—yes, I know people think I abandoned them, but I didn't. Truly, I haven't. I just don't make my attentions too obvious. I dislike people who make their children the center of attention. That happened to me, you know."

"You must have been a lovely child," he said without considering what he was saying.

"Yes, I was." There was no vanity in her voice, just plain fact. She would have been paraded and indulged. Not the best upbringing for a child. He'd never considered that before, and now guilt suffused him when he recalled how wrapped up he was in his own concerns, his own importance. He'd wanted Honoria, so naturally she would come to him.

Ben ducked his head. "I'm sorry. I've misjudged you."

"Society does that." The matter-of-fact tone hurt. She was right, especially where women were concerned. His jewel of a wife had been judged too tall, not pretty enough, and then too old. And she'd been forced to accept that fate. Yet she had intelligence, grace, and beauty—yes, beauty.

Honoria continued. "I will return to my parents and take the girls with me." Her lips twisted. "My father will probably have me married to someone else before the end of the year, but at least the girls will be safe. Whatever happens, they'll stay with me." She gave him a wry smile. "I have to admit you made me angry when you arrived at dinner with your new wife. But it is your choice, and the deed is done. Isn't it?" She sent him a questioning look.

Ben nodded. "I'm very happy."

"At least one of us is."

A thought occurred to him. "The estate still holds several small properties. Louis didn't sell them all. You could take one of those."

"No." A bitter tone entered her voice, and she blinked. "If it wasn't for William, he wouldn't have had to sell half of what he did. At least half. We spent, but we bought furniture, jewels, clothes, and they can be sold again. They were investments."

His breath caught in his throat. "What does William have to do with it?"

She stared at him as if he knew something he did not. Except he did— he had just discovered it. Honoria had dropped the final piece onto the chessboard. Now he could see the whole game.

The penny dropped, heavily. Understanding shot through him with the force of a bullet. "When did he incur the debts?"

She rolled her eyes. "When did he not? Every time he went on campaign. Once he had the taste for it, he rarely left the tables before dawn."

Military men were renowned for betting. Wagers on everything under the sun, even which of their company would die first, although of course that particular wager was banned. It didn't stop them doing it. "Cards?"

"Dice."

The word fell like a hammer of doom between them. "So Louis felt obliged to pay his debts?"

She nodded. "The estate he inherited from his father is largely sold, or mortgaged. If Louis inherited, he could have paid off William's debts and found a way to stop him gambling."

So William had never conquered his habit. He had merely kept it quiet and told people that he had done so. The youthful folly that both Ben and Louis had grown out of as they found other interests had remained with William and grown to command his life.

And with Louis's death, that source of income was cut off. If William got the estate, he would wager away the unentailed parts in a fortnight.

Ben had seen men—and women—taken with gambling fever. Once it got into the blood, there was no going back, no stopping. William would end his life in a debtor's prison, perhaps the Fleet, where that fraudulent cleric had pretended to marry Ben's parents. A strange irony, that.

Ben tried to tell himself he didn't care, but it wasn't true. When he'd thought he'd left the estate in safe hands, he was happy to move away. But the blood of his ancestors flowed through his veins. How could he leave the estate for someone to throw away?

He had to. He had no choice.

A drop of black ink fell from the pen he was still holding to the paper below. The one that had revealed the debts had been worst when William was in the field with the army. Only when he'd recalled the pattern of military disputes in the last few years, and where William's regiment was stationed, did he see it.

But that wasn't enough to prove anything. Even if he could prove William was a complete and utter villain, Sir James wouldn't find against him. Primogeniture ruled his thinking. A shame a man couldn't choose his heir, but even if he could, Ben's technical illegitimacy would rule him out.

If he couldn't find the records of his parents' marriage, he would lose the title and see the estate disgraced. His father's legacy would be ruined. If he'd considered William worthy, Ben could have walked away with a clear conscience. He couldn't do that now.

Those records existed; he was sure of it. What if—what if William had found them? Or even Louis?

"Did you help Louis destroy the proof of my parents' second marriage?" He was taking a chance in assuming that, but it was all he had.

Honoria spun around in a whirl of skirts, facing away from him, toward the door. "I don't know what you mean. Papers?" She gave an artificial laugh.

She knew, all right. Swiftly, Ben rounded the table and moved in front of her, blocking her exit. He was no longer afraid she would strike him. She was not the murderer, merely a coldhearted woman. "What happened, Honoria?"

Their gazes met. He wouldn't look away. Let her do that. Let her deny what had happened.

Her shoulders slumped. "Louis didn't destroy them. He said he'd hidden them in case he needed them. Don't ask me where, because I do not know. He said the fewer people who knew, the better." She sighed. "I'm sorry, Ben. I couldn't tell you before Louis..."

She couldn't become the marchioness now. And now he was convinced she hadn't killed Louis or persuaded someone to push the cherub off the roof. She certainly hadn't tried to shoot him at the duck hunt, because she wasn't there. Louis could have done that, but he had not.

William had done it all. If he, Ben, died, Sir James would find for Louis, which meant William would have his debts paid and be in a position to gamble more recklessly. If Louis died, William would become the marquess. Without the papers, he still would, but if he'd killed his brother, Ben would have to drag the family into a scandal it would never recover from. And his wife, the person who meant more to him than anyone in the world.

For a heartbeat he stopped thinking clearly. But he had to go on.

"Do you think William killed Louis?" He hated putting the question so bluntly, but he needed to know. Honoria understood the men best.

"I don't know. He could have, but I was asleep." She hung her head. "I find laudanum helps me to sleep better, and I've been getting headaches of late. That's why I heard nothing."

Her explanation made perfect sense. A person could sleep through volleys of gunfire under the spell of that drug. "I think they might have argued. They've been doing that a lot recently." She waved helplessly, her gesture graceful even now. "Louis was at his wits' end. That's why he took the papers. He only did it after we knew you were back."

Ben narrowed his eyes. "Where was he likely to hide the papers? Can you think of a clue, something he said?"

She pursed her lips in thought. "He said I would never find them because it was the one room in the house where I never went."

A man hurtled in without warning. Schultz, his hair ruffled, his face a mask of horror, most unlike his usual calm self. "Sir, madam, one of the footmen heard a cry for help from the library. Then a scream. But the doors are locked. We can't get in." He swallowed.

The library! Honoria was not fond of reading, so that was the room she never went into. He'd arranged to go up there later, after he'd finished with the accounts. His wife was in the library.

Pushing past Honoria, he headed for the door at full tilt, his shoes hammering the stone passage as he made his way to the stairs. Behind him people shouted.

If they hadn't broken that door down by the time he reached it, heads would roll. Not least William's.

Chapter 28

Dorothea clutched the loose papers to her chest. She no longer doubted what she held. The parish register fell to the floor, landing with a crash that shook the floorboards. It was a big book. "I have the proofs of marriage, do I not?"

"Yes, you do. I'm so sorry, Dorothea, but I must have them."

"Why?" She furrowed her brow. Why would he want the title, when he'd been passionate about his army career?

"Because only inheriting will save me."

That didn't make sense. "You wanted to go back to the army. You were to become a colonel."

He nodded. "And I still will. I can go back. I wouldn't be the first peer of the realm to serve in the army."

She held the future of William and Ben in her hands. And her own, come to that. She had no doubt she was holding the only official records of the second marriage between Ben's parents; the one that made him the true heir to the title. The papers crackled as she held them closer to her chest. "I need to show these to Ben and Sir James."

William raised the stakes when he drew a pistol out of his capacious coat pocket and leveled it at her.

She opened her mouth to call out, but warned him first. "I have a footman outside. He will come at my call." Surely, he wouldn't risk being caught like that.

William shook his head. "I sent him away. After all, I am the marquess-elect. And the door is locked."

She swallowed. That meant he would have time to get away after he'd killed her.

The click of him drawing back the hammer sounded loud in the spacious room. Dorothea fought to keep her breathing steady.

Dorothea took only a second to make her decision. She wouldn't give him the papers. "You won't use that here. They're already looking for Louis's murderer. They'd think you did that if you shoot me."

Even now, looking at his handsome face with all the kindness stripped away, she couldn't believe William had killed his brother. She read desperation in his eyes. She didn't know why he was doing this, but he was determined.

"He always had a temper, my brother, and he never could control it properly. Ask your husband. Why do you think that duel took place? If they'd let themselves cool down, it would never have happened. So I pushed Louis a little. Only a little."

"Why would you do that, William? And you can't kill me." Trembling began deep inside her, and she had to fight to control it. "You know you can't." She tried to keep her voice calm and reasonable.

"I can. They won't look to me because I won't be here." He jerked his head. "There's a secret passage from the library to a small outside door. We used to use it as children, but nobody remembers it now. Except me. I told Schultz I would take a walk in the gardens, since the rain has cleared. I was never here."

So he would shoot her, take the documents, go outside and dispose of them, this time for good, and come back in again, pretending innocence? No doubt he could find someone to blame.

An icy chill flowed over her, like the sea coming in. Had he done this with Louis? And the statue too? He'd been on the roof when they were talking. He'd gone on the duck hunt.

Why didn't matter as much as stopping him from doing it. But surely, he should have fired by now?

A click from behind her told her somebody else knew about the secret door. She was standing with her back to it. As it opened, William lifted his gaze.

Someone stood behind her. She didn't have to turn around to know it was Ben. She felt his presence.

"Put that pistol down, William. Either that, or shoot me, too. And Schultz. Do you have enough weapons to deal with us all?"

The room was still, as if time itself had stopped.

William shook his head. The tip of the pistol wavered.

"You could have come to me to settle your debts. Or confessed the whole to Miss Childers and arranged a schedule of repayments. Instead, you chose to murder people."

"You couldn't have saved me."

"Why kill Louis?"

William shrugged. "He refused to help me anymore. Enough, he said. So I took him at his word."

So William owed money? Realization hit Dorothea with the power of a lightning bolt. He'd been the one who gambled. That, plus Louis's extravagance, had brought the estate to its knees. She gaped.

Louis's extravagance could be viewed as investment, if the gambling debts were discounted. Her world turned on its axis.

"I'm wealthy enough to cover your debts. Not that I would have, but I could have helped you."

Her husband spoke sense, but even now Dorothea was glad he hadn't offered to pay off William's debts.

William's mouth twisted in a sneer. "And have me live like a pauper for the rest of my life? Unable to face my peers? No." He returned his attention to Dorothea. "I'm sorry," he said. "Turn away."

And as the shot rang out, Ben dragged her into his arms and shoved her face against his chest, so she didn't have to watch.

Epilogue

Two years later

As the agonized scream came from behind the closed door, Ben could bear no more. Throwing off Hal's restraining hands, he flung himself into the bedroom and went straight to the bed. Ignoring the scandalized screams of the women attending his wife, he reached for her.

Dorothea gripped his hand so tightly that his knuckles ground together, but he took no more notice of it than if a breeze had swept across him. Because his gaze was fixed on the bundle in the arms of the maid. His baby was squalling noisily, but that did not give him pause.

If she had delivered their child, why was she still in pain?

Something was wrong.

Her knees were raised, the sheets tossed off, her night rail stained with sweat and blood. "Dorothea, my darling!"

A midwife was bent over her, but she sent Ben a poisonous glare. "You should not be here, my lord."

He took no notice.

Dorothea scrunched up her face and bore down, grunting with the strain. What was going on?

"Here it is, my lady. Keep pushing!"

Bewildered, Ben hung on. This wasn't what he'd expected to see, what he'd dreaded witnessing.

A sharp cry broke the air and Dorothea gave one scream before she sucked in a deep breath. The maid mopped her brow with a clean cloth.

"Another fine boy, my lord," the midwife announced, straightening. She held a naked, bloody baby, unmistakably squirming in her arms and letting out lusty cries. The midwife handed the child to another maid, who took it to a table and commenced cleaning it. "We'll have them both swaddled in an instant, then you may see them."

"No!" Dorothea's order snapped sharp and clear.

Ben knew what she meant, and he reinforced her request. "No swaddling." The practice wasn't approved of by the experts they'd consulted in London. Wrapping a baby up tightly could lead to suffocation, and doctors no longer considered that a baby's limbs needed straightening.

Desperately determined to keep his beloved safe during her pregnancy, he'd taken her to every midwife and physician he could find. They had all declared her strong and healthy, but Dorothea had been more eager to discover the latest advice for the babies. No swaddling, and she should try to feed them herself. Ben had still engaged a wet nurse, the respectable wife of a sailor who had her own baby to feed, but could take care of two.

They would need her now, because taking the wet nurse's own baby into consideration, they had three to feed.

Now he knew why Dorothea had been large in the latter part of her pregnancy, which had worried him desperately, but he hadn't shown it. Knowing his concerns, she'd taken pains to reassure him, which had shamed him.

"Twins?" Saying it didn't make what had just happened any more real. He was dreaming this, he must be.

The midwife looked up. "Aye, my lord. A little small, but no smaller than twins should be. They're fine boys."

Dorothea was lying on the bed, smiling. Her legs were still up, the sheet tented over her knees, and there was no mistaking the blood staining the bedding. But nowhere near the flood he'd feared, that he'd witnessed before. Dorothea's fair hair, darkened with sweat, was sticking to her forehead and cheeks.

She'd never looked so beautiful. Not on her presentation at court as the Marchioness of Belstead, nor at the ball held at their London house to celebrate its reopening. Not at his office at the Pool of London, a forest of masts outside the window, dressed as plainly as any City merchant's wife. Nor even with him in bed, laughing in delight as they made love.

Someone shoved a chair forward and he sat, still holding her hand. The midwife and her assistant made themselves busy with the boys, who by now had begun to cry in tandem. "Now you know she's well, my lord," the midwife snapped, "would you leave the room? This is a woman's work."

"No." He would not budge. He wanted to see their sons the instant she did. And he wanted to ensure she was all right. "You are wonderful." He leaned forward, giving her a gentle kiss. "I love you so much."

"I love you too."

The women moved around, cleaning up, helping deliver the afterbirth.

Too intent on his wife, Ben was barely aware of them changing the linen and putting Dorothea into a fresh night rail. She shoved her hair back with shaking hands. Ben took a damp cloth from someone and cleaned her face. He couldn't seem to stop smiling.

Then the babies were put into her arms.

That was when they both cried with sheer happiness.

Author Biography

Lynne Connolly was born in Leicester, England, and lived in her family's cobbler's shop with her parents and sister. She loves all periods of history, but her favorites are the Tudor and Georgian eras. She loves doing research and creating a credible story with people who lived in past ages. In addition to her Emperors of London series and The Shaws series, she writes several historical, contemporary, and paranormal romance series.

Visit her on the web at lynneconnolly.com, read her blog at lynneconnolly. blogspot.co.uk, find her on Facebook, and follow her on Twitter @lynneconnolly.

References

For a list of references and books I used, check my website, or contact me directly.

The Girl With the Pearl Pin

Founded by the wealthiest woman in London, an unconventional crime-solving club brings together single lords and overlooked ladies from every rung of society. It's a perfectly scandalous match . . .

As London's most sought-after bachelor, the Duke of Leomore stuns society when he announces his engagement to a woman who has just been branded a thief. Yet as his painfully shy "bride-to-be" understands, it is merely a ruse until The Society for Single Ladies apprehends the true culprit—and a ploy to further delay Leo's obligation to wed. For him, marriage will be a purely practical affair. Still, why does a stolen kiss with his faux fiancée conjure such tempting visions of romance? . . .

As if being falsely accused weren't mortifying enough, Phoebe North is now the talk of the town. And while she knows Leo did the honorable thing to protect her reputation, she can't help but long for more. It would be an impossible match given their unequal stations, and Leo has made his view of marriage quite clear. Yet his kiss and flirtatious ways say something else. If only she could persuade him of how delightful it would be to thumb their noses at convention—and become fools for love . . . .

Chapter 1

April 1750

Phoebe North was about to experience the most romantic episode of her life. Quite unexpectedly too. The Duke of Leomore, "Call me Leo," leaned into her with the evident intention of fastening his mouth to hers. And Phoebe, surprised but completely in agreement, prepared for the onslaught.

Then merry hell exploded outside the secluded grotto they were sharing. Screams and the sound of running feet interrupted them.

The duke jerked back, gray eyes gleaming in the moonlight, and took her arm, urging her to retreat. Phoebe shook him off. Somebody out there was in trouble. This was no time for discreet withdrawal.

She took a couple of quick paces to the pillared entrance and went down the two steps to the main path, lifting the skirts of her new ball gown in a graceless manner her hostess would definitely not approve of. The sound of running came closer, and the ground under her feet trembled with the coming onslaught. Around the corner hurtled a man dressed in drab street clothes, his cocked hat pulled down low over his forehead. Something glittered in his grasp. He was too large for Phoebe to block with her body, but as he raced past, trailing the aroma of well-used clothing and body odor, she grabbed at his hand, trying to wrest away whatever he was carrying. The sounds of shouting and "Stop thief!" grew closer.

The bully shoved Phoebe, and she caught her heel in her skirt, tumbling backward.

Strong arms hauled her up, and she found herself drawn close to a hard, male chest. Her breath gone, she needed a moment, but she should really pull away.

A woman's shrill cries centered on her. "There she is, the thief! Look what she has in her hand!"

A soft male voice from behind her countered her ladyship's words. People crowded around, abandoning the brightly lit ballroom beyond. "I fail to understand how you draw that conclusion, ma'am. My betrothed and I were merely snatching a few quiet moments together."

Betrothed?

* * * *

Earlier that same evening, Leo's grandmother glared at him over the dinner table. Leo wouldn't have been surprised if the delicate china and gleaming silverware had turned to stone, followed in short order by himself. "You must not marry to oblige me. You must do it for the title and estate. You cannot be the last Leomore in the direct line." She tapped the crisp linen tablecloth twice to emphasize her point. She spoke with a vigor that belied her seventy years, but the walking cane propped within her reach told a different story.

"Pay heed, Leomore, if you do not make a decision for yourself soon, I shall do it for you."

He tried for frozen hauteur, although trying that with a woman who had personally hauled him out of trees on the estate and punished him for it made ducal reserve difficult to assume. "I will find a bride, Grandmama, never fear. I'm fully aware that you deserve rest and comfort, not to be obliged to act as my hostess and work for the family."

A smile curved her thin lips. While his grandmother barely topped five feet, every inch counted. Nobody overlooked her delicate form, nobody turned away when the Dowager Duchess of Leomore entered the room. She had all the dignity and grace of a queen and deployed it to great effect.

She softened her tone. "I know that, my dear, but you should also be aware that I will prevent it, if your selection is not suitable. I failed to do that with your father, but I will not shirk my duty a second time. While I cannot force you on to your knees in front of an eligible female, I can arrange matters to make it impossible for you to go ahead with an engagement to an unsuitable candidate." Her expression gentled, her gray eyes revealing more than most people saw. "Indeed, I regret the necessity, since you are content with your bachelor state. If your heir had lived, I would have remained content to let you take your time. Now the insufferable Erasmus has become your heir, you must do something to prevent him taking the dukedom."

Leo knew she was right. His cousin and heir up until the end of last season had died in a boating accident. John would have made a very good duke, had Leo died, without issue. On the other hand, John's younger brother, Erasmus, had absolutely no interest in family obligations. Not his own, at any rate, although he cared passionately about the Caesars. He would have the estate, its employees and dependents bankrupt in no time, despite the wealth the title carried, by buying the contents of Rome, and probably Athens, too. That must not happen, not after the depredations of Leo's parents.

His father had married for love. She was from a good family with a reasonable portion, but after Leo's birth they set about ruining the estate with their high living. The duke gave her everything, and then they had died together. Smallpox had taken both of them in a week, and because of the risk, Leo hadn't been allowed to see them.

They left a wrecked inheritance and a small, bewildered, half spoiled, half wild boy to carry on the venerable dukedom. Leo owed his grandmother more than he could ever repay. But that didn't stop him trying.

Leo picked up his glass of wine, watching the dark liquid glimmer before he took a sip. "I know it, ma'am." He would not keep her in suspense. "I intend to look about me this season. Did you compile the list I requested?" He would not have his grandmother upset, so his first criterion was to find someone the dowager liked, or at least could tolerate. The omissions would tell him what he needed to know. Nobody knew society better than his grandmother, even though she rarely ventured abroad these days. She did not need to. Society came to her.

She flourished a sheet of paper. "Here."

Silently he perused it until he got to a name near the bottom. "Miss Angela Childers?" He glanced up. "That's long odds, to say the least."

His grandmother lifted her chin. "The woman said she would never marry, but have any dukes asked her before? Dukes of your consequence?"

"Apart from the title, I can offer her nothing she cannot get for herself." He liked Miss Childers, the daughter of what society haughtily referred to as a mixed marriage. Which was to say, her grandmother had been a duchess, and her grandfather on the other side a wealthy City man. Leo had not seen the beautiful banker since the autumn of last year, but he recalled his pleasure in her company. And her rejection of any man who tried to get closer to her. "She refuses to marry, and I cannot imagine she will change her mind." But his grandmother had a point about the title, and he could not deny he liked Miss Childers. "I daresay everyone who is in town will be at her house tonight."

"She cannot hold the ball on her own," the duchess said, her lips primming in disapproval. "Asking men to her house when she lives there alone is not done."

"Her uncle reluctantly serves as host on these occasions, I believe."

Stuffy rules. As if Miss Childers would ever behave in a way to draw opprobrium. In a few years, society would consider her an old maid, and then she could do as she wished, or so she had declared last year. Protecting women was one thing, but the ridiculous unwritten rules society lived by irked him excessively. "I will have a chance to look over most of the women on your list." All the people his grandmother considered "everyone," at any rate. "Do I escort you, ma'am?"

His grandmother reached for her cane, her hand trembling. Old age had hit her hard the past few years, and now her hands were twisted with arthritis. Leo would marry the devil himself if he could get her the rest she deserved. "I received an invitation, but the event will be a sad squeeze, and I am in no mind to go. However, you may give the lady my warmest regards."

The dowager duchess's regards were hotly sought after. Leo duly promised to pass them on. He glanced down the other names. His grandmother had listed ten young ladies who would no doubt be eager to receive his attentions. A few weren't there. He would not trouble them, not caring enough about any of them to make a fuss or defy the dowager's wishes.

He knew what he wanted for himself. A sweetly amenable woman of good character and high birth who would not expect the close intimacy that had no place in a rational marriage. He allowed a certain measure of affection from his mistress, but his wife should be aware of her position in the world and behave accordingly. Recent family history made that requirement even more important.

He would do everything in his power to give his grandmother a tranquil old age.

"Leo, you must not marry without affection," his grandmother said, "but ensure your feelings for your bride are no more than that."

Leo nodded. He and the dowager agreed on that point. "Liking will be enough."

"Indeed, you may lavish affection on your mistress," Her Grace said. She shifted a little, enough to make the footman standing behind her chair hurry forward to help her stand. Not that she needed it, but she appreciated an attentive servant.

"I did." Leo shuddered, recalling La Coccinelle's final tantrum. Final for him, that was. He had sent her the deeds to the house he'd bought for her, and she could consider their affair at an end. He would certainly not return there.

Getting to his feet, Leo tossed his napkin down on the table before making his bow. "I will uphold the dignity of the dukedom, never fear."

"I know you will. You always do."

* * * *

"You look lovely," Angela said. "You'll do well tonight, Phoebe, mark my words."

Phoebe let her mouth tilt up in a doubting smile. "I'll d-do well enough." She flourished her fan. "At least I m-mastered that part." Her relatively plain gown marked her as inferior, so she didn't expect any special notice. In fact, she'd positively dislike it. They were standing outside Angela's bedroom door, ready to go downstairs and greet her guests.

Angela took her hands in hers. "You've come a long way since you escaped from your odious suitor in the country. Now you may enjoy yourself."

Phoebe smiled back. Yes, she had. Sir Marcus Callow, a bold, handsome, overbearing man had set his sights on her in the provincial Assembly she regularly attended. He was unexceptional, except that he wanted his own way in everything. Phoebe had avoided him. When he'd tried to press his suit by forcing a kiss on her so rough that it split her lip, Phoebe had grabbed Angela's invitation to visit her and escaped. All the way to London. With any luck, when she returned, Marcus would have settled on somebody else. Having a retiring nature did not mean she was compliant or weak, as many people supposed. And she would not marry Marcus. Not if she had to remain a spinster for the rest of her days.

Phoebe waited for Angela to lead her down the stairs and into the brilliantly lit hall below. Angela's Uncle Harold, who acted as host at times like this, waited for his niece. He was, as always, austere in the darkest of blues, his fashionable white wig firmly in place.

This was Phoebe's first society ball. She'd attended a few affairs in the week between Easter Monday and today, and now she was glad of it, because this was society at its most glittering.

This spacious London house took her breath away every time she went down into the main reception rooms, although Phoebe knew enough by now not to gawk. She bobbed a curtsey to Angela's uncle. "Good evening, sir." He gave her a smile and a nod.

Phoebe followed Angela through to the main chamber, the biggest drawing room, which was acting as the ballroom.

Forced up to the highest echelon in society, she was still overwhelmed by the grandeur and sheer luxury everyone displayed with a carelessness that concealed their wealth. Everyone except Phoebe. She'd come from a small town in Buckinghamshire, where her mother was the resident queen of local society to—this.

This being hundreds of candles in glittering chandeliers, precious gems around the women's throats, expensive French lace at every elbow—three rows of it—the most sumptuous fabrics used in careless profusion and a plethora of liveried servants ready to attend one's every need. And the sound of chatter, noisy and loud, buzzing in her head. The ball had only just started, and already the rooms were full. At least Angela had decreed no receiving line. This was more a rout than a ball, apparently. Not that Phoebe was entirely sure she knew the difference.

People crowded forward, eager to meet Phoebe's cousin.

Phoebe's stomach swooped, and she slammed her foot to the floor as the other slipped forward, and she nearly lost her balance. She should have roughened the soles of these shoes, but in her haste she'd forgotten. Now it was too late, and the parquetry floor was polished to a high shine. The servants hadn't even put French chalk on the part of the floor meant for dancing. If anyone else had shoes with shiny soles, the result could be interesting.

Angela responded to everyone, and Phoebe curtseyed when people deigned to notice her. Which they did too often for her liking. Her head spun with the names of all the earls, dukes, marquesses, and Lord knew who else flocking to the house for this ball. They politely enquired after her welfare, but their gazes never rested on her. They drifted past her to Angela. She doubted any of them would know her if they passed her in the street if she was here on her own.

The humiliation of that careless disregard annoyed her, but she could do nothing. As she was stiffening her shoulders, someone stopped. Lady Hamilton smiled and met her gaze. "Good evening, Miss North." She'd even remembered Phoebe's name. "Are you well?"

"Tolerably, I thank you," Phoebe said, dipping into a token curtsey, warming to the lady. "Is your daughter here tonight?"

Lady Hamilton wafted her fan in the vague direction of the dancers. "I believe so. But my son has arrived from the Continent. Do you think Miss Childers would like to meet him?" Not would Phoebe like to meet him, because who cared about her?

A sigh threatened to escape. And she was actually thinking that someone wanted to talk to her! How foolish she was. "I daresay she would, my lady. I'm sure she will enjoy meeting him." She would have to warn Angela before Lady Hamilton trapped her.

Angela headed, as she always did, to the group in the corner. The women and girls who sat together for company, chattering and pretending that not being asked to dance was exactly what they wanted. She always said she was one of them, even though she could obviously have any man she wanted for her husband. She chose not to, that was the difference.

Phoebe followed her.

This was where Phoebe belonged, with the older sisters who had not taken in society, women of little fortune, or those who genuinely did not care for dancing and popularity. This was the natural home of companions, the employed, or poor relations. A few widows, wealthy and otherwise, were sprinkled in for interest. Phoebe felt more at home there than anywhere else in a fashionable ballroom. When Angela left the group, Phoebe would stay.

Angela spoke to a few women, then took a seat, ignoring the stares from the more exalted guests. Fans fluttered, enough to make the flames of the hundreds of candles flicker in their holders. "Ladies, it does my heart good to see you."

They didn't titter or giggle. The women here were beyond that. They sat, a phalanx of the rejected, keeping each other company and pretending they didn't care. Some truly didn't, of course, and scorned society. Others did.

The lady next to her froze, and Phoebe lifted her gaze. And also froze.

A dark shadow in male form loomed up. His Grace, the Duke of Leomore stood and waited politely for Angela to notice him. He always made Phoebe shudder, and she did not know why. She had seen him before, since he attended most society events, or the ones that would amuse him. This season, or so gossip said, he intended to find a bride, which explained his attendance at parties he usually avoided.

He wore his hair naturally, a raven's wing tied back in a black bow. His eyes were dark gray, his frame large. But it was the intensity of this gaze that gave her pause, the way he saw through everything to the person beneath.

As far as she knew, he'd never actually noticed her.

Her heart pounded when he came to stand close to her. He bowed, not making his obeisance too deep, as gentlemen sometimes did, intending their bows as mockery rather than gestures of true respect.

Angela turned her attention to him with one brow raised slightly and met his smile of greeting with one of her own.

"Madam, it is always a delight to see you looking in such good heart," he said. "Would you do me the honor of dancing with me?"

"I'm afraid my hand is bespoken, sir." Angela could beat anyone at elaborate courtesy if she wished, which she rarely did. "May I present my cousin, Miss Phoebe North?"

The duke bowed to her, his expression stony. Fobbed off on the companion!

Phoebe nearly burst into laughter but sealed her lips firmly until she had risen to her feet and curtseyed to the exalted being. Although her reaction lasted but a second, she had the disconcerting impression that he'd noticed her amusement. Why should she care when he evidently thought so little of her? She should not, but she couldn't prevent her reaction to him.

At least he hadn't turned his back on her, even though Phoebe had fully expected him to do so. She was perfecting her bitter laugh. Perhaps she could use it on him.

But he didn't turn away. He gave her a bone-melting smile. "Would you do me the honor of favoring me with the next dance?"

A duke wanted to dance with her? Angela had adroitly turned him to her, but Phoebe was not sure this counted as a favor.

"Do you feel quite well, Miss North?" he enquired gently as she stifled her amusement.

Good Lord, this man was observant. She forced a smile. "Quite all right, th-thank you, Your Grace." The highly polished marquetry floor slid under her feet.

"I saw that," he said. "When you came in and you slipped. Take care, Miss North."

He'd noticed her faux pas? Who else had seen it? Were they already laughing at her?

He held her hand properly, that was to say, barely at all, and led her in the first steps of the country dance. Phoebe took her courage in both hands, finding his manner daunting. The perfection of his moves, the way he stared down his nose at everyone, marked him as the kind of person she preferred to avoid. "May I call you sir, or d-do you prefer that I use your proper title all the time?"

"Leo will do," he said carelessly. Of course, he would not care what she called him. She was well below his notice.

"I cannot c-call you by your first name," she said. While she was mindful of the correct address, she knew young ladies did not refer to gentlemen by their given names. "I c-cannot p-possibly call you something so familiar." She would call him "sir," as was proper.

"My given name is George. Nobody calls me that, or I might be confused with a dozen or more other men here tonight. My title is Leomore, and since I inherited, people call me Leo."

"Of c-course. L-like the lion. But I would not presume."

He cleared his throat—or was that a laugh? "Perhaps when we're in private you might consider doing so." Was that a gleam of answering challenge lighting his gray eyes?

Before they separated in the dance, she had time to reply. "I feel c-convinced that will n-never happen, sir." Curse it, her stammer had broken in once more. She thought she had overcome that burden. It was the bane of her life. She rarely stammered in private, but in London, where she did not feel comfortable, it had started up again. The harder she tried to overcome her stammer, the worse it became.

As the dance demanded, she moved on to her next partner.

Well, if she'd seen interest in him, she had certainly doused it now. An awkward, stammering woman, dressed in one of the plainest gowns possible and wearing a ribbon around her throat instead of jewelry—he wouldn't be interested in anyone like her. Moreover, one who could not keep steady on her feet.

Country dances involved little skips and hops. Every time her foot left the floor, Phoebe held her breath and prayed she would land safely. She managed very well, even though when they changed partners, the men looked over her head or to one side, as if she was not good enough to meet their gaze. She wasn't imagining the way they didn't look at her. Their unspoken snubs only made her straighten her spine and dare them to meet her gaze. If they wouldn't look at her, she would stare at them. Dare them to continue to ignore her. Which they usually did successfully.

Did she feel excluded? Yes, because they meant her to. For that reason, she would never show them how deeply the treatment affected her.

Eventually this torture of a dance would end. With relief she faced the duke once more, because that meant the dance was drawing to a close. He gave her his hand with no hesitation, his manner impeccable. His expression was warm without condescension. Leomore had such perfect manners that he quite cowed Phoebe, whereas she felt only defiance to those without such address.

After the dance he would return her to the corner of the room from where he'd collected her, thank her for her company, and never give her another thought. Women glanced at him, sending him flirtatious glances, but he took no notice. His manners were far better than most other people in the room, despite him being a duke, which meant he could probably strip naked in the middle of the dance floor and everybody would treat it as a mild eccentricity. Or that he was setting a new, amusing fashion.

She should not have brought that image to mind because now her cheeks heated, and her breath came shallower. He was tall, broad-shouldered and with no trace of padding in his clothes to make up for a lack of muscle and shape. He was wonderfully good-looking. With the excuse of the dance, Phoebe could examine that blade of a nose, the flashing steel-gray eyes, and surprisingly full lips. His cheekbones were as high as his station demanded, and he moved gracefully for such a large man. His clothes, while dark in color and sober compared to the popinjays here tonight, were nevertheless of the best quality. The buttons marching down his waistcoat and coat were probably real gold. Disdaining the fashionable wig, he had adopted the new style of gentlemen wearing their hair naturally, but most did not draw it back so simply. The black velvet bow behind his head absorbed the light from the chandeliers.

Thinking about the duke naked had fatally distracted her. Phoebe hit the floor awkwardly. Her stomach opened into a bottomless pit as she skidded, more like a skater on a frozen lake than a graceful dancer. The sickening sound of ripping fabric rent the air, piercing the melody of the quartet in the corner, quickly followed by a clatter and a crunch as she dropped her fan and promptly stepped on it. Someone sniggered, but she was too busy trying not to fall to discover who.

The duke's hand slid from hers, and Phoebe's heart plummeted along with the rest of her. She would land with a decided thump and have to leave the floor ignominiously on her own, running the gauntlet of amusement.

He was as bad as everyone else, and she was mistaken thinking him a gentleman.

Except she steadied when he grabbed her lace-covered forearms and simply lifted her off her feet. He set her down so gently she hardly felt it and had to force herself not to flail as if she was falling once more. The next moment, he touched her elbow. "Come with me," he said softly.

Phoebe glared down at where her feet peeped out from the hem of her gown. Those new shoes had let her down at last. The rest of the season loomed in front of her, terrifying and ominous. She would be known forever as the clumsy stammerer who could not keep her feet in a simple country dance.

He supported her, one hand firmly under her elbow. "Keep your head up. Smile."

His voice was so low she hardly heard it, but automatically she responded to the command inherent in his tones, and she did as he bade her, even though her ankle hurt like the devil. Doors either side of the ballroom opened to stone staircases that descended to the garden. She counted every one and ensured her foot was well planted on them. Her care did her no good, because on the second to last, she stumbled.

With a curse, the duke swung her into his arms and carried her off, as if she was some kind of princess who couldn't walk.

She squeaked in alarm. "I can manage."

"Be still," he commanded as she struggled.

"This is ridiculous. I'm not hurt. Please, sir, put me down." She could not call out. Someone might hear.

"If you stumble again, we will never get that ruffle repaired. It's early in the evening, and a chilly night. Nobody will see you. Don't you think this is better than people watching and speculating?"

Printed in the United States
by Baker & Taylor Publisher Services